playing with fire

RIA WILDE

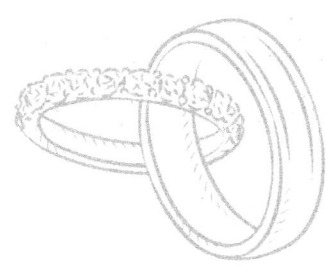

Copyright © 2024 Ria Wilde
All rights reserved

The characters and events portrayed in this book are fictitious. Any similarity to real persons, living or dead, is coincidental and not intended by the author.

No part of this book may be reproduced, or stored in a retrieval system, or transmitted in any form or by any means, electronic, mechanical, photocopying, recording, or otherwise, without express written permission of the publisher.

Cover Design: Ria Wilde
Formatting: Ria Wilde
Edited by: Amanda Wallace

ISBN: 9798322055006

Playlist

Sin So Sweet - Warren Zeiders
Superhero - Aim Vision
Horns - Bryce Fox
Be My Queen - Seafret
Like You Mean It - Steve Rodriguez
My Strange Addiction - Billie Eilish
All The Good Girls Go To Hell - Billie Eilish
Flowers - Miley Cyrus
Give - Sleep Token
Rain - Sleep Token
Something In The Orange - Zach Bryan
Power Over Me - Dermot Kennedy
Work Song - Hozier
Only Love Can Hurt Like This - Paloma Faith

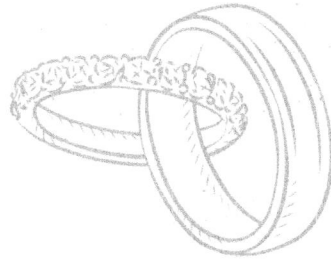

AUTHOR NOTE

Playing with Fire is a standalone dark romance intended for readers aged 18+

It includes content some may find triggering, distressing, or simply you may not like. This includes the following:

- Arranged Marriage -
- Blackmail/bribery -
- Graphic, on page violence -
- Torture -
- Revenge Porn (Not by MMC) -
- Spanking -
- Spitting -
- Forced Orgasms -
- Orgasm Denial -
- Rough Sex -
- Use of restraints -
- Somnophilia -
- Coercion -
- Controlling behavior -
- Abduction -
- Use of weapons including guns -
- Alcohol -
- Medications -
- Forced Sedation -
- Organized Crime -

The MMC in this book is a walking red flag, he won't be for everyone and that's okay.

But if you're reading this like a shopping list, then buckle up, baby. Malakai is ready for you now.

Happy reading.

Ria ♡

Sometimes revenge doesn't have to be bloody and brutal. Sometimes it can be swapping sugar for salt, or putting ketchup in your new husbands Prada shoes.

Stay petty, queens

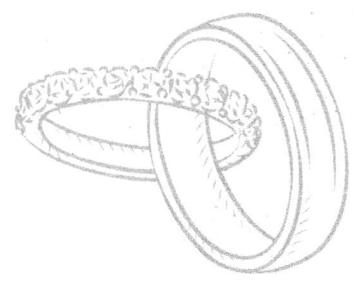

1
Olivia

I like pretty broken things.

That's what he had said when this farce of a marriage was arranged. If that wasn't warning enough, then I don't know what is.

I still signed that contract though; it's my name scribbled on the dotted line tying me to the devil himself.

I am under no illusions, however, about the man I am about to marry.

Malakai Farrow is dangerous. Brutal. Controlling. Sitting on a throne made of blood and violence.

But I had to save my sister, and this was the only way.

"I don't know, Oli," Willow, my best friend, says with a wince, "I really don't like this."

She knows about the wedding. Not about who Malakai really is, because I won't bring her into this mess and endanger her, but she knows it's an arranged marriage.

"Arranged marriages happen all the time," I shrug as if it's no big deal, "you know that, Wils. It's not an uncommon practice where we come from."

"I know," she huffs, angrily folding a t-shirt before she throws it into the open case, "But a year ago you would have revolted at the idea. What changed?"

So much. *Everything*.

"My dad died, and Arryn already does so much. She deserves to be happy. I need help with the hotel, he can offer that while also fulfilling his duties."

I've practiced that over and over in the mirror, so much so I've almost convinced myself that the words are true. They're not lies per se, except for that last bit about the hotel. I can manage my late father's empire just fine on my own.

"You don't even know the guy."

Willow Stanton has been my best friend since kindergarten, ever since she pushed a bully off the swing set in my defense. We've done everything together, college, travelling, heartbreaks, all the highs, and all the lows. She's my family as much as Arryn, my older sister, is. I depend on her.

"It'll be fine."

"I guess he is hot," she giggles, helping to pack the last bits in the bedroom into the boxes and cases. I roll my eyes.

Sure, Malakai is hot, scorching hot, but it's the type that burns. There's darkness in those blue eyes, brutality in his face, everything about him screams danger, from the sharp lines of his cheeks and jaw, to the dark mess of hair on his head. He is death in a suit and pain with a smile.

A tremor works through me.

Terrified doesn't even cut how I feel about this marriage and the impending living situation. I'm moving in with him today and I haven't stopped shaking since I woke up this morning, but I know I'll do it, despite the fear and dread.

He had a hand in my father's death, threatened my sister and the man she loved, but gave me the option to stop it if I just agreed to this marriage. So, I did.

Now my sister is living on this dreamy little island with a man who worships her, and friends who love her, so if it means letting her have that taste of happiness, then I'd do it again.

Of course, my sister fought me on the decision, tried to convince me not to do it, but in the end, we all knew this was the only way out. You can't run from a man like Malakai. He is *power*. The quiet kind, the deadly kind.

"I think that's it," I blow out a breath and look around the room. This penthouse has been my home for three years, it's the only home I've made for myself, a sanctuary I'm sad to see go. I doubt I'll ever see it again once I step out this door and move in with Malakai.

The intercom buzzes and I hit the accept button, the front desk calling up.

"Your moving vans are here, Miss Lauder."

"Let them up," I approve and push back the sting of tears.

Playing with Fire

"Come here." Willow drags me into her arms knowing exactly what I need, and she rubs my back as the first tear falls.

I hate crying. What was the point in tears really, when all they do is make your eyes sore and your face wet. They didn't take away the pain, they just showed everyone your vulnerabilities and weaknesses. I swat at them angrily, huffing out an impatient breath, and try to get myself under control before the movers come in to haul my life away.

"You don't have to do it, Oli." Willow assures me. "You don't."

"I know," I lie, but I do have to, there is no get out clause, no loophole.

It takes an hour at most for the movers to get everything I own out of the apartment. There's no point taking furniture or anything like that, so it's being left and sold with the penthouse. Everything of value is in my boxes, clothes neatly packed in suitcases and bags. I stand at the side of the road as the vans pull away, watching as they disappear around the corner.

I don't know what to expect. I haven't yet been to Malakai's house, have no idea where it even is, which is a daunting thought on its own.

In the weeks after the agreement, after he let my sister and her boyfriend go, he was silent, letting me fall into a false sense of security, but then I received a message from him a few days ago. I was expected to move back and be ready to relocate by the end of the week. I'd procrastinated for a few days at the start of the week, but when Wednesday rolled around, I knew I couldn't put it off any longer.

Willow stands at my side protectively as a car pulls up, and a stoic looking man climbs out. Dressed in a dark suit with sunglasses covering his eyes, he steps onto the sidewalk, ahead of the two of us. I can't see his eyes, but I know they're assessing me, judging me.

"Miss Lauder?" He asks, voice deep and no nonsense. My internal alarm bells start to ring, heart thumping chaotically inside my chest.

"That's me," I hate the shake in my voice but there's no hiding it.

"I'll be your driver today," he opens the back door to the Mercedes idling at the side of the road, "Mr. Farrow has requested I take you straight to Silver Lake."

"Speak now and I'll get us out of here." Willow hisses in my ear, her tone giving away her own fear for me.

"I'll text you," I tell her, giving her one last hug.

She pleads with her bright blue eyes, but I take that step away from her, scanning her features like this will be the last time I see her. I memorize the exact shade of her red hair, and the smattering of freckles she's always hated, remembering the blue of her eyes and the pink gloss she loves so much, she wears it every day.

"See you soon." I tell her before I turn my back and get into the car, the heat chasing away the January chill that had settled on my body.

My driver says nothing as he climbs into the front seat, pulling into traffic. In the silence I watch the city roll by, people going about their lives, laughing, and drinking coffee, wrapped up tight in their thick coats and bundled under layers of hats and scarves and gloves. The sky tumbles with grey clouds, an ominous feeling sinking into my gut as the car weaves through the city.

It's when we start hitting the outer limits, the buildings becoming less and less that the fear and anxiety truly settle in. They roll like a swarm of angry wasps in the pit of my stomach, making my palms clammy and my legs ache with the urge to run.

It's another hour before the car begins to slow, and the only thing that surrounds us is open space on one side, and a sprawling forest on the other, the road quiet and seemingly abandoned.

We stop at a set of large black gates, a wall over ten feet tall bracketing either side, and the driver punches in a code before the gates start to slide open.

I have no words as the tires roll through, bringing us into a place that can only be called *paradise*.

I've grown up with money, I'm used to wealth and privilege, used to the glam and the prestige, but this is a whole other league. The road we currently idle down is bordered by pristine, well-tended lawn; trees bare as they make a line around the perimeter to hide the imposing wall that surrounds the whole area. A large marble fountain sits in the center of the lawn, the water off since the harsh winter will only freeze it, but I can imagine how beautiful it would be in the warmer months. I see stables in the distance, horses out to graze in the meadows that are just beyond a line of wooden fences, separating that part of the estate.

But up ahead, right in the center, with a backdrop of what appears to be a never-ending forest, is probably the largest house I have ever seen.

It's in a U shape, made up of red brick and black beams with a Tudor style feel to it. A deep-set porch draws my eye, leading to a huge oak wood door. Chimneys let out smoke that slithers into the sky like snakes and warm light spills from the large windows, cutting through the gloom.

It's not what I had been expecting at all.

There's a circular drive at the front of the house with several expensive vehicles parked around it, but I can also see a seven-vehicle garage to the side, which no doubt houses more luxury cars.

But despite the size of the property, despite the cars and the light, there is not a single soul to be seen.

My breath is caught somewhere in my throat, both awe and fear wrapping around me as the car comes to a gentle stop and the driver gets out.

My door is opened, but my body is frozen to the leather seats.

"Welcome to Silver Lake Estate, Miss Lauder, Mr. Farrow is expecting you inside." My driver says, those dark glasses still covering his eyes, even with the lack of sun.

I still don't move, swallowing the nausea that churns in my stomach.

I can't do this.

This can't be my life.

Less than six months ago, I was traveling the world with Willow, learning, exploring and now I am here.

"Miss Lauder," the driver gets my attention, and I know I have to move.

While I don't fully understand the business my future husband is involved in, or how it works, I do know that he is dangerous. I know he has hands in every pot and people in all the places, even the ones you least expect. It's likely my driver is just as deadly, and I am not stupid enough to test his patience just to see what could happen.

I do have some survival instincts after all, and this isn't a battle I'd win.

My heels touch down on the smooth pavement and as I climb from the car, a wind so cold it feels like it touches my bones, sweeps through the estate.

Even the weather is warning me to turn around, high tail it out of here and hide.

I flinch with the sound of the car door slamming. I expect the driver to leave but he doesn't, instead he steps up next to me and guides me forward, a hand at my back but not touching, almost like he knows I'm flighty and is preparing to grab me in case I decide to run.

I glance at the shiny black Louis Vuitton's on my feet and stifle a laugh. There's no way I'm running in these shoes, and the gravel on the drive will just tear up my skin. The grass, however, could work, but then I'd have to figure out how to scale that ten-foot wall surrounding the estate. It's tempting, but logically I know there is no escape.

My mind is still conjuring escape plans as my feet hit the top step of the porch and the front door swings open immediately, drawing my focus. An older woman with silver hair threaded throughout the dark strands steps out, as if she was waiting behind it this whole time, ready for the right moment to announce her presence. She's dressed entirely in black, age lines her face but I wouldn't put her much past her fifties, even if her expression, the downturn of her lips and the sneer, makes her appear much older.

"Mr. Farrow is waiting in the drawing room," she says, her voice as cold as her expression, "Follow me."

I step over the threshold, the warmth of the house immediately chasing away the cold. It is entirely unexpected inside as much as the outside was, homely is the only way to describe it. I am not sure why I anticipated an almost sterile environment; I had an image in my head of all white walls with little personality, not this.

The foyer is decked with greenery, the walls an off-white color and a stag horn chandelier hangs from the ceiling. Art is mounted on the walls, paintings of forests and snowcapped mountains, and a lake that draws my attention more than the others. I find my feet pulling toward it, the hues of greys and whites and blues almost hypnotizing. It's a huge lake painted in winter, with snowy shores and huge, towering pines that border it like sentinel guards. The sky is light grey, and the artist has even managed to paint little pockets of snow between the trees. If I couldn't see the delicate strokes of paint, I'd believe it was a photograph.

"Miss Lauder," I startle at the stern way she calls my name, "This way, if you'll please."

"Right," I nod, flicking my eyes some more around the space. Ahead of me is a huge staircase that leads to a level that then splits off left and right, but I can't see further than that. There's a closed door to the left that we don't go in and more rooms down a dark hall next to the stairs.

I follow her down a separate corridor with more closed

doors before we come out into a huge kitchen. Oak wood counters wrap around the space with every appliance you could ever need, a huge double fridge dominates one wall and in the center is an oak wood island, red velvet stools placed around it. A vase full of flowers sits in the center and the space is lit by spotlights placed in the ceiling. There is a set of French doors that looks to lead out onto a patio and as much as I want to go there, I can't as the woman steers me down *another* corridor toward a door that is ajar at the end.

This house is huge, I can imagine how easy it would be to get lost in it. It smells of burning logs and cinnamon, a cozy scent that wraps around me and tries to put me at ease. I have enough wits about me not to fall for it.

The woman taps her knuckles on the door even though it's open and his deep voice calls from the other side.

"Come in," he says, his tone a rumble that zaps down my spine. It has a similar feel to that first sip of whiskey, it burns a little but warms you as you take it down, leaving behind a tingle that makes you crave more. My skin prickles as I take a step forward, my hand barely touching the door as I push it open.

The first thing I see is the fire crackling in the hearth, the flames strong and warm as they lick the bricks on the inside. My eyes follow the line up, seeing a mantel made of oak, a gleaming gold statue of a stag resting in the center and hanging in the middle of the flute is a huge painting of a woman, she has no features, and her back is facing me, her head turned to look over her shoulder. The background is black where she is bright, like a light in the shadows, her white dress hugging the curves the artist has painstakingly painted. Her hair is pulled up but wisps float around her face.

I focus on that instead of the desk to the right where I know he is sitting.

There's a set of leather couches and chairs on the left side of the room, surrounding a dark wooden table. In the corner sits a grand piano, the gleaming black making my fingers itch to press on the ivory keys. I haven't played for a while but it's a skill one doesn't forget.

With nothing more to look at, I finally draw my eyes to the man that makes the room feel much too small.

Malakai remains seated in his huge high back chair, the thing resembling more a throne than a desk chair, behind his obnoxiously large desk. A laptop is in front of him, the lid pulled down but not closed. There's a stack of papers, a leather bound notebook with an embossed symbol on the front I can't make out from here, and a tray with crystal glasses and a decanter of whiskey. But that's it. Despite the absolute size of the desk, there's barely anything on it.

A feline grin tugs up the sides of his mouth and his eyes lick down the length of me.

I'm hit with just how stunning the man is, but his beauty comes with a price. He's a predator, a monster and as the door clicks closed, locking me in the room with him, I suddenly feel like I've become his prey.

"Olivia," he purrs my name, finally standing from behind the desk. I remain still, barely breathing, my feet rooted to the spot as he stalks toward me. His finger curls beneath my chin and he tilts my face up to keep his eyes on mine. He has over a foot on me in height, and if he hadn't tipped my chin up, my eyes would have been level with his chest.

I can't breathe with him so close, his scent invades my

senses, a mix of citrus and spice and despite the sheer size of him, his hand on my chin is gentle, the rough callouses on his fingers scratching my skin.

He leans in, close enough I feel his breath fan across my lips.

That grin stretches higher, something dangerous flashing in his eyes as he whispers in a voice barely louder than the crackle of the fire. "Welcome home."

2
Malakai

Two hours earlier

"When will she arrive?" I twist the watch on my wrist, the Prada shoes on my feet clipping against the shined hardwood floors of Silver Lake Estate. My home.

"The moving vans have collected her belongings; they are making their way here now. Dennis is collecting Miss Lauder as we speak."

I dip my chin with a nod, the drawing room which doubles as a second office for me, warmed by the fire burning in the hearth. "Have the guest room made up next to mine," I advise Miranda, "Tell the staff to have all her items put away in my bedroom, any items that do not belong in the bedroom, leave in the boxes, and put them in the closet. When Miss Lauder arrives, please show her through. I'll be here for the next few hours."

"Yes, sir," Miranda nods obediently, not another word spoken as she turns on her heel and exits, going to follow the orders I have given her.

After the sound of her footsteps disappear down the hall, silence settles around me, the only noise coming from the crackle of the logs as they burn in the pit. I press open my laptop, an image of my future wife staring back at me.

I had everything on her at my fingertips, there isn't a secret she can keep or a skeleton she can hide. There is no denying that Olivia Lauder is a stunning creature. With her fathomless eyes, so dark they can pass as black and pair them with her raven black hair, she has the type of alluring beauty men would go to war for. Did I manipulate, scheme and plot to force her hand into agreeing to this marriage? Of course I did, and it was fucking easy too.

All I had to use was the family she cared so deeply for.

In her defense, I would have killed them all if she hadn't agreed, and she knew it too.

And I'd do it again to make her mine.

I flick through the images of her, ranging from photos taken at galas where she's dressed to the nines in designer dresses that appear to be made for her body, others when she's been captured unaware, dressed in tight as fuck leggings and cropped tees, that mane of dark hair pulled into a dead straight ponytail that hangs at the back of her head.

My hand itches with the urge to wrap those thick strands around it, to tug her head back, stretch out her neck for my teeth to sink into while my hands and cock punish her.

With time, I tell myself. I may be a man with very little morals, but *that* I will not take from my future wife until she comes crawling to me herself.

And *crawl* she will.

I have her now, it's only a matter of time.

Leaning back in my chair, I reach for the decanter of whiskey I keep at the edge of my desk, but the sound of heels on my floors reaches my ears and my eyes narrow at the door, waiting for them to show themselves.

There's a tap but they don't wait for my invitation to come in, instead they push it open and step inside.

I stifle the groan at the woman who now stands in my space, a scowl on her face and her painted red lips turned down in a frown.

"You're joking, right?" She snaps, glaring at me.

Good fucking lord, I can't be dealing with her shit today.

Ever since her uncle died and I got an out from the wedding with *her*, she's been on my ass. Granted, it wasn't easy to dismiss her, not when her father sits on the panel with me. I may sit on the throne, but my reign will only last as long as I have the loyalty of my men.

Regina Ware and I were supposed to wed, a deal I struck up with her uncle. I needed a wife, and she was available, she comes from a high family, understands the life, and would have been a good wife if she didn't get on every last nerve I have. But now her uncle is dead, and I have no bargain to fulfil, so Regina was left high and dry when I decided to end the engagement and choose Olivia instead.

Her father understood and accepted my decision, but

Playing with Fire

little Regina here can't come to grasp the fact that all that power she would have had as my wife, has slipped through her fingers.

I would tell her it's because she's a money seeking bitch who is never happy with anything. Not the thousand-dollar dresses or the designer shoes and purses. Not with the estate or the horses or the cars. She wants more. Always more.

And quite frankly, she can go take a walk off a high cliff if she thinks she can control a man like me. I took the quickest route out of there. I mean I could have put her up, gave her everything she wanted, sent her away overseas and just had the marriage certificate to satisfy the centuries old rule that told us we must be married to secure our lead over the organization, but that would have meant I wouldn't have pretty little Olivia moving into the manor this afternoon.

"I hadn't realized I'd told a joke, Miss Ware." I glance at my laptop, those stunning black eyes staring back at me.

I'd told her when we agreed to this marriage that I liked pretty broken things, but I have a feeling the woman coming into my home in just a few short hours is not going to be the demure little bride I am expecting.

I suppose it could backfire on me; I could have another Regina on my hands, but I guess we will find out. There are always other means to end a marriage.

"You know what I am talking about Malakai," She huffs, annoyed.

"Have you come to try and renegotiate?" I ask, bored.

"You're breaking contract!" She stomps her foot like a petulant child.

"No," I pick up the decanter and a glass, watching as her eyes follow the movement. She frowns even more when I don't offer her a glass too. "I made a deal with your uncle; your uncle is now dead. Your father has not renegotiated, leaving me free to do whatever the fuck I like."

"You didn't give him time." She shoves her hands to her hips, "and now you're marrying some uptight little whore. She doesn't belong here like I do."

I quirk a brow at her tone and whatever she sees in my expression has her shrinking away. Am I like the leaders that came before me? No. No I am not. A lot of people assume that's a weakness but all it does is reel them in, let them feel like they're safe before they're in too deep with no way out.

I have just as much blood on my hands as all those that came before me, but where their kills came with screams, mine come with calculation. I never go into a situation without knowing the whole picture. How do they think I secured Olivia Lauder after all? Not only do I have a wife, I have her late father's empire too.

"We would have been so good together," She pouts, widening her eyes as she tries, and fails, to give me a puppy dog face that she should know would never work on me. I'm not easily manipulated, especially not by people like her.

I scoff at those words, sipping a little from my glass. The burn down my throat is almost as satisfying as sinking into a tight, hot body.

Placing the glass down, I check my watch, "You've taken enough of my time now, Miss Ware. I am expecting a guest so you should see yourself out."

"Is it *her?*" She sneers.

My patience is sitting on a precipice, one wrong nudge and I'm not sure what I'll do. Maybe bury her next to her uncle in that unmarked grave somewhere out in one of the meadows that surrounds the estate.

She must read my thoughts through my expression because she backs down, a placating smile stretching up her mouth. Her voice lowers and her body softens as she turns back into the *lady* the world knows her to be.

"Well," Her hands run down her pink dress, "I guess I'll see you at the wedding, save me a dance."

And with that, she breezes out of my office, the sound of her heels grating on that last nerve.

I take the rest of my whiskey in one gulp, slamming my crystal glass down onto the desk hard enough it splinters, the crack running from base to rim. Impatience runs through me as I glance at my watch once more, seeing barely any time has passed so I choose to get up, exiting my office to wander the house. It's brimming with staff, but no one is around, not in these parts at this time anyway. I can hear faint thuds upstairs as a bedroom is prepared for Olivia, can hear footsteps somewhere else but right here, I am alone.

This estate has been in the Farrow family for as long as our history has been written. The base where the organization first started.

Listed as Farrow Industries, we hide behind a guise of buying out businesses and flipping them to make a profit, we own several chains of hotels, and restaurants and bars but deeper than that is a river that fuels our lives. I couldn't give two shits about the businesses tied to the Farrow name, as long as they're making money, what I care about is the individuals that keep me powerful.

I own them all.

It's dark and it's dirty and it's mine. It's all I've known. I own the city and the people without them even knowing it's me. I see it all.

Death is no rarity in my life, if I don't see it at least once a day then it's a quiet day but it's always been this way. I know life no other way.

I let out a whistle as I bury my hands into my pockets, strolling casually through the house that sits atop the bodies of those who tried to stop us.

Death is lucrative. Death pays.

It's why I have over five thousand hitmen under my employ, scattered across the globe. It's why I own a database full of hits, targets and marks.

It isn't just us Farrow's that thrive off of death, there is a panel, a council if you will, that sit alongside me. It helps keep the organization off the radar, keeps us underground and all important decisions are made through votes. There are rules, laws that only we abide by, but it's worked for hundreds of years and will continue to work for hundreds of more, with a few changes I plan to implement.

It's one of those rules that has this wedding being prepared.

It's obviously dated and not something that fits in today's society, but nonetheless, we abide by it, meaning if I want to keep the throne I sit on, I will be marrying Olivia. It tells us we must marry within the first six years of leadership or lose the seat. Why? Fuck knows, but it didn't matter much to me.

As I hit the foyer, I notice a number of my staff directing the moving people through the house, boxes and bags being ferried through the rooms and deposited upstairs.

It's almost time.

My palms tingle with her almost in reach.

I knew the moment I saw Olivia that I wanted her. There wasn't a question of *if* but *when* and the day is finally here. I gave her some time, it's more than what I would give anyone else and now she belongs to me.

She signed that contract on the dotted line, placing herself right in my hands. The little broken doll will be fun to play with, if only to see how far I can *push*.

With a smirk playing on my mouth, I head back to the drawing room, lowering myself back to the chair. My broken glass has already been cleaned up, a new one placed on the tray along with the decanter.

And then I wait for the little kitten to come to me.

3
Malakai

My fingers drum against the pristine wood of my desk, the sound of her heels a rhythmic tap in the otherwise silent house.

Miranda knocks twice and I wait a beat before I call, "Come in."

The door swings open silently and Miss Lauder steps into the room.

Her eyes don't immediately come to me, so I take a moment to appreciate the beauty before me.

Dressed in a tight black skirt and white blouse, she screams elegance and sophistication, not a single wrinkle can be seen in her clothes. Her raven black hair is left down, dead straight and pulled away from her shoulders so it falls down her back like a curtain made entirely of the night sky. Her skin has a glow to it, like the sun has recently kissed it and her eye makeup is so dark it makes her already dark eyes even more fathomless, long lashes and plump lips painted a plum color, slicked with a gloss I itch to taste.

She holds her delicate hands in front of her as she stares at the painting above the fire. Everything about her screams timidness and politeness, even the way she stands, back ramrod straight, shoulders squared with her legs posed in such a way it looks uncomfortable. Someone clearly didn't forget their etiquette lessons from when they were a kid.

Sweet little Olivia.

Fuck, she's going to be fun to rile.

Finally, those dark eyes fall to me, flicking back and forth as she takes in the space I am currently occupying. It feels like forever before they finally land on me directly.

So damn pretty.

So put together.

I feel my grin as it pulls up my mouth, my eyes eating her up from across the room.

"Olivia," I purr, standing from the desk.

My steps are slow, languid as I cross the space between us, wondering if she'll turn and bolt but I'm pleasantly surprised when she roots herself to the spot, though she keeps those pretty eyes down. With a curl of my finger beneath her chin, I tip up her face, the scent of her invading my senses. Like raspberries mixed with something floral, it's so sweet it makes my mouth water for a taste.

She stiffens under my touch, her breath stuttering to a

stop as I lean in closer, feeling the heat of her wrap around me and then I'm barely a breath away from her.

My smile only widens when she doesn't move.

"Welcome home," I whisper, the words landing against her mouth as I speak them so quietly, I wonder if she'll be able to hear them over the crackle and pop of the fire.

For a few long seconds she does nothing, says nothing, doesn't breathe or blink but then it's like the words sink beneath her skin, her brain finally catching up and she jumps away from me, wobbling on those heels.

"Home?" She spits, tipping up her chin in a show of defiance, "This will never be my home."

I stifle my laugh, "The contract you signed says otherwise, darling."

I head back to the desk and lower myself into the chair, reaching for the decanter and two glasses, pouring two fingers of whiskey into each. I then push one of those glasses to the edge of the desk, tipping my head down to it in offering to her.

She narrows her eyes, stomping across the room to snatch it off the desk, any elegance she had just shown is gone with her anger.

"Contract or no contract," She hisses, "This'll never be home for me."

"What a very sad life that will be," I tease, "The estate is beautiful, I should imagine any number of people would dream of calling it home."

"So why not ask one of them to come live here?" She quirks a brow, bringing the glass to her lips before she knocks the whole of it down. I almost wince. This is a

Playing with Fire

whiskey to be savored not downed like a cheap shot in a shitty nightclub.

"Well, if I did that, Olivia," I toy with her, "How else would I have made a bargain for your precious sisters' life?"

A lick of fire brightens the darkness of her eyes as rage twists her face, "I vow to you, Malakai," Never has my name sounded so good coming from a woman's lips. "I am going to make your life hell. Miserable. You're going to regret ever thinking you're going to get a quiet, obedient little wife with me."

As excitement works through me, my cock twitching in anticipation, I take a tender sip of my drink, leaning forward until my elbows rest on the desk, "I sure hope you don't disappoint me, kitten."

Her nose flares as her teeth bite down and she slams the glass down on the desk. "Where am I staying?" She hisses.

"For now?" I lean back, smirking, "I have a room being prepared for you."

"And my things?"

"They're here." I confirm without telling her they're being placed in the closet in *my* bedroom. It's her room now too, after all.

"May I leave?" She grits out, her politeness outweighing her anger.

What a shame.

"Sure, kitten."

"Stop calling me that," She snaps, turning on her heel and heading toward the door.

"You'll get lost in a house this big," I warn.

"I'll take my chances." The door slams on her way out and I let out a low chuckle. Perhaps I wasn't expecting the fight so soon and I'm pleasantly surprised by it.

I wander through the house sometime later, listening to the roar of the fires I have going throughout the house. The coffee machine whirs in the kitchen, and I can hear my staff preparing for the evening in the various rooms.

It takes me five minutes to find Olivia.

She is sitting on the very top step, her head cradled in one hand as she swipes through her phone with the other. Her groomed brows are drawn low, her face twisted into a grimace.

"No luck?" I tease.

Her head snaps up and her eyes narrow, "No one will talk to me."

"That is because I haven't given them permission to do so."

"You're an ass." Olivia turns her attention back to her phone, dismissing me.

I take the steps two at a time, but she doesn't move at my approach, even though she stiffens. She's putting on a good front, trying to play it cool like she isn't terrified to be here, with me.

I snatch the phone from her hand, locking the screen before I shove the device into the pocket of my pants.

"Hey!"

"If you'll follow me," I gesture with a curl of my finger, not stopping even when I don't hear her following.

I count in my head, getting to ten before her heels stomp after me.

"Give it back!"

I ignore her, pushing on until I come to the door next to mine and step inside, finding the bedroom ready for her. A fire burns in the hearth that sits opposite the four-poster bed, fresh white linens tucked in tight across the mattress. The window has a view of the stables and the meadows, and I know that just beyond that band of trees sits the lake the estate is named for. She follows me inside, stopping just inside the door.

I throw her cell onto the bed, turning to her.

"Dinner is at six," I step toward her, "Don't be late."

"I won't be joining you," She snatches up her phone.

"You will," I demand, "Or I'll drag you down there. Oh, and Olivia." I pull the thick cardstock from my pocket, tossing it onto the dresser near the door, "This is for you."

I leave before she can pick it up and am halfway down the stairs when I hear her scream my name.

4
Olivia

You are cordially invited to attend the wedding of Olivia Lauder and Malakai Farrow.

My palms are sweating as I stare down at the invitation in my hand. An invitation to my own wedding. This Sunday.

As in one day from now.

One fucking day.

What the fuck!?

I'd screamed his name the moment I realized what I was holding but the prick never came back and like fuck would I be leaving this damn room to chase him down. One, I'll likely get lost because I was too angry at him for stealing my phone to get my bearings on which halls we went down, and what doors we entered when he brought me to this bedroom, and two, he seemed to be getting off on riling me up and I don't want to give him the satisfaction.

I won't be leaving this room until they drag me out, that's for sure.

It had everything I needed anyway, an ensuite, stocked fully with creams and lotions, soaps and shampoos. There's a mini fridge with snacks and drinks, including wine. I can just pretend I'm staying in some fancy country manor hotel, and this isn't really happening.

I text Willow, letting her know I'm fine – as much as I can be anyway – and go to the closet, assuming all my things have been unpacked already since there are no boxes or bags laying around. But the closets are empty save for a long bath robe hanging from the pole, and the drawers are too. There isn't a single item of mine here.

Maybe it hadn't arrived yet and Malakai was just fucking with me when he said they were here? I think, as I kick off my shoes and head over to the bed in the center of the room, sitting on the soft surface and placing a foot onto my knee so I can massage the arch. All that walking through the house did a number on them. No one would talk to me, not properly anyway, they just kept telling me to speak with *Mr. Farrow,* it didn't matter that I didn't know how to get back to the pretentious idiot.

It's how I ended up at the top of the stairs, sat on the hard floor as I scrolled Instagram.

But a wedding... already?

I groan as I fall down onto my back, sinking into the bed. Why so damn soon?

Either way, he can screw off if he thinks I'll be joining

him for dinner.

No. You know what I'm going to do?

I'm going to make use of that huge claw foot tub in the bathroom and sink to my nose in a bubble bath.

Decision made, I start to strip, unzipping my skirt before I pick it up and fold it on the bed, I do the same to my blouse and walk in my underwear to the bathroom.

I am going to make his life a living hell. How, I'm not sure yet but I'll figure it out.

I am not a violent person, I never have been, but I'll think up ways that'll hurt in every sense but physically.

With the water running, I rifle through the drawers looking for a hairband to tie my hair back and once that's found, I make use of the cleansing oils to remove my makeup. I should probably question why he has all this stuff but that would mean talking to him. My father used to tell me my stubbornness would get me in trouble one day and I guess that day has come to test the theory.

The bathroom fills with steam and the scent of lavender, thanks to the oils I added to the water and when it's ready, I strip the rest of the way down, climbing into the boiling water. It's almost too hot to sit down in so I hold my breath, sinking slowly beneath the bubbles.

I have no awareness of how much time passes as I lay in the tub but it's long enough for my fingers to prune and the water to become more lukewarm than hot, so I get out, dry off and use the robe in the closet since I have no clothes in here. I wasn't getting back into that skirt today, no thank you!

The sky has since turned a deep shade of periwinkle,

Playing with Fire

the evening drawing in. I couldn't wait for the days to be longer. I love summer over anything else, the heat, the freedom it brings.

Crouching in front of the mini fridge, I find an expensive bottle of white wine but no glasses anywhere in the room.

Was it acceptable to drink it straight from the bottle? There's a small glass in the bathroom, which I assume should be used to rinse your mouth out but I've drank out of worse so I let my feet slap over the hard floors, noticing that they're warm under my soles, and grab it, going back to the bed to make it up so I can watch videos on my phone.

With wine in my hand and a film playing on the tiny screen of my phone, I settle into the pillows, finally feeling somewhat relaxed given the circumstances.

I'm barely through the opening credits when a loud knock sounds on the door. I startle, the wine splashing over the rim.

"Who is it?" I yell, pulling at the edges of the robe.

"Miranda," Comes a huffed reply.

"Miranda?" I say under my breath, "Do I know a Miranda?"

"I showed you through to Mr. Farrow."

Oh, the lady who seemed like she never smiled.

"Um, what is it?"

"May I come in?"

"I'm not decent."

I swear I hear her sigh. "Dinner will be served in the

dining room in five minutes, Mr. Farrow has requested your presence."

My lip curls, "Tell him I'm not coming."

"Miss Lauder," Miranda starts sternly.

"I am unwell," I fake a cough, "I can't make it."

I wait, and I wait some more for a reply but when none comes, I figure I'm in the clear and get comfortable again, pressing play on the paused movie. The fruity flavor of the wine hits my tongue with a sigh, and I glance to the window, the sun setting so beautiful here. I can see the meadows, bathed in a wash of gold as the night chases away the final traces of the sun.

If the house and estate wasn't owned by an absolute ass of a man, I might actually say this is a place I'd like to explore.

I'm about ten minutes into the film when the door opens so abruptly, I scream, throwing my wine across the sheets and my phone to the floor.

Malakai stands in the doorway, his eyes narrowed in on me where I'm poised in the middle of the mattress on my knees. The sleeve of my robe is wet with wine, and I can feel my knees getting wet too where the wine soaks the sheets.

"Sick, huh?" He growls, eyes flicking to the open bottle of wine on the bedside table and then to the floor where the film still plays on the tiny screen.

He cocks his head and then curls his finger, "Let's go."

"You can't make me," I sit back on my heels and cross my arms. Yes, I was being petulant, but fuck him.

"Should we test that theory, Olivia?"

The way he says my name sends warning bells ringing inside my head. It's part threat, part purr, the tone of it licking down my spine as the rumble of his voice vibrates through me, all the way to my bones.

He steps forward, making good on that promise.

"Fine!" I snap, snatching up the bottle of wine from the bedside unit.

"There is wine on the table," He sighs impatiently.

"Well, I want this one."

I may as well stick out my tongue at him with the way I am acting.

He sucks his tongue against his teeth before he throws out an arm, letting me go first.

My feet slap loudly as I walk, the wine held by the bottleneck in a death grip. It feels like I'm doing my death march down this long corridor, but I hold my head high and turn left at the end, turning down *another* long hallway. This place is a damn maze.

Malakai clears his throat behind me, and I spin, ready to snap at him but he's gesturing in the opposite direction I'm heading.

Head held high, I stomp back the other way, avoiding any part of my body touching any part of his. The wine sloshes around in the bottle as I take the stairs down to the ground floor, the smell of the food instantly hitting me in the face.

Oh, fuck that smells good.

"This way, kitten."

"Stop calling me that!" I huff.

"But it fits you so well," He's suddenly behind me, his proximity sending zaps down my spine, "Especially when you're stomping around with your claws out."

His deep chuckle has my eyes narrowing. God, I hate him.

"Through here," He guides me, "Pick any seat you want."

I step into a room that is completely dominated by a table that can seat at least twenty. Bookshelves line one wall of the room and on the other side is just a wall of windows that stare out into a forest. It's almost fully dark out but I can make out the trees that stretch into the sky, the bare limbs like skeleton hands clawing for the clouds.

There's a spread of food on the table and a few members of Malakai's staff standing at the edge of the room. A blush creeps up my neck and warms my cheeks as I realize I'm still in the robe and I am very naked underneath.

I choose a seat in the middle of the table, assuming Malakai will take his place at the head, but much to my absolute dismay, he chooses the seat directly opposite me. He grins at my scowl.

"You make it too easy, darling," He plucks the covers off the dishes, and I'm hit with the direct aromas of all the food. Beef in a type of red wine sauce, sauteed greens and creamed potatoes all sit steaming in the middle of the table.

"Please help yourself," he tells me, leaning back in his chair as he picks up his glass with two fingers of amber liquid. I wonder if it's the whiskey I threw back earlier. That stuff was good, after it stopped burning of course.

Playing with Fire

I pour myself a glass of wine from the bottle I still have a strangle hold on and reach for the potatoes.

He watches the entire time, making my stomach knot with unease.

For a man who holds death like a set of playing cards, he sure doesn't act like it in his home.

At the hotel where the deal was made, that man was the devil. He manipulated me, dangling my sister's life in front of me, like she was tied to a string. Her or me. That was the choice. This man here though, sitting in front of me right now, they're not the same. I fully understand it's all a front, a disguise and it's keeping me on edge, wondering when the *real* him will come out.

With a plate of food and a full wine glass I go about getting through this dinner quickly. I keep my eyes down, my fork moving as I shovel food into my face. It's not lady like, it's not elegant like I've always been taught. It's messy. I'm pretty sure I have red wine sauce dripping down my chin and let's not start with how the white wine and this food doesn't pair.

But I'm not trying to impress him. I'm trying to *repulse* him.

I glance up, wondering if it's working but all I am met with is a smirk.

The staff standing at the back of the room can hardly contain their horror, but Malakai is clearly finding this highly entertaining.

I grab the napkin and wipe my mouth.

"You're fucking adorable." He cocks his head as if studying something.

"And you're a fucking asshole," I give him my sweetest

smile, fluttering my lashes like the pretty doll he thinks I am.

How do I make this man suffer!?

With his eyes on me, I watch him straighten the cutlery around his still empty plate and place his glass down meticulously on the slate coaster set up at the side. He spins his glass before he settles it down again, eyes on me the whole time.

They're a deep blue around the edges, like dark denim which make them look a lot darker than they are, but in this light, I can see the almost neon centers, so blue they look electric.

Pretty, I think.

But then you pair them with the dark lashes, deep set brows and mess of dark hair, he looks menacing.

Okay, now I'm staring.

Dropping my eyes, I reach for my wine, downing the rest of it to the chorus of his laughter.

5
Malakai

Her cheeks burn with a furious blush as her eyes dart away quickly. I can't help but let out my chuckle, watching as I rattle her.

I knew it wouldn't take much to rile her and I'm looking forward to finding all the buttons she has.

She hasn't mentioned the invitation yet though, so I bring it up for her, "You'll be going into the city tomorrow."

That gets her attention, "Excuse me?"

"You need a wedding dress." I spin my glass before I pick it up and take a sip.

Her nose flares, "I'll wear this."

My eyes drop down her. I can only see her top half, but the robe has separated some, showing off the tan skin of her chest. I couldn't see any straps or clothing peeking out which leads me to believe she's naked under that thin piece of material.

"Exactly as it is?" I ask smoothly, "No panties and all?"

"Nope!" She stands abruptly, "Not doing this."

She grabs the half bottle of wine and starts for the door.

"Sit down, Olivia." I order, voice edged in that steel she witnessed back when we made this deal.

Her legs stop moving.

"Sit." I say again.

With a grumble, she trudges back to the table, dropping down into the chair farthest away from me.

"Dennis will take you into the city at nine a.m. You have an appointment, my card is on file, pick whatever you want."

"Do I have a choice?"

"No. When you return, we can discuss the schedule for Sunday."

"Where are my things?" She asks, changing the subject.

"Where they belong."

"*Where?*"

I get up from the table, having not eaten a thing. Needling her was too much fun for me to give her what she wants so easily, even if it is as menial as her belongings. This is the most entertainment I've had in months.

"Good night, kitten."

"Malakai!" She screams after me, her bare feet slapping against the floor, "Malakai!"

I glance over my shoulder, watching her as she storms toward me, the bottom of her robe parting and swishing around her bare legs. Long, toned legs that could wrap around my waist while I bury –

"Hey!" She grabs my arm, nails sinking into the material of my suit. "I need my things."

I glance at the hand still on my arm and as if remembering herself, she snatches her arm back and crosses them over her chest.

"Head into the room next to yours," I tell her in a low tone, "They're in the closet."

"Why are they in there and not my bedroom?"

"Because that isn't your bedroom. Goodnight Olivia."

She doesn't continue to fight me and allows me to walk off, heading for the drawing room. I can hear deep voices filtering out through the gap in the door, quiet laughter and glasses being clinked.

I push the door to the room open, finding Sebastian, my right-hand man, drinking from one of my crystal glasses, three other glasses on the table while a pile of poker chips sit in the center.

Bast looks up to me, a shit eating grin splitting his face. Fucker.

"How's the bride to be, Kai?" He taunts.

I narrow my eyes, "Settling in." I lie.

Mirth dances in his green eyes, "Is that so?" He swipes a hand over his mouth while the other men around the table look on, "She sounds a little screechy."

My mouth kicks up as I remember her blush and then the anger that bloomed almost immediately after. "Concentrate on the game, jackass," I snatch the decanter from them, "You're losing." I eye the meager stacks he still has in comparison to the rest of the guys.

I know them all, there's Dean, sitting in the chair closest to the fire, a dangerous man who has been in my inner circle since I took over nearly six years ago and my lead hacker, Killian his brother is opposite Bast and then there's my cousin, Stefan, in the chair closest to me. He watches me more intently than the others, likely waiting for a slip up since he's up next to take over should something happen to me, or I don't go through with this wedding.

Our relationship, at most, is tense but since I have no choice but to keep him high on the pyramid, I deal with it.

"You buying in?" Killian leans back, placing his cards down on the arm of his chair.

"Not tonight," I take my seat behind the desk and straighten up the items on top, adjusting the leather-bound notebook and run my hand over the embossed family crest on the front. It's an image you'll see throughout the estate, a shield with a crown at the tip, a raven perched on the left with the family initial in the center and the motto, artistically scrawled in black letter in a ribbon below.

Memento mori.

Remember death.

"Trouble in paradise already?" Bast pushes more.

As much as the fucker annoys me, he's been my closest friend since we were kids. Killian, Dean and Bast are the only men I trust other than Abe who's unusually missing. He always plays on poker night.

"Where's my grandfather?" I ask.

It's Stefan that answers with a shrug, "Old man said he

had business to handle. Canceled last minute."

Abe Farrow was the only Farrow to never sit on the imaginary throne of this industry. When his time came, he decided to hand the reins to his younger brother instead. He's always been a member of the council, just never the lead despite our traditions. Since his brother never had kids, after he retired, the throne went to my father, Abe's son, and now it's with me after my father found himself in an early grave six years ago now.

I have no siblings.

Abe and Stefan are the only remaining family I have left. And I'll be dead before I let Stefan take this business over. The slimy bastard will ruin it.

When my time is up, I plan on having an heir to take it over from me, I guess I just have to convince Olivia long enough to spread her legs for me to put a baby in her.

I shake my head, dislodging the thought as I pull out my cell and fire off a text to my grandfather. He's old, almost eighty, but the stubborn fool refuses to lessen his duties.

Unfortunately, it isn't as easy as sitting back and watching the world fall at our feet. There were appearances to be had, balls and galas and interviews that were required so we could masquerade as the law abiding citizens the world believes us to be. There are thousands of businesses under the Farrow branch, each one serving one purpose. To clean the money we make through the hitlist database.

And Abe likes to put on a show. He always has.

I pinch the bridge of my nose, trying not to imagine

what ludicrous stunt he's attempting to pull. It'll have something to do with the wedding, I know it.

Add meddling to his list of qualities.

"I guess you and little Olivia didn't hit it off straight," Bast throws a couple chips in the center of the table, "And you thought she was a quiet little lady."

"She is," I say, "I expected some push back initially, but we're still getting married on Sunday and it's her in my rooms upstairs."

"But not *your* room." Killian quirks a brow.

"Give it some time," I kick back, "It won't be long before I have her on her back."

Sebastian lets out a chuckle, "Now this is a bet I'd like to put money on."

I shouldn't. *I shouldn't.*

"Yeah, how much?"

Did I need the money, no, I didn't, but would I make the bet just to shut him the fuck up? Absolutely.

"Five thousand." He offers.

"Is that it? Come on, make it worth my while." I roll my eyes.

"As if bedding that woman would be such a hardship," Bast tuts, "Fine, a hundred."

"A hundred grand?" I contemplate.

"Sure, why the fuck not," Bast jokes and then goes all in with his chips.

I almost forgot they were playing poker in the first place.

"Time frame?" I ask.

"A month."

I scoff, "I've got it in the bag."

"Oh, I saw her," Sebastian grins as he shows his cards to the rest of the table, "That girl wants nothing to do with you."

For now. She wants nothing to do with me, *for now*.

"You're on," I get up, walking across the room to shake his hand to seal the deal. His palm slaps on mine in a quick shake before he turns his attention back to the table.

Two aces lay face up, winning him the pot.

"Who's losing now, fucker?" He brags, dragging all the chips to his side.

He has too much money to play with. With a shake of my head, I head back to the desk, opening my laptop. Her image stares straight at me.

How do I get Olivia to fall in love with me?

It's dangerous. A game I shouldn't be playing but I had to wonder what her love might feel like. It'll be a pity to break her heart when she realizes that's not my end goal with her.

I just need a wife. And an heir. A pretty little thing to warm my bed.

But I guess it's hardly a hardship for her, she's got a comfy life now, though I had a feeling it'll be a cold day in hell when she accepts that.

I watch the men ahead of me argue of the ethics of Sebastian's win since they're all now on their last legs and he's got a pile of money ahead of him, money they'll have to pay up by the end of the night, and wonder if she ever did get the courage to go searching for her things.

I'd be able to tell if someone was in my bedroom. It's a sanctuary. Everything has a place so if one thing is out of order, I'll know her dainty little fingers had touched it.

And as I replay our interactions from today, I don't doubt my decision to scrap Regina and replace her with Olivia.

She'll come crawling. I have no doubt about it.

6
Olivia

The moment I realize exactly whose room I am in, I freeze. Part of me wants to tuck my tail between my legs and hightail it out of here but then…

This is *his* space.

We're not going to address his comment about my things being where they *belong*, he can shove that up his ass if he thinks I'll be spending time anywhere near him and his bedroom.

But this room tells a whole story.

It's so *tidy.*

There isn't a single item out of place, no dress shirts hanging over the back of the chaise lounge, no old water glasses on the side or cufflinks on the dresser. My feet pad over the plush grey carpet, sinking into the soft warm fabric. It smells like him in here, warm and almost comforting which is a surprise since there isn't a single inch of that man that's inviting. White walls with black accents, it's modern in comparison to the rest of the house.

There is only one painting in this room, hanging above the bed which is more abstract than the rest of the ones I've seen dotted through the house, the colors a mix of greys and whites and blacks. His huge bed sits in the center of the room, king size with a leather black headboard and monotone sheets that are tucked in and straightened to within an inch of their life.

The bedside units hold a single lamp each, but nothing else, I can't even see a cellphone charger plugged in. It's like no one lives here. I might have questioned if I was in the right place if I hadn't headed to the walk-in closet to find shelves and shelves of his clothes and shoes. They dominate one wall of the closet, which is huge in its own right. All his clothes are color coordinated and then hung by designer.

I nearly laugh at how meticulous it is, with the shirts and the jackets all hanging without a single crease. His shoes are lined neatly in little cubbies and next to that is a large cabinet which showcases his array of designer watches, cufflinks and rings. There's a drawer full of ties, folded neatly.

"Surely not," I open the first drawer and find that even all his socks are folded and sorted by color. Only black and white of course because clearly the man can't have any other color.

Shock runs through me, this is not what I had expected but then I think back to the short time I spent with him at the dining table, how he had fiddled with his cutlery until they all sat in a line and how he spun his glass around every time he picked it up before he set it back down.

Someone likes a little order in their life.

A smile works up my mouth.

Order can so easily be interrupted.

Closing the drawer, I head down the line of hanging clothes, running the tips of my fingers over the softness of them. Money oozes from the fabrics, luxury soaked into the very walls, and I just grab the first shirt I find.

It's huge which is hardly surprising when the man towers over me but then I walk back down the line, tucking the shirt between two suit jackets. Petty? Definitely. But do I feel better about it? Yes. Yes, I do.

I turn and find all my things put away opposite his. It's the same set up, my clothes organized and put away based on color and what they are. Even my underwear has been folded into the drawers and my jewelry placed delicately in the cabinet. My shoes are all lined up and cleaned and the only reason I know that, is because the nude pair of Prada heels I wore a few days ago had a scuff on the toe from where I tripped in them, and now that scuff has been buffed out.

Rolling my eyes, I find the drawer with my pajamas, grabbing the first set on top, and then pick out an outfit for tomorrow, with a pair of shoes to match. I don't want to have to come back here tomorrow. I locate my makeup in a box on one of the shelves and grab everything else I might need before I walk out of the closet, purposely leaving on the light as I cross the room to the bed. Grabbing the corner, I rip the sheets down and then I leave.

The satisfaction it's given me, just to fuck with his system a little, is well worth it.

Shutting myself in the bedroom next to his, I strip out of my robe and get into the comfy pajamas I grabbed before I sink into the bed. Warmth envelops me as I tug the blankets up to my chin and pluck up my phone, playing the film I'd started before I was forced to dinner.

But it's not long before fatigue works through me and I fall asleep barely half way into the movie.

A heavy, irritated knock wakes me the following morning, my phone buried under the sheets and my arm numb since I slept with it above my head the whole night.

"Miss Lauder." A stern female voice I now recognize as Miranda's, filters into the room. "Miss Lauder."

Her impatience stresses me out.

Grumbling, I trudge to the door, "Yes, Miranda?"

"Breakfast." Is all she comes out with before she spins on her polished black shoes and heads back down the hall.

She reminds me of my old etiquette teacher. So grumpy all the time.

With a yawn, I head back into the room and get ready for the day. I dress in a pair of blue denim jeans and a turtleneck sweater before I tie my hair back and apply a small amount of makeup.

When I head downstairs, memorizing the way from the night before, I go to the kitchen where I can smell fresh food being cooked. Miranda is nowhere to be found but there is a man in a chefs uniform whizzing through the kitchen.

"Well good morning, sunshine," He beams at me when

he spots me in the doorway staring at him. He has an accent, French maybe and age lines his face, the smile lines around his eyes and mouth instantly putting me at ease. "You must be Olivia."

"Um hi," I give him a little wave which makes me feel ridiculous.

"Mr. Farrow made me aware of your stay here at the estate," He smiles, "I'm Louis, but you can call me Lou if you like."

He goes back to whatever he is doing on the counter.

"You work here?" I ask, wandering further into the kitchen.

"All my life," He says with enthusiasm, "Here. Sit. Sit." He ushers me to one of the stools around the island. "I hope you like salmon."

Before I can even open my mouth, a plate is placed in front of me, sour dough bread with crushed avocado, water cress and smoked salmon sits in the center, while two steaming, freshly poached eggs rest on top.

"I – uh, thank you."

"Dig in!" He claps his hands with a grin.

I pick up my cutlery and cut into the bread, making sure to get a bit of everything on my fork and shove it in my mouth. He watches the whole time which is a little unnerving. But then flavor hits my tongue, the sour lemon with a kick of pepper on the smokiness of the salmon, and I have to stifle a groan.

"Nothing like a classic," he says, clearly satisfied with my reaction despite not using any words, and goes back to cooking.

I take another bite before I start talking again. "You made dinner last night too?" I ask.

"Yes, Ma'am," He tells me, nodding, "I hope it was to your liking. You will need to let me know of any dislikes so I can make sure not to give you them. And any allergies."

"No allergies," I say before I ask, "Do you always cook for Malakai?"

"Five out of the seven days, yes." He places a fresh glass of orange juice on the counter, "Coffee?"

With a nod, he starts making coffee while something continues to cook on the stove. I won't lie, he stands out in a place like this and after dealing with Malakai and Miranda, I don't know what to make of him.

He's too…nice.

"Eat up, sunshine!" He places my coffee down, "I hear you have a big day!"

I resist the urge to roll my eyes, "Apparently so."

"The caterers will be coming today to set up ahead of tomorrow," He goes on, "I love weddings."

"I love them even more when they're not my own."

"Now, now, kitten," I jump at the sound of Malakai's voice, "No need to have your claws out so early in the day."

My teeth sink into my lip so hard I taste the metallic tinge of blood touch my tongue. He prowls across the room, heading right for me.

"Your breakfast, sir," Louis passes over a plate as Malakai takes the stool right next to mine. He immediately digs in while I still gnaw relentlessly on my lip, making it sore within minutes.

Finally, he drags his eyes from his food, flicking them to me before they drop to my mouth. And I freeze when his hand raises and his thump gently presses against my bottom lip, forcing me to let go of it with my teeth. He rolls his thumb across the bottom lip, all the time I'm sitting there silent and frozen.

When he pulls his thumb away, I see the smear of red on the pad, but it's gone a moment later when he sucks it into his mouth and then continues on with his breakfast like nothing happened.

What the actual…

Shaking my head, I focus back on my food, cutting around the crusts on the bread to get the rest of the food as I finish it up, leaving the crusts on the side. I don't care what anyone says, the crusts on the bread are the worst!

"Thank you, Louis," I say, climbing off the stool and picking up my plate, "That was delicious."

"What are you–"

I drop the plate in the sink and turn on the tap, grabbing the dish soap before I squirt it onto the sponge I pluck from the side.

"You'll have to teach me how to mash the avocados like you do," I tell him, "I can never get it smooth like that."

"Olivia, we have staff for that." Malakai interrupts me.

"I can do it," I grumble to him, focusing back on Louis, "Will you teach me?"

"I mean, sure, of course."

"Thanks!" I beam.

I finish washing up my plate and pop it in the drainer before I head back to the coffee waiting on the counter next to Malakai's plate.

His eyes are on me, the neon blue somewhat dulled in the morning light.

"Dennis will be picking you up in five minutes," he tells me, narrowing his eyes.

"Yay for me," I take a sip of my coffee, staring at him over the rim.

His mouth kicks up, but it isn't a kind smile or one that has any warmth to it, "Did you sleep well, kitten?" He asks.

I bristle at the nickname, "Fine after I barricaded the door." I lie.

He chuckles low, taking a mouthful of food, "You didn't barricade the door."

"And how would you know?"

My only answer is a flick of his eyes.

I go to demand a response when the same man that brought me to the estate the day before enters the kitchen.

"Ah, Dennis," Malakai wipes his mouth with a napkin and climbs from the stool, "Olivia is ready for you now."

Fuck no I'm not, but I don't fight him as he guides me toward the foyer and ultimately the front door. With no other choice, I start to follow Dennis but a hand around my waist snags me to a stop.

"Next time kitten," Malakai rasps in my ear, "When you turn down my sheets, make sure to strip off and climb beneath them. It was disappointing to find you not in my bed."

For all of two seconds I am stumped and then I am furious.

"Fu–"

My words stop when he presses his lips to my forehead and walks away.

7

Olivia

"Where are we going?" I lean forward, shoving myself between the two front seats as Dennis drives us through the city. He side-eyes me before shuffling himself slightly over as if he can't bear to be this close to me. I choose not to be offended by it.

"We have one stop to make," He tells me, voice cold and indifferent, "And then we will move onto our next destination."

I recognize where we are, the streets and houses surrounding us right now are ones I could navigate with my eyes closed. We are on Willow's street. Her penthouse is in the apartment building on the corner right here.

The car rolls to a stop right outside and Willow breezes out the double doors, a huge grin on her face. Dennis climbs out, rounding the car to open the back door for her.

"Oli!" She beams as she throws herself inside, instantly

wrapping her arms around me.

"What the hell is happening?" I breathe.

"I got the message last night!" She tells me, "I didn't know we were going dress shopping today!"

"I found out yesterday," I tell her, "How did you know?"

"Malakai had a message sent to me, told me the time and told me to be ready and here I am! I guess he knew his future wife couldn't pick a dress without her best friend."

I glance to Dennis in the front who happens to already be looking at me in the rear-view mirror. He quickly diverts his eyes to the road, driving carefully through the streets toward the shopping district.

"I can't believe you're getting married tomorrow, Oli!" Willow continues, "It's crazy."

I just nod my head in agreement because she isn't wrong, but I have nothing to say. Malakai arranging for Willow to come wedding dress shopping with me was actually nice of him to do. And that just makes me mad at him.

Firstly, how the hell does he even know that Willow is my best friend!?

But then he is a criminal, isn't he? He has eyes everywhere. It wouldn't surprise me if he'd had me investigated.

Fuck, I'm about to marry a monster.

We pull up to a luxury wedding boutique ten minutes

later, the streets surrounding the shop quiet, and Dennis climbs out to come around and open the door. I would say he was a gentleman, but I'd tried the handle and found the doors were locked.

Willow links her arm with mine as Dennis guides us to the door. Once inside, I'm suddenly hit with just how quiet it is.

This particular store is popular for wedding gowns, it's always busy and I only know that thanks to the number of weddings we've held at my father's hotel – sorry, late father's hotel, now mine.

"Why is it so quiet?" I whisper, afraid to disturb the silence.

"Mr. Farrow paid to have the shop closed today to the public. It is yours exclusively."

My eyes snap to Dennis as Willow's widen, my lips parted as words fail me. It's then that one of the store attendants joins us in the front, her smile wide and eyes twinkling.

"Miss Lauder," She says kindly, "Pleasure to meet you."

Before I can question Dennis, I'm being guided toward the back, Willow on my heels.

I haven't said a word in minutes, but the woman continues anyway, "We took the liberty of picking out some dresses we think would suit your body type."

Okay, weird.

"However, you can try on any dress you like. Champagne?"

Still, I haven't said a word. A flute is pressed into my

palm before the woman floats away, leaving me and Willow standing in the center of the fitting rooms.

"Breathe, Oli," Willow hisses, "Breathe."

Her eyes are lit up with amusement as she sips on the champagne.

I suck in a breath, "Fuck me." Is all I manage to stutter out.

"It's very last minute," Willow comments, walking towards the row of stunning dresses that are hanging there, "I can't imagine having to pick my dress for a wedding which is happening literally the next day. We have to find you something perfect."

"Where did the, *'you don't have to do this',* feelings go?"

"I know you, Oli, you'll do it regardless."

I didn't have a choice.

"Okay, Miss Lauder," The lady returns, "If you'd follow me, we have you set up in room three. It's the biggest. Annabelle is in there ready to help you into the dresses and we can guide you out here for your friend to see."

My flute is plucked from my hand as I am ushered into the large fitting room, a young blonde woman smiling at me as the curtains are pulled behind me.

"Hi!" She chirps but that's all she says as time whirls around me, my clothes are stripped, and I'm bundled into a dress that weighs more than I do! There's layers and frills and lace, the top half a corset style that's pulled so tight it restricts my lungs and pushes up my breasts until they're touching my chin. It's a ballgown style, but bigger, heavier, and covered in glitter. I hate it.

I can barely walk in the thing as I make my way to Willow.

"Don't!" I warn her when I see she is two seconds away from bursting out into laughter.

"Not this one," I grumble to the attendant who nods and helps me back.

Getting it off is much harder than getting it on and I break out in a sweat as the dress is tugged and pulled until I'm finally free and can breathe.

"No ballgowns," I tell them.

She glances to the rack and winces, "I'll be right back!" She says as she grabs four of the dresses and drags them from the room, leaving only two behind.

I collapse onto the velvet bench inside the dressing room, cradling my head in my hands as I try not to overthink this.

By this time tomorrow I'm going to be married, and then what? What happens next?

She returns a little while later with several other dresses, "To be honest, I didn't think you were a ballgown type," She tells me, "I think mermaid will be best for you."

I nod as if agreeing and watch as she takes a pure white gown from a hanger. It's silk with no adornments at all, but it doesn't need them. There is so much beauty in the simplicity of it that it almost takes my breath.

She grins when she sees me staring, "This is from our new collection, it's technically not on sale yet but I just knew you'd love it."

My fingers reach out to touch the material of the dress, breath in my throat. I would wear this. "Let's get it on." She says.

She helps pull the dress over my head, adjusting it down my body and it feels like heaven against my skin, so soft and silky it brings goose bumps up across my body.

The straps are thin, and the dress is form fitting, lining every curve like it's a second skin. It has a cowl style neckline that droops low in the front allowing the space between my breasts to show, almost down to my naval and the back is completely open, leaving me nearly bare to my ass. A series of small buttons then work down the back of the dress before it sweeps into a long trail.

"I don't think we need to try on anymore," The woman says on a whisper.

I shake my head, agreeing with her.

"Let's go show your friend!"

At this point, it didn't matter who I'm marrying, this dress is stunning.

"Oh shit!" Willow gasps, standing abruptly, "Oli you look…"

I blink as I turn to the bigger mirror to get the full picture, the one in the fitting room didn't do this dress enough justice.

The material is snow white but almost pearlescent, a shine to it that throws off hues of pink and purples and it fits like a glove. I'm still staring when the woman starts pulling at my hair, clipping it back to show off my shoulders and long neck, drawing attention to the bare skin of my chest.

"It's a dress that doesn't need any jewelry," She tells me, "Maybe a pretty pearl clip to tie up your hair, did you want to try a veil?"

"No veil." I shake my head.

"Do you want to try on more?"

"No," I tell her. "This is the one."

"I just can't believe you're getting married *tomorrow*" Willow breathes, blowing at her coffee before she takes a sip. Dennis hadn't argued when I'd asked if we could go for coffee since the dress fitting barely took any time at all. The dress was being shipped to Malakai's house this afternoon, along with the shoes and accessories I'd chosen to match.

"You'll be there, right?" I panic, leaning forward as I feel my eyes go round.

"Well obviously," She scoffs, "The invitation was attached to the message I got about the dress fitting. I'm your bridesmaid."

"Really?"

"Yeah," She shrugs, "I didn't say no since I knew you would have asked me anyway."

That's true. I guess I could give Malakai a little grace, I didn't want this wedding but at least he's making the day a little better for me by allowing my best friend to be with me. I wonder if he's invited my sister too though it's unlikely, considering the history.

"Do you have a dress?" I ask.

"Mm," she nods, sinking back into the chair, "Blue."

"Well okay, I guess," I look towards Dennis who stands outside, leaning casually against the car but he's watching us, like a goddamn guard dog. He's barely said two words all day and just stands there and scowls like the world has wronged him.

"So, what's it like?" She asks, "What's *he* like?"

I drag my eyes to my best friend, "I hate him."

She chokes on a mouthful of coffee, sputtering the liquid all over the table, "What!?"

"I hate him." I repeat. "Like *hate* him."

"Shit, Oli!" She rapidly shakes her head, "Do we need to like, buy plane tickets or something?"

I shake my head. Even if I did, he'd find me, I'm sure.

"No, but it's okay," I nod, more to myself, "Everything will be fine. After tomorrow I'm just going to actively avoid him." *And make his life hell.* But I leave that part to myself.

"That's not a marriage," She grimaces.

"It's an arranged marriage. It's a farce anyway."

"You always dreamed about finding love," She pouts, "I remember that journal! The one where you planned your wedding day when you were twelve!"

"That was when I believed in fairytales," I laugh. "We live in the real world."

She rolls her eyes, "You know what I mean. You can't see this going anywhere? At all?"

"With Malakai Farrow?" I laugh at how ridiculous that would be. Me and him? Absolutely not. I'd rather swallow glass than ever give that man the time of day. Not only did he manipulate me into agreeing to this marriage, using blackmail and threats as his weapons, he's a dangerous man. One that kills for fun. He owns a whole damn business designed for people exactly like him. He's terrifying. Brutal.

"If a day comes when I tell you I have feelings for him, put me out my misery. I will never," I meet her eyes, showing her how serious I am, "*Never*, fall in love with him."

8
Malakai

Heading to bed last night to find my room fucked with was not on the list of ways I wanted to end the evening. I expected a little tampering, it's human nature to look without invitation, but it was only supposed to be a drawer not closed properly or the toiletries in the bathroom misaligned.

It wasn't even the bed. It was the clothes in the closet, the misplaced shirt, the light left on. She calculated it based on how organized I liked to be. She watched me, calculated her move and played it seamlessly.

It's amusing. But she'll have to try harder than that.

And whispering in her ear this morning, telling her to strip and get into my bed sank so much satisfaction into my stomach I don't know how I survived this long without her. It's been too long since I've had any sort of amusement in my life.

She's been gone since this morning, but I know she's finished shopping since the bags and boxes arrived thirty minutes ago.

I dial Dennis, putting my phone to my ear and he answers on the second ring.

"Where is my bride?" I growl into the cell.

"Having coffee with Miss Stanton." He replies immediately, "I have eyes on them right now."

"Why isn't she here?"

"Sir?"

I glance at the clock and note barely any time has passed since she left to go shopping. I just assumed it had been a few hours already.

"She finished quickly," I note.

"Yes sir."

"She asked to go for coffee?"

"Yes sir," He answers robotically.

"Fine," I grumble, "Bring her back within the hour."

"Yes sir."

I roll my eyes and hang up, heading through to the kitchen where several people are. The caterers are setting up for the wedding tomorrow, while the planners guide their staff into where things need to go.

The wedding will take place in the Garden room, it's located in the west wing of the manor house, a sprawling space made up entirely of windows that look out onto the forest that hides the lake. The reception will then go ahead in the Grand room attached to it which is currently being converted to house the many guests that will be in attendance.

I don't just have the council to appease with this wedding, I have the press too. I have no qualms in telling the world that little Olivia Lauder is now mine.

The wedding is to be witnessed by every council member, old and new, the record noted in the Farrow archives and the tick box checked that I am fulfilling old traditions which will further secure my seat.

I don't bother checking on the status of things, instead I head to the drawing room. I had an office upstairs, but I've always preferred this room above all else.

A fire is always going inside, warming the space through the harsh winter and I guess I spent so much time in here as a kid, it's become my sanctuary, second to my bedroom.

Except when I push open the door, I find I'm not alone.

My grandfather, Abe, sits in my chair, the old fuck drinking from my decanter. What is it with the people closest to me taking my things!?

"Get out my chair," I grumble to my grandfather.

But he just grins, the lines in his face sinking in deeper as he does, "Malakai, my boy. Is that anyway to speak to your pops?"

I roll my eyes and despite my demand for him to vacate my chair, I perch on the desk, staring down at him. How does he look older already when I only saw him a few days ago? There's a milkiness to his eyes, a papery thinness to his skin that wasn't there the last time I saw him.

"You missed poker night."

"I was busy wrangling the press. They caught wind of your upcoming nuptials." Despite the age clearly lining every inch of him, the glint in his eyes tells a different story.

"Oh, I wonder who told them about that." The press was needed but only one or two, not the army my grandfather has likely tipped off.

"Who knows," He shrugs innocently, "So, where is she?"

"Who?" I tug at my shirt sleeves.

"Olivia!" He stands abruptly, "I need to welcome her to the family!"

I stifle my laugh. I can only imagine how that might go down.

"She's out, pops, wedding dress shopping with her friend. She'll be back later."

I talk about her like there isn't a single thing wrong between us but realistically, we didn't know each other, and I didn't plan on knowing her further than how I can rile her up and how to get her in my bed. My grandfather doesn't need to know that though. He's a real love kind of guy, always has been. My grandmother had been his first and only his entire life. She passed some years back now, but I'd grown up knowing them together. He worshipped the very ground she walked on.

Sucker.

"Well, I'm sticking around," He shrugs and lowers back in the chair with a groan, "No point heading back tonight when I need to be here bright and early. Will I still be walking her down the aisle? She has no father, right?"

I stifle my wince. I had a hand in her father's death, even if I wasn't the one to pull the trigger.

Playing with Fire

It started when Regina's uncle wanted more in his business. He owned a long line of luxury hotels and had expanded but the Lauder's were in his way. He wanted their business too. At the time I needed a wife, and agreed to help him take down his competition. It gave me more places to run my money through anyway.

But as it turned out, Olivia's father was feeling the pressure and had hired one of my own guys to take out the competition too.

Funny how the world works that way.

But things went wrong, Olivia's father died, and her sister witnessed it.

That's how I ended up with sweet Olivia in my grasp.

"Yeah, pops, you're walking her down the aisle."

"It doesn't seem right to walk her down when I haven't even met the girl!" He tuts, drinking from his glass, "We will all have dinner tonight." He declares.

Shit.

I barely got her downstairs last night, how the fuck am I to get her down tonight? Throw her over my shoulder and take her there myself?

Now that I think of it…

"What's that grin for?!" Abe frowns.

"Just thinking about how much you're going to like her," I pat him on the shoulder, "Go freshen up, I'll make sure you meet her this evening."

It's a little past three in the afternoon when Olivia returns to the estate. She appears lighter in herself than yesterday, the constant scowl isn't on her face and there's a pretty tilt to her lips as she walks through the front door.

It immediately drops when she spots me waiting for her.

"I assume you got everything you need," I say, even though I know she did. It's all waiting for her in her room ready for tomorrow.

"I spent your money, if that's what you're asking," She gives me a fake smile, "About five hundred grand of it."

"Good," I throw back, "It's yours."

Her eyes narrow, "Well that'll be the first and last time, Malakai," She starts to unravel her scarf, eyes never straying from me, like I'm a predator she needs to keep an eye on. Show her back and she might just get eaten. "Figured I'd rather use your money over mine when it's for something I don't want."

"You wound me, kitten," I purr. "And here I thought you were besides yourself to get married to me."

She rolls her eyes but then she begins to walk toward me, cocking her head as she looks at me from beneath her lashes. Her heels clip on the floor and her tongue peeks out to trace across her bottom lip. Once she's in front of me, she walks her fingers up my chest, the feel of her this close stuttering my breath in my throat. She smells too damn good, and with those dark eyes, and those thick lashes fluttering delicately she looks like the perfect amount of innocent and sinful.

Playing with Fire

"Malakai," she whispers my name, a slight rasp edging her tone, and I swallow, blood shooting straight to my cock. Surely it hasn't been *that* long since I last got laid that the mere close proximity of a woman will leave me hard. But I guess it's just *her*, this gorgeous specimen of a woman staring up at me with those doe eyes and plump lips.

"It will be a cold day in hell when I want a man like you."

Her words should be like an ice-cold bucket of water but if anything, it just heats my blood more. What a delicious challenge she's laying out for me, and she doesn't even know it.

"You're playing with fire, darling," I rasp, "Careful not to get burned."

Her nails scrape down the front of my throat as she drops her innocent mask, eyes narrowing as she stares through her lashes at me, "You may scare everyone else, Malakai, but you don't scare me. I vowed to make your life hell and I've never not kept a promise."

"I look forward to it, wife," I whisper.

"I still have twenty-four hours of not being your wife," She steps away from me, plastering on that fake smile once more, "You don't get to use it yet and by the time I'm done, the last thing you're going to want me to be is your wife."

I quirk a brow, reveling in this fire she's burning in my direction. I'm basking in the glow of it, these little verbal sparring matches feeling a little like foreplay. I can only imagine how it'll be when we get past all these walls.

Explosive comes to mind.

"I'm going to watch a movie in my bedroom. Unless the house is falling down around me, leave me alone." She wiggles her fingers as her goodbye and struts away, her hips swaying hypnotically in those tight as fuck blue jeans.

I'm a simple man at heart and the sight of a plump round ass will leave me a little dumb.

She's long gone by the time I snap out of it.

9
Malakai

The dining room is set, my grandfather is in there chatting with Miranda – he seems to be the only one who can get her to smile – and I'm waiting for Olivia to come downstairs.

She was called on over thirty minutes ago and while I'd decided to give her time, I knew she wasn't coming.

So just like the evening prior, I go up to fetch her.

I find her just like the night before, tucked into the mammoth bed, still dressed, which is a surprise, drinking wine out of a cup, but she's snacking on Cheetos now, the orange dust staining her fingers.

She glares over at me where I stand in the door, hands in my pockets.

"What?" She snaps.

"Just wondering when you'll be joining us," I say nonchalantly, leaning on the door frame.

She rolls her eyes, one day I'm going to punish her for

that. I'm sure her pretty ass will look even better with a large red handprint on it. "I won't be."

"Wrong answer, kitten."

In three strides I'm across the room, grabbing her ankle to drag her to the edge of the mattress.

"What the fuck!" She screams, using her other leg to try and kick at me. Everything about her is small, her tiny feet, her dainty hands, it makes me think she's fragile, but then she kicks me straight in the gut, knocking the wind right out of me.

I grab her other ankle, sucking in air as my stomach aches with the kick she landed. She flails and lashes out and I can't fucking get her to stop. With her screams echoing through the house, I get on the bed, pinning her on the mattress with my body.

"Stop fucking fighting me!" I yell.

"Fuck you!" The little kitten even tries to headbutt me, but I manage to move before her forehead connects with my nose. It would have been hard enough to break it. I straddle her thighs, keeping her pinned as I shove her hands above her head, glaring down at her.

"Are you going to behave?" I ask casually.

She blows out a breath, trying to move a strand of dark hair from her eyes, "Fuck off." She huffs.

"Fine." Moving her wrists into one hand, I take hold of them with a firm grip, almost losing it when she wriggles and thrashes but then one of my hands falls to her waist, to the slither of skin on show from where her sweater has risen up. Her flesh is warm and soft under my palm, and I can't help it, I give her a little squeeze, watching as my fingers make indents into her. It's not

Playing with Fire

the time for another damn hard on.

"What are you doing?" She begins to panic, shaking her head frantically, "Please no!"

Shit.

"Stop it," I growl, "I am not going to force myself on you, Olivia."

She swallows, tears welling in her eyes and just for a minute a bloom of regret takes root in my chest. Not enough however to stop me from doing what I am about to do.

With her frozen, I quickly get off, dragging her with me before I hoist her up and over my shoulder.

The air rushes out of her lungs with a grunt and I'm almost out the door when she comes back to me.

"Get the hell off me!" She screeches, "Put me down, you asshole!"

Her tiny fists pound into the bottom of my back but I don't shift her, I continue down the halls and then the stairs with her over my shoulder, her screaming bloody murder the whole time. It's not until we get to the dining room, and I dump her ass into one of the chairs that she stops.

"I am going to kill you!" She wails.

Abe clears his throat, amusement lining his aged face.

"Olivia, I take it?" He muses, grinning like a fool at her.

She snaps her eyes to him, them widening as she realizes we have company to witness her little tantrum.

"Uh, hi?" She swallows, cringing.

"Don't you worry about me, sweetheart, go ahead and

drop him down a peg or two," Abe leans back as Miranda scurries from the room to let the kitchen know we're ready for dinner.

"I'm sorry, who are you?" She flicks her eyes to me and then back to my grandfather.

"Name's Abraham," he gets up and walks towards her, "You can call me, Abe, I'm his grandfather."

"Grandfa – shit, hi!" She gets up promptly, grasping his hand in a firm shake. Well at least she's nice to someone. It's just me she doesn't like.

Abe chuckles fondly, patting the top of her arm, "Come, come," he gestures for her to follow him before he drags out the chair next to his and waits for her to sit before tucking it into the table and taking his own.

Stifling the roll of my eyes, I take the seat opposite them, spinning my glass on the coaster.

"Big day tomorrow," My grandfather starts, "You nervous?"

Her shoulders stiffen but the manners that were taught to her, her whole life win over, "Not nervous per se," she rolls her lips, "Hesitant."

I chuckle into my glass, taking a sip as she struggles to remain polite.

"Mm," Abe agrees, "I would be hesitant too if I was marrying that buffoon."

"I am your grandson," I point out, "You're supposed to sing my praises, not offend me."

"Are you offended?" Abe asks.

"No."

Playing with Fire

"Exactly."

Before he can continue his tirade to my future wife, dinner is brought in, an Italian dish my grandfather requested earlier in the day. Olivia is served first, then my grandfather and me, before a bottle of wine is placed in the center of the table.

I get up to grab the chilled bottle, leaning across to pluck up Olivia's glass to pour it in.

"Thank you," she says quietly, accepting the glass as I pass it back to her and go about pouring for my grandfather and me.

"I'll be walking you down the aisle tomorrow," My grandfather casually announces, "Don't worry, I won't let you trip."

"You will?" She gasps.

"Malakai tells me you don't have much family," Abe says, digging into his food, "it would be an honor to hand you over to my grandson."

"Oh." Is all Olivia responds with.

The rest of dinner is mostly spent in silence with the casual words being had here and there and when the plates are cleared, I expect Olivia to run away but to my surprise she accepts another glass of wine and settles into an easy conversation with my grandfather.

I just choose to watch them, listening to her talk about her father's hotel, which she is now the owner of, and all the travels she has taken with her best friend. It's an unfiltered view of the woman in front of me, giving me a subtle glimpse into *who* she is.

My grandfather has always been a people person, he can get anyone to talk and be comfortable around him.

It's a gift, he likes to say, and a weapon. Secrets, he tells me, they're the greatest currency and making someone trust him enough to spill their secrets is the best arsenal to have.

Olivia lights up as she speaks with him, especially when talking about her sister and best friend, but it makes me wonder just how many people are in Olivia's life. After I'd looked into her, the only two names that were relevant were her sister and Willow.

She didn't have many people in her corner, I realize and it's probably part of the reason she so willingly threw herself into my hands to save her sister. If you don't have much, you fear losing it far more greatly.

"I'll see you at the end of the aisle," Abe stands from the table with a soft smile aimed at Olivia.

She nods, "Yeah." The word comes out as a whisper, "You will."

"Chin up, sweetheart," Abe knocks her chin fondly, "He's not that bad."

The most adorable little snort laugh leaves her at his words, and she flicks her eyes to me, letting them roll down my body with a mixture of disdain and disgust, "I'll take your word on it."

My grandfather chuckles, slaps me on the shoulder and exits the dining room, heading to his bedroom in the east wing of the house.

Olivia sips the remainder of her wine quietly, looking everywhere else but at me.

"Your stylists will be here at nine a.m." I say, filling the silence, "Willow has been invited to join too."

"Okay," She answers.

"The ceremony shall begin at eleven in the garden room," I keep going, finding it hard to stop just so I can keep her here for a bit longer. I know she's about to flee at any moment.

"I'm sure I'll make it there," She replies dryly, "And if not, someone can drag me."

I clear my throat, scrubbing a hand across my mouth to hide my grin, "Kitten, I've no problem throwing you over my shoulder to get you to the altar. You're mine, no matter which way I have to make it happen."

"Pig," She snaps, getting up from the table abruptly.

"Goodnight Olivia," I call after her.

Her response is flipping her middle finger over her shoulder, and I can't help the chuckle it brings.

And when I head to bed that night, I'm delighted to see she's upgraded from simply turning down my bed.

My pillows are thrown across the floor, the sheets a balled-up mess tossed into the corner with some sort of liquid on them that looks like shower soap from my en-suite, and my mattress is somewhat half on and half off the bed base.

Olivia's tantrums seem to be chaotic, like she tries hard to be destructive but the most she can do is a little bit of mess that'll take no time to clean.

It doesn't even register on my scale of annoyance, not when I can smell that sweet scent of her still lingering in my space.

I straighten out my bedroom and then cross the hall. I'd gone in the night before while she was sleeping, just to see, just to watch as she dreamed but I won't have such luck tonight.

The door doesn't budge when I push on it this time, and since there isn't a lock on this door, I wonder if she barricaded it like she said she did the night before.

Such a shame.

But it doesn't matter now. I could go the next seven hours without seeing her. After tomorrow, as soon as that ring is on her finger she won't be in a separate room. She'll be in my bed. Under my sheets.

There will be no hiding from me.

10

Olivia

To say I'm sick with nerves is an understatement, my stomach hasn't stopped churning all morning and the thought of ingesting anything right now makes me feel ten times worse.

"You're looking a little green," Willow cringes.

I press my hand to my stomach, "I'll be fine."

The artist presses the powder puff to my cheeks, setting the makeup she's placed on my skin. She's done an incredible job, keeping it light but I have this subtle glam look going on, which I'm not mad about. My hair has been pinned back and the small flower shaped accessories I picked up at the boutique have been intricately woven into my black strands.

The only jewelry I have on is a bracelet Willow lent to me for the day, my something borrowed, she said. After she'd given it to me, she pulled out a lacy little lingerie set, wagging her brows, "Something blue and something new," she shoved it into my chest and told me to put it on.

Since the dress is backless and strappy, I can't wear the bra, but I appease her and put on the lacy panties.

Now my feet are being slipped into the strappy white heels we had picked to match the dress, and Willow is reaching for the gown hung up by the bedroom door.

The house for the past few days has been quiet, barely a whisper but now I can hear commotion, voices and laughter, footsteps and furniture being moved. I know there are hundreds of people downstairs waiting.

I haven't seen Malakai today, I had gone for breakfast early this morning, even though I couldn't stomach anything, but he was nowhere to be found. I'm not sure if that made me happy or even more nervous.

"Let's get this on you," Willow whispers, helping to ease the dress over my head, avoiding my makeup so we don't mark it and once it's over my head, I shimmy a little, letting it fall in a swish of material down my body, soft like a cloud as it goes.

Despite my lack of excitement for this wedding, this dress really is stunning.

The buttons are secured at the back, the dress fitting like a glove.

Willow lets out a whistle, "Damn girl."

She looks stunning herself, in a cobalt blue dress that makes her skin pop, it hugs all her curves. She's gone light with her own makeup, using gold and browns to compliment her blue eyes and the dress and her red hair is curled, framing her face perfectly.

"You ready?" She asks.

My chin barely moves with my nod.

Playing with Fire

She reaches for the door but before she can get it open, a knock sounds.

"Who is it!?" Willow's eyes widen in panic.

"Sebastian."

"Who the fuck is Sebastian?" She hisses.

"Fuck if I know!" I whisper shout.

"I'm the best man," He calls a moment later, "I'm here to escort Miss Stanton down the aisle."

"Oh shit!" She snaps.

"Did you know about this?"

"Yes!" She hops on her toes, "I forgot!"

"How do you forget! I can't go down there on my own!" I grasp her hand, holding it tight.

"Uh, bitch," She tries to snatch her hand back, "You're gonna break my hand!"

"Don't leave me!" Panic surges through me, that churning of my stomach becoming so heavy I can feel myself on the verge of vomiting.

"Nuh uh!" Willow grasps my shoulder, "You look too pretty to puke. Suck it up, honey!"

"Don't make me go down there on my own!"

"That Abe dude is walking you down, right?" She nods, her voice calm and soothing.

"Yes, but he isn't here! And I have to go down there! There's so many people, Wils, what if I fall down the stairs!?"

She opens her mouth to speak but I'm already talking over her.

"Oh god, what if he stands me up!? Could you imagine!?" I let go of her hand, ignoring how she shakes it and then cradles it to her chest, "I don't even want this wedding but I'm doing it anyway. He's going to stand me up, isn't he? He's going to humiliate me. The asshole!"

The door opens a touch and Willow shoves her head out, "Oh!" She breathes but immediately admonishes herself and snaps out, "Wait focus!"

"Willow!" I hiss.

"Sorry, he's hot," She shouts back, "She's spiraling. I'll meet you downstairs, okay?"

"Spiraling?" I hear him repeat in that deep voice of his.

I've not even met him! Shit.

I can see the hair and make-up artists staring at me, but they know better than to speak right now. I'm in a big old hole and I can't find a ladder to climb out of it.

Shit. I can't do this. I can't fucking do this.

"I'll get her downstairs," Willow vows, "I'll meet you down there!"

Then she shuts the door and is back in my face, "Oli," She says my name sternly, "Breathe."

I shake my head frantically.

"Do not cry!" She demands, "We are going to walk out of that door, I am going to hold your hand the whole time, so you don't fall down the stairs, and I'm going to take you to Abe. He's going to walk you down the aisle to where Malakai *will* be waiting, do you understand me?"

"He'd do it, you know," I point out, "Stand me up just

to humiliate me."

"He's down there!" I hear Sebastian yell through the door, "I just saw him."

"See?" Willow rubs the tops of my arms, "It's going to be fine."

I nod, more to myself than to her. I mean if he stands me up then I'm free, right? It'll be fine.

Why am I even panicking about this!?

"There you go," She smiles, "You ready?"

"Yeah," I reply, voice wavering.

She grasps my hand firmly, tugging me toward the door. When she opens it there's no one in the hall and we begin to move down it slowly. Noise filters up from downstairs, but it's almost drowned out by the sound of my thumping heart, my blood pounding inside my ears.

Don't throw up. Don't throw up. I chant it over and over in my head as we descend the stairs, one step at a time, our movements slow, Willow's grip on me tight as if she knows I'm going to bolt at any second.

Just before we hit the bottom step, Abe comes into view. I can't help but smile at him. He'd instantly put me at ease the night before with his charm, it didn't matter that he was related to the devil because he's nothing like his grandson. There's a kindness to him Malakai lacks, and he almost reminds me of my father when he wasn't drowning in work.

"Olivia, sweetheart," He says when I reach the bottom, "You look beautiful."

"Thanks, Abe," My voice shakes, giving away my nerves. He takes my hand from Willow, not giving me an inch to even think about running.

"Chin up," he taps my chin with a crooked finger, "Shoulders back," I find myself obeying his words, straightening my shoulders, "One foot in front of the other so you can go knock my grandson on his ass."

A quick burst of laughter escapes me and some of that tension leaves my chest, making it just that little bit easier to breathe.

"You good?" Willow asks me just as a man steps up behind her.

He's fucking huge. Dressed impeccably in a blue suit, it stretches over broad shoulders and thick arms. His white shirt is tucked into blue slacks and his dirty blond hair is styled to perfection atop his head. Dark green eyes, thick lashes and he's clean shaven which highlights how sharp his jawline is, his cheeks high, his brows low.

He throws me a dazzling smile, winking before he takes Willow's arm and leads her away from me.

"Sebastian?" I ask.

"The one and only," Abe grumbles, "Troublemaker if you ask me."

"Is Willow safe with him? Is he… is he like Malakai?"

"Yes, sweetheart," Abe pats my hand, "We're about to walk into a nest of snakes, assume everyone is venomous, because they mostly are. Trust no one except Malakai and those he keeps closest to him."

"So, Sebastian?" I push.

"Yes, as much as I loathe to admit it."

I'm not about to tell him I'm never going to trust him or

Malakai. The only person I can trust is myself.

"You ready?" Abe asks.

"I don't think I have much choice," I admit honestly, "Let's get it over with."

11
Malakai

Soft instrumental music begins to play as the room rises to a stand at the first sight of Sebastian and Willow. They walk toward me, looking quite the pair and acting as if this wedding isn't between two people who barely know each other.

They make it to the end but just before they take their places to the side, Sebastian leans in, a shit eating grin on his face.

"You're so fucked," He chuckles under his breath, "She's killer man. Fucking *killer*."

Willow stands on the opposite side, holding a small bouquet of white flowers, while Sebastian takes his place behind me, that grin still splitting his face.

I already know how stunning Olivia is, I don't see how today makes any difference – oh shit.

She finally comes into view, my grandfather at her side, arm linked with hers.

Devastating.

I hear a quiet murmur start in the room, hushed whispers between parties as they discuss everything that she is. Her hair, her dress, the makeup she has chosen to wear. They'll rip her apart like the damn vultures I know they can be.

But Olivia truly is stunning.

Her dark hair pulled away from her face to showcase her long delicate neck, the neckline of the dress low that I get a peek at the mounds of her breasts, barely being held in by the silk that hugs her body like a second skin, flowing over her curves. She holds a bouquet of blue and white blooms, her grip on them so tight her knuckles have turned white.

She doesn't look like she's breathing much at all and instead of looking at me, she stares straight ahead at the wall behind me. Camera's flash, a mix of the paparazzi that had been formally invited and some of my council members wanting documentation for the archive.

The garden room has been transformed to be able to seat over three hundred people, the space decorated to perfection to match the color scheme the planners had come up with. It's a damn good wedding even if the bride looks like she'd rather be anywhere else but here.

Finally, they make it to me, and my grandfather gently presses a kiss to the top of her hand before he places it in mine. Still, she doesn't look at me, her eyes to the floor.

"Eyes on me, kitten," I whisper, "Give them all a show."

Her eyes snap to mine, blazing with so much swirling

heat that resembles something like resentment.

"You are breathtaking," I tell her.

Her jaw pops as she clenches her teeth and the officiant steps up and she diverts her gaze to him, her hand trembling within mine. I stroke my thumb over her knuckles, hoping to soothe her, focusing on the tender caresses of my thumb over her delicate skin, so soft under the roughness of mine. The tremors seem to ease but they don't go completely but I'll take it as a win, nonetheless.

As the officiant goes through the spiel, the room is silent around us, I keep my eyes on her. Tracing over the line of her jaw, down her throat, her collar bones and shoulders. I stare at the darkness of her eyes, framed by impossibly long black lashes and how her skin has a slight shimmer to it beneath the gold lights in the room. It's gloomy beyond the windows, the frost that fell overnight has not yet melted and it leaves the landscape around us a wash of white and grey. Perhaps if we were on better terms, I would have whisked her off somewhere hot for a honeymoon, but I can't guarantee she wouldn't try to murder me while we were away and claim it as an accident.

I repeat the vows provided to me, slipping the platinum ring, embedded with diamonds onto her finger. Her thumb instantly starts to play with it, spinning it around her finger and as she repeats the vows, her voice shakes.

She slides the ring onto my finger, staring at it.

"You may kiss the bride!" The words are yelled and for just a moment the world stops spinning.

Olivia's wide eyes latch to mine, panic seizing her, so I

Playing with Fire

step in, closing the gap between us and take her face in my hands.

Her eyes bounce between mine, the room around us silent save for the rapid breaths she expels from her lungs.

And then I lean, keeping my eyes on hers until my mouth whispers across her plump lips. A breath whooshes from her and her lips part just enough for me to take hold. I crash my mouth to hers, tasting her for the first time, my tongue tracing the seam of her lips in request for access.

I'm delightfully surprised when she parts and lets me in.

I deepen the kiss, not giving a single fuck to the hundreds of eyes staring at us or the frenzy of flashing cameras as I claim her right here, in front of them all. Her hands grip my wrists and I tilt my head, forcing her to do the same as I slide my tongue into her mouth. She tastes like devastation, like the sweetest ruin, and I'm starving for her.

She makes it damn hard to breathe.

Someone clears their throat and it's enough to startle her. She snaps out of my hold, putting the distance between us again and then she glares at me, her kiss swollen mouth looking far too appealing in this moment.

"Savor it," She whisper hisses at me as I step up and link her arm with mine, "That'll be the only kiss you'll ever get from me."

I chuckle low as I begin the walk back down the aisle, "Scratch and bite all you want, kitten," I say to her,

"But you're now mine. *My* wife. Make sure you remember that when you look into the mirror and reminisce what it felt like to kiss me."

She scoffs, turning her attention ahead of her as we make it out of the room. I direct her down the hallway toward the grand hall where the reception is being held and guide her to the head table, pulling out her seat as she lowers herself, reaching for the wine already in an ice bucket between our two places.

"We've got a long day ahead of us," I warn her, watching her fill her wine glass to the rim, "Pace yourself."

My eyes narrow, the need to punish her making my fingers itch as she lifts the glass, downs half of it and then flips me her middle finger, finishing it all off with a saccharine smile.

My teeth grind together as I take my place next to her, watching the guests file into the room.

Sebastian comes to take his seat next to me while Willow places herself next to Olivia.

"Regina is here," Sebastian whispers in my ear, adjusting the cuffs of his shirt, "she's already spreading the rumor you two are still an item behind Olivia's back."

I roll my eyes, "Where is her father?"

Sebastian points to the greying man, rotund in shape and balding on top, Hank Ware is as much of a slimy asshole as Kenneth, Regina's uncle was. He just happens to sit on the council making it harder to dispose of him.

To be honest, he's been a good sport about not having his daughter married to me, it's a power move, one I know he wanted so I couldn't be too angry at him, even if he couldn't keep his spoiled daughter in her place.

"I'll speak with him," I tell Sebastian, "Keep Regina away from Olivia."

He nods, looking over my shoulder at my new wife. "That was quite the kiss."

Lowering my voice, I chuckle, "Scared of being a hundred grand lighter now?"

"Nah," He leans back, "She came to her senses pretty quick."

I roll my eyes, the commotion in the room settling so I turn my attention back to Olivia. She's moved her chair further away from me, closer to Willow and is sipping her wine. The whole glass is almost gone.

That just won't do.

Grasping the chair, I yank it back, the wine in her glass spilling over and splashing against the tablecloth.

"What the fuck!?" She growls at me.

"We just got married," I tell her, "Putting a mile between us is hardly selling it."

"You got the wife," She replies, "we never agreed that I had to sell it too."

"You keep pushing me, kitten." I warn.

"What?" She flutters her lashes, "You'll tell me off?"

"Don't fucking test me."

"Or what, Malakai?" She challenges, a devious little glint lighting up the darkness of her eyes. "What exactly are you going to do?"

I open my mouth to speak but a photographer steps up

to the table, "A photo for the city paper," He says with a grin, "Say cheese."

I place my arm around Olivia's shoulder, pulling her in close as I rest my mouth against her hair, the camera going off as he captures a moment that looks intimate but is anything but.

She goes to move away, but I don't give her an inch, "Olivia, darling," I purr, voice quiet and only for her, "When you give yourself up to me, when I have you spread beneath me, naked, wet, and panting, I'll remember every moment you defied me. Every challenge you threw at my feet, and I'll deliver it back." She stiffens under me, "Your ass will be sore, your cunt throbbing but I won't stop, even when you beg me to."

"Congratulations!" The photographer scurries off and I finally let her go, reveling in the blush that has risen to her chest, turning her skin pink.

She practically leaps away from me, keeping her eyes off me as she reaches for the wine, scoots her chair toward Willow and tops up both their glasses.

"You're so fucked," Sebastian laughs.

"We'll see," I reply, staring at the back of my wife's head, "We'll see who breaks first."

12
Olivia

I am fucked.

My head is light, the alcohol working through me, warming my blood and loosening my nerves but I'm struggling to stand up straight.

"Okay," Willow holds me up in the bathroom, "No more wine for you."

"What?" I slur, "Why not?"

"It's three p.m. You didn't eat any of your food and can barely stand up. I'm pulling the card, no more drinking."

I pout, "Boo."

She shakes her head, manipulating my body until I'm leaning on the counter so she can wash her hands before we exit the bathroom.

She has her arm around me as we make our way to the room still brimming with people, but she suddenly stops, pulling me to a halt with her.

"Water," I tell her, "I need water."

"Hold on!" She snaps. "Who is *that*?"

With blurry eyes, I search the space in front of us until I can just make out the shape of two people. Malakai stands outside of the room, with a woman.

A very pretty woman. In a red dress, her lips painted the same color. Strawberry blonde hair and a body to die for, yeah, this woman is a knockout. And she's standing really close to Malakai, her hand on his chest.

"Bitch." The word slips out before I can tell my tongue to stop, and I slap a hand over my lips. But too late, Malakai is staring at me, a frown tugging on his brows, and I have the strangest urge just to smooth out the crease that forms between them. He grips the woman's wrist and tugs her hand off him before he stalks toward me, head cocked as if trying to keep my eyes since I'm tilting.

Strong arms band around me and I feel Willow let go, giving me to him. Traitor.

"Who's she?" I ask, unable to stop myself.

"No one you need to worry about," He hoists me up, his arm around my waist strong and firm but he turns us away from the hall and toward the stairs.

"Where are we going?" I ask, stumbling over my words.

"You're going to bed."

"No." I dig my heels in.

"What do you mean, no?" He groans.

"I'm going back in there. We're putting on a show."

Playing with Fire

"No, you're making a fool of yourself," He snaps.

"Oh, fuck you too," I snatch out of his arm and stomp toward the hall. But his arm is there again, dragging me back until my spine hits his chest.

"Olivia," He warns.

"You're not scary." I tell him.

His laugh is like smooth whiskey, so deep and warm it sends a zap down my spine that then coils low and hot in my stomach. It's the alcohol, I tell myself. It isn't *him.*

"If it's not fear making you shake, kitten, please enlighten me to what it is you're feeling right now that is making your body tremble so badly."

I flare my nostrils, dragging in air, trying to clear this fog out of my head. The wine was a bad idea, I should have been smarter, now my thoughts are lagging, and my body is betraying me.

I wiggle out of his hold, point my finger in his face and promptly do... nothing. I've got nothing right now. In a huff, I spin on my pretty strappy shoes and beeline for the hall, making it all the way to find Willow getting comfy in Sebastian's lap.

"Hussy," I grumble, "They're the enemy!"

She rolls her eyes, "Drink your water."

I snatch up the glass and down the whole thing, pinching the bridge of my nose between my fingers. I need more.

The pitcher in the center of the table is empty and feeling more confident than earlier, I feel like I can make it across the room without falling flat on my face.

"Where are you going?" It's Sebastian who asks the question.

Fingers wrapping around the handle of the pitcher, I shake it in his direction, "To get water. I'm on a wine ban."

"I'll go," He offers, moving to pick Willow up off his lap.

"I'm good," I point at him, "You stay."

His brows twitch as I keep pointing my finger at him like he's a dog and not a very real man, but he lets me go. Malakai has yet to reappear which is a blessing. Not sure I could have handled another second with him in this state, mainly because I can't control my tongue and I'm not sure if I'm going to say something I'll regret.

I make it to the bar that's been set up, and drop the pitcher on the counter, blowing out a breath as I wait. A few people talk to me but I'm not focusing enough to remember any names or anything they've said and when I get the water, I turn back to the table only to be doused in a cold liquid.

I suck in a shocked breath, the pitcher of water falling from my hand and smashing on the floor, scattering ice cubes and soaking the end of my dress in ice cold water.

And when I look up, I see the same woman who was in the hall with Malakai.

"Oops," She gasps in mock horror, the grin tugging up the side of her mouth making it very clear she just did that on purpose.

Red wine is seeping through the thin silky material of my dress, soaking my skin beneath it and blooming as it grows across my abdomen. It's macabre, the deep crimson stain on a white gown, spreading and growing and all I can do is stand there and watch it happen.

Everyone is staring.

The woman is just standing there.

Behind her I can see Sebastian moving toward me, this big bear of a man shoving people out of his way as Willow stares on in horror.

But it isn't Sebastian that gets to me first.

It's Malakai.

"What the fuck are you doing?" He growls, his anger palpable, thickening the air around us.

"I– I–" I stutter out my words, my eyes on the growing stain. The dress is ruined. They'll be no saving it and everyone saw her do it, but no one is helping.

It seems ridiculous to cry over it. I'm blaming the alcohol for the sting of tears I feel welling up in my eyes.

"Not you," He softens as he speaks to me, "You!" He points to the woman. "Get her the fuck out of here. Now!"

There's a sudden flurry of movement as several large bodies move in.

"Mal," She says sweetly, "It was an accident. She's drunk, she wasn't looking where she was going."

"Bullshit," Sebastian is here, and he's glaring. Oh shit, he's scary, like *terrifying*. He looks like he wants to rip her apart and throw away the pieces.

"Get her the fuck out of here." Malakai orders, the voice coming from him right now not one I've heard him use. This is the real him. Not the pretend pieces he's given me these last few days, this man right here is the devil in the flesh, and I'm frozen in his orbit.

People move at his word, they cower and bow, at his every beck and call.

"Olivia," He speaks so gently to me in comparison to the way he just commanded the room, "Darling?"

"My dress," Is all I manage to squeak.

I can feel myself flushing hot all over, embarrassment making me want to curl up into myself with everyone still watching.

"Breathe," Malakai whispers, hands up as he steps toward me, like he's soothing a frightened animal.

Don't cry, I tell myself. Don't embarrass yourself further.

"Olivia," Malakai says my name again. My vision swims as I bounce my eyes back to him, frantically shaking my head. The dress is sticking to me now, my skin soaked and cold, chasing goose bumps over my body.

"I've got you," Is all he says before arms are swooping beneath me, taking out my legs before another cradles me beneath my spine. I don't even have it in me to fight, I just want to hide. I can fight him all I want but with hundreds of eyes on me, whispering, gossiping, I can't help but feel like a frightened little girl.

I've been in a position like this before, granted it was much worse than this but all those feelings flood back, the humiliation, the way everyone stared...

I bury my face to hide from their eyes as he carries me from the room, sure, strong steps away from the

Playing with Fire

masses. And he doesn't stop until we're closed away in a bedroom, the noise blocked out, the warmth of the room fighting to take the chill off my skin. He gently places me down, helping to lower me onto a soft, plush seat.

"Wait here." He orders gently. I watch his feet walk away from me, the soles sinking into the carpet. If I wasn't so drunk, I might have fought him about coming into his bedroom, but I'm tired. I'm wet. I'm humiliated.

I hear the shower turn on a moment later and then Malakai is back and he's kneeling in front of me. My lips pop open in an O shape as he lifts my foot to rest it against his muscled thigh, pushing the dress up enough to get to the straps holding the heels to my feet. He removes one, gently placing my foot back onto the carpet before he lifts the other one, and once they're both off, he helps me to stand.

"Can you undress yourself?" He asks.

I wince, "Yes."

"I'll get Willow for you."

But I shake my head, "No. Don't. I just…"

He nods, understanding, stepping out of the way to give me a clear path to the bathroom. Steam rolls out of the open door and I beeline for it, shutting myself inside as I press my spine up against the wood.

A mirror sits before me, and while it's fogged up in here, it's clear enough to see the huge red wine stain on the front of my dress, and the dark strands of hair at the sides of my head that stick out messily.

I look awful.

Reaching behind me I manage to fiddle with the buttons to loosen the dress enough I can slip the straps off my shoulders and let the dress slide down my body. Droplets of red wine stick to my skin and even the top section of my new underwear is stained red.

Shaking my head, I slide out of them, dumping them on the ruined dress and climb under the hot spray of the shower. My fingers work through my hair, pulling the little flower pins from the tresses, releasing them from their hold and the pins make a little *ting* noise as they hit the floor at my feet. I scrub my face free of makeup and shampoo my hair, and then I turn my face to the wall and just exist.

I let the water run over me, soaking my hair to my head, let the water catch in my lashes and in my lips and I just stand there and breathe.

Overwhelmed.

Overstimulated.

There was too much going on too quickly that I couldn't keep up with it.

But here, I can breathe. The sound of the water on the tile is loud, it drowns out my thoughts, washes away most of the effects of the alcohol though I still feel buzzed. And nauseous.

I am going to have a serious hangover in the morning.

For a few more minutes, I let the water cleanse me before I reach for the button and switch off the water. I wrap a heated towel around me as I step from the shower but freeze on the bathmat as I realize the ruined dress and panties are gone from the bathroom floor.

I didn't hear anyone come in at all.

Playing with Fire

Swallowing, I tiptoe to the door, opening it as quietly as I can to peer out into the bedroom.

It's dim in there now, the main light switched off in favor of the two lamps at the bedsides and a fire is going in the hearth, smaller than the ones in the rest of the house but it's warm and cozy and drags exhaustion to the front of my mind.

My feet leave wet prints on the carpet as I head to the pile of clothes waiting on the end of the bed.

They're my pajamas, a long sleeve shirt and flannel pants combo and I quickly dry to get into them, wanting that familiar feel of my clothes against my skin. I don't bother drying my hair, just choosing to give it a towel dry and look at the mammoth bed.

I should go to my room, get into the bed I've been sleeping in for the past couple days but this one looks so inviting.

I climb onto the mattress, sinking into it and when my head hits the pillow a sigh leaves me. I'm wrapped in his scent, it lingers in the sheets and despite knowing better, I drag them to my nose, smelling that masculine fragrance that warms something inside of me.

Before I know it, sleep is claiming me, sinking me into a slumber not even the devil himself could wake me from.

13
Malakai

"Get me Hank!" I demand, "Now!"

The ruined dress dangles from my fingers, the cloying scent of the red wine only fuels my rage more. I'd grabbed it from the bathroom while she was showering, not wanting her to see the spoiled dress after she'd finished cleaning up. The house has pretty much cleared out, after that show in the grand hall I'd ordered Sebastian to start getting them away. I didn't want anyone here.

It was bad enough the photographers had caught her in that state, but everyone just fucking stared.

"Farrow," Hank saunters up to me, his eyes a little glassy, cheeks reddened from the alcohol he has consumed.

"So help me, Hank," I growl, "If you do not put your daughter in her place, I fucking will."

His eyes widen, "Excuse me!?"

"She went after my wife." My voice drops to a low timbre, a deadly kind of calm settling over me, "At her wedding. Embarrassed her in front of everyone. And don't you dare for one minute tell me it was an accident. You forget I have security tape."

His nostrils flare, "Careful, boy," Hank swallows, showing off the fear he is trying so hard to mask, "We put you on the throne, we can take you off."

"Shall we put it to a vote?" I bluff. "I'll call the council in right now."

He huffs, "We can hardly be surprised at Regina's reluctance to accept your new wife."

"Regina is not part of this organization," I remind him, "she was only ever a pawn. A pawn that got discarded for a prize much better."

"You took away her power."

"She had no power!" I roar. "She never would have either, as my wife or otherwise."

He steps back at my slip of anger, "You know how Regina can be." He stammers.

"I don't give a fuck, Hank," I step up, closing that gap between us, "Sort it out or I will. We buried your brother not long ago; it'll be such a shame to have another funeral so soon."

Sebastian pushes off the wall to join me as I storm from the room, leaving Hank staring after me.

Losing my temper with a council member is not how I wanted the day to go. There are ramifications to disagreements within the council, and I knew some of the members sitting around that table have questioned my leadership for some time. Unfortunately, it is not as easy to get rid of disloyalty. I have few close to me, and there is a reason for that.

"I want eyes on him at all times," I tell Sebastian, "I don't trust him."

"And Regina?"

My teeth snap together at her name, "Where is she now?"

"Ran the moment you lost your shit."

"Perhaps it was what was needed to keep her away," I roll the statement around and instantly know it's not true. That snake is relentless and I'm just glad I managed to find an out before she sank her teeth into me.

Sebastian knows it too.

"Olivia?"

"Last I checked, she was in the shower." I rub at my temples, hoping to keep the headache that is knocking at my skull at bay.

"I should have got the water myself," Sebastian rubs at the back of his neck, "Sorry, man."

"We can't coddle the woman," I say, "She'll only kick back more."

"Man," Bast laughs to himself, "I can only imagine what Olivia would have done if she were sober."

I roll my eyes. Would she have done anything? She fights me but it's always in private, no witnesses but today she froze up.

I want to know why.

"Get me the copies of every photo taken after the incident. If a single image leaks of Olivia with her ruined dress, I want the person who leaked it in the cells. Understood?"

He nods and goes to walk away.

"And Bast?" I call after him.

He stops to look over his shoulder, waiting.

"If you're gonna fuck Olivia's best friend, make sure she knows you're not committing. The last thing I need is for my wife to have more ammo against me because you can't keep your dick in your pants."

He scoffs a laugh, "Sure, boss."

I end up back in the drawing room, the house around me quiet as I rewatch the footage from the security camera. Anger runs through me as I watch her spill the wine on my wife but it's Olivia that keeps all my attention.

She completely shuts down as everyone stares on, a deer caught in headlights as she did nothing but stand there. My eyes flick to the ruined wedding dress hanging in the corner of the room, the red stain looking offensive. She looked so stunning in that dress, it's such a shame it's now ruined.

And the underwear, sitting in the top drawer of this desk, had a red stain on the waistband, nothing too serious but the fabric is light and it's unlikely it'll come out. A waste.

Dropping my eyes to my computer, I open my email and fire off a message to the boutique it was purchased from. Even if she never wears it again, I want her to have another one.

Closing the laptop, I spin the glass before I lift it and down the remaining whiskey inside. It's late now, the darkness beyond the window impenetrable and I walk slowly down the halls of the manor home I've lived in since I was a child.

These walls have seen a lot, death, secrets, betrayal but it is home. As I get closer to the central point of the house, the sound of the cleaners fills my ears, tidying up the garden room and grand hall but I don't check on them. I take the stairs two at a time before I come to a stop at my bedroom door.

Will she be inside?

Granted, she wouldn't be able to get back into the bedroom she was using since I'd had locks installed and only I had the key, but that didn't mean she didn't go wandering and fell asleep in one of the many other vacant rooms in this house.

I compress the handle slowly, staying quiet as it opens up into the room.

And there she is.

Curled under the sheets in the middle of the bed, her midnight black hair a stark contrast to the white pillows beneath her head. She has her back to me, her breathing even, body still.

I slowly walk around the bed, coming to a stop in front of her as I lean in and gently brush a silky soft strand of hair from her sleeping face. Her lashes flutter at the whisper of my touch, a sigh parting her plump lips. She's in the pajamas I'd found for her, the sheets pulled up to her chin.

My eyes on her, I start to strip out of the shirt I'm wearing, unbuttoning each button slowly before I tug it off my shoulders and throw it toward the hamper in the corner of the room. My pants come off next and follows the shirt to the washing, leaving me in just a pair of boxers.

I lose track of time as I stand there watching her but eventually, I go to the bathroom and take a shower before I grab some flannel pants and pull them on.

It's been a fucking long ass day.

She's still in the same position when I come out of the bathroom, a cloud of steam following me and my feet sink into the carpet as I move around the bed, climbing in behind her.

A small sigh escapes her again and then she turns, settling onto her back, a small little frown creasing her brow. I resist the urge to smooth it out and flick the lights off, laying there with her beside me in the darkness.

My thumb spins the new wedding band on my finger, round and round as I inhale her scent, the natural fragrance of hers now mixed with my own, thanks to the products she used in the shower and her body rubbing up against my sheets.

It's a heady mix and a somewhat primal feeling blooms in my chest. My woman. My wife. Smelling like me.

She shifts again next to me, turning onto her side and her hand lands on my bare chest as she scooches closer. My muscles stiffen at her touch, her soft skin on mine and when I feel her breath tickle the side of my neck, her lips so damn close, I almost break.

I remember every second of the kiss we shared at the altar, the way she tasted, the way she yielded to me. Her fingers curl, nails digging into my skin, and I have to stifle a groan, blood shooting straight to my cock.

She snuggles in further, relaxing once more as I lay there deathly still, my cock rock hard.

And I settle in for a long fucking night.

14

Olivia

A headache pounds inside my skull, the kind of throbbing that makes it hard to focus on anything else. My eyes hurt, my ears hurt, *everything* hurts, and I know it's completely self-inflicted thanks to the amount of wine I drank the day before, but god, this is hell.

I keep my eyes closed, waiting for the headache to abate enough for me to move and go in search of hydration and pain meds. At least I'm comfortable, and warm and something smells really damn good. I let my hands run over the sheets under me until my fingers bump into something hard.

Huh?

That doesn't seem right.

Popping one eye open, squinting through the light that floods the room, I finally latch onto what or rather *who* is lying next to me.

That is a man chest. A very nice man chest, his pecs and abs defined so perfectly it's like they've been carved from stone. Swallowing, I let my eyes drift down, taking in every dip and curve before I see the waist band of flannel pants and the sheets.

Shit.

My eyes bounce up, only to find Malakai smirking down at me, one dark brow quirked, his blue eyes twinkling.

"Oh my shit!" I move so quickly I get wrapped up in the sheets, dragging them from him as I scramble, tangling myself up more. I'm in such a panic, I don't see the edge of the bed and I'm tumbling off the side before I can right myself. I land in a heap on the floor, the sheets locking my limbs together, my hair falling over my face.

A deep chuckle has every hair raising on my body and I blow out a breath, trying to move the hair from my vision so I can start untangling myself.

I'm still struggling when Malakai's feet land on the floor next to me and I look up to find him leaning his head in his hands, elbows resting on his knees as he watches me struggle, that damn smirk on his face.

"What the fuck are you doing here!?" I snap.

"This is *my* bedroom," He cocks his head, analyzing me.

"What!?"

"How's the head, kitten?" He asks as he stands up, raising his arms above his head to stretch out his unfairly beautiful body. So many muscles, flexing and popping as he moves and I forget how to talk, letting my eyes drag down him. I've even stopped fighting with the sheets just to let myself drink him in, the six pack and the muscles at his sides, the veins that snake down his forearms and the V that carves up his hips. A trail of hair leads from his naval down to the waist of his pants and disappears beneath, right to his –

"That's a dick!" I scream, coming to my senses as I scramble away, taking the sheets with me. That's a very hard, very big cock tenting the front of his flannel pajama pants.

"Well, you can hardly blame me, kitten," He steps toward me as I crab crawl backwards until I have nowhere else to go, my back hitting the chaise lounge, "Especially since you were rubbing yourself all over me all night."

His finger curls under my chin, bringing my eyes to his.

"I was not!" I snap in indignation.

His tongue traces his bottom lip, "How are you feeling?"

"Can you please get your dick out of my face!"

He rolls his eyes and steps away, heading toward the bathroom, "I asked you a question, Olivia."

I glance to where he's disappeared into the bathroom, leaving the door open and I scramble to remove myself from the sheets, getting to my feet quickly. The headache is still knocking at my temples and my stomach is rolling, reminding me I really need to eat something and drink a gallon of water.

But first escape.

I look to the bathroom again, slapping my hand across my mouth when I see he's dropped the pants and is currently brushing his teeth completely naked. His toned ass is staring right at me.

Fuck. Fuck. Fuck.

The water turns on as he spits into the basin, almost finished with his morning routine so I bolt.

"Olivia," He sighs, catching me making my escape. I throw the bedroom door open and run to the one I was staying in only to bounce right off the door. I shove at the handle, but it doesn't budge and then I feel his body press up to mine. The warmth of his chest leaks through the shirt I'm wearing, searing my skin. I glance subtly behind me, loosening a breath when I see he's at least put a towel around himself, so his cock isn't rubbing up all on me.

"This room is now off limits," He whispers close to my ear, "It's my bedroom or nothing at all."

"I'd rather sleep in the stables," I grumble stubbornly.

"That's not what it looked like last night," He drawls.

"I was drunk," I hit back, "Drunk me and sober me are not the same person."

"Get back in that bedroom," He orders.

"No."

"Olivia."

"Malakai."

I can hear his teeth grinding together, "Your dentist must hate you with all that grinding." I point out, "Maybe you should get some of those guards or something."

"You are the most irritating woman I have ever met."

"Aw," I pout and look over my shoulder, fluttering my lashes at him, "Thank you."

Playing with Fire

His gaze narrows before he drops it to my lips and it's right about now, I'm going to nope the fuck out of there. I slip under his arm and bolt back into his bedroom, slamming the door before he can get inside, twisting the lock to keep him out.

His fist slams into it. "Olivia!" He roars.

"Yes, Malakai?" I call, heading to the closet.

"Open this fucking door, right now!"

"Sorry, I can't hear you." I pull some clothes from the racks inside our shared closet, choosing some leggings, an oversized sweater and a pair of knee-high socks since it looks like it's going to snow today. A frost covers the ground, and the sky tumbles with grey clouds.

"Olivia!" He yells, pounding his fists hard.

I roll my eyes; he's being *very* dramatic.

I strip out of my PJs, throwing them onto the bed and reach for the underwear I got out at the same time when I hear the wood of the door splinter, a cracking sound that zaps awareness down my spine. If he gets through that door…

"Shit," I hiss, rushing to get my underwear on. I hop on one foot as I drag the leggings up my legs and shove my head through the hole in the sweater. I'm out of breath as I tug my long hair into a messy bun and then I'm rushing to the door.

And breathe…

I unlock it and throw it open, "If you wanted in," I say sweetly, "All you had to do was ask nicely."

I pat his chest condescendingly as I saunter down the hall away from him. I can feel his glare boring into my spine and knew I'd find burning anger etched into his face if I were to look back.

Poking the bear probably isn't the wisest idea but getting him riled up and out of control gives me a thrill. Payback, I like to think of it as. Getting some of my own control back.

I find Louis in the kitchen when I make it downstairs, cooking up something that smells good for my neglected stomach.

"You're like an angel," I whisper, drifting towards him.

"Mrs. Farrow," He beams at me, "Good morning."

"Well, you *were* like an angel," I pout, "Why did you have to go and say that for?"

His brows tug in confusion, "Sorry?"

I wave my hand, "Don't worry, do you know where the painkillers are?" I ask.

"Are you okay?"

"Too much wine," I say by explanation.

"Ah," His face softens in understanding, "Well sit down, let me get you some and then something to drink."

I breathe a sigh of relief as I take a seat at the island counter, rubbing my temples. He places a glass of fresh orange juice in front of me alongside two little pills which I take immediately, and then he places a plate of bacon, eggs and French toast on the counter, and I don't wait a second to devour it.

Playing with Fire

I am *starving*.

He watches with amusement for a while, "Will Mr. Farrow be joining?" He asks.

I shrug, "Maybe, I don't know."

"I will be," His voice sounds from the doorway behind me and I purposely keep my head forward and down, focusing on the eggs on my plate.

The stool scrapes across the floor as he pulls it out, grating against the headache still to abate, sitting right next to me. I see one dark suited leg and one high shined Prada shoe resting on the cross beam of the stool. He's dressed impeccably, and that scent that is inherently him is stronger now, wrapping around me.

"You should cut down on the cologne," I tell him, "It's stifling."

The lie falls so easily from my tongue that I can't help but glance at him, seeing a smirk tugging up the corner of his mouth.

"I'll be going into the city today," He tells me, thanking Louis for the food he passes over, "Try not to get into any trouble."

"Wouldn't dream of it," I roll my eyes.

I feel his eyes staring into the side of my face but when I don't give him what he wants he relents, starting his food. We sit in uncomfortable silence, the sound of our forks scraping the only noise between us. The tension is enough to even make Louis uncomfortable who finds an excuse to leave the kitchen.

"I'll be back in a couple of hours," Malakai places his empty plate next to the sink and I shake my head at him.

"The dishwasher is right there," I tell him.

"Goodbye, Olivia."

With him looking elsewhere I let my gaze travel down him. He's just as beautiful dressed as he is undressed. It's unfair to make a man like him *that* attractive. Dressed beautifully in a black suit and black shirt, the clothes fit him like a glove, showing off those threateningly broad shoulders and the dark fabric contrasts with the neon blue of his eyes.

"I can feel you staring."

"Goodbye Malakai." I snap back at him and then all I'm left with is the lingering echo of his chuckle.

15
Olivia

"But what does he do?" I ask Miranda for the fifth time, following her around the huge living room I haven't even had a minute to admire. There's a whole wall of books, from floor to ceiling and it even has a ladder – I've only seen that shit in movies!

But I'll check that out later. I need intel.

"Mrs. Farrow, please," She huffs impatiently, "I have work to do."

"You've fluffed that pillow three times."

She gives me a withering stare and moves on, "Don't you have something to do?" She presses.

"Nope, I'm free as a bird." I tell her. "I just need like a routine or something?"

"Why?"

"I'm his wife," I say, lying about my motivations, "I should know my husband's schedule."

"It didn't seem like you wanted it this morning when he

was bashing down the door."

I cringe, "Yes well," I wave a hand, "That was then, and this is now."

She narrows her eyes suspiciously, "He works a lot." Is all she gives me.

Work? Pfft, that isn't work. That's preying on the helpless.

"And when he is here?"

"He rides the horses. Works out. That's it."

I know she's bullshitting me.

"Is there a gym here?"

She nods.

"Where?"

"Mrs. Farrow, if you'd please let me get on with my work." She dismisses me, her chunky heels stomping on the floor as she runs away from me.

Fine. Before I go in search of someone else more willing to cooperate with me, I wander toward those towering shelves. So many books, there's some ancient ones on the shelves, with leather spines and crackled gold lettering, newer works and biographies. It's a book worms dream. I let my hands trail over the works, admiring the array of colors on display. It's the main feature in this room, not the grand fireplace dominating the other wall, or the several plush sofas or the expensive sculptures.

Deciding I'll revisit and select a few books to read since I'm sure I'll have plenty of time on my hands, I go in search of someone else.

And find no one.

This whole house is filled with staff, they're always around and yet I can't find a single one. Miranda probably told them all to avoid me though I have no idea why they'd want to keep the information from me.

It's the first day I've been truly alone here.

Pulling out my cell, I dial Willow's number and she answers on the first ring.

"Bitch!" She hollers down the phone, "What the fuck happened!?"

"What?" I frown.

"You disappeared and then Malakai had everyone leave. He cleared the whole place out."

"What are you talking about?"

"After that hoe bag threw her wine on you," she says by explanation.

Oh. That.

"I passed out." I admit.

"You passed out," She repeats, "Malakai was pissed, Oli. Like scary mad."

"Just showing you the real him," I shrug even though I'm wondering if that's even true. Which version of Malakai is the real one?

Shaking my head to myself, I wander upstairs to the bedroom. It's been cleaned since this morning, new sheets fitted, the hamper emptied, and the bathroom tidied like no one has even stayed in here.

It's nothing like my apartment. Sure, I had the penthouse, and I loved it, the space, the view but it was lived in. I had dirty glasses in the sink and laundry in the basket. There was dust on shelves and limp looking plants on the sides. It was a home but this, this just seems like a show room. You can look but don't touch.

Shaking my head, I take a seat on the end of the bed before I flop down onto my back, looking up at the white ceiling.

"I don't know," She answers my previous statement, "He doesn't seem *that* bad."

I roll my eyes though she can't see me, "I woke up next to him this morning."

"What!?" She squeals.

"Nothing happened. I fell asleep in his bed and when I realized I freaked out so bad I fell out of it. Then his dick was in my face."

"Wait. Hold up. Nothing happened but you had that man's penis in your face?"

I laugh to myself as I remember how ridiculous it was, "Sure did. It was hard for it not to be. I was on the floor; he was stood up."

"But you didn't put it in your mouth?" She hedges.

"No!"

"I bet that man is packing some serious heat, am I right?"

My cheeks burn with the memory. Those flannels didn't hide much, and Willow isn't wrong. Thick, hard, long…

"Oli!?" Willow snaps my name, bringing me out of my own head. "Were you just picturing his dick?"

"Stop talking about his dick," I sit up, fidgeting to try and disperse some of this tension in my muscles.

"Okay but can you confirm first? I need to know for research purposes."

"Research?" I scoff incredulously.

"Yes." She states matter of fact.

"Fine. Yes." I give up the information reluctantly, wiping the back of my neck.

"I knew it!"

"Okay new topic, did you fuck Sebastian?"

"No," I can hear her pout through the phone, "He told me I was too drunk and to go home and sleep it off."

"Wow."

"Mmhmm," she grumbles. "I don't like this topic."

I laugh, "Well I'm bored out of my mind. Malakai is off in the city and all the staff here are avoiding me."

"I see you're making friends," she says sarcastically.

"Whatever. I'm going now."

"Don't be sour," she laughs, "You'll settle in soon enough."

"Yeah, we'll see," I say, "Love you, bye."

"Loveyoubye!" She says it so quickly all the words roll together and then the phone disconnects, leaving me in a silent room.

Snow is gently falling beyond the window, settling onto the already frozen ground but as peaceful as it is, I can't relax. It has a lot to do with this morning. Now I'm a woman who has control over herself, one bad experience some years ago sort of forced me to do it, but seeing Malakai like he was this morning…

All those muscles, that lazy feline grin on his face, the hard length of his erection.

I squirm, the heat building in my core making my thighs ache.

"Don't do it, Oli," I talk to myself, "You're not getting off to images of the husband you didn't want."

But fuck, I'm horny.

Rolling my neck side to side I walk into the closet, searching through all my things for the little box I know I packed and sent here. There wasn't much inside, a couple of vibrators but they did the job, now where is it?

I rifle through the whole closet, but I don't find it anywhere. Where would they have put it? Fuck. Did they open it?

I'm too turned on at the moment to give a shit.

"Fuck it," I grumble, crossing the room to the mammoth bed, I crawl up it, settling myself into the mountain of cushions as I let my hand slip beneath my leggings.

My eyes shutter closed at the first swipe of my fingers against my pussy, the wetness there helping the glide as I work myself slowly. I feel ridiculous, to be so worked up over something so miniscule so I decide I'm putting it down to how long it's been. I slip a finger down, sinking it inside of me as I press the heel of my palm to my clit, allowing myself the friction as I work my finger in and out of me. My other hand trails up and under my sweater, sliding over the warm skin of my abdomen until I cup my breast, squeezing my nipple between my thumb and finger.

My little whimper seems obscenely loud in the silent bedroom, but I work my hand faster, applying more pressure as my muscles begin to spasm. My hips lift from the bed as if searching for more and I add a second finger, pushing myself over that edge with a loud moan.

I keep my hand moving until the aftershocks of my orgasm subside and slowly pull my hand from my leggings, releasing my breath.

"Quite the show, kitten," his voice startles me enough I let out a scream and my eyes snap to him. He's leaning on the door, legs crossed at the ankles but when my lips part and heat floods my cheeks, he pushes away from the door, prowling toward me. There's a heat in his eyes and determination in his steps.

I'm lost for words.

He watched it. *He watched it all.*

Frozen solid and slowly dying a little inside, I can't take my eyes off him as he moves to the edge of the bed closest to me, grasps my wrist gently and brings my hand toward him. My eyes widen as a new wave of arousal floods me when his lips wrap around the fingers I'd just had inside of me, and his tongue licks them clean.

I'm completely floored, even when he steps away, straightens his suit jacket, and leaves the room.

"Meet me downstairs," He calls before he can completely disappear, "You're due a tour."

16
Malakai

I can taste her on my tongue, the flavor of her so damn addictive I'm immediately craving more. I should have made my presence known, especially when she was so lost to her pleasure, she didn't hear me enter. But when I saw her hand moving beneath her leggings, her other caressing her breast, I lost all ability to speak.

She looked divine as she pleasured herself, chin tilted toward the ceiling, hand moving expertly against herself as she brought herself to climax. And the sounds, the little whimpers and gasps, I'd instantly been hard.

I'm *still* hard, cock pressing achingly against the front of my slacks, throbbing with need. I was driven by pure desire when I crossed that room, seeing her glistening fingers, wet with her arousal, that pretty blush staining her cheeks. I needed a taste more than I needed the air in my lungs.

And the moment I had her fingers in my mouth, my tongue lapping up every last drop, I knew it wasn't

Playing with Fire

enough. It's why I got the fuck out of there as quickly as I did.

I stand at the kitchen counter, glaring out the window at the snow that falls, the house around me quiet until I hear her timid footsteps slowly approaching.

They stop when she reaches the threshold of the kitchen and I subtly glance behind me, finding her wringing her hands in front of her, face pointed toward the floor in something akin to shame. Embarrassment.

I turn to her, swallowing, trying to banish the images from my head, "Olivia." My voice is roughened by desire, rasping out of me thickly. "Eyes on me, Olivia."

Slowly, so fucking slowly, she lifts her eyes but not her head so she's looking at me from beneath her lashes. You'd think she'd just been caught doing something she shouldn't and was now here to receive her punishment.

I certainly wanted to punish her, but purely for her smart mouth, her stubborn tendencies and accurate pokes to my patience but *that...* I wanted to praise her for that.

"Don't be ashamed, kitten," I tell her.

She drops her eyes proving to me that's exactly what she's feeling.

I cross the room in a few steps, closing the space between us so I can curl my finger under her chin, tilting her face up, "Never be ashamed, Olivia. I've never seen something quite as beautiful as you pleasuring yourself."

She swallows, eyes bouncing between mine. I want the feisty girl back, I want the confident, sexy little kitten with the claws and the insults.

"Let me know when you do it again," I push, "I'll pull up a chair to get a better view. See how pink and wet you are."

The attempted slap is a nice little surprise. I grab her wrist before she can make contact, gripping it firmly but not hard enough for it to hurt her. She burns with rage, her eyes are alight with fury, her little body trembling violently in my grip.

"You're a damn pig," She growls, teeth grinding together.

"Oink," I grin at her.

She snatches out of my hand, putting that distance between us as she goes to the fridge and grabs a bottle of water.

"I hear you've been curious, darling," I drawl, "You'd like to know more about me, huh?"

"Just trying to work out where to hit you where it hurts the most," She gives me the sweetest little devilish smile.

She wants to play with fire I'll make sure to give the greatest flames.

"Follow me, kitten," I crook a finger, "Tour begins now."

I don't wait for her as I walk away, my shoes clipping rhythmically against the shined wood floors. I hear her scurry after me, feet scuffing on the floor.

"We'll skip all the rooms you already know," My voice is monotone, flat. I skip the grand hall and garden room, the living room and drawing room as I follow the maze-like corridors through the house.

"How many rooms does this place have?" She asks behind me.

"I forget," I wave a hand, "a lot?"

Her brows shoot up, "A lot, that's all you got?"

"Seventeen bedrooms," I tell her, "Four living rooms. Two kitchens."

Her eyes widen as I go on, listing all the rooms in the house. I come to the media room, opening the door to show her the huge TV, the rows of plush couches and loveseats, a bar set up at the other end, stocked fully with every beverage and snack anyone could ever want. It's a waste since it never gets used. Her lips are parted as she looks around, but I cut off her view as I close the door and move along, skipping a few of the downstairs bedrooms which get used sometimes by my inner circle and the council members when our monthly meetings run over.

I stop at the game room, showing her the pool tables and dartboards, another bar that never gets used.

"Can you play?" She asks.

"Pool?"

"No, the violin," She deadpans.

I smirk, "Yes, I play."

"Interesting," She spins on her heel, "So where to next?"

"This way," I take her down towards the sunroom, an extension on the south side of the property that faces the thickest part of the wood. There's a patio with a grill out here but then there are two paths, one that leads down to those woods and further in, taking you to the lake, and the other stretches around the property, bringing you back to the main yard where the gym room and pool are.

She sucks in her breath, spinning in her spot to stare at the walls of windows that surround her, the snow unable to settle against it thanks to the heat pushing up against it. A telescope looks out toward the sky and a grand piano dominates one corner of the room, the rest of the space taken up by couches, a rug covering the floor.

"This one," She breathes, "This one is my favorite."

"It's yours whenever you want it to be," I tell her, watching her face light up in awe. There's nothing really special about the room, it's the view that steals the show.

"Is this everything?" She asks.

"We have the gym and pool rooms," I tell her, "Unless you want a tour of all of the bedrooms."

She narrows her eyes.

"Keep your mind out the gutter, dirty girl." I chuckle at her sigh of annoyance, "Follow me."

She looks less than impressed by the gym room. I can't see why; it's decked out with everything anyone could ever want. I've spent countless hours here, working out anger, building strength. The wall of mirrors opposite us shows the two of us, her tiny build next to mine, her little hands fisted at her sides as she glares at the side of my head.

Rolling my eyes, I continue, opening the door joining onto the pool room, complete with jacuzzi and sauna.

"Feel free to use it whenever you want." I tell her, checking my watch.

There's a council meeting in thirty minutes but I know members will start to arrive soon.

"I won't be joining you for dinner," I tell her as we walk out of the gym and back toward the house, the short walk outside enough to make Olivia start shivering.

"What a shame," she says dryly.

"I have taken the liberty and requested Willow come keep you company." I tell her.

"Wait, what?"

"All I ask is that you stay away from the meeting room on the first floor."

"Why?" she asks suspiciously.

"Because it would please me," I tell her seriously, holding my breath to see what she will do.

It takes a few seconds but then a quick burst of laughter spills from her lips. I can feel the scowl settle onto my face the longer it continues.

"That was probably the wrong thing to say to me," She giggles, holding her stomach.

"I'm serious, Olivia."

My tone halts her laughter.

"The men coming here tonight are not the company you want to be around."

I can see the color drain from her face, the whites of her eyes getting wider.

"Stay away from that room, Olivia. Do you understand me?"

She gives a barely there nod.

"Good." I check my watch again, "Willow will be arriving any minute. Go and greet your friend. I will see you at the end of the night."

She mumbles something that I don't catch and walks away from me, the sway in her hips drawing my eye.

With her gone, I head through to the back of the house, opening the door to see several cars already parked on the gravel. They would have already let themselves in, so I don't wait. I don't want Olivia running into any of them and I need to contain them to the meeting room.

This gathering needs to be over and done with as quickly as possible, there will be no lingering in the house as usual tonight.

For as long as I can, I will keep Olivia from the shadows of my life. From the blood money and death and the men that deal it like master gamblers.

I'm not blind to the fact that I am just like them, if not worse. I'm as highly trained as any of the assassins in my employment. I know she understands the role I have in this business, but she doesn't fully understand the depth in which that root grows.

"Gentlemen," I greet as I open the meeting room door. As large as any corporate office, the room boasts a large oak wood table with chairs to seat twenty, not including the two high backs on each end of the table. I always sit at the back of the room so I can see everyone and the door, and Sebastian takes the seat at the other end, closest to the door so he can be the one to call in my inner circle and the others should anything go wrong.

There's only been one time in Farrow history when the council members turned on their leader and that was a long time ago, but things happen, and I already know I am pissing people off.

They don't like my age for starters. The youngest Farrow to sit on this throne ever. But they also don't like my leadership style, don't like that I am taking away their control, questioning the old rules and laws.

I don't need them. They need me.

And I have no issues reminding them of that fact.

17
Malakai

My fingers tap on the table, eyes scanning the room of men. Sebastian sits opposite me, doing the same. One of the reasons the man is my second is his ability to turn from playboy joker to ruthless killer in a matter of seconds.

People second guess themselves when he steps into a room.

He's loyal. Smart. Brutal.

He's been the same way ever since we were kids.

"If you've all stopped gossiping like a bunch of teenage girls in a playground, we can begin," I address the room, the stern tone of my voice zipping their lips.

"Someone a little eager to get back to that pretty wife?" My eyes fall to the man who spoke, the son of a now deceased council member and that's the only reason he has a seat. *Fucking traditions.*

No one laughs.

"I can't remember your name," I say to him, "Remind

me."

The color drains from his face, "Samual."

I click my fingers, "That's right, Samual."

His eyes dart around the room, waiting for someone to step in but they won't.

"Do you know why you have that seat, Samual?"

"It is my birthright," At this, he puffs out his chest.

I nod, contemplating, "You're right, but let's not pretend you deserve it."

"I was trained for this!" He sputters.

I laugh, "You think your father was in any position to train you? The man was a drunk, it's how he landed in an early grave. His poor liver."

The end of his nose turns red, embarrassment flooding his cheeks, "You can't talk to me like that!"

"But you can make comments about my wife?" I retort.

My grandfather, seated next to me to the right, clears his throat, "If that'll be all. I'm not getting any younger here."

"While we are on the topic of your wife, Malakai," an older gentleman stands a few seats down from my grandfather. Iwan Mcdonal, a long-standing council member and giant pain in my ass.

"Yes, Iwan?" I glare at him, warning him on his next words. I don't want Olivia to be a topic of discussion at this table. Ever.

"This organization has a long-standing history of arranged marriages happening within this circle," he says.

"Okay."

"While it is not part of the rules to marry within, it is preferred." I glance at Hank who's smirking like he just won something. Prick.

The wedding to Regina, while not arranged through Hank, but his brother, Kenneth, would have given him more power. Perhaps he was more pissed than I realized. I glance at Sebastian who leans forward, ready and waiting.

"What are you trying to say, Iwan?" I sigh impatiently.

"Olivia is a liability. She requires an initiation."

I lean back in my chair, tracing my bottom lip with my finger, "Please do tell when this organization became a fraternity."

"It is not a hazing, Malakai. It's collateral. It's for the best interest and protection of this fine establishment."

"And what do you propose we do with *my wife,* strip her naked and parade her through the streets?"

Someone clears their throat, mumbling something under their breath that I don't catch.

Stefan sits at Hank's side, the slimy bastard sporting a smirk like he knows something I don't. Things needed to change around here. Fast.

"Malakai, this is a serious matter. Your age is showing."

I laugh without humor, "Out with your ideas, Iwan." I click my fingers, "I don't have time for this."

"We require something on her." He speaks.

"Collateral." Hank inputs so helpfully.

"What?"

"Something that we can keep on her that will keep her quiet should anything happen."

"You suspect my wife will betray me?" I ask.

"She is not part of this lifestyle; we cannot simply trust her word."

"I will not be putting my wife through any kind of *initiation*," I growl to the room, "And it is not a topic I will discuss further."

"She is married to a murderer," Stefan buffs his nails on the breast of his suit jacket, "Perhaps it'll be fitting to have her kill for you. It would be good material to keep her in her place."

My anger begins to boil, simmering under the surface of my skin as it slowly heats and heats.

"You expect me to tell my wife she has to murder someone so you can lord it over her head for as long as she lives?"

"She is a woman," Iwan tuts, sitting down and reaching for the whiskey on the table, "She'll do as she is told."

"You'll keep my wife and her name away from this table, and out of your mouths. *She is not up for discussion.*"

"Then explain to the council how you ensure your new wife won't betray you or us."

"You forget I have her family on a string." I spin my glass, bones physically aching from the restraint I am holding myself under.

"It is not enough. You are putting this organization at

risk because you're weak for a pretty face," Hank comments.

Sebastian's spine goes ramrod straight, his eyes falling to Hank, filled with a cold quiet fury that I mirror. He subtly begins to reach beneath the table, likely for the gun he has strapped there but I catch his eyes and shake my head.

"We all see it," Hank smirks, "Just see what happened on your wedding day. Ended early because your wife's feelings got hurt over a little spilled wine. All we are asking for is a little protection."

"If my wife betrays me or this organization," I grit out, "I'll kill her myself."

I know, not even that, will satisfy them, and all I'm doing is solidifying their dislike for me. I see my cousin smirking, a look of satisfaction on Hank's face as unease rumbles through the room. It doesn't matter and I don't care. I'll have to be dead for any of them to take this from me.

They don't know what I've done, how I've secured this seat and this organization. I could annihilate them all with ease without question.

I'll kill them all, consequences be damned.

"Stage it," Someone suggests and at this point, that simmering anger has turned to boiling but they're too blind to see they're pushing me to an edge none of them will come back from, "Have her attacked with no option but to kill them. It looks like an accident, we stay safe."

"Are you really suggesting I have someone attack Olivia?"

My grandfather slams a fist against the table, surprisingly hard enough to rattle all the glasses, "That's enough!" He snaps, "Malakai has spoken, he has given you your answer, and as your leader, and the man between you and those fat bank accounts that you think keep you protected, that should be enough to end this conversation. Your damn disrespect is showing. Olivia will not be brought up again and should I hear another whisper of her name at this table, I'll kill you myself. I'm an old man, I have nothing to lose, so please, test my word."

18
Olivia

I jump onto the couch, sinking into the mountain of cushions, the pile of snacks between me and Willow scattering.

"God, this is too good," Willow howls with laughter, "He actually caught you fingering yourself!?"

My cheeks burn at the memory even if my anger at him far outweighs my embarrassment, "Yes." I grumble.

I've purposely left out the part where he sucked my fingers into his mouth, she'd eat that shit up and I don't want to have that conversation. Or how it made me feel for that couple minutes after.

The shock turned arousal tore through me like a hurricane but in true Malakai fashion, he stamped out those flames pretty quickly. He infuriates me.

But I am secretly thankful for the tour since I never would have known about this media room without it and it's now the scene for mine and Willow's night while Malakai is off doing god knows what with god knows who.

I gnaw on my lip as an array of possibilities swim through my mind, but when the thoughts spiral to other women, namely the woman from the wedding, I shut it down. Did it matter if he had a mistress? This isn't a real marriage after all, just a piece of paper to satisfy whatever it is he requires.

"You got that little line between your brows that tells me you're thinking really hard about something. And you're grinding your teeth." Willow pops a skittle into her mouth, grabbing the remote to pause the movie we haven't watched a minute of. "What is it?"

"Oh no," I lie, "It's nothing."

She purses her lips, not believing me, but she knows when to push and when not to, and thankfully she drops it, changing the conversation. "Are you ready for the event?"

"Event?"

She flicks her eyes to me, "Yes. The winter ball. It's at *your* hotel, Oli. How do you not know about this? Malakai organized it."

"Of course he did," I pinch the bridge of my nose, a headache suddenly knocking at my temples. "God, he fucking annoys me."

"Just sounds like you need to get a little pay back," Willow shrugs.

I pause, looking at her, "What do you have in mind?"

"I was just going to suggest some good old-fashioned hate fucking but I see that look in your eye, Oli. You want to raise hell with him."

"Damn right, I do."

She chuckles, "Just make his days a little less easy. Small things to drive him mad."

A smirk tugs at my mouth as ideas begin to form.

"You're a genius," I smack a kiss on her cheek.

"No, no," She wags her finger, "I had nothing to do with this, in fact, I have no idea what you're talking about."

"Is that your way of saying to keep you out of it?"

"Exactly," She laughs, "I'm not playing these games."

"Spoil sport," I roll my eyes.

"No, I just don't want to be the third wheel when it eventually leads to the hate fucking."

"There will be no hate fucking or fucking at all."

"Mmhmm, if you say so."

Dennis drives Willow home sometime after eleven, and with the house quiet I decide to go to bed myself. I haven't seen Malakai once this evening and I hope to be asleep whenever he decides to come to bed.

I take a quick shower before I change into my pajamas and then grab a few of the pillows to build a wall down the middle of the bed, tucking them in tight with the sheets, clearly dividing the bed in two.

There'll be no waking up on his chest again. Or dicks in my face.

When I wake up the following morning, it's way before

the sun has even risen, the pillows dividing the bed are a mess but still in place and in what little light there is, I see him.

He's led on his back, chest rising and falling steadily as he sleeps.

If it were lighter, I might have studied how he looks when he sleeps. Were the severe brows relaxed now? The scowl on his face gone or do those things stay with him, even in sleep?

I don't have time to find out.

I may not have the sway he does or the power, but I can be a petty bitch. And I'm okay with that.

As quietly as I can, I climb from the bed, creeping into the closet to grab some clothes for the day before I lock myself in the bathroom where I do everything I need to, to get ready for the day.

Dressed and somewhat presentable, I sneak back out into the bedroom, the room growing lighter as dawn begins to break, transforming the dark sky into hues of oranges and red as the sun sets fire to the clouds.

It's almost eerie being up in the house before the day has yet to begin but even though it's barely seven thirty, I can hear a few people wandering the huge mansion. Voices travel through the walls and footsteps echo down the halls, making it seem that people are close but whenever I turn to see if I'm being joined by one of the many staff Malakai employs, I'm met with empty space.

It runs a shiver down my spine, even though there is a logical explanation for it. It's that same feeling when you turn off all the lights downstairs and have to bolt to your bedroom because all those childhood fears of monsters under your bed, and in your closet, come back to haunt you.

I race down to the kitchen the rest of the way. It's still dark when I enter, but I can hear whistling coming from the pantry.

"Hello?" I call, trying to be quiet but not wanting to startle whoever it is.

"Mrs. Farrow?" Louis's voice travels out from the open door and I relax a little at the friendly company.

"Olivia," I correct.

He comes out with an armful of ingredients, a smile on his face, "Olivia," He widens his eyes dramatically, "You're up and ready bright and early today."

"I'm a morning person." I lie with a shrug.

If he doesn't believe me, he doesn't call me on it, "Pancakes?" He asks.

"I'd love some."

I make myself some coffee, eyeing the pot of sugar stationed next to the machine, "Does Malakai take sugar in his coffee?" I ask, wrapping my hands around the fresh cup.

"Two," Louis replies absently, mixing up the batter.

"Does anyone else?"

Louis shrugs, "Not sure, Olivia, the staff have a separate kitchen with their own supplies."

I try to stifle the grin that attempts to pull on my mouth. I just needed to get Louis out of the room for like five minutes.

Playing with Fire

He's busy at the counter while I drink my coffee, the sun almost fully risen beyond the windows and the house still caught in that sleepy state between night and day.

"Oh," I click my fingers, coming up with a plan I hope will work. Guilt eats at me for manipulating Louis since he's just so nice, but I needed him out of the room. "I saw a bunch of boxes and crates in the foyer when I came down." I tell him, "Looked like a delivery of some sort."

He frowns as he checks his watch, "The food delivery isn't supposed to be here till this afternoon. Honestly, these people can't get anything right. Did you know they left a whole delivery of perishables outside the door in the middle of August?"

"No," I feign horror, that guilt swirling heavily in my stomach.

"Mm," He grunts, "Let me go check that quick. You good in here?"

"Perfect," I give him my best smile and watch him leave the room before I'm rushing toward the pantry. I find what I'm looking for pretty quickly and I'm back out in less than a few seconds. Grabbing the sugar, I dump it into a cup and hide it before I empty the contents of what's in my hand into the jar.

It's juvenile and ridiculous, but I can't find it in me to care.

"Hey Olivia?" Louis calls just as I'm putting the lid back on the sugar pot.

"Yeah?" I answer.

"Where did you see those boxes?"

"In the foyer, are they not there anymore?" My teeth capture my lip nervously.

"I didn't see anything."

"Maybe someone already got to them then," I shrug, heading to the island to take a seat on a stool.

I have a stack of pancakes in front of me when Malakai strolls into the kitchen, dressed in a grey pair of sweats and a form fitting white tee and I almost choke on the piece I have in my mouth. I've only seen him in suits, I didn't even know the man owned casual but *own* it he does.

Fuck, he looks good in that. I can see the ridges and dips of his muscles through that skintight tee, his hair still messy from sleep, the growth around his mouth and up his cheeks thicker than it was the day before like he's just rolled out of bed and threw on the first thing he found.

I like this just woke look, it makes him seem more human.

My eyes don't stray from him as he heads to the coffee machine, placing a cup down before he presses the button and drags the sugar pot towards him.

And I continue to watch as he drops two heaped spoons into the freshly made brew and brings it to his lips.

19
Malakai

I feel her eyes on me, and I'm not going to lie, it feels fucking good.

After the shit show of a council meeting that just kept going from bad to worse the longer it went on, I was disappointed to find she had separated our bed. Did I expect to hold her all night? Absolutely not but I'd found comfort in that scent of hers and it was muted because of all the damn pillows in the way.

Then I woke to an empty bed, her side long cold.

So, coming down to the kitchen to find her in a pair of blue jeans and cropped sweater was a sight. She looks good. Edible.

The moment I saw her I'd had an image flash in my mind of her spread out on that kitchen island, naked and sweaty and writhing while I got myself another taste of her. I can only imagine how divine it would be directly from the source.

And now her eyes on me, devouring me like I was her in my mind. Who knew it would be a pair of grey sweats that caught her attention?

I make my coffee, grabbing the sugar to drop in a couple of spoons and stir it in, cradling the cup in my hand as I turn and lean on the counter, capturing her eyes.

She cocks a brow defiantly, a tiny devilish smirk toying on her mouth.

"Good morning, kitten," I address her.

"Malakai," She replies coldly, tucking back into the stack of pancakes with fresh berries sprinkled over them in front of her.

She flicks her eyes to me as I bring the cup to my lips but the way she looks makes me pause.

"What is it?" I ask.

She shakes her head, "Nothing."

"That look suggests otherwise."

I make a note not to invite her to our poker nights because that poker face is the worst one I've ever seen.

"Just didn't know you owned sweatpants, Malakai."

"You saw the gym." I tell her, finally taking a sip of the coffee.

Only to spit it out, spraying the hot liquid across the shiny floor.

Olivia roars with laughter, clutching the edge of the island as if it's the only thing keeping her seated. The salty taste in my mouth makes my tongue itch.

"What the fuck!?" I bellow.

She just laughs harder.

Playing with Fire

"You *poisoned* my coffee!?"

More heaving giggles leave her clutching her stomach, tears rolling down her cheeks.

"That depends," She laughs so hard the anger in me almost dissipates. *Almost.* But I'm too furious right now to truly appreciate that laugh. "You allergic to salt?"

I glare at her and then flick my eyes to my chef, "Did you have something to do with this!?" I roar at him.

Louis's startled eyes bounce between us, his face paling.

Olivia sobers immediately, jumping up to step between me and my chef as if to protect him from me. "You leave him out of this. He had nothing to do with it."

"So, all you then, kitten?" I step toward her, and she takes a step back.

"All me," she taunts, giving a big show even though she is backing up. "Can't take a joke, Malakai?"

My eyes narrow on her, homing in on the way she tilts her chin up defiantly and plants her feet.

"Don't fucking mess with my routines, Olivia." I warn her.

A fire lights up in her eyes, "Whatever you say, Malakai."

A deafening silence settles in the space between us while Louis hovers, still pale in the background. She messed with my coffee to get a reaction from me, and I'm giving it to her.

"I'm going to the gym," I growl, dumping my coffee into the sink and grab a bottle of water before I storm from the room, leaving her and my chef behind. I'm around the corner when I hear the sweet tinkle of laughter and my own lips quirk at the sound.

My fists slam into the bag, over and over again, my breath coming out in short quick bursts as I push myself to the limit. The sound of my fist on leather echoes in the empty gym around me, my sweat rolling down my face, down my back and chest. Bare feet move effortlessly across the mat, eyes focused on the target ahead of me.

I've been in here for hours, pushing myself to the point of pain to try and ease some of the tension I feel coating my body, but nothing has helped. I knew ninety percent of this stress is stemming from the damn council and their need to drag Olivia into my world, but the other ten percent came from my very reluctant wife.

For as long as I can, I will keep her away from the shadows that surround me, away from my enemies and the death that follows. I'd thought it would be easy, that the council would drop it now that I satisfied the old tradition, but apparently I was wrong.

My fists move faster, harder, pounding into the leather bag with determination and quiet rage.

You'd think they'd be happy.

They have more money than they know what to do with because of the organization my ancestors built. They have their big houses and expensive cars because of us Farrow's, but these fuckers are always greedy, and they just love to corrupt the innocent.

Like fucking demons stalking through the darkness waiting to suck the life out of something.

And Olivia is innocent, as devilish as she can be with her quick words and cold stares, she is too much of a bright light to be corrupted by my darkness.

I'd thought her broken when I arranged our marriage, thought her this sweet little doll I could have wrapped around my finger, but I realize I simply jumped too soon. And I don't regret it.

Perhaps my life would be easier if I had chosen a quiet little demure bride, but when have I ever enjoyed the silence? She's ten times the woman Regina is, and I don't even have to know her to see that. Where one would suck whatever soul I had left in me, the other lights it up, crafts it and challenges it.

Having Olivia is both a gift and a curse.

And as I think about it, think about her with her sweet smile to accompany those sharp claws, I wonder what I have to do to make her want me as much as I am starting to want her.

I grab the bag to stop it from swinging like a pendulum and rest my forehead on the warm leather, breathing hard as I slowly begin to regain my equilibrium, feeling the rapid thumps of my heart beating inside my chest.

The sound of heavy footsteps draws my attention to the door, and I watch my second in command stalk toward me, his face thunderous, brows drawn low.

"We have a problem." Sebastian says in way of greeting.

"Just what I fucking need." I walk to him where he's stopped at a row of benches and as I get there, he throws down a brown folder, several images falling out. I'd recognize that spill of dark raven black hair anywhere.

"The fuck is this!?" I growl, snatching up the photos, my throat growing tight as I flick through each one.

Olivia on her knees, eyes unfocused, skin rosy. Her on her back, legs spread, eyes closed. There are over ten photos of her in various positions. She looks younger in these images; her hair is shorter and she's wearing heavy makeup. There is a man in each one, but their face is cut off, revealing nothing about them except that he has his dick in my wife.

"Who?" I growl.

Sebastian shakes his head, "Delivered this morning."

"Here?"

"To me. Found it on the windshield of my car. Asked around to see if anything had been delivered here today but no one has seen anything. Killian and Dean haven't had anything, nor any of the other inner circle members."

"Why you?"

"My guess," Bast starts, "I'm your second, your closest. They knew I'd come to you immediately. They didn't deliver here because there's too much risk of being seen but at my apartment? There's plenty of areas one can go to avoid security."

"Fuck," I roar, unable to take my eyes from the photos.

"Does she know?"

Sebastian shrugs, "I don't know, Kai."

Why the fuck would someone dig this up about Olivia? Where the fuck did these photos even come from? They never came up in any of my background checks on her.

And how exactly do I address it with her?

20

Olivia

Every time I think about this morning, I laugh. I've been giggling all damn day as I picture the way he spat out his coffee and immediately thought he'd been poisoned.

Poor Louis though, he was a mess for a good thirty minutes after Malakai skulked off to lick his wounds in the gym. It took a lot of convincing to assure him he wasn't about to lose his job.

It's been a few hours since then and despite not having anything to do in this damn house, I'm in a cheerful mood. I took a swim this morning and picked a book from the library in the living room before I'd sat in the sunroom and read for a while, but then I became restless and now I'm wandering the halls.

No one speaks to me still but that's okay, I'm finding comfort in the silence.

That is until I find Malakai in the kitchen.

He's now in a suit, hair styled, and face freshly trimmed, his shoulders looking impossibly wider with his hunched over stance. There's a folder in front of him.

I calm my heart as I walk into the kitchen, heading for the coffee machine.

"Sit down, Olivia." His voice startles me, not because I wasn't expecting him to talk but because I wasn't expecting that deep stern tone to come out of him.

"I'm getting coffee," I grumble, reaching for a mug.

"Sit. Down."

Someone's still sour about the salt. It just makes me want to do it more.

"You don't tell me what to do." I snap at him.

"Olivia," He growls.

I hear footsteps behind me and glance over my shoulder to find Sebastian blocking the way out.

Okay...

"Fine," I drop onto the stool and cross my arms, "What's got up your ass? Is this about the salt? It was a joke, Malakai, get over it."

"Salt?" Sebastian queries.

"It isn't," He turns with the folder in his hands, cocking his head as his eyes run down the length of me. "I have a question."

"Well ask," I sigh impatiently, "And if I think you deserve it, I'll answer."

I hear a quickly stifled chuckle from behind me, but I don't turn to confirm it, not when Malakai glares at Sebastian in a look that could maim a man.

"Is there anything in your past you might want to tell me about?"

I feel my spine stiffen but I quickly relax, shoving down the emotion that rises with that question like I have done many times before.

"I stole an orange from the market when I was five," I widen my eyes dramatically.

"Olivia," he says my name like he's scolding a child.

"Malakai."

"Try again," He grinds his teeth, making the muscle pop in his jaw.

I tap my finger on my lip, fighting off memories from a time long ago, a time I've buried and try my hardest not to think about. It's not even overly bad but it is *humiliating,* and that feeling is not one I like to feel. I hide all that behind a mask of indifference.

"No, I don't think there's anything you should know about me." I say without emotion, "Or anything I want you to know either."

He tosses the folder down onto the counter, "Open it."

"Malakai," Sebastian steps forward, "Perhaps…"

"Open. It."

Nerves flutter through me as my fingers grasp the edge of the folder. Suddenly a hand slams down on top of it. "I'm stepping in here." Sebastian snaps, "Not like this, Malakai."

"Move, Bast," Malakai steps forward and I'm suddenly sandwiched between two very big men, Sebastian at my back, Malakai at my front. This is a lot of testosterone.

"You're making a mistake." Sebastian warns.

"How I handle my wife is none of your concern."

"Um, I'm right here," I wiggle, trying to free myself, "What the hell is going on?"

Sebastian pleads with me when I meet his eyes but for what, I don't know.

"What's in the folder?" I ask.

"Open it and find out."

Sebastian shakes his head.

Oh, for fuck's sake, whatever it is can't be that bad!

I snatch the folder off the side and rip it open, several pages falling out and onto the floor.

All three pairs of our eyes drop to the photo laying face up in the middle of the kitchen.

I think I squeak as my very naked body stares back at me.

"Where did you get these?" I breathe, feeling tears prick my eyes, those memories pushing at my wall I have erected in my mind to keep them back. It's not that bad. *It's not that bad.*

"Someone kindly delivered them this morning."

"Malakai," Sebastian warns.

"Who?"

Silence. I finally drag my eyes from the image still on the floor, no one bending to pick them up.

"Who?" I ask again.

"We don't know." It's Sebastian who answers.

"I have an idea," Malakai says.

"I don't understand why you have these." I swallow, rubbing my eyes to try keep them dry.

Playing with Fire

It was a long time ago, back when I drank too much, partied too hard and trusted the wrong men.

It took a lot of effort, money and begging to have these buried. Six months of my life was chaos because of these images.

Frantic need to bury them again spurs my moves as I drop to my knees and start to gather all the photos. My eyes are blurry with the tears I can't keep back now all those feelings that come with this time in my life, rush to the surface. Humiliation. Betrayal. Regret. And deep-rooted sorrow that I let myself trust people who didn't deserve it.

"Shit," I hear someone say through the roaring in my ears. "Kitten."

Hands touch mine and I flinch away, shoving everything in the folder before I get to my feet and I run.

"Olivia!" I hear him roar behind me.

But I need them to be gone.

I feel them chasing me, hear them call my name but I don't stop, not until I'm back in that grand living room with all the books, a roaring fire right in front of me.

I toss the folder into the flames, the cardstock catching immediately as it begins to eat away at the folder and all the images inside.

"What are you doing!?" Malakai hisses behind me.

"They have to go." I say quietly.

"What happened?"

I shake my head, back and forth probably too many times it makes me look a little manic.

Only Willow and my sister know the story. They were the ones who helped me bury it, quickly and quietly so my father never found out, so the world didn't see.

There were people who did see them, a whole room of people but they were dealt with, served legal papers that forced them to keep quiet.

I wanted to hurt Malakai for bringing these up. For finding them and using them against me.

"Olivia," It's Sebastian who touches my arm, but I move away from his touch, watching the flames eat at the evidence of my humiliation.

"You're a fucking prick, Kai." Sebastian growls at my side.

"I'd like to be alone now," I say quietly.

But they keep arguing, shouting at each other but I don't hear them.

So, I just walk away, and they don't follow.

21
Malakai

I fucked up.

Sebastian warned me, but I still fucked up.

Shit.

She's been sitting in the sunroom since this afternoon and now it's dark beyond the windows, the moon casting a silver glow across the frosted estate. I stand in the doorway, watching her as she sits beneath a blanket and watches out the window. I don't know what she's looking at but whatever it is, has her complete attention. She didn't even stir when I announced my presence twenty minutes ago.

With a sigh, I go to her, sitting in the chair opposite as I rest my elbows on my knees and wait for her to give me those big brown eyes.

When five minutes turns to ten and then fifteen, I realize she isn't going to and I'm going to need to get her attention.

"I'm sorry," I say thickly, "I did not handle that with

care."

Her lashes flutter a little but still, she continues to watch out the window until finally her lips part and she speaks.

"He was my boyfriend." She says it so quietly I have to lean closer to be able to hear her. "We'd been together for nearly a year at the time. I was still in college, and we were at a party. I was drunk."

The hair on my arms stands on end, something unsettling dropping into my stomach.

"I was a virgin when I met him, and I made him wait. I didn't want to just lose it to anyone, so I made him wait and he did."

I open my mouth to speak though I don't know what to say, so it closes again.

"On the day of the party I told him I would give it to him that night. It was just after midnight when he took me into one of the rooms in the frat house. I didn't know he had a camera set up. We had done other things but never went the full way, but I was pretty confident. I got on my knees and gave him a blowjob. He was recording the whole thing."

Fury rolls through me and my fingers curl into the palms of my hands, nails biting in with how tightly I fist them.

"It went on for a couple hours and when it was done, he took me home and I passed out. When I woke up the next day, I'd forgotten the whole thing."

I want his name. I want him dead. Now.

I almost demand it from her, but she continues speaking.

"About three months later I caught him cheating on me, so I broke up with him and I thought nothing of it until my birthday a few weeks later. Willow had arranged for us to go to a club. She'd hired out the upstairs to throw a party for me and when I arrived all my friends were there, some of them being from when I was still with him. Even after we broke up, we stayed friends, and he tried but I didn't want anything to do with him."

I swallow knowing what is coming.

"I walked in and immediately I saw the big screen and it started to play a recording. It was an hour and a half long. And in it is me, completely naked, he's fucking me, and everyone is watching it. I couldn't stop it; I didn't know how." She pauses, swallowing, blinking rapidly as if trying to clear the images I know are playing inside her head. "And then he came out and everyone was standing there and staring at me. They were just watching." She sucks in a ragged breath, "I broke. It *broke* something in me."

"Olivia," I whisper her name, hoping to bring her back to the room instead of wherever she's gone inside her head.

"Everyone saw and they did nothing. They just stared and it felt like the whole world stopped moving at that point, like time stopped. And when you look at it, in the grand scheme of things, it's not even that bad, right? It's just a little sex tape."

My teeth grind as she tries to brush it under the rug, of course it's a big fucking deal. It's a big fucking deal because some jackass humiliated her in front of all her friends, it's a big deal because they stood there while she had to watch herself in the most intimate setting with someone she trusted.

"Willow managed to stop it," She finally says, bringing her dark eyes to me, lacking that light that usually sparks within them, "She got everyone out, but some people had recorded the whole thing. They uploaded them onto porn sites and my ex had done it too. It took six months to get it all taken down and we buried him in court but I'm sure there are still versions of it online. The internet is forever after all." She sighs, looking away again, back out the window. "I guess the whole thing knocked my confidence and I struggle in crowds a little because of it. Like everyone in there has seen it and I can feel it boiling up inside of me. The humiliation. The betrayal."

"I'm sorry, Olivia," The words are sharp unintentionally while my mind comes up with ways to end the fucker's life. "What was his name?"

She quirks a brow and scoffs a laugh, "Bradley Vermont the Third." She cringes to herself, "Even his name sounds pretentious."

"I'll find who got the images," I promise her.

She shrugs, "I don't care."

I smell the lie for what it is. She pretends she doesn't care but this distant version of herself says otherwise.

But it made sense now, how she froze up after the wedding, when she almost shrank into herself while everyone watched. It only made me want to fuck them all up, rip out their eyes for staring and doing nothing.

She doesn't say another word to me and doesn't look in my direction, pretending I'm not here so I take the hint and leave her alone, ordering one of the staff to take her a drink and some food in the sunroom.

I'm dialing Sebastian the moment I'm locked in the drawing room.

"Malakai," He answers.

"Find me Bradley Vermont," I spit his name, "The Third."

"With a name like that, it won't be hard. Any other details?"

"He's the one who filmed Olivia." I swallow down the acid on my tongue. "I want him dead."

Silence greets me from the other end of the phone. "I'll handle it." Sebastian eventually says.

"Make it look like an accident." I order, "No questions. And I want tech online, any traces of the video I want removed."

"I don't know if that's possible," Sebastian says, I can hear him walking, his steps echoing which tells me he's in the underground parking lot of his apartment building.

"Make it possible," I demand, "I don't give a fuck how, just do it."

"On it." Is his only reply.

I hang up and let out a harsh breath, pinching the bridge of my nose between my fingers. This stinks of the council, their tantrum targeting my wife. What else will they attempt to do? What did they hope to achieve with these images?

Another meeting needed to happen, because clearly, I am not being loud enough in my demand to leave my wife out of this damn business.

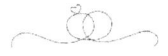

With the council meeting invitation sent, I head to bed but not before I check the sunroom. It's empty save a still full glass of wine and an untouched plate of food, the blanket she was using draped over the arm of the chair.

I switch off the lights and walk quietly through the house, up to the bedroom which is dimly lit by the light spilling out from the bathroom.

And there she is, fast asleep in my bed with that damn wall of pillows dividing the bed. She's facing the windows, her hair braided and lying across the pillow. She doesn't stir when I climb on my side of the pillow barricade after showering and once again, when I wake the following morning, she is no longer in the bed.

22
Olivia

It's while Malakai is in the gym, I decide to enact my next piece of revenge. I grab everything I need and then disappear up the stairs before anyone can spot me.

I woke up this morning feeling like shit. The memories plagued my every thought, dragging my feet and watering my eyes but it was a long time ago. The event fucked me up enough when it happened that I made the decision I wouldn't let it affect me anymore. I could mope and whine if I wanted, or I could make my husband's life a little harder like I promised to do.

The latter is far more enjoyable.

So that's how I end up in our shared closet, perusing the shelves of shoes. There's sneakers and loafers, and a couple of pairs of boots but it's a specific pair I'm looking for. He has several different pairs of loafers but it's the black Prada ones I've noticed he favors the most.

I pull them out and take them through to the bathroom, almost feeling bad about it. Not because they're his, but because they're expensive and rather beautiful for a pair of man's shoes.

But I don't feel guilty enough *not* to do it.

Picking up the bottle of ketchup, I pop the cap and tip the shoe, toe pointing down as I empty a good portion of the ketchup into it, being careful not to spill any down the sides. I then do the same to the other one.

When I feel they are thoroughly coated in the condiment, I carefully place them back into the shelves where I found them.

Standing in the middle of the closet, my eyes scan the rest of his things, wondering what else I can do until I hear the handle go to the bedroom.

My eyes bug out of my head. He wasn't supposed to be back yet! He was in that gym for several hours yesterday, but it's only been an hour today!

I rush out of the closet, spotting him immediately. He's dressed in only a pair of dark sweats, topless, barefooted, and sweating. His damp hair falls over his forehead and perspiration makes the tanned skin of his chest glisten.

"Olivia," he says, as shocked to see me as I am to see him.

The ketchup bottle is still sitting in the middle of the counter in the bathroom. Where he's probably about to go for a shower.

I say nothing as I sprint for the bathroom, slamming the door behind me and locking it.

He knocks a moment later, "Olivia." His voice is soft, almost gentle and it makes me feel uneasy.

I grab the bottle, ignoring him as I search the bathroom,

looking for somewhere to hide it where he isn't likely to look. The only storage is beneath the counter, everywhere else he will see it. And I'm not sure what kind of answer I could give him as to why there is a bottle of ketchup in the bathroom.

"I'm sorry, okay?" He calls through the door. "I handled everything yesterday terribly."

Shit.

"Don't worry about it!" I yell back. I'm still pissed at him throwing that folder in my face. I'm not entirely sure why I told him the whole story, I guess I didn't want another person looking at me like all those people did. He made me feel dirty.

If there was any guilt left about the shoes, those thoughts burn them away. He deserves all of this.

"Olivia, you can't avoid me." He growls through the door, his tone changed.

I roll my eyes and crouch, shoving some things out the way inside the cupboard as I shove the bottle right to the back and then pile up things in front of it, just in case he does decide to look in here. I rush to stand, smacking my head on the counter as I rise.

"Ow!" I yell, rubbing the spot.

"Are you okay?!" His fists slam on the door, "Open the door!"

His fists hit the wood so hard the whole door rattles. I unlock it and throw it open, Malakai immediately stepping into me, his sweaty chest pressing into mine. I hold my breath as his hands come to my body, checking for injury.

"Jesus Christ!" I slap his palms away, "I'm fine, you overbearing buffoon." Abe is clearly rubbing off on me.

"What happened?" He doesn't stop searching.

"I bumped my head," I slap his hands again, "Get off me."

"Show me." He demands.

"Fuck off!" I hop away from him, "You're being ridiculous."

He shoves his hands into his pockets, tilting up his chin as he looks down his nose at me. "What were you doing?"

I narrow my eyes, shoving my hands on my hips, "Can't a girl have some peace in the bathroom?"

"Sure, she can, but only when she doesn't run in there like her ass is on fire."

I huff, "I'm going out. I need a change of scenery." I decide there and then, heading into the closet for a change of clothes.

He doesn't answer and locks himself in the bathroom. I pick out a cute, knitted dress with some tights and my knee-high boots, laying them out on the bed. I glance at the bathroom door, still hearing the shower, so quickly change out of my leggings and oversized sweater and into the new clothes. By the time I'm done and running my fingers through my braid to loosen it, Malakai comes out of the bathroom, a towel wrapped around his hips.

"I'll come with you." He tells me before he turns into the closet and returns with an all-black suit and those ketchup filled Prada shoes.

I'm not sure I want to be around when he puts them on.

"I'd rather go alone," I quip, zipping up my boots and heading for the door.

"It wasn't a request."

"It wasn't an invitation." I bite back.

I hear him getting dressed behind me and purposely keep my back to him to save getting an eyeful. Granted it'll be a pretty view, but I have to keep my wits. There's a reason the devil is beautiful, he likes to lure you in with pretty promises and a dazzling smile only to eat your soul when you end up in his grasp.

Sure, I'd fuck Malakai in a heartbeat, have done several times in my head, but that's where that'll stay. Imaginary. Because I already signed my soul over, he isn't having my body too.

When it's been a respectable amount of time, I turn to him, finding him sitting on the bed, one shoe in hand.

That's my cue.

"Have a great day, Malakai!" I flee out of the room and I'm just at the top of the stairs when his bellow chases me down them.

"Olivia!" He roars.

A quick giggle leaves me as I sprint toward the door, throwing it open and slamming right into a hard chest.

I fall back, landing on my ass in the doorway as I stare up at Dennis.

"Mrs. Farrow?"

"Dennis!" I rush, getting back to my feet, "Just the person. I need to go into the city."

He nods but doesn't move.

"Now?" I urge him.

"Sorry Mrs. Farrow, I'm here for Abe."

"Okay but can I come with you? You can just drop me off."

He shakes his head and looks behind me, dipping his chin in greeting as I feel the press of a warm chest to my spine. A hand curls around my shoulder.

"My grandfather is in the kitchen. Go ahead and collect him, Dennis."

With a gentle hand, Malakai pulls me back and out of the way so Dennis can enter and when we're alone, I feel him lean in.

"Ketchup, really?" He says close to my ear. "Do you live to fuck with me, kitten?"

"I did promise I would," I whisper, breath caught in my throat as his scent invades my senses.

"You owe me a new pair of shoes."

"I'm sure you can afford another pair."

"I can," He agrees, "But payback is making you come with me to get some."

"What!?" I spin, "No!"

"Let's go, kitten." He grasps my hand and yanks me toward the door and despite me fighting him, he's stronger than me and far more determined. We head around the building, my legs going twice as fast as his as I try to keep up with his pace, his grip firm but not hard. He stops at the row of garages, pressing his thumb to the keypad and one of the doors begins to slide up.

Playing with Fire

"Get in the car, Olivia," He demands, dragging me toward the matte black Maserati sitting pretty in the garage.

Malakai opens the passenger door and then stares at me blankly, waiting for me to climb in. "You're such a prick." I snap at him but climb in, crossing my arms as I watch him walk around the hood and get in beside me.

He starts the engine, the purr echoing inside the garage. It's sleek and modern inside, the chairs comfortable as I sink into them, keeping my eyes forward.

"Seatbelt." He orders.

I ignore him.

"Seat. Belt." He grinds out.

I flip him the finger.

"You're such a fucking brat!" He growls, suddenly leaning over me as he grasps my belt and yanks it over me. I fight him, but he doesn't relent, his body pressing against mine, his mouth close.

"Malakai!" I yell but he doesn't stop until it's buckled and then he grabs it, pulling it tight to pin me to the chair.

"One fucking day, kitten," He rasps, his lips a mere inch from mine, blue eyes burning, breath whispering against my skin, "One fucking day, I'm going to punish you for pushing me. Have you spread across my lap as I tan your ass red."

My breath ceases to exist, eyes widening as heat pools hot and heavy between my legs.

"You lay a finger on me," I warn breathlessly, eyes dropping to his mouth, "And I'll cut off your dick."

His mouth kicks up into a devilish grin, his own eyes staring at my mouth as his tongue traces his bottom lip, "You'd like it wouldn't you?" He purrs, "Having my handprint on your pretty ass. Would you be dripping, Olivia? Like you're soaking your panties right now?"

I tilt my chin up, forcing my body not to squirm. He leans in just a touch further, his lips a whisper against mine and my own part, lashes fluttering.

"You fucking would," His words are spoken right against my mouth and I almost sigh when his tongue touches my bottom lip, "Just know, I'd fucking love it just as much."

My eyes close as I move forward to try and press my mouth firmer against his but then there's suddenly nothing in front of me except thin air.

His deep chuckle sounds next to me and my eyes snap open, flicking to him as his hands curl around the steering wheel and he floors the pedal, peeling us out the garage and down the long drive of the estate.

23
Malakai

My cock fucking aches.

Having her so close, a small taste of her on my lips and I'm about to blow right in my damn pants. Fuck she blushes so damn pretty and the way she pressed her thighs together, squirmed under my touch, it took everything in me not to strip her out of her clothes and fuck her right there in the car.

She hasn't said a single word the whole drive, her hands held tightly together in her lap, knees pressed together, face turned to look out the window as the scenery bleeds from woods and open space to skyscrapers and heavy traffic.

My fingers twitch where I have one resting on my leg, itching to reach over and take her thigh in my grip, while my other hand controls the car.

I pull us into the lot close to the shopping district, turning off the engine after I've pulled into a space. Olivia gets out the moment the car is stopped and stands at the hood, not giving me a chance to open the door for her.

I take her hand in mine, ignoring how good she feels when she's in my grip and I don't give her a chance to pull away as I begin walking, forcing her to follow.

We come out on the main strip, people milling about all around us and paying us no attention. She stays close as I take her toward the mall, but she stops suddenly with a gasp.

I follow her eyes to a magazine stand and right there on the front page is the two of us on our wedding day.

Olivia Lauder, New CEO of Lauder Hotels and Resorts marries business tycoon, Malakai Farrow in a super-secret wedding at Silver Lake Estate.

"They wrote an article about us?" She picks up the magazine, flicking to the full article a few pages in.

"We're high profile," I tell her, "And there were press in attendance at the wedding."

Her nose scrunches up as she reads the article and I glance over her shoulder.

Olivia Lauder, youngest daughter of the late Victor Lauder has done some questionable things in her short life, but marrying one of the most eligible and wealthiest men in the city has to be the topper.

Is it power? Status? Money?

Read on to find out how Olivia sunk her claws into one of the cities greatest men as a source close to the couple spills all.

I snatch the magazine from her hand and shove it back into the stands.

"They think *I* trapped *you*!?" She squeals.

"Let's go, Olivia," I start to drag her away.

"The fuck!" She growls, her steps quickening with her anger. It's adorable that something so small can harbor so much fury. I still have her hand in mine when we enter the shop, instantly being greeted by the overly happy saleswoman.

"Good morning, how can we help you today?" She asks chirpily.

Olivia comes to an abrupt stop, her anger still radiating from her.

"My future ex-husband is looking for a new pair of shoes."

I choke on air.

The woman's eyes widen, and she opens her mouth and closes it, desperately trying to figure out what to say.

"Your future..." She stutters, "Husband. Shoes."

I shake my head, clearing my shock as I give her hand a squeeze, "My wife has a sense of humor." I tell her, "Just here for a pair of black Prada loafers."

"I really don't," Olivia says, rolling her eyes like the brat she is. Fuck, it makes me hard.

She walks off before the assistant can guide her and I cock my head, watching her go, her steps sure and determined. Likely to get the fuck away from me.

"We can handle it," I tell the woman before I follow Olivia, slipping further into the store. I find her down the men's aisle, eyes scanning the row of boxes as she looks for the pair I'm after.

"Your future ex-husband," I purr in her ear, watching as she stiffens with my proximity.

"I just figured I'd let you know now, wouldn't want

you to be surprised when I eventually leave you," She smiles at me sweetly, pressing up onto her toes to reach a box on the top rack. "I guess a size eight?" She flutters her lashes.

I roll my lips together, not biting at her clear tease and reach above her, pressing my chest to her spine. "Twelve."

"Weird flex," She breathes, "But okay."

I shake my head. Fuck, I feel on edge around her, like control is right there but out of reach. I thrive on control, live for organization and a clear outcome but she blurs all the lines. One minute the tension between us is thick enough to slice it with a knife, the next, she's cold and distant, making it hard to believe she reacts to me at all.

But I can't forget the way her breath stutters from her chest when I'm close, or how her eyes devour me. I can't scrub the image of her pressing her thighs together, leaning closer to press our lips together only for me to take it away.

What a fool I was.

I try the shoe on before I take the box to the counter, Olivia hanging back.

"Let me take you to lunch," I tell her.

She scrunches up her nose, "I'll pass."

"Okay," I growl, "I'll rephrase it. We are going for lunch."

"Sorry, do you want me to bark too?" She snaps at me.

"No, but I wouldn't mind you crawling."

Color blooms on her cheeks, "Pig." She spins and

storms from the store and I let out a chuckle as I follow her.

I take her to a small hole in a wall pizza place downtown, away from the busy streets and heaving traffic central city is known for. She sits on the opposite side of the little round table, manicured fingers playing with the hem of the white tablecloth.

"Malakai!" Gina, the manager beams as she walks to the table, "Hi!"

"Hi, Gina," I greet her. She's been the manager here for years, too many to remember.

She shoves her hand toward Olivia, who hesitates only for a moment before she accepts it, "I'm Olivia," she tells her politely.

Gina's eyes go round, "Oh! *The* Olivia!"

My wife sinks down in her chair, cringing a little.

"Those damn magazines," Gina continues as if she doesn't see Olivia currently trying to sink under the table, "Anyway, what can I get you? The usual?"

Gina has no idea what I do, she doesn't need to. I pay her wages and she runs my business, though this pizza place isn't one on the Farrow books. This one is just mine. It's one of the many *clean* businesses I own.

"Yes," I give her a smile, "Olivia?"

She selects something from the menu and reaches for her water.

"I need to go back to the hotel," she says eventually.

"Why?"

"It's *my* hotel. It isn't going to run itself."

"You have a board. And staff. Of course, it's going to run itself."

"Is this something you're going to take from me too?" She captures the inside of her cheek between her teeth as she glares at me from across the table.

"Go ahead, Olivia." I lean back, "You want to work, work."

Her brows drop into a frown, "That easy?"

"You're not a prisoner. You're my wife."

"And the Winter Ball?" She asks, "Were you going to tell me about that? Or that my hotel is hosting it?"

I shrug, "Figured it would give you something to do." I lie.

"Liar." She calls me out immediately.

I chuckle, "I figured it would be a good event to use as our first official public appearance. At a hotel you own, where you're known."

"I guess so," she says quietly.

The meal between us is done so silently, no conversation, no eye contact and it's becoming harder to figure out how to win this woman over.

Despite the tension and the sexual chemistry, it's pretty clear she hates me. You can want to fuck someone and still despise them.

And I am not completely opposed to a little hate fucking.

24

Olivia

Just because he forced me to go shopping with him after I ruined his shoes, doesn't mean I'm not going to continue to fuck with him.

It's why I have a pair of scissors in my hand and I'm cutting off all the buttons on his shirts with a satisfied little grin on my face.

But I am sad I'm not going to be able to see his reaction because sure to his word yesterday, Dennis is taking me to my hotel this afternoon. Malakai is out somewhere, I didn't ask, and he didn't tell me where, but he had left with a stern, *"don't fuck with my shit."* So naturally, I'm fucking with his shit.

With the final shirt now buttonless, I hang it back up in the closet and smooth my hands down my pencil skirt, slipping my feet into the nude heels I forgot I even owned. It's been a couple weeks since I've been back to the hotel, and I'm nervous to go. The staff know who I am, they know I'm now the boss and they didn't treat me any differently the last time I was there, but I'm now married to Malakai, and I'm worried about what they might think about me.

It's not like they know he was involved in my father's death or that he threatened my sister. For all they know, Malakai swooped me off my feet and we couldn't wait to get married.

The thought makes me want to gag. I can't imagine Malakai swooping anyone off their feet, not with his constant scowl and severe need to have everything in control. But then his chuckle is to die for, this deep, warming sound and he smells like sex and sin, an intoxicating aroma that has made me brainless a couple of times.

And the way he talks, the deep baritone of his voice strips you bare, and those neon blue eyes that feel as if they're looking right through you, seeing all of you. And his hands, his skilled hands, long fingers and –

What the fuck am I doing?

I shake my head to clear the thoughts and turn, walking out of the bedroom. My heels clip against the floors and when I get to the foyer, Dennis is already waiting.

"Mrs. Farrow," He greets professionally.

"Just Olivia is fine," I tell him.

He doesn't answer me or even move his face out of that stoic expression, so I just follow him out to the waiting car.

"Do you always drive around whoever Malakai tells you to?" I ask him after he's closed my door and climbed into the front. His eyes flick to me in the mirror before focusing back on the road.

"Yes."

"Do you drive him around?"

"Sometimes."

So chatty. I resist the urge to roll my eyes, "He drives himself?"

"Sometimes."

I loosen a breath, "Why doesn't anyone want to talk to me?"

Those eyes move to me once more, staying longer on me in the mirror than before, "It isn't you." He eventually says.

"Did Malakai tell them to ignore me?"

"You ask a lot of questions," He focuses back on the road as the gates slide open at the end of the long drive.

"That's because no one tells me anything," I lean back against the warm seats, "Of course I'm going to be curious."

"Malakai didn't tell them. The staff are hesitant with you because the previous woman who was in the house treated them like shit. Plus, they know you're messing with his order, and they worry they'll be blamed."

"Malakai is very aware it's me doing it," I roll my eyes, "And whoever she is, I'm nothing like her. Ask Louis!"

"I know, Mrs. Farrow," Dennis sighs.

"Olivia," I correct, "Say it with me, Olivia."

A smirk tugs on his mouth, "Would you like music, Mrs. Farrow?"

I let out a disgruntled huff, "Yes."

He laughs as he presses a button on the dash and music begins to play through the speakers.

There is a constant stream of people coming in and out of the hotel, the reception filled to the brim with people as staff scurry back and forth trying to accommodate them. Dennis parks the car out front, in the spot reserved for me and gets out to open my door.

"I'll be here when you're done," He tells me.

"Thank you, I don't know how long I'll be."

"Take your time," He gives me what can only be an attempt of a smile, but it looks more scowl like. I shake my head and walk toward the doors, letting a couple out before I slip in the open door.

It smells like home here. My father never once changed the scent of lilac and honey that had been a constant here, or the burgundy walls and gold trimmings. The décor was a bit outdated if you asked me, but the guests seem to like it.

I head to the front desk, finding Meredith, one of our oldest members of staff, smiling behind the computer.

"Hi, Mere," I greet her, walking around the desk to give her a hug.

We grew up here and this woman had been our babysitter on more occasions that I could count.

"Oli!" She beams, jumping up far quicker than a woman of her age should be able to manage. She's due to retire… actually I think she was supposed to a few years back, but she never did.

She wraps me up in a warm hug, the feel of her arms around me easing some tension that had been lining my body for a week now.

"What are you doing here?" She asks, "Shouldn't you be off on some romantic honeymoon still?"

"You saw the papers?"

"Of course I did!" She tuts, "Well, I went to read them, then they pissed me off because they couldn't be more wrong about you, so I just looked at all the pictures. You looked stunning."

"Thank you, Mere," I touch her arm, "But no, no honeymoon. I actually came in to see if there is anything I can do. I know dad has been gone a couple months now and things seem good here."

"They are," she goes back to her chair, "Management have been great with the transition."

I nod, "Well I guess I'll just go do paperwork then."

She gives me a smile and greets the waiting guests as I wander through the staff only doors, my heels clipping on the tiled floor until I come to a stop outside my father's office. It used to be his name in gold on a plaque on the door but now it's mine.

My finger traces the name, *my* name. Lauder, not Farrow.

With a sigh, I push on it, finding the office exactly how my father left it. There's still a half empty bottle of whiskey on the shelf and a box of cigars on the desktop. His laptop sits in the middle of the desk, a fine layer of dust settled on the top. People had been in here but only to deposit paperwork. I wipe off the dust and pop the laptop in the top drawer before I tackle the mountain of paper in front of me.

It's just HR business and some legal papers to sign and I get through them quickly. I wasn't needed here, not really. It's my hotel, my name above the door, but this place thrives on its own. My father had made it that way, but he was a businessman. He lived for this place, especially after my mother died when I was younger.

But I'm not my dad, I'm not savvy in the business world.

I just have a pretty face and an expensive last name.

I've only been here an hour or so, but I feel out of place. This hotel used to be a second home, but it no longer feels that way, this office doesn't belong to me, the staff may be employed by me, but it isn't me they report to.

Shuffling all the papers, I get up from the desk, a droop in my shoulders that wasn't there before as I head down toward the small offices we have toward the back. I can see people working behind their desks, ensuring the smooth running of the hotel.

"Miss Lauder!" A girl from the HR department announces my presence with shock which quickly turns to a grimace, "Mrs. Farrow, I mean, my apologies."

"Miss Lauder is fine," I assure her. I didn't plan on being Mrs. Farrow for long so it would be easier if everyone just called me by the right name, "I have some paperwork here, who should I give it to?"

"Oh, I'll take that," She smiles, holding her hands out for the stack.

I hand it over, glancing around the room but my attention gets caught by the small conference room. The door is open and a large whiteboard dominates the back wall and on it are images and color schemes, and across the top are the words, WINTER BALL, all in capitals and underlined several times.

"Oh, is that the plans for the ball?" I ask, stepping closer.

She cringes, "It is, or at least it was."

"Was?"

"Our event coordinator quit last week," She fiddles with her hands, "She's the third one in the last year."

I wince, "Shit, really? Why?"

"Too much work?" The girl shrugs.

"Sorry, I didn't get your name," I tell her.

Her eyes widen as her cheeks pinken before she shoves her hand out, "It's Nora!"

"So, these plans are no longer usable?" I shake her hand as I put my attention back to the board.

"They are but we have no idea what we're doing." She admits, "Between that, trying to recruit a new event coordinator and our daily jobs, I don't know how we are supposed to pull it off."

"I know how," I beam at her, "Me."

"What!?"

I shrug, "Why not? I've planned plenty of events and god knows I need something to do."

"Are you serious?"

"Absolutely," I start for the room, heels clipping on the floor as a newfound confidence lifts my shoulders, a sense of purpose settling in, "I'll start right now."

"Miss Laud – I mean Mrs. Farrow, are you sure?" She chews her lip, "I mean isn't this, I don't know, beneath you?"

I scoff, "Absolutely not. I'd love to do this."

"Well okay," She follows me into the room, "The portfolio is on the table," She points, "I don't think everything is ready though. I'm worried we will have to postpone it. It's next week!"

"I've got it," I assure her, "We won't be postponing. Did Mr. Farrow have specifics on the event?"

"No, just that it's held here."

"Perfect," I nod, mostly to myself.

"Can I get you coffee?"

I shake my head, "I'm good, I'll grab one in a minute. Just leave it all to me."

She gives me an unsure smile and heads off with the paperwork, leaving me staring at the mess on the board. Nope, this just won't do.

First coffee, and then I'll get to work.

I'm at the coffee machine in the staff kitchen when I get a call.

Pulling out my cell, I grin at Willow's name, excited to tell her I'll be planning the event. She'll get involved; I know she will.

"Oli," she says before I can get in a greeting, sounding breathless.

"You okay?" I ask, concerned.

"Fine," She huffs, "Did you hear?"

"Hear what?" I hit the button to begin to pour my coffee, watching the dark liquid sputter out the nozzle.

"Bradley." She says his name with a bite, but it's not as coated in venom as it usually is. She usually refers to him as the '*prick who shall not be named*'.

"What about him?" I mentally swat at the memories that instantly bloom with his name, tackling the fresher ones from the recent images that had been dug up.

"He's dead."

25
Malakai

"Skiing accident," Sebastian leans back, a cruel grin spreading across his face, "How tragic."

Killian chuckles as he throws down the folder onto my desk, Dean following him in. They both take their seats on the couches in front of the fire, Sebastian still grinning like a fool.

"You did the job?" I ask Killian who reaches for the whiskey in the middle of the table. I made sure to put out a bottle, so the fuckers don't touch my shit.

"Pushed that fucker right off the edge of the cliff," Dean tells me proudly.

"Well, I asked for an accident," I shrug, flipping the cover on the folder.

The gruesome image of Bradley Vermont, the Third, with his head busted open, blood staining the pristine white snow is the first thing I see. His body is contorted at an awkward angle, skin pale with dark splotches, eyes wide open as he stares unseeingly toward the forest.

"Poor guy," Killian shakes his head, "Never saw the drop coming. You'd expect more for a seasoned skier."

Sebastian chuckles.

"I should be worried about how much fun you sick fucks have on a job," I grin, closing the folder and open my laptop, hitting the button to wire over the money, split between the three of them.

Killian shrugs as he sips his whiskey and then reaches for the poker set beneath the table.

"What's that beautiful wife of yours doing?" Sebastian asks, quirking a brow in my direction.

"Keep your eyes to yourself," I warn him.

"Just saying how it is, man," Sebastain slaps his knees, "You definitely married up."

This fucker.

"If you must know, she's at the hotel. She wanted to go back to work."

"To get away from you," Sebastian laughs, "How's the new shoes?"

I shake my head, I should never have told him about the damn ketchup in the shoes. Killian and Dean look at me curiously and before I can tell them not to bother asking, Sebastian goes ahead and tells them.

"She put ketchup in the boss's Prada's." He laughs boisterously, "He then put them on!"

Killian laughs while his brother does the sensible thing and *tries* to contain it. He fails but at least he tried.

"She put salt in his coffee the day before that," Sebastian tells them like it's school gossip on the playground.

"Looking more like Bast is gonna win this bet," Dean chuckles.

I shake my head and don't say a word since I can't tell him he's wrong.

"So, what did she do to you today?" Killian asks, "Since fucking with you seems to be a theme."

"I'm almost scared to find out," I get up from behind the desk, "I haven't checked out our bedroom yet but everything else seems to be clear. Maybe she skipped a day."

She did not, in fact, skip a day.

I pull the shirt out and then the next and the next finding every single one is missing all of their buttons.

It's so absurd I can't help but laugh.

I'm still in a towel, fresh out the shower, my hands on my hips as I stare at her handiwork when she breezes into the bedroom, a grin on her face and a light in her eyes that wasn't there this morning. It almost puts me on edge wondering who put that smile there.

"Where have you been?" I growl.

She stops abruptly, her eyes widening, "Excuse me?" She snaps back, "Just who the fuck do you think you're talking to?"

Shit.

"You've been gone all day," I try again.

Her eyes glance to the pile of shirts on the bed before they bounce back to me, "And?"

Yeah, I had nothing.

"Besides, you know where I've been since you had your guard dog wait for me outside *all day*."

That's true. He'd checked in a few times, just letting me know Olivia was still at the hotel.

"You're smiling," I point out.

Her brows knot in confusion, "What the hell is wrong with you?"

Fuck if I know. I don't say that to her though.

"Your handiwork?" I point to the shirts.

She flutters her lashes, "I have no idea what you're talking about. Perhaps you shouldn't be so careless with your clothes."

"You're a real piece of work, you know that?" I step toward her and revel in the way her eyes dip down my body, snagging on the muscles of my abdomen, still wet from the shower.

She swallows and then looks back up, straightening her spine and tipping up her chin, "Only for you." She replies sassily, moving past me toward the bathroom.

"Did you have a good day?" I call after her.

She pauses in the bathroom door, looking back at me, "I did, actually. Thank you."

"What did you do?"

She grins, showing teeth, her whole face lighting up, "I saved your winter ball."

The door closes with a quiet click, leaving me confused. The coordinators were supposed to be handling the ball.

Leaving the shirts on the bed, I head back into the closet and grab a turtleneck sweater, pairing it with my slacks and a dinner jacket. Not my ideal wear for a council meeting but I have little choice.

When Olivia returns from the shower, she does so in just a towel, her face bare of any makeup, hair pulled into a messy bun atop her head. My movements stop as I stare at her, water droplets still clinging to her skin.

"Oh," She stops, "You're still here."

"This is our bedroom," I point out.

She pouts, "Dinner date?" She eyes my attire.

"A meeting."

"Okay well, don't wait up." She disappears into the closet, "I'm going out with Willow."

She returns with a slinky black dress and a pair of strappy silver heels, dumping them on the bed, on top of my shirts.

"Where's the rest of that dress?" I growl, scowling at the offensive material.

"Don't worry," she fingers the fabric, "I can fight. Now get out, I have to get ready."

Glancing at my watch, I grumble knowing I don't have time to fight her on this.

"Have Dennis drive you," I order.

"That'll be a no." She says, "but have the night you deserve, Malakai."

I open my mouth to argue but my cell begins to buzz in my pocket. I pull it out seeing Sebastian calling.

"What?" I snap into the phone.

"Where the fuck are you?" He hisses back, "They're here already."

"I'll be there in a minute." I hang up and look back to my wife who just happens to be slipping on a pair of black panties underneath her towel. She quirks a brow, challenging me to keep watching and find out what'll happen.

And as much as I'd love to stick around, I can't.

Fuck.

"What's the reason for this?" Hank demands the moment I walk into the room.

Ignoring him, I head down the length of the room, pulling out my chair before I grab the whiskey and pour a drink. My grandfather sits stiffly in the chair next to mine, having been filled in on what happened – or at least most of it, he's just as pissed as I am.

He's only known Olivia for a short time yet he's already protective of her, and I'll always be grateful for that.

I move my eyes over every face in the room, slowly taking a draw from my drink, letting the burn of the whiskey flow down my throat.

"I thought I made it clear," I say to the room, "That my wife is off limits."

Someone fidgets. Another clears their throat.

"What are you talking about, Farrow?" Hank scoffs, throwing up a hand, "You called an emergency meeting for that little wife of yours?"

Stefan smirks at his side. I'd really like to take a knife to that damn cocky smile and cut it right off his face.

Accidents happen all the time, if only I could figure out a way of taking out half this room without raising suspicion.

I don't want to outright say what has been dug up on my wife, but I know one of these vultures went behind my back.

"I have it on good authority someone in this room dug into her past," I tell them, omitting the details as I scan their faces. The trouble is, every single man in this room is a trained liar, their poker faces strong so I can't expect to find the guilty party based on their expressions. "I called this meeting as a warning."

"A warning?" Iwan pipes in, "And what warning is that, exactly?"

"That when I find out who disobeyed my direct orders, they will be dealt with."

"Are you threatening the council?" Iwan snaps incredulously, standing as he raises his voice, "We are your backbone, boy, and we don't take kindly to threats."

I simply stare at him with boredom, "No threats. Only promises. To disobey my command is as good as treason in my eyes and the only rightful punishment is death."

Silence falls as Iwan goes red in the face, "Savor that seat while you're in it," He lowers his tone, "It won't be long before someone throws you off it."

"Is that a threat? With witnesses too." I tut with a smirk, "How sloppy of you, Iwan."

I click my fingers and Sebastian stands, moving toward him.

"I have been on this council for seventeen years!" He swats Sebastian's hands away but pales when Dean and Killian enter. "What are you going to do, Malakai!?"

"Escort you off the premises, of course, you're clearly not feeling like yourself, Iwan. Get some rest." I give him a wink for good measure, taking great pleasure in watching my men haul him out of the room. I have no patience to deal with his level of hate this evening. Especially not when my mind is picturing my wife in that slinky little dress grinding up against some fuck in a night club.

"Things are going to change," I tell the room, "The old traditions, the old rules, you can kiss them goodbye."

Everyone starts to argue all at once, talking over each other with raised voices, all directed at me of course. I look toward my grandfather who has remained silent throughout, but he gives me the smallest of nods, like he approves so I look back to the men around my table.

I don't blink, don't talk as I lift my whiskey glass and take a casual sip, draining it before I throw the glass at the wall. It shatters on impact, raining shards of glass over the men closest.

"It is not up for discussion." I roar, "and if you don't fucking like it, get the fuck out of my council meeting and kiss your lives goodbye."

Silence falls quickly.

"And as I said before, when I find out which one of you

fucked with my wife, you'll be answering to me. So, I suggest you make your amends now. It's only a matter of time."

26
Olivia

The drinks spill over the rims of the glasses as I shove my way back through the pulsing crowd on the dance floor, the dark lighting with the flashing strobes making it hard to see exactly where I'm going.

I finally push out of it, finding Willow in the booth I had left her in. She grins at me and accepts her drink.

"It seems kind of like bad karma to celebrate someone's death," I cringe.

She shrugs, "It seemed like bad karma when he leaked your sex tape."

"True," I agree, sucking up my drink through the red straw when my cell buzzes in my purse.

Pulling it out I see a text from an unknown number.

Unknown: Where are you?

Me: Who is this?

Laying my cell down, I focus back on Willow, finally

getting round to telling her about my involvement with planning the event. But my damn cell just keeps buzzing.

"What the fuck?" I growl, snatching it off the table.

Unknown: Malakai. Where are you?

Unknown: Answer me, kitten.

Unknown: Olivia.

"Jesus Christ," I pinch the bridge of my nose.

I quickly save the number, and reply.

Me: Go away.

Future ex-husband: I can find you, kitten. I would just prefer you to let me know where you are.

Me: So, you can come fuck up my night?

Future ex-husband: No, so I know you're safe.

Rolling my eyes, I show the texts to Willow. "That's some weird foreplay, but alright, whatever floats your boat."

"It is not foreplay," I shove her playfully.

Me: We're at Sinners. Happy now?

I wait for a reply, but it never comes. I can see he's read the message, but I get no response. I guess just knowing satisfies him enough to leave me alone.

I wonder idly if he'd found my last little gift for him. I'm sure I'll find out later if he had.

"Do you want to dance?" I call over the music.

"Is that even a question you need to ask?" Willow downs her drink and grabs my hand, yanking me up from the booth and shoves us into the crowd, pushing people out the way until she finds the perfect spot. It's busy tonight considering it's a weekday and it had been a while since Willow, and I have done this.

After my father died, I didn't do much of anything.

My skin becomes slick with perspiration as we move to the music, my grin broad, body relaxed until I feel hands slip around my waist.

My eyes widen and I lurch forward, but they hold on tight, yanking me back. Panicked, I search for Willow, but she's gone.

Shit.

Attempting to snatch out of their hold but failing, I choose to spin instead, my hands going for the chest, "I'm married, dickhead!" I yell.

Malakai grins down at me, "You have no idea how good it sounds to hear you say that, kitten"

My mouth drops open, "You're here."

His eyes dip down me, heating as they take in the dress, "I never got to see the dress before you left."

My eyes narrow, "So you came here?"

He nods, hands sliding around my waist to press into my spine, bringing me flush with his body. I choose to ignore the flash of heat it brings, how my heart picks up and my core begins to ache.

We don't want to fuck this man, no we do not, I tell myself, but I hear my own laughter mocking me, *okay maybe we do. But only in our heads.*

There's a whole list of reasons why it would be a bad idea to let him between my legs.

But even as he begins to move us to the music, our bodies grinding together, his intense blue stare never leaving mine, I'm finding it hard to remember the reasons.

"Turn, kitten," He purrs close to my ear, not waiting for me to comply before his hands start to spin me. He doesn't let me get far; he brings my ass back against him. His hips grind forward as his hand splays on my abdomen.

"What are you doing?" I ask him.

"We're dancing, kitten."

My breath is coming out in quick short bursts, my heart pounding so hard it feels as if it might break through my ribcage.

Bad idea! This is a bad idea.

Yet, I don't stop him when his hand slides up my abdomen, through the valley of my breasts to my throat. His fingers wrap around my neck, while his other hand holds my abdomen, keeping me pinned to him.

"Look at you, kitten," He rasps, "You're not fighting me for once."

"There's still time," I breathe, lashes fluttering closed as his breath whispers at my ear and goose bumps rise on my skin.

He chuckles, "Just let me have this."

I open my mouth to say no, but my head is nodding already.

"Good girl," He growls low, the vibration of his voice doing all sorts of crazy things to my body. I'm wet, I ache and I really, really want to be alarmed.

"Relax, my darling kitten," He purrs softly, tempting

me with that voice of his, "Dance with me."

And so, I do, until I'm breathless and sweaty, the fine hair at my temples sticking to my skin, my dress feeling too stifling.

"I need a drink," I tell Malakai, stepping out of his hold. It's hesitant but he lets me go but not far as his hand links with mine and he begins to stroll through the crowd. They seem to part for him, none of the fighting like Willow and I had to do and I'm not mad about it.

I probably should be but I'm not.

At the bar he's served immediately, and he glances to me, a silent question, "White." I tell him.

He calls the order to the server and as he's waiting, I turn to the crowd, searching for Willow, guilt blooming since I'd all but forgotten her while I was dancing with Malakai.

I start to drift away but Malakai tugs me back, "Where are you going?"

"I can't find Willow."

"Sebastian has her." He tells me, handing me my glass of wine while he holds what I guess is two fingers of whiskey.

I don't get a chance to ask where, when Malakai tugs me through the crowd again, but we don't stop. We continue on until we come to the roped off section of the VIP area and the security guy lifts the rope without a question. I follow Malakai up a short set of black wide stairs, and I spot Willow the moment we're at the top. She's sitting between three massive guys. Sebastian is on her right while two men I've never met before sit on her left. She's laughing at something Sebastian is telling her while the other two watch on.

"Well damn," Bast turns to us, "I thought we were all gonna get a show with the way you two were grinding all up on each other on the dance floor. A nice change from her wanting to murder you, hey, Malakai?"

My cheeks bloom and I slide my hand out of Malakai's, cradling my wine to my chest. I don't miss the glare Malakai shoots at his friend who only responds with a shrug and a wink. Malakai guides me into the booth next to Sebastian, sliding in beside me.

I make sure to put space between us as I look past Sebastian to Willow who is already staring at me in concern.

"You okay?" She mouths.

I shrug because fuck if I know right now.

"This is Killian," Malakai points to the guy closest to Willow. He's around Malakai's age with thick black hair and a beard. His eyes are the color of steel sat beneath dark brows. "And this is his brother, Dean."

Dean is much like his brother, younger and without the full beard, more like stubble, but his hair is just as dark and his eyes a similar shade, more storm cloud over steel.

"Hello." I greet them.

They give me smiles but they're not warm, curious maybe?

"Get out your head, kitten," Malakai whispers in my ear. "I just need a night where everyone in the room doesn't want me dead. You can hate me again in the morning."

I study his face, noting the crease between his brows, the darkness beneath his eyes.

Something in me softens toward him and I know damn well it's a mistake. Know it's the beginning of the fucking end, but I nod.

"Okay," I tell him in a whisper.

27
Malakai

"Ow. Ow. Ow." Olivia winces with every step she takes at my side. The wind is bitterly cold, howling down the narrow streets of the city and there's still snow on the ground. She has my jacket over her shoulders, her arms wrapped around herself.

"I don't know why I fucking do it," She growls, mostly to herself. "Heels during the day are fine, heels on a night out? Torture."

Stopping abruptly, I bend, sliding my arm behind her knees, the other around her back and I lift.

She lets out a shrill scream that echoes down the street. "Put me down!"

"No."

"Malakai!"

"Your feet hurt."

"So?" She struggles in my arms, but I just tighten my hold, continuing the walk to the Maserati I parked around the corner, "You said it was close!"

"It is." I agree.

"Put me down!" She demands again.

I ignore her, continuing down the sidewalk until my car comes into view.

"Okay, you can put me down now," she says, eyes on the car and the warmth it promises. But I don't let her down, keeping her close until I'm at the passenger door. It's a struggle to get it open but I manage, bending to deposit her in the seat.

"I can get in myself, you know?" She scowls.

"I know, I just wanted to do it," I give her a quick kiss on the forehead before I can think better of it and then shut the door, her face still slack with shock when I climb behind the wheel.

It takes a good few minutes for the car to warm up and for the shock to wear off.

I feel her stare on the side of my face, but I'm really trying to focus on the road and not on the creamy skin on show, the black dress having ridden up her thighs, barely covering the center of her.

"This is a nice car," She eventually says. "Can I drive it?"

"No," It comes out quick and harsh and I wince at myself, "Sorry, no."

"Men and their toys," She sighs, "It's just a car."

"One, it's limited edition." I tell her, flicking my eyes to her face and definitely not her legs, "Two, this entire interior is bespoke and upgraded with the latest technology. And three, no one but me drives this car. Ever."

She rolls her lips, her eyes sparkling before she breaks out into a full grin, giggle and all. I need to focus on the road, but the sound, fuck it's mesmerizing. Sweet and melodic and that damn smile will be the death of me.

"You should've married the car, Malakai," She giggles, "Since you love it so much."

I roll my eyes with a shake of my head, focusing back on the road.

It's a long drive back to the estate and when we come out of the city, the roads are less taken care of, more treacherous and icier in this weather. I slow my speed, carefully taking the corners so I don't spin on any black ice.

"I can drive quite well, I'll have you know," She turns to face me, curling her legs onto the seat and that damn dress rides up some more, "This baby would be in good hands." She pats the dashboard for good measure.

"Absolutely not," I flick my eyes to her, my lips wanting to tug into a smile at the pleading look on her face. "How about I'll buy you one. Whichever one you want."

"I don't need you to buy me a car," She rolls her eyes, "I can buy my own car."

"Maybe I want to buy you a car," I counter.

"No," She orders sternly. "I don't want your money."

And that just makes me want to give it to her more. Keeping my eyes on the road, I reach into my pocket and tug out my wallet, handing it over.

"Well, it's yours anyway."

"Put it away, Malakai," She huffs, crossing her arms

over her chest.

I chuckle as I pop the wallet in the holder between the seats, settling in for the rest of the drive home.

"You look beautiful tonight," I say after some time of silence.

She lets out a long breath, "Thank you."

Twenty minutes later, I pull to a stop at the gates until the camera recognizes my plate and the gates begin to open, and then I let the car roll quietly down the long drive. It's so dark out here that you can barely see much beyond the windows. It used to scare me as a child but now I just find peace in the darkness, it's harder to see the stains on your soul when you can barely see in front of your face.

Once the car is in the garage, I walk around to Olivia's side, opening her door and offering my hand to help her out. Her fingers slide into my palms as she climbs out and she promptly bends, unstrapping her shoes and kicking them off.

We walk in silence through the house, the staff long gone to bed in the quarters provided for them, some stay here on the estate while others choose to commute, but either way, there's not a soul awake in the house save for the two of us.

In the bedroom, she heads straight for the bathroom, dropping her shoes in the doorway of the closet. I follow behind, picking them up to put them on the shelf.

While I wait for the bathroom, I strip out of the jacket, putting it on a hanger to place back in the closet and then slip out of the turtleneck, tossing that into the hamper for laundry.

"Um, Malakai?" I hear Olivia call from the bathroom.

"What's wrong?" I'm immediately at the door, pressing on the handle to get inside but it's locked. Would it be wrong to remove the lock? I wonder while I wait for her to respond.

"Um," She says uncertainly, "My zip is stuck."

"Open the door, Olivia."

After a long pause, I hear the lock disengage but she doesn't open, so I let myself in.

She's gnawing on her lip when I get inside, her hands cradled together in front of her body.

"Turn around," I order gently.

"It's stuck," She rambles, "It's too tight for me to just pull it off and I can't get it."

"Turn around, kitten."

She jerks her head in a resemblance of a nod but doesn't turn.

I step up to her, gently taking her arms to turn her around and her eyes meet mine in the mirror. I tower above her, like a looming shadow behind her back. Dropping her eyes, I look at the zipper on the dress, seeing it's just snagged on some material. My fingers work to free it, unhooking the material and then I slide it undone, the sound of the metal on the teeth loud in the quiet bathroom.

"Thank you," She breathes, pushing back on the fingers that whisper across her bare back.

"You're welcome," I rasp, focused on the way my

hands look against her, the roughness of my fingers offensive against the softness of her flesh. I raise my eyes to meet her once more in the mirror as I flatten my palm, slipping my fingers under the edge of the dress where it's parted. Her curves fit so perfectly in my grip, and I trace the shape of her, letting my hand rise until I'm trailing it over her shoulder blade and then onto her shoulder, slipping under the material there where it clings to her.

I gently push it off, blood pulsing through my cock, the mere sight of her enough to leave my dick aching and leaking.

Her chest rises and falls heavily as she holds my eyes in the mirror, her cheeks blooming with color.

"Tell me to stop," I warn her.

She shakes her head and I slip the sleeve of her dress down her arm. It takes the rest of the dress with it, and the material slips from her body, leaving her bare save for the lacy black panties covering her.

Her nipples are peaked, the rose-colored buds moving as she breathes deeply, lips parted.

I reach around, letting the tip of my finger trail up the center of her abdomen until I can follow the curve of her breast, watching as my finger moves over her skin and brushes over the sensitive peak of her nipple.

Her breath stutters from her lips, eyes fluttering closed.

"Eyes on me, kitten," I demand roughly, watching my hand completely cover her breast, my thumb rolling over her nipple. She falls back onto my chest, eyes on me just like I asked.

"Look at you being such a good girl," I praise, leaning down to scrape my teeth across the soft, sensitive skin between her neck and her shoulder. Her head tilts to let me in further and I look up from beneath my lashes to watch her pleasure in the mirror.

So fucking pretty.

"Can I touch you, darling?" I rasp against her skin.

She gives me a gentle nod and sucks in a breath when I let my other hand curl around her hip, squeezing it gently before I move it to the band of her panties, dipping only a little beneath the lace.

Her hips twitch in anticipation and my tongue licks across her skin as I sink down further, letting my one finger part her lips, feeling the slick wet heat of her pussy coat me.

"You're so fucking wet for me, kitten," I gently move my finger up and down her folds, smearing her arousal all over her before I move back up, right to the apex and gently circle her clit with the barest of touches.

A sweet little moan tumbles from her lips as one hand snaps up to wrap around my wrist, not to pull me away but to keep me in place.

I keep the pace, teasing that sensitive little bud but never going too far, keeping her at the edge. I want to be inside this fucking woman, want to feel her convulsing around me, crying out my name.

She cries out when I move away from her clit, using two fingers now as I go lower, slipping to the entrance of her.

"You want them inside, kitten?" I ask, teasing at her hole, spreading her wetness.

"Y-yes," She stutters.

"As you wish," I rasp, sinking my teeth into her shoulder at the same time I penetrate her with my fingers.

Her moan bounces off the tiles, her nails digging into the skin on my wrist as I thrust my two fingers into her as far as they'll go, the heel of my palm adding the friction to her clit she's so desperate for.

"Look at you falling apart for me," I lick over the bitemark on her skin, "You feel how wet you are for me, kitten?"

She nods, her whimpers only adding to the ache in my cock as I grind into her ass.

"Shit," She breathes, "I'm going to come."

"Let me have it," I demand, keeping up the pace, keeping the grind but this time I pinch her nipple between my fingers.

Her knees shake as she cries out loudly, pussy convulsing around my fingers still thrusting inside of her as her head tilts back and she falls apart in my arms.

I gently ease her down from her climax, softening my strokes until I pull out of her completely.

My hand glistens with her arousal and keeping my eyes on her in the mirror, I bring my fingers to her soft lips, smearing the wetness across the seam of them.

"Open up, kitten," I rasp, "Taste what I do to you."

Her lips close around my fingers and she sucks them clean, lids hooded and glassy, the orgasm zapping her of energy.

Gently I lift her, cradling her against my chest and unlike back on the street, she doesn't fight me. Her head lands against my shoulder as I carry her to the bed, laying her down onto the mattress.

Her sleepy eyes watch me for a moment, fighting sleep but when I step back, they fall closed and by the time I'm finished up in the bathroom, she's passed out cold in the bed.

28
Olivia

I should have heeded my own warning.

Letting him have even an inch will be my ruin.

I'm pretty much naked in our bed, makeup still on, hair a mess and there's an unmistakable ache between my legs. It's been a while since a man has been anywhere near me and I'm certainly feeling it now.

What did I do!?

I can't even blame alcohol for my behavior. Stifling a groan so I don't wake him, I glance toward him where he lays next to me. There's space between us despite there not being a wall separating our sides, and even in sleep, he's fucking delicious.

Asshole.

Slowly, and quietly, I climb from the bed, wrapping an arm around me to cover my naked breasts and tiptoe toward the bathroom. My cheeks heat as the memory of his fingers working through me shoves itself to the front of my mind. Fuck it felt good, to be touched like that, to be caressed and looked after, his skilled fingers using precision to bring me up that peak I was more than happy to fall right off of.

But it shouldn't have happened. It crossed a line.

Maybe I can pretend it just never happened.

I jump in the shower, washing away the traces of makeup left on my face and give my hair a good deep condition before I brush my teeth and sneak back out of the bathroom.

Malakai still sleeps but he's rolled onto his front, one leg kicked out from the sheets and arms buried beneath the pillow. It's actually kind of adorable, with his sleep mused hair and sheets tangled all up around him. I figured he would have been, a sleep on his back and don't move kind of sleeper, he just gives that vibe, but I guess I was wrong.

I dress quickly in a pair of sweats and oversized hoodie before I flee from the room and follow the smell of coffee wafting up from the kitchen.

I'll go into the hotel again today; I have some calls I want to make for the event, and I need to try and coordinate the last minute changes I decided to put into place after I'd looked over the plans.

It'll be a grand evening, full of all the magic winter can offer. Sure, it's a little later than I would have had it, but it is still winter, so it's fine.

I greet Louis with a smile and slide onto the stool after I've fixed a coffee.

"You're positively glowing!" Louis comments with a grin, eyeing me.

"What?" I blush, "No I'm not."

Playing with Fire

I swear if he mentions some weird after sex glow myth to me, I will actually die.

He quirks a brow as if he knows but thankfully keeps whatever comment he wants to say to himself.

I don't make conversation today, just accept the breakfast he makes gratefully and eat in silence, wondering just how last night happened.

It was the dancing and the playfulness in the car. It was the way he held me because my feet were hurting and gave me his coat because I was cold.

Shit. This is bad. Very bad.

Once I've finished my breakfast, I clear away my dishes and make another coffee, sighing as I take a sip but then I hear his steps and my spine stiffens, my stomach swirling with butterflies.

He stops in the doorway, eyes finding me immediately, "Did you really cut holes in the toes of *all* of my socks?" He says in way of a greeting.

Oh shit. I forgot I did that.

I hide my smile behind the rim of my mug, "I don't know what you're talking about."

His eyes narrow, "You're a terrible liar, kitten."

"I'll be sure to pick you up some new ones in the city today!" I put the mug down, "And on that note, I have to get ready. See you later!"

I try to flee past him to get back to the bedroom now that he's out of it so I can fully get ready for the day, but I have no such luck.

His arm captures me around my middle, and he draws me in close, "You used my wash." He inhales deeply.

"I have to say, kitten, I like my smell on you."

My body remembers. It remembers the pain from his teeth and the soothing caress of his tongue and how he played my body like an instrument. My core clenches in response, thighs aching as desire heats me from my center.

"I ran out," I force my voice not to waver, put on a good show of not being affected by him. "But if you don't mind," I wiggle, "I have things to do."

"Is that what we're going to do, darling?" His mouth drops to my ear and his breath sends a rush of goose bumps to rise on my skin.

"What?"

"Ignore what happened?"

"Nothing happened," I lie.

His chuckle is quick and short and not at all filled with humor.

"I was drunk," I lie, "It was a mistake."

His arm drops so quickly you'd think my ass was on fire. I look at him, keeping my expression purposely blank. His jaw pops as he grinds his teeth, any softness or light he had in his eyes when he came down is now gone.

Because of me.

Everything in him has changed in a second, standing in front of me is not the man I watched in the mirror last night, no, this man right here is the current leader of a deadly group of assassins. This man is a killer.

I step away from him, fear working in at the edges of my emotions. I'd be stupid not to be scared of this man.

Playing with Fire

I can't let his soft strokes and pretty words fool me.

My husband is not a good man. Pushing him and fucking him is one thing but whatever I just hit with my words has had an entirely different reaction than I was expecting.

His eyes remain on me, but he doesn't say a word and he doesn't stop me as I start to edge away from him, putting distance between us.

I feel his eyes on me even when I'm halfway up the stairs and still feel the phantom burn of them long after I've locked myself in the bedroom.

I change quickly into more appropriate clothing for the hotel, a nude pencil dress with black heels and dry my hair before I use my flatiron to tackle the wavy mane. I leave my makeup light but give my lips a burgundy gloss, then I grab my purse and head out.

When I return downstairs, Malakai is no longer in the kitchen.

"Where did he go?" I ask Louis.

He winces, "Gym."

"Did you hear?" I ask.

"The boss cares for you," He says, his back to me, "And he doesn't care for anyone."

I scoff, "No, he just likes the challenge. He doesn't know me well enough to care for me."

Louis shrugs, "If you say so, Olivia. Dennis is waiting outside for you."

"Okay," I nod, looking toward the patio doors that would lead me to the gym, "Could you let him know I'll be right there?"

I cross the space in the kitchen, opening the doors and shivering against the cold bite of the wind.

"Mrs. Farrow, perhaps now isn't the right time to see him," Louis suggests.

But I ignore him, closing the door behind me as I hurry over the stone path in my heels, trying not to get them stuck in any cracks so I don't break a damn ankle. As I get closer, I can hear this kind of rhythmic thumping, and I pause at the door, waiting to hear anything else. When I don't, I carefully crack the door open.

The door is far enough away from the main hall that contains all the gym equipment that I can see through without being heard.

And Malakai is right there, in the middle of the gym, bare feet moving over a mat as he pounds into a punching bag, the leather sack swinging roughly with every smash of his fist.

Sweat pours from him, dampening his hair and bare torso and he's completely focused, brows low, eyes on the target.

He has that same pissed off expression marring his handsome face, and guilt gnaws on me as I realize I shouldn't have said it was a mistake.

Being a bitch isn't necessarily the goal here, but I panicked.

Letting out a breath, I backtrack out the door, gently closing it behind me and then take the path around the house, finding Dennis waiting just like Louis said.

"Hi Dennis," I smile but it's short and not entirely all real.

"Mrs. Farrow."

"Olivia." I correct.

His lips twitch as if to smile but it never comes and he opens the back door for me, waiting until I'm inside and safely buckled in before he shuts it behind me.

"Where to?"

"The hotel," I stare back toward the gym, "I'll be a few hours again today so there's no need to wait for me. I can call you when I'm done."

"I'm all yours for the day," He pulls away from the house, "I'll just wait."

"I know it's useless fighting you," I say, "Actually before we get to the hotel can we stop at the mall?"

He nods and then switches on the radio, cutting all conversation as he drives me into the city.

29

Olivia

I come out of the mall with a bag and two fresh coffees, handing one to Dennis before he can reach for the bag to take it from me.

"I figured you were a black coffee kind of guy," I say, sipping at my own latte.

He nods, "Thank you."

"Welcome!" I chirp, slipping into the back seat of the car, dropping the bag onto the seat next to me, "Hey, Dennis?"

"Yes, Mrs. Farrow?"

"*Olivia,*" I pronounce it like I'm talking to a child, "Can I ask you a question?"

"I might not answer it," He admits.

"That's fair." I nod, contemplating if I really want to ask this. It's none of my business and I don't really care about the answer, do I? *Do I?*

"Has Malakai had many women at the house?"

Playing with Fire

Dennis's eyes snap to mine in the mirror, his thick brows pulling low, "What makes you ask that?"

"Just curious."

"No. He hasn't."

"Girlfriends?" I pry.

"No."

"Are you trying to tell me he's celibate?"

He scoffs, "Hardly."

I purse my lips, glancing out the window as the coffee warms my hands.

"What has stirred up these questions?"

I shake my head, "No reason. Just curious, like I said."

He narrows his eyes at me but doesn't press further before he focuses back on the streets as he navigates them, heading toward the hotel.

I spend the day holed up in the tiny office room at the back of the hotel. No one has bothered me, except Willow once when she called to ask about dress shopping for the event, and I've managed to get a shit ton done.

The caterers are confirmed and paid, the DJ replaced since the last one was just arrested for god knows what and I've set up an auction to raise funds for the local charity. I've called a few of the city's event decorators but have yet to hear back so that's where this could all fall apart.

Glancing at the clock I decide to call it a day and grab my purse, heading through the hotel. I greet a few of the staff on my way out and offer courtesy hellos to a few guests who spot me, but I'm almost relieved when I climb into the back of the car.

My back aches and my feet hurt thanks to the heels last night. I need a foot rub, stat.

"Home?" Dennis asks.

Rolling my lips, I nod and settle in for the quiet drive home.

It's almost dark when we pull through the gates, the house ahead lit up, warm light spilling out from the many windows.

"Thanks Dennis," I pat his chest, holding my purse and the shopping bag I grabbed from the mall and head inside, smelling dinner the moment I enter.

I'm immediately greeted by Abe.

"Olivia, sweetheart!" He smiles broadly, leaning in to kiss my cheek.

"Hi Abe," I smile. The sweet old man was a literal ball of energy that I don't even possess half the time.

"Join me for dinner?" He asks, already guiding me toward the dining room.

"Where's Malakai?"

"Oh, the boy has been sulking all day," He rolls his eyes, "Did you tell him off?"

Stifling my cringe, I shrug, "Sort of?"

"I like you," He pats my arm affectionally, "He's always needed someone to put him in his place, god knows I tried when he was just a lad, but that boy has never been one to listen."

"Oh, he doesn't listen to me," I assure him, "I just piss him off."

"Keep him on his toes," He nods.

I'm pretty sure I can do no wrong in Abe's eyes, he'd probably pat me on the back if I were to tell him about the petty pranks I've been pulling and say something like *Malakai needs a little fun in his life.*

It is obvious he loves his grandson, and despite this sweet man holding my arm, I know he's likely just as ruthless as Malakai.

We eat and talk, but Malakai never joins us and when I decide to head to bed, I lay there in the dark waiting.

I was going to put up the barrier but decided not to, it didn't feel right so I'm just laying here.

Eventually I get too tired to stay awake any longer and when I wake the following morning, it's to an empty bed.

I vaguely remember him coming into the room, I remember a soft hand against my cheek, but it could have been a dream since there is no evidence he's even been here.

I dress as normal and go downstairs, finding him in the kitchen, already dressed for the day.

Which means he would have found what I replaced all his socks with.

Sitting next to him, I grin when Louis passes me a coffee he already had prepared.

"No breakfast today," I tell him softly. "Not feeling it this morning."

"You'll eat," Malakai says gruffly at my side.

Subtly I glance down at his ankles, hoping to see if he's wearing the neon pink socks I provided. They're the only pairs in the drawer so it's not like he had many options, but I can't tell since his pant leg covers them.

"I said I'm not hungry," I grumble.

"Louis, make her breakfast. I have business in the city. Don't wait up."

And then he leaves, and it remains like this for the next couple of days.

Asshole.

30
Malakai

There's no barrier in the middle of the bed when I get home though I definitely expected there to be. The way she glared at me this morning suggested there would be, if not poison in my coffee but no. There she is, curled in a ball on her side of the bed, facing the windows as she sleeps soundly.

A soft light kisses the side of her face, but the sting of her words still rests upon my skin.

I was likely being a prick about it, but I didn't give a shit.

Showering, I clean off the day of meetings I've had. Stuffy offices are my least favorite places to meet but buying out big corporations and blackmailing CEOs can only be done in certain environments.

Today I won one of the city's biggest financial corporations, purely using blackmail. That's a feat on its own, most of the wealthiest in this city truly believe their money can buy them out of anything, but I had proof in black and white of the *extracurricular activities* that not only would have lost them every penny in their vaults, it would have landed him a hefty prison sentence too. No amount of money he had would have got him out of it, I would have made sure of it.

Now the company is mine and an extra route for me to clean the money made through the assassins under my roster.

The bed is warm when I climb in beside Olivia, leaning across to inhale that scent of hers. She may have pissed me off but there's something about the way she smells that eases the tension in me.

I can't put my finger on what it is or why, but it's as addictive as any drug.

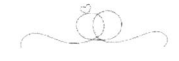

She's out of bed and in the kitchen by the time I get up and dress for the day. And to my surprise so are my men.

Sebastian leans on the counter chatting with Olivia, his grin wide. I know that fucking grin and it makes me want to wipe the damn thing off his face. The man can't *not* flirt. Olivia giggles – fucking giggles – at something he says while Killian and Dean scoff down the food Louis provides.

"I didn't realize I extended an invitation for breakfast to you fuckers," I grumble, drawing the attention of the whole room.

Olivia rolls her eyes and plucks up her coffee, averting her eyes from me while Sebastian smiles at me. He knows what he's doing and the next time we're in the fucking gym I'm going to slip with a dumbbell.

Playing with Fire

Prick.

"We have shit to do today," Dean says past a mouthful of bacon, "Figured it'll be easier for us to come here."

All the legal and technical shit needed to be done for the company I gained yesterday.

"Tell me more about your dress, Olivia," Sebastian goes back to the conversation with Olivia. My ears perk at the conversation.

"I haven't got it yet," She tells him eagerly, "I only saw it in the window. I'm going back today!"

"Is this for the event?" Killian asks her.

She nods, "I've been working on the color scheme, we are going white, black and red so take note, you'll need your tuxes fitted in one of these colors."

"There was no color requirement," I say.

She flicks her eyes to me and instantly dismisses me again, "There is now."

"Where was my approval in this?" I'm being a dick and we all know it.

"I don't need your approval." She picks up a piece of crispy bacon and takes a bite, smiling at me sweetly. If only I could fuck that attitude right out of her.

She wouldn't be able to give me that little devil smile with a mouthful of my cock.

How pretty she would be choking on it, tears on her cheeks and her hair in my fist.

"The fuck you don't."

She scoffs, "Get over yourself, Malakai. All this egotistical shit really makes you appear small." To really hammer in her words, she lifts her hand and holds her finger and thumb close together while her eyes drop to my crotch.

Killian chokes on a piece of fruit while Dean clears his throat and Sebastian laughs.

"Since you're so interested in my size, kitten," I rasp, kicking out a leg, "Why don't you come check it yourself. See if it'll *fit*."

Her eyes widen and she snaps her head around, grabbing her coffee to drain it.

"It's *my* hotel." She continues, clearing her throat as if I didn't say anything at all. "I'll do whatever the fuck I want with the event *I* am now planning."

Wiping her mouth on a napkin, she hops down from the stool, "See you guys later," She smiles at the guys and then her face morphs into a scowl as her eyes drop down my body and then drag back up. "Nice socks." Is all she says to me.

"If you're going shopping for a dress," I reach into my pocket for my wallet, "You can buy it on my card."

Her lip curls, "No."

"Let me buy you a fucking dress." I growl.

"I don't want nor need your money, Malakai. I don't owe you anything. You're my husband in title only, nothing more. You have no other rights to me."

"By being your husband gives me every right to buy you a damn dress."

She smirks as my temper flares as if she gets off on pissing me off. The smile only gets me hard as I think about everything I'll do to her as punishment for this

Playing with Fire

damn attitude.

"Olivia," My voice is all growl, gravelly and rough.

"Malakai," she says as she plucks up her coat and purse. "I'm going shopping. Don't wait up…" She licks her teeth, "*Darling.*"

The word is said so sweetly it could rot teeth and then she's breezing out of the room while the four of us stare after her.

"You are so fucked, man," Dean whistles, "I want one."

"Empty it." I snap, my voice carrying alongside the clip of her heels as she exits the house, her smug, saccharine smile playing behind my eyes.

"Sorry?" One of the guys says, which one I don't know, and I don't fucking care.

"Empty it. Empty her bank account. Now."

"Kai," Sebastian hesitates, "I'm not sure that's a good idea."

I snap my eyes to him, "Good thing I didn't fucking ask for your opinion on handling *my wife.*"

If its war she wants, it's war she's going to fucking get.

"Empty it now." I order, "*Now.*"

"I'll get on it," Dean says, grabbing his laptop.

"You do that," I grit. "Now give me the files for the company." I tell Sebastian.

He provides them quickly, sensing my mood is not to be fucked with right now. When his arm is close enough, I grab his wrist and tug him closer, "Flirt with my wife again, Bast, and I'll hurt you, understand?"

He quirks a brow and smirks, "Sure thing, boss."

"It's done," Dean tells me, "Empty."

"Good. Let's see how she survives without my money now."

"Don't you think that's maybe a little bit too far?" Killian advises.

Probably. "She's my wife, what's hers is mine and what's mine is hers."

I see their glances at each other, silently agreeing that I'm a prick right now for doing what I just did, but I am already looking forward to the fiery argument to come from her. I just know it'll be damn explosive.

31
Malakai

I hear her before I see her.

The guys have all left, the house is quiet, but she is *very* loud.

"Malakai!" She screams.

The door slams open and in she comes, her fury so violent it could rival a storm.

"Wife," I purr, leaning back in my chair.

"You!" She growls, her eyes wide, face contorted with her anger. She's still fucking stunning. "How dare you!?" She crosses the space between us and slams down her palms on my desk.

I rub together my fingers as I watch her, my smile feline, "I just wanted to buy a dress, kitten."

She grabs one of my glasses and tosses it, as hard as she can at the wall, raining shards of glass across the room. I abruptly stand, leaning over to grasp the back of her neck, "Easy now, kitten."

Her breathing is ragged, her eyes filled with so much

venom, "I fucking hate you."

"No, you don't," I rasp.

Brown eyes drop to my lips and then her mouth crashes against mine violently. My fingers slide into her thick hair, gripping it as I tug, stretching out her neck as I plunge my tongue into her mouth. Her fingers curl into my shirt, tugging me closer but this damn fucking desk!

Not separating us or removing my hand from her hair, I manage to manipulate us until we're at the end of the desk and then my hand is on her waist, biting into her flesh as I yank her closer.

Nothing about this is slow or sweet or romantic, this is violent. This is dominance. A challenge. *This is fucking us.*

Her hands quickly start tugging at my shirt and once it's out of my pants, her hands shove up under it, her nails clawing at my back. I hiss into her mouth as the pain registers and she uses it to her advantage to sink her teeth into my lip, drawing blood.

I break away from her, breathing heavy as my tongue laps up the blood welling on my bottom lip.

"You little fucking brat," I growl, my hand coming up to wrap around her throat, her eyes widen as her hands shoot up to grip my wrist. I don't squeeze or constrict her air, but a twitch of my fingers tells her I can.

"Fuck. You." She spits.

Desire rushes through me, my cock aching, "Get on your knees."

She doesn't move so I coax her down with my hand on her throat, "Take out my cock, kitten."

Playing with Fire

Her hands release my wrist and fly to the button of my pants, yanking at it before she tugs them down and has my cock in her hand in the next second.

Releasing her throat, I bring my thumb to her chin, pushing it to open her mouth while her hand works my shaft slowly.

"Look at you being a good girl right now," I praise her, "Such a shame you couldn't be a good girl for me before. Good girls get rewards, bad girls choke on my cock."

Her eyes widen as I press the head of me between her lips, forcing her to widen and relax her jaw. When she's wide enough, I thrust in, going to the back of her throat. Her hands slap against my thighs while mine go to the back of her head, keeping her right fucking there while I fuck between her lips.

"That's it, kitten," I rasp, reveling in the bite of her nails on my skin, "Choke on it."

Her eyes stream and her tongue swirls around my shaft, flicking against the sensitive area underneath and I groan, fingers flexing in her hair. Her teeth begin to scrape dangerously against my shaft, and I widen my eyes in warning, gripping her hair tight enough for it to hurt.

Tears stream down her face but despite them, she glares at me, her anger so hot it burns. She challenges and threatens, even when she is on her knees.

"Don't you fucking dare bite me, kitten."

She grins around my cock and withdraws me from her mouth only to lick up the seam of me, making my damn knees wobble.

"Suck me, Olivia," I rasp.

Her lips close around the crown of me and then she pushes me all the way to the back of her throat, one hand skirting up the inside of my thigh where her nails then run, with a light pressure against my balls.

Oh shit.

I groan as I tip my chin toward the ceiling, so damn close. My hips thrust into her mouth, and she takes all of me eagerly. I'm about to fucking come.

"Do not fucking swallow me," I drop my head to look down at her as my fingers flex on the back of her skull and then I thrust all the way, my orgasm spilling into her mouth. Her nails dig in, but it doesn't deter me, not as I flex and feel her gag, drawing out every second of the pleasure before I withdraw from her.

"Show me, kitten," I demand, pressing my thumb against her bottom lip, "Tongue out."

Eyes on me, she parts her lips and sticks out her tongue. My come coats it, dripping off the tip.

"Well can't you be a good little brat," I commend, "Now swallow it."

With a devilish grin, she closes her mouth and swallows me down before she stands, and her mouth is on mine once more. The kiss heated and rough like before, teeth clashing, tongues dueling. Barely able to think, I keep a tight hold on her as I reach blindly behind and swipe my hand, throwing off the entire contents on top of the desk. It all crashes to the floor, glass smashes, pens and paper scatter and Olivia jumps in my arms but then I'm lifting her, planting her ass on the desk.

I break the kiss, stepping back from her, "Lay back,

Playing with Fire

Olivia."

Burning eyes on me, she lowers her spine to the desk, and I reach out to grasp her ankles, lifting until the heels of her feet rest on the edge of the desk. I let my hands run up the inside of her calves until I stop at her knees and then I push them apart, the pencil skirt she has on rises until it bunches at her hips.

She's barely covered by a strip of lace, and I run a finger over them, feeling the warm wetness of her pussy coat the tip of my finger. "Fucking soaked."

Her hips twitch as my fingers run back up and I flick my eyes to her face, seeing her eyes closed, lip caught between her teeth.

"Are you aching, kitten?" I ask, leaning down to blow my breath on her cunt, "Tell me."

"Yes." She breathes, spine arching.

"Should I fill you up, Olivia?"

I add a little pressure to her, pushing into the lace and she whimpers, her fingers gripping the edge of the desk as she groans.

"Use your words, Olivia," I demand.

"Please!" She snaps.

"Please what?"

"Please fill me up, Malakai. Please fuck me."

"Such a good fucking girl."

I begin to unbutton a few buttons at the top of my shirt before I grip the hem and rip it over my head and then I shove down my pants some more, and grip her hips, pulling her toward me and reach into my pocket for the utility knife.

Her eyes snap to me as I whip out the blade.

"What are you–"

"Hush, pretty girl," I rasp, using two fingers to bring her panties away from her soaked pussy.

Her breathing comes out in rapid bursts and unease, and fear widens her eyes as I bring the blade closer to her.

"Stay fucking still, Olivia." I warn.

She holds her breath as I hook the edge of the blade under the band of her panties and a quick tug slices it clean in half. I do the same on the other side, watching as the lace slips away, revealing her sweet, dripping cunt.

"Fuck me," I breathe.

"What?" Her voice wobbles.

"Shh," I soothe, gripping my already hard cock as I force her legs wider to accommodate me.

Using my hand, I guide the head of me through her lips, coating myself in her wetness before I slide myself to her entrance, pushing in just an inch.

"Eyes on me, kitten," I demand once more and when she obeys, I slam forward, impaling her on my cock, filling her so completely with me, I can't fucking see where I end, and she begins. She's so fucking tight, so damn wet.

Her scream echoes through the room but I don't stop, I pull out and slam forward, thrusting into her. She holds on to the desk as I fuck her, but it doesn't stop her from shifting up the desk, away from me.

Playing with Fire

"You'll never fucking escape me," I grasp her thighs and yank her toward me, slamming forward at the same time, "You're fucking *mine*, Olivia."

"I hate you!" She hisses but then moans, so damn prettily.

"Yeah?" Thrust, "You hate it when I'm fucking you like this?" Thrust. "You hate it when I fill you up and stretch this tight fucking cunt full of my cock?"

"Shit," She hisses, "Don't stop!"

"You're a brat, Olivia," Sweat coats my skin, "I'm going to fuck this attitude right out of you."

"Fuck you, Malakai."

"You are, darling," I purr, fingers digging into the soft flesh of her thighs before I bring one hand around to press a thumb to her clit. She jerks against me and lets out this sweet little fucking whimper. "Now fucking come all over my cock, Olivia, and sing for me."

I circle my thumb on her clit, pumping into her hard and fast until I feel her begin to convulse around me, her whimpers turning to moans, her pussy spasming beneath me.

"Oh god," She cries as she clamps around my cock.

"Fuuuuccccckkkkk," I groan, my thrusts becoming jerky until my balls are drawing up tight and I spill right into her, filling her up with me.

When I pull out, I watch as I slip out of her, my come leaking from her. I scoop it up, watching her twitch and jerk as I slip it back inside, thrusting my fingers into her, "If you think I'm fucking done with you, kitten, then think again."

Gripping her thighs, I drag her until her feet land on the floor and then I haul her up, her lax body falling against my chest.

"You're fucking mine now, Olivia. *Mine.*"

32

Olivia

Fucking Malakai Farrow is an out of body experience.

No that isn't right. I feel everything, every touch, every caress, every ounce of his possession.

"Take it off," He growls, his skin glistening with sweat, his eyes a little feral, hands balled up into tight fists. "Strip for me, Olivia. Right fucking now."

My hands tremble as I bring them to the buttons on my blouse, popping open each one. But I'm fumbling, my fingers not working the way they should. My pussy throbs, sore with how hard he fucked me against his desk but deliciously clenching, begging for more. Fuck, I need more. More of this unhinged, uncontrolled side of him.

"Too long," he growls as he snatches forward, hooks his fingers into the blouse and rips down. The buttons pop off, scattering across the room, leaving the blouse open and half tucked into my pencil skirt.

"That was a Valentino," I try to add bite to my words,

but it comes out more like a breath.

"I'll buy you another one," His hands turn softer as he pulls out the rest of the blouse from the skirt, "Turn around."

Slowly, I turn, giving him my back and then his fingers are at the zipper on the back of the skirt, gently tugging it down. Without the tightness around my waist, the skirt slips off my hips, pooling at my feet.

He helps me turn and offers his hand to help me step out of it. Now I'm just left in a torn blouse, a bra and my heels.

"Look at you," He runs his thumb across his bottom lip, eyes devouring me, "Lose the blouse and the bra," He orders, "Keep the heels."

Swallowing, I obey, slipping the blouse off my shoulders and letting it fall to the floor, joining my skirt and then I unhook my bra, exposing me entirely.

"So, you can be a good girl," He cocks his head, taking me in like I'm something to be bought. He reaches forward, running a finger from the center of my clavicle all the way down, over my sternum, down toward my naval and then lower. His finger stops at the apex of my pussy. "Who does this belong to?"

"Me." I hiss.

His brow quirks and a smirk pulls on the edge of his mouth, "Does it now?"

"Yes."

"Is that not *my* come dripping down your thighs, kitten?" To prove his point, he leans down slightly, and his finger runs up my inner thigh, gathering the sticky come to smear it over my skin. "Is it not me leaking

Playing with Fire

from you right now?"

"If I let every man have a little bit of me every time they fucked me, what would be left for me?" My own smile lifts my mouth, a challenge that he bites at so fucking easily.

"No fucking man matters now, Olivia. It does not matter who has been between these legs anymore, it's just fucking me. I own this cunt, this body. I own your fucking soul, Olivia."

"For now," I taunt.

His hand snatches out so suddenly, I gasp, startled, and his fingers wrap around my throat, pressing in hard but not hard enough to choke me. *Fuck, if only he'd choke me.*

I don't want soft with him. Soft means feelings, hard means hate. It doesn't matter that it makes no sense. It's how I'm dealing with this. I want him, have wanted him, and I am only allowing it with these very clear boundary lines I'm putting in place. Hard, fast and rough.

"That all you got, Malakai?" I taunt, my voice only a little stifled by his hand, "I always knew you were a fake. You put on a big show but you're weak. Fucking weak, Malakai."

His fingers tighten and I grin at him.

"Show me the monster," I challenge, "Show me why I should be afraid of you."

"Olivia," He warns.

I laugh, balancing in my heels, furious at myself, furious at him, "Are you scared, Malakai?" I taunt, "Scared you've met your match?"

Suddenly he's pushing me back, my feet barely able to keep up with his long, determined strides until my spine slams against the wall hard enough the painting in the frame beside my head rattles.

"Don't fucking push me, kitten," He warns.

"What will you do!?"

Something comes over him, something dark and slightly terrifying. A thrill works through me as the hand around my throat tightens, my own hands flying up to wrap around his wrist.

His knee shoves between my thighs, forcing them apart and my precarious balance becomes even more wobbly with the move.

"You won't like me if I do what I want to do to you, Olivia."

"I don't like you now," I manage to get out.

He laughs but it's not filled with amusement, this dark laugh is filled with violent promises.

"Turn around." He suddenly releases my throat and I lurch forward, not expecting the freedom. He doesn't catch me.

He stares at me, unforgiving as he waits and I turn, chest heaving, heart pounding until I'm facing the wall.

"Put your hands on the wall."

I reach out my arms, placing my palms flat against the wall, having to bend slightly to be able to do so.

"Good girl," He praises, "Now step back, bend over for me, kitten."

Playing with Fire

I walk my hands down the wall as I bend, adjusting my feet at the same time. I'm bent over, vulnerable, and I've never felt more alive.

There's a quick, hard slap against my ass cheek that makes me gasp and jerk up but his hand flies to the back of my neck, forcing me back into place. "Stay fucking still, Olivia."

My ass stings from his slap and my pussy throbs, something hot and heavy coiling tight inside of me. I wanted another one.

And he delivers.

His slap resonates through the room, joining the crackle of the fire as the skin on my ass cheek burns just as hot.

A groan slips from my lips, turning to a moan as his long, skilled fingers massage over the sting.

"I always knew this pretty ass would look good with my handprint," He muses, a single finger tracing the outline of his fingers and palm.

"More," I whisper, the plea slipping from my lips.

"More?" He chuckles, "What a dirty little slut you can be, Olivia," his hand squeezes punishingly against my ass cheek, "You want me to treat you like my whore, kitten?"

"Just more, please," I hear my voice crack, desperate to ease this ache inside of me.

His slap stings against my other ass cheek and then I feel the head of him pressing against the entrance of me.

"More, kitten?" He asks, "I'll give you fucking more."

His cock penetrates me so suddenly I can't help but cry

out. He fills me so abruptly my body has no time to adjust or relax into him. The burn of the stretch leaves me screaming, calling out as his cock thrusts in and out of me, not giving an ounce of mercy. He impales me on him from behind, his hand coming down onto the back of my neck to hold me in place as he uses me.

His fingertips bite into me as he thrusts, pushing me further against the wall until I have to bend my arms and start to fight back. He fucks me like he hates me, just how I want it. So fucking hard I hear the slap of our skin, feel my pussy stretching and yielding to him.

"Just like that," I moan, pushing back against him.

And then his palm slaps against my ass cheek again, the pain a sudden burst that shoots heat through me, making me extra wet, extra needy.

"Yes!" I hiss, my skin is stinging, my pussy soaked, and he just fucks me harder, pounds into me relentlessly. It's brutal and messy, my inner thighs soaked, the arches of my feet aching. Palms caress my ass cheek before he slides his hand toward my crack, his thumb running down the center of me there, before his thumb presses into me.

"Has anyone had you here, kitten?" He grits.

I don't have a chance to answer, not when he suddenly spits on me, using it as lube to apply more pressure, as if to enter but he just lingers there, the threat of it enough to make my pussy start to twitch.

He chuckles, "They haven't but you want it, don't you?"

The tip of his thumb enters me, the intrusion foreign but not entirely unwelcome.

"You want it that much you're ready to come all over my cock for it."

In he goes further and that does it. I detonate, the scream is ripped from my throat as he thrusts through it, his thumb mimicking his cock as he fucks me in both holes. "Fuck me, Olivia, you're so fucking tight."

My orgasm settles but he's not close to being finished, not when he's still fucking me violently and his thumb is still inside my ass. My knees are shaking, my spine aching with the position but like fuck will I give up first. He can fuck me half to death and I still won't let him win.

"Such a pretty little brat," His tongue suddenly licks up my spine, making me shiver, fingers digging into my hips. His thrusts start to turn jerky, and I lift slightly, looking over my shoulder. His face is turned toward the ceiling, muscles in his neck pulled taut.

"Goddamn," he moans, the bruising hold on me only tightening more and then he's spilling himself into me, filling me up.

I cry out at the feel of him, dropping my head when he pulls out, leaving me wobbly and unbalanced.

But then his arms are suddenly around me, holding me up while he sinks onto the floor, pulling me into his lap to cradle me against him. I'm sticky, sweaty, I can feel him leaking out of me, but he just holds me, stroking back my wild hair, holding me as I continue to tremble.

"Are you alright?" he whispers.

"Yes," my voice is hoarse, throat tight and raw.

"Can you stand?"

I nod, and start to climb off him, wincing as I feel more of him slip out of me and down my thighs, but he doesn't seem to care, not when he then lifts me. I don't have the energy to fight him on it and then he's walking us out of the drawing room and through the halls of his house.

I momentarily panic since we're both naked, but no one comes out and we make it up to the bedroom without incident.

"Why are you doing this?" I whisper. This side of him is in clear contrast to the man that just fucked me in his office.

"Shh," He says as he sits me on the vanity and reaches for the heels on my feet.

He takes them off gently, throwing them behind him, and then he's back, hands on my inner thighs, pushing my legs apart.

His eyes drop to my pussy and his thumb gently strokes over the sensitive flesh of me, "Look at you," he muses as I whimper at the sensitivity, "All swollen and full of me."

I hold my breath, watching his face, at the rapt attention he is placing on me, watching his own fingers as they part my lips and run through the come soaking me.

His eyes finally flick up to my face as he brings his hand away and still watching me, he leans across and switches on the shower.

"I'm not done with you, kitten," He warns in a low voice, "Not fucking done at all."

33
Malakai

Her body is a work of art, so finely constructed, not a single part has been missed. She's devastatingly stunning, from her big doe eyes to the soft curves and long legs. She is perfection in human form, a feast for my eyes and a delicacy on my tongue.

My hands smooth the sudsy water over her soft skin, across her breasts as her head leans back against my shoulder, the water running over her, steam filling the bathroom.

She whimpers when I move my hand between her legs, "What a needy little thing you are," I muse proudly, "My wife is as desperate for it as I am."

She mumbles something inaudible as my fingers part her, moving through the slick heat of her. She's still swollen, likely sore but she takes it as I slip my fingers into her.

I hold her to me as I start to thrust my fingers, one, then two, working her up with the heel of my hand to her clit.

She reaches around and grasps my hard cock that was resting against the curve of her ass and squeezes, stuttering my breath.

"Fuck," I hiss as her hand begins to pump at the same tempo of my fingers pushing inside of her. Fucking her is quickly becoming one of my favorite things to do.

I slam my hand down on the button to shut off the shower and then have her out of it in the next minute. A fire is burning inside the room, keeping it warm so I don't bother with the towels as I capture her mouth with mine and walk her backwards into the room, kissing her like she is the very air that fills my lungs.

She kisses me back with as much fervor, nails scraping over my biceps where she holds me. When I feel the bed hit her legs, I stop, grabbing her to spin her before forcing her down onto the mattress on her knees. She lets out a yelp, but I manipulate her body into the position I want, face down, ass up, spine arched as I force her knees to spread, opening her right up.

With her pussy and ass in the air, I grasp her cheeks, spreading her before I bury my face between her legs, and I fucking eat like a damn man starved. She lets out a startled cry as I suck her clit into my mouth, flicking my tongue against her enough that she starts to push back on me.

"Malakai!" She moans my name and my fucking cock jerks at it.

"That's my name on your lips, kitten," I come away from her pussy, sinking a finger into her, "Mine."

"Please," She whimpers.

"Beg for it," I demand, "Say my name and beg for it."

She doesn't say another word.

I chuckle and give her a long lick, punching my tongue into her before I draw away again.

"Say. My. Name." I order, squeezing her ass. There are still light red marks on her cheeks from my slap, the outline of my hand making me want to give her a permanent mark. A branding. Showing everyone, she is mine. My wife. My kitten. My little fucking brat.

But I don't slap her ass this time.

I slap her dripping cunt.

I grin at the scream, the smile stretching when she begins to move away from me only for me to drag her back.

"Say it."

"Fuck you!"

I pinch her clit between my fingers, and she moans loudly, arching her spine further, showing me her ass.

"Give me what I want," I roll the tip of my thumb against her, teasing her, "And I'll give you my cock, baby. I'll fill up this needy little cunt just like you want."

I move my fingers, keeping the touch so light it'll only keep her at the edge but never push her over, no matter how hard she tries to push back and add more pressure. She's fucking dripping for me, her pussy glistening, slick and hot and my own cock is leaking, ready to be back inside of her.

But not until she gives me what I want.

"Come on, darling," I coax.

"Please," She begs.

"Please what?"

"Please *Malakai*!" She cries, a bite to her tone, "Just fuck me."

I chuckle and grip her hip, pushing her onto her side before I grasp her leg and yank it up, situating myself between them so I'm straddling one leg while the other is on my shoulder. Gripping the base of my cock, I slide it over her pussy, coating myself with her before I nudge the head of me into her body.

Her eyes roll back, fluttering closed.

"You look at me when I fuck you, Olivia," I tell her.

Her eyes open and then narrow in on me, glaring but then I thrust, stretch and fill her and they widen, her mouth parting in a silent scream.

"No one else will ever see you like this," I rasp, looking down to where I'm buried in her body, "You are mine. Mine to fuck. To please."

She doesn't answer me, not like I expect her to, but she does keep her eyes on me, watching as I fuck her. Watching as I own her.

Now that I've had her, felt her, I don't know how I'll go without it. She's so perfect for me, pushes when I pull, opens for me, but never backs down.

Her vitriol turns me on. Her attitude even more so.

I thrust into her before I move us again, helping to lower her leg and move her onto her back, my body fitting into the cradle of her thighs as I lower, softening toward her as my mouth latches onto hers. She slides her fingers into my hair as I continue to move, rolling my hips so I can catch her clit with every grind. She shudders beneath me, her legs coming around to tighten over my hips.

"Come for me, Olivia," I whisper against her lips.

Her eyes search mine, her face a mask of pleasure and confusion and I cradle her cheek in my hand, something stuttering inside my chest.

"Come for me, my beautiful girl," I kiss her gently, rolling my hips to give her everything she needs, "That's it," I praise when her lips part and her pussy begins to convulse on my cock.

"You're so beautiful, Olivia." I tell her, "So perfect."

Her teeth sink into her bottom lip as she stifles her cry, and her lids fall closed. I don't demand for her to look at me this time, I just watch her, watch as her brows knot and her eyes squeeze, her perfect pussy fluttering and gripping my cock with her orgasm. I keep thrusting through it, until pleasure zips down my spine and I groan, dropping my head into the crook of her neck. I suck her skin into my mouth, biting down as I come in her, filling her up once more, marking her both inside and out.

Her nails scratch at my scalp, her breaths coming out hard and fast and when I'm spent, I take a moment, my cock jerking inside of her as I hold my weight off her.

Then I slip from her, pushing up to stare down at her face. She looks up at me lazily, lids hooded over dark eyes, fatigue relaxing her features. My thumb runs over her bottom lip before I push up, walking to the bathroom.

When I return, warm wash cloth in hand, she's in the

same position, sleepy eyes watching me.

I gently part her legs again, swiping up the insides of her thighs, removing the evidence of me from her skin before I then wipe over her pussy, cleaning her up.

"Thank you," She breathes.

"Get into bed," I order her softly.

She shuffles and wiggles, moving over the mattress until her head hits her pillow and she sighs into the comfort.

I head to the bathroom again, tossing the cloth into the sink as I wash myself up and then I'm back at the bed, pulling back the sheets, making her move since she's spread out on top of them. Her hair is still wet, but she doesn't seem to care.

When we're both beneath the sheets, I reach for her, hesitating since this is new but when she doesn't flinch or move away from me, I bring her closer. Her arms are wedged between our bodies, fingers pressed just beneath my clavicles and her face is buried in my neck where she inhales deeply, seeming to settle even further.

I smooth down her hair, trying to detangle the knots for her though my fingers can only do so much. I should brush it for her, I think, but I won't move her now. Another time. I'll do it for her another time.

"I still hate you," She whispers, pressing her lips to my Adams apple.

My mouth kicks up into a smile, "I'm sure you do."

"You can buy my dress," she says, snuggling in further.

Playing with Fire

"You're going to let me buy you a dress?" I say incredulously, "If only I knew fucking you into oblivion would make you more agreeable, I would have done it a long time ago."

She huffs, "I want my money back."

"I'll have it transferred tomorrow," I promise her. "But I'm still buying the dress."

"You can still buy the dress," She agrees.

"Will you show it to me?"

"Not until the event," She admits, "It's a power move."

I chuckle, "That good, huh?"

"That good," She nods softly, "Good night, Malakai."

I sigh, twisting a wet strand of hair around my finger, my other hand flexing where it rests on her hip. She feels too damn good in my arms, like this is exactly where she belongs.

My wife.

Bringing my hand away from her, I twist the wedding band on my finger as I kiss her head and inhale the sweet scent of her. "Good night, kitten."

34
Olivia

Me: Dear future ex-husband, I loathe you.

My message is read instantly, three little dots appearing seconds later.

Future ex-husband: Dear Wife, your claws are out early today. I like it.

I chuckle to myself, tossing my phone down onto my coat that rests a few feet away.

"This dress on you," Willow whistles, "Malakai is going to go nuts."

As I promised, I'm letting him pay. I have his card in my purse and the dress is being fitted right now, the seamstress pinning it to fit me like a glove. The red is vibrant, with a subtle sparkle and it's off the shoulder with a sweetheart neckline and a low back. It fits every curve of me, from my breasts to my hips before it follows the lines of my thighs and then flows out in a mermaid style.

Playing with Fire

The moment I saw it, I knew I needed it.

"You okay?" Willow asks when I don't respond.

"Me?" I point to my chest, "Fine. Why?"

She frowns and then shrugs, "Seem distant today is all."

Perhaps it's because of the complete dick down I got last night. I'm still sore from it, every inch of me marked in some way, either physically with finger shaped bruises or internally with muscle aches. There's a damn hickey on my neck that I've had to work some magic on to cover and I'm silently thankful to all the tutorials and videos I've watched on color correcting makeup. It's hidden right now under layers of makeup. I don't need the whole world to know how thoroughly Malakai owned me last night.

I'm not even sure how I feel about it.

My phone buzzes and I reach for it, bending to pick it up.

Future ex-husband: Show me the dress.

Me: No. You have to wait.

Future ex-husband: Color at least?

Me: Red. You're wearing black entirely.

I drop my phone again, lifting my eyes to the mirror. I'm exhausted but after this I needed to go to the hotel to finalize a few details and pay the remaining amounts outstanding for the services I've hired for the event.

But I'm also avoiding going back home.

Malakai was up before I was this morning, he didn't even join me for breakfast but when I checked my account, like he promised, my money was back where it belonged.

I didn't go searching for him after I dressed and had Dennis bring me here, but I also felt weird and vulnerable. It's why I texted him.

I feel like a teenager again, having a crush on some boy.

A part of me thought he wouldn't text back and then the delight when I saw that he had, startled me. I don't want to be catching feelings for my husband.

"There," The seamstress smiles, clasping her hands together, "This is perfect."

I glance at the mirror and can only agree.

There are only a few days left to go before the event. I've closed off the main ballroom for the decorators to come in and transform the space. Everything is finally organized, paid for and confirmed. My heels clip through the hotel confidently, the last of the invoices ready to be filed and I'm ready to get back to the estate to rest. I haven't stopped aching all day and I need a damn nap.

When I've finished doing everything I need to, I grab my purse and head through the lobby, stopping short when I see Malakai waiting by his Maserati and not Dennis.

"What are you doing here?" I brace for the cold, my brows tugged low, "Where's Dennis?"

Malakai checks his watch and then grins at me, "Get in, we have a reservation to catch."

"Now!?" I gasp.

"Now, kitten," he opens the passenger door for me and

offers me his hand which I take, careful not to slip on any ice as I climb into the car. Warmth envelopes me and I sink into the plush seat, sighing. I can't even be mad that he's here, not when this chair feels like heaven.

I'm so freaking tired.

Malakai climbs into the seat beside me, flicking his eyes to the mirror before he pulls into traffic. It's late, not quite dark yet but it won't be long.

"What's wrong?" Malakai asks after a few minutes of silence.

"Other than you completely bulldozing my plans to sleep, nothing. I'm just tired."

I look over to him to see his brows lowered in concern, his mouth a grim line.

"Don't start that," I grumble, "We don't care about each other, remember?"

He scoffs, the sound is so sudden and unlike him I'm caught off guard by it.

He doesn't say anything though and I settle into the seat, maybe I can get a few minutes sleep while he drives us to wherever we're going. I close my eyes and rest my head back, using my hands to pillow my face.

I jolt awake what feels like only minutes later when Malakai is sliding his arms under me.

"What are you doing?" I clear my throat, trying to get my bearings. He attempts to lift me, but I wiggle, and fidget and he growls in annoyance.

"Do you always have to fight!?" He snaps.

"Stop trying to carry me everywhere! Everyone will

see!"

"We're at home," He deadpans, not amused.

"Wait, what?" I blink rapidly, "Why?"

"You're tired."

"I thought we had a reservation."

"Another day," He steps back to let me climb out of the car and places his hand on my lower back as we walk into the quiet house. It appears no one is here, not even the staff.

"Where is everyone?"

"I gave them all the night off," he grumbles.

"You're mad," I accuse.

"No."

I roll my eyes and slip away from his hand, tucking my arms around me. "I'm just going to go to bed." I tell him.

"Did you eat?" He stops me, cocking his head when I turn back to him.

"Well, I –"

"It's a yes or no, answer," He quirks his brow, "Did you eat."

"This morning," I admit.

"Get changed and come back down, you can sleep after you've been fed."

He doesn't wait for my reply when he strolls off, disappearing into the kitchen. Confusion has my head swimming, but I continue up the stairs and quickly change into a set of fleece pajamas. Bare footed, my mouth

Playing with Fire

stretching in a yawn, I head back to the kitchen, climbing tiredly onto the stool.

Malakai is at the counter, chopping vegetables.

"Didn't figure you'd know how to cook."

He rolls his shoulders as a response but keeps his back to me. Whatever he is preparing smells good, spicy but warming, and I'm hypnotized by the way he moves around the kitchen. I definitely assumed he had no idea how to cook, especially since Louis has cooked every night since I've been here and well, I guess I just never expected he taught himself how. I figured everything has always been done for him.

I have my head resting in my hand when he slides a plate in front of me, It's a curry with fluffy rice on the side.

"Huh," I chuckle, inhaling the spicy aroma of it. He doesn't sit next to me, instead he heads for the pantry to grab the loaf of bread.

"You have bread with your curry?" I ask.

He dips his chin with a nod and slices a few pieces before he grabs the butter and joins me.

I take the first bite and my brows shoot up, "Wow, it's good."

"You sound surprised," He huffs, grabbing some bread before he starts to tear off the crusts and then my mouth drops open when he places it next to my plate.

"Why did you do that?" I blink rapidly.

He glances to the bread and then me, and then back at his plate, "You don't eat the crust."

"How do you know that?"

It's a thing I've done since I was a kid, my friends and family used to make fun of me for it, but I never did like the crust.

"I noticed," He shrugs, taking a big bite of his food before he reaches for the bread again, butters a slice and starts mopping up some of the sauce at the edge of the plate. But I'm still in shock. No one has taken the crust off for me before.

I'm stunned silent, following his lead by buttering the bread and mopping up the sauce and carefully take a bite. I have nothing to say, so I eat in silence, Malakai doing the same.

When we're finished, he clears the plates and grabs two bottles of water from the fridge.

"Let's go." He waits for me.

"Go where?"

"To bed." He frowns.

"I am so confused right now," I follow him up the stairs and head for the bed once inside while he goes to the closet, dropping the water onto the bench outside. He returns in a pair of flannel pajama pants, topless and the dim light from the lamps kisses each peak of his muscles, shadowing the hollows.

I could stare at him all day, run my fingers over those muscles and trace each severe line of them. I shake my head, the fuck is wrong with me?

"Drink your water," He passes me a bottle and then climbs in next to me.

"Are you tired too?" I ask, downing half the bottle before I put it on the bedside table.

Playing with Fire

"No." He pulls the sheets over us.

"Why are you in bed then?"

"Because I want to hold you," While his voice is stern and strong, his eyes are not. There's a hint of vulnerability there, an edge of something uncertain flicking in his expression. "Is that a problem?"

Seeing him like this, that steely hardness to him pushed down to show this softer side, I don't have the heart to say no. So, I shuffle closer to him and when he lifts his arms, I tuck myself against his side, hand falling to his abdomen. For a few minutes we lay there silently, as if getting used to the feel of it, the feel of each other.

I won't lie and pretend it doesn't feel nice. He holds me tightly, his fingers absently tracing up and down my spine while his chest moves evenly beneath my cheek. His heartbeat is strong under my ear, the thump of it somewhat soothing to my exhausted mind.

My own fingers begin to move, following those lines I was tempted by earlier, my nails lightly scraping against his tan skin.

His muscles jump under my touch, but I don't stop, even when my eyes grow heavy and start to sting. I'm ready to give into it, let the exhaustion I've fought all day finally take its hold.

I'm at the edge of sleep, the fog seeping in quickly and thickly when I hear his voice.

"You may not care about me, kitten," His chest rumbles, "But I'm certainly finding I care an awful lot about you, certainly more than I ever expected I would."

35
Malakai

A groan slips past my lips as pleasure whips down my spine. Something warm and wet is moving over my cock, stroking it eagerly.

My eyes open and I dip my chin, finding Olivia between my legs, my cock in her mouth. She flicks her eyes to me, and she grins, her teeth scraping up my shaft.

"Fuck," I growl, my fingers slipping into her hair. She bobs her head and then one of her hands slides up my inner thigh before her nails scrape across my balls.

My hips jerk, my cock thrusting further into her mouth, causing her to gag, but she just takes it, even when her eyes water. Her tongue swirls around me messily, and when she cups my balls and squeezes, almost so tight it hurts, I nearly fucking spill down her throat.

But if she's waking me up by sucking my dick, you can damn well know I'm not coming in her throat. I'm filling her up so she can start her day where she fucking belongs.

I grab a fistful of hair and pull her off me, making sure I

don't hurt her when I pull. She lets my cock go with a wet pop of her lips and then frowns at me, pouting like I just took away her lollipop.

A feral grin stretches my mouth as I sit up, shoving my pants down the rest of the way before I reach for the shirt on her. She lifts her arms for me, letting me remove it but I don't discard it.

"On your back, take off your pants."

She moves as I ask, removing her pants until she's completely bare for me. Something primal rumbles up inside of me when I drop my eyes to her cunt, finding it glistening with her arousal.

"Arms up." I demand as I start to twist the shirt, making it thinner so I can use it to bind her wrists. I wrap the material around her hands, pulling it taut and stretching up her arms where I keep the shirt tucked in my fists and then anchor my fingers to the bed.

I hold her like that while my other hand reaches down between us, swiping through her lips as I gather that wetness before I start to roll my fingers over her clit.

"Did sucking my cock get you this wet, kitten?"

"You were hard," She breathes, "Figured you wouldn't mind."

"You're a dirty little thing, aren't you," I praise, slipping my hand down her pussy further so I can enter her with my fingers.

She whimpers as I thrust, stretching her, making sure she's ready to take me.

"If you lose feeling," I tell her, referring to the makeshift binds I have her wrists in, "Tell me, okay?" She nods her understanding as I grab the base of my cock and start to slide the head of me through her pussy. Her eyes roll back, and I don't wait a second longer to thrust into her, her body opening right up for me.

"Malakai!" She screams, her fingers curling into her palms.

"Open your legs wider, kitten," I demand. She spreads her thighs more for me, and with one hand still holding her arms above her head, I use the other one to hold down her hips as I drill into her, her tits bouncing with every hard, powerful thrust.

Fuck me, she's like damn heaven. I watch my cock disappearing into her cunt, watch as it comes out covered in her, she's so damn wet that she soaks me completely.

"My needy little wife," I praise, jaw slackening as pleasure propels me forward, quickening my hips as I fuck her. Her eyes are squeezed shut, her skin slick with sweat. I move my hand to her clit, using my thumb to caress her and her whole body shudders, her eyes snapping open.

"Yes," She hisses, "Fuck!"

I focus on her pleasure, focus on bringing her to the edge and I can feel it when she gets there, her pussy fluttering around my cock so I keep going, reveling in the cry as she falls apart for me. I follow her over the edge, hips jerking as I empty myself into her, losing myself to the feel of it.

"Goddamn," I breathe, letting go of the bedframe so her arms drop above her head, still bound by the shirt. She lays there for a moment, completely limp, eyes hooded as she follows my movement as I roll off her and land at her side, taking a moment to breathe myself.

When I've caught my breath, I reach up and start untangling her wrists, bringing her arms down to start massaging at the red marks left behind.

She watches the whole thing silently, and when I'm done with her wrists, I move my hands down her body, touching, feeling, following every curve of her before I cup her pussy, my fingers getting drenched by a mix of me and her.

Her lips part as I lean in, whispering my mouth against hers, "Mine." I growl before I let go completely and sit up.

She sits up beside me, bringing the sheets up to cover herself.

"Can I have your keys?" She asks me, leaning on the headboard.

"Can you have my what?" I tug my pajama pants back on and stand.

"I want to drive today."

"No."

"You can't have Dennis take me everywhere. I want to drive the Maserati."

"Absolutely not."

She pouts, "We're married. You have to let me."

I chuckle, "No, I don't." I start to walk toward the door, "I'll grab a shower in another room. See you downstairs for breakfast."

Olivia joins me in the kitchen sometime later with a

pout on her face. She's dressed impeccably in an all-black pant suit, the blazer is over sized and done up at the middle, but she's wearing this lacy little thing underneath, teasing her cleavage. She's slicked back her hair severely, letting her ponytail fall down her back, dead straight and tempting to wrap around my fist. All in all, she doesn't look like the woman I had thoroughly fucked on the bed this morning, all limp and sated.

"You're not wearing that."

Her eyes burn where they touch me, a glower on her face, "And fuck you too."

"I'm serious."

"So am I."

She smiles at Louis gratefully as he passes her a bowl of berries and yogurt before she scowls again in my direction.

"Get changed." I demand.

"No." She spoons some yogurt into her mouth before she takes a sip of her coffee and checks the time on her watch. She quickens her eating, before she downs the rest of her coffee. "I've gotta run. Nail appointment to catch."

"Olivia," I warn.

"Have a good day, darling," she flutters her lashes as she makes a move for the door. I'm going after her in the next breath.

"You're showing everything," I growl.

"Like a give a single fuck," She snatches away from my hand, "Stop fucking trying to control me."

My nostrils flare, "I don't want every man looking at

you, Olivia."

She scoffs, "So what if they look?" She quirks a brow, "What does it matter?"

"You're mine."

"And if another woman looks at you?" She flicks her eyes up and down me, "There's plenty of women who love a man in a suit. Go change."

I open my mouth and then snap it shut.

"Exactly," She clicks her fingers, "Your argument is invalid and honestly, annoying. You don't get to tell me what to do, Malakai and you need to get over that."

"Just do up another button," I compromise but she slaps my hands away when I reach for the blazer.

"Be a good boy," She pats my hand, "And try not to think about all the men getting an eyeful of my tits, and maybe I'll let you fuck me again."

"Olivia," I rasp.

"Have the day you deserve, Malakai."

And then she walks out with me watching after her. Fuck me sideways, that woman will be the death of me.

I trudge back into the kitchen pinching the bridge of my nose. Louis looks away immediately, filling up my coffee mug before he busies himself with food prep.

"Your wife ever do as you ask her?" I ask the man.

"Nope," He laughs, "I stopped trying. But I do know you shouldn't tell your wife what to wear."

I glare at him but he just shrugs, "It'll do no good." He continues, "And she'll only wear something worse just to piss you off."

Yeah, I could see Olivia doing that.

"Fuck me." I grumble.

"She's your partner, no?" Louis continues. "You compromise."

"Olivia isn't the type to compromise." Neither was I to be honest. I like things my way or no way at all. Everything is controlled, precise, planned out. But she came in and blew it all up.

"Miss Olivia is a very sweet woman," Louis continues, "She has big feelings."

I grunt noncommittedly and finish my coffee.

And then I spend the rest of my day trying *not* to think of all the men looking at *my wife*. I had a feeling if I knew just how many even dared, I'd be digging a lot of graves.

36
Olivia

My nails match the red color of my dress perfectly, and with the event happening tomorrow, I'm now back at the hotel approving the final decoration.

Everything is set up exactly as I had designed. Black silk drapes along every wall, interweaved with splashes of red. The ceiling has been transformed and now gothic style black chandeliers hang from it. There's a DJ booth set up in the corner and a large space reserved for dancing, but the rest of the space is filled with round tables. Large bouquets of red roses center the tables along with white pillar candles and black tablecloths.

I wanted something different for the event, it's always black tie and so pompous I never enjoy the evenings. But this room, looking a little gloomy with all the black provides the perfect atmosphere.

Happy with how it looks, I lock up the room and decide to call it a day. I won't be back here tomorrow until the event begins and was planning on getting ready with Willow.

Dennis is waiting beyond the doors for me, and I give

him a grin when he opens the door, "Mrs. Farrow," He greets.

I've given up trying to get him to call me Olivia.

He's much too professional to do it.

"Hello, Dennis," I say when he's in the front seat.

"Home?" He asks.

"Sure," I settle into the back seats for the journey back, my stomach knotting in anticipation. After waking up Malakai this morning by sucking his dick and then getting fucked by him, only to be followed by yet another argument, I was a little nervous to see him.

I don't think they'll ever be a day we don't get into some kind of fight and after his controlling ass this morning trying to make me change, I want to fuck with him some more.

He doesn't get to tell me what to wear. Ever.

And punishing him for it needs to be more than ketchup in his shoes or cutting the buttons off his shirts. No, this one needs to hurt him a little.

And I have the perfect idea for it.

Dennis pulls through the gates and drives up to the house, getting out once he's parked to open my door for me.

"Is he home?" I ask.

His chin dips with a nod.

I wave him goodbye and head into the house, eyes already searching for him but when I don't find him in any of the rooms, I figure he'll be in the drawing room.

I head that way but the closer I get, the more I hear

voices.

Namely a female voice.

Interesting.

I don't bother knocking as I enter, shoulders back and prepared for everything.

Malakai's eyes snap to me and then run the length of me, and I swear I see his shoulders lower, as if he's just let out a shit ton of tension that's been harboring in his body since this morning.

"Olivia," He says my name fondly and I try to hide the way it surprises me and affects me. I like how it sounds. Which only means trouble.

The woman in the room is one I recognize, with her strawberry blonde hair and upturned nose. She's very pretty, lithe, and expensive looking and she looks down her nose at me, eyes in slits.

"Regina was just leaving," he says, pointedly looking at the other woman.

My brow quirks when her lips turn up, her scathing look probably an attempt to intimidate me but she won't catch me off guard again, not like at the wedding.

I didn't figure I'd ever see her again but clearly; I wouldn't be so lucky.

"I'll see you tomorrow, Malakai," she says to him softly, fluttering her lashes before she turns for the door. I step to the side when she clearly has no intention of going around me, and while I have no issues slapping a bitch, I refuse to fight this woman over a fucking man. I don't even know her, and she doesn't know me.

"Tomorrow?" I face Malakai when I know she'll be

away from the room and not in earshot.

He sighs heavily, "She will be at the event."

"Wonderful," I say sarcastically. "Better keep her away from the red wine. She seems a little clumsy."

His mouth quirks up at the side, "I didn't hear you get home."

"Entertaining guests will do that," I lick my teeth, this unwelcome feeling in my stomach making me feel a little sick. I am not jealous. What is there to be jealous of?

Other than the fact that she clearly wants him and seems much better suited for him than I ever will be. She'll probably be the perfect little wife Malakai wants.

"You know what?" I click my fingers, turning for the door, "I just realized I forgot something at the hotel. Bye!"

"Olivia," Malakai's stern voice stiffens my spine. "Eyes on me, kitten."

I huff out a breath and plaster a smile on my face, "Yes?"

"Are you jealous?"

I narrow my eyes, "Me? Jealous?" I scoff. "No."

He cocks his head as if he's studying me, the move animalistic. "Did another man touch you today?"

"What!?" I snap my head back.

"You look good enough to eat, Olivia. Any man would want you."

"Stop it." I face him fully, "Firstly I wouldn't *let* another man touch me. Secondly, there is such a thing as decency and respect. I haven't left the hotel once today and everyone knows me there."

"Okay."

I roll my eyes, "You're such a control freak, you know that?"

He nods, "Yes, I know."

"Okay good, at least you're not delusional."

"You have an attitude." He leans back in his chair, "Need to fight it out?"

My teeth grind.

"Come here." He orders.

"No." I snap as I throw open the door and start to storm away from him. I'm about to kick off my shoes so I can move faster – heels aren't the best footwear when you're trying to dramatically walk away from a man, but a sudden hand on my arm stops me.

My chest presses into the wall and Malakai's hand pins me there by the back of my neck.

"I've warned you before, kitten," he whispers in my ear, "I've warned you about what I'll do to you if you keep giving me fucking attitude."

"You're not fucking me after you've just spent however fucking long entertaining another woman."

"Entertaining another woman?" He laughs humorlessly, it's low and violent, a promise, "You really think I'd *entertain* another woman?"

My nostrils flare, "Well I don't know, Malakai, especially since that's the same woman who had her hands all over you on our fucking wedding day."

"I've thought about nothing but you all fucking today, Olivia. I have barely been able to concentrate when all I can think about is this damn body, and your fucking moans and when I'm going to fucking see you smile again."

I push back on him, hoping to get him off me, "How romantic." I deadpan, "You've thought about fucking me all day." I skip over the smiling things because… well I can't use that right now. It's not dramatic enough.

His fingers flex on the back of my neck and he doesn't relent.

"Yes, I've thought about fucking you." He admits. "And if you've eaten. Or had water. I've nearly fucking lost my mind thinking about another man being near you when you're wearing this fucking outfit. And I was watching the damn clock, waiting for you to get home just so I could fucking see you."

His nose presses into my hair as he takes a breath, "Regina is nothing and no one. She's a spoiled little bitch who is throwing a tantrum because she didn't get what she wants."

"So why is she still here? Why not send her away?"

"You have no reason to be jealous, Olivia. And I apologize that you feel like you do. I assure you," his mouth presses to my temple, "I want no one but you and I haven't wanted anyone else since we made this arrangement weeks ago."

My heart pounds inside my chest, "Let me go, Malakai."

His hand works away from my neck and down my spine, but his body keeps me pressed to the wall. He slides his hand around my waist until he flattens his palm against my abdomen, his fingers slipping beneath the flap of my blazer, so his skin burns against mine through the sheer lace of the bodysuit.

"Letting you go, kitten, is the last thing I want to do right now." He whispers, voice layered with gravel, edged with a deep roughness that scrapes against me in the most delicious way. I shiver against him.

Memories of this morning assault me, the way he bound me and fucked me damn senseless blooming heat low in my core. His cock grinds into my ass, his breath tickling the shell of my ear.

"What will it be, kitten?" He rasps, "Let you go or let me fuck this attitude out of you?"

"You'll never be able to fuck the attitude out of me," I push back on him.

"You're probably right," His teeth scrape threateningly across my neck, "But it'll be fun to try."

"Give it a go," I breathe, moving my head to the side to open my neck up for him, "Just know I'll hate every second of it."

He chuckles, the sound vibrating against my back. "You tell such pretty lies, Olivia." The hand that was pressed on my abdomen starts to lower, deft fingers quickly working the button on my suit pants before it then slips inside. "Your body betrays you, kitten."

My breath stutters from me as his fingers shift beneath the crotch of my bodysuit and slips through me. I already knew I'd be wet. But he doesn't remain there like I expect him to, instead he pulls his hand out, releases my neck and gently pulls my pants down. They fall to my feet, leaving me in just the bodysuit and blazer.

Fingers trail up the back of my thigh before they go back to my neck, forcing me forward. My cheek rests against the cold surface and my heart pounds in my chest as my ass sticks out.

"You're beautiful," Malakai whispers, palming my ass cheek before he suddenly spanks me.

Hard.

A mix of a moan and a cry spills from me.

"Will you lie again?" He asks, caressing the sting.

"Don't play games, Malakai," I snap, my arousal intensifying to the point of pain. "You don't fuck me? I'll fuck myself, I really don't care."

"Then go fuck yourself, Olivia." He steps away from me, cold air suddenly bringing goose bumps to my skin. "Because while you're acting like a little brat and pretending you don't want me just as much, you're not getting my cock."

My breath saws from my chest, cheeks heating in a mix of indignation and humiliation but then he makes it worse by bending, grabbing my pants and pulling them back up my legs. I stay still, grinding my teeth while he buttons them and then walks away, the door clicking closed behind him, ass cheek still stinging from his slap.

The problem with glitter is, no matter how careful you are, that shit gets everywhere.

And I was definitely careful not to touch anything as I

Playing with Fire

snuck back through the house and got straight in the shower but there's still a slight shimmer on my skin and in my hair and if you stand at the right angle, there's specks of glitter all over the carpet and bed.

I doubt he'll notice.

After I dry my hair, I climb into bed.

I've decided to be strong. I'm not going to touch myself out of pure stubbornness. Yes, I'm horny as fuck, yes, I lied and said I could fuck myself better, but he doesn't get to work me up and then leave me hanging.

He hasn't left the drawing room and I bet he has cameras in here and is watching, just waiting to see if I'll do it. I won't give him the satisfaction.

If I ache, he can ache too.

With a huff, I roll onto my side, facing away from the door. I've gone way longer without sex, several months in fact, a few days of good sex isn't going to suddenly turn me into some sex maniac. He's crazy if he thinks I'll cave and admit I want him too. I mean it's pretty obvious without words.

But with him being the control freak he is, he wants that damn validation and onus on me.

For good measure, in case there are cameras, I throw my arm up to the room and give it the middle finger, showing him exactly what I think about that.

And then I force my eyes closed, thinking of everything else but the unhinged, god of a man downstairs.

37
Malakai

I didn't go to bed because I couldn't trust myself not to fuck her in her sleep.

Honestly, I thought she'd cave but I should have known she's much too stubborn and prideful for that. So, I slept on the couch in the drawing room, fucking lonely as shit. I should have just fucked her despite the hit to my ego.

My wife knows where to strike me.

Even the mere thought of her gets me fucking hard and there's only so much my hand can do. Since I've jerked off three times since last night, with the picture of her pressed to the wall, round ass sticking out and reddened by my palm playing inside my head, I'm going to need something a little more satisfying.

I switch the shower to cold as fresh images of her harden my cock and avoid touching it as much as possible. The next time I come, it's going to be all over her fucking skin. She'd look so pretty with my come dripping off her.

With a groan, I shut off the shower, forcing my head to focus.

The event is today, I have a few things to do before that, but Olivia is going to be mine tonight. On my arm, our official first event since she became my wife, and I can't fucking wait to have the little beauty right where she belongs.

At my side.

I have some other things planned for her too, things that'll make the evening far more interesting.

I head into the bedroom after being out of it since yesterday to find the bed pristinely made and Olivia nowhere to be seen. She's an early riser, I've noticed that since we've been sharing a bed and is likely downstairs with Louis having breakfast.

I pull a suit from the closet, a charcoal grey one and a new white shirt – since she ruined all my others and then grab my socks, shaking my head at the neon pink. I could have replaced them already, yet I haven't, and refuse to look into the why of it.

Twenty minutes later, I stroll into the kitchen, finding Olivia giggling at something Louis is saying, dressed in a pair of grey sweats and this frayed, severely cropped sweater that has more holes than it does material.

The view of her tan skin and soft curves makes my fingers itch. Her hair is up in a messy bun, but it can hardly be contained, strands falling out and sticking all over the place. Fresh faced and bright eyed, she looks fucking stunning.

"Good morning, kitten," I greet her and nod at Louis.

She flicks her eyes at me, but there's no scowl, and the smile remains on her face, "Hello, Malakai." She says formally.

I kiss her temple before I take a seat at her side, shocking her enough that her mouth drops open.

When Louis turns to prepare more food, I lean in close, "Keep your mouth open like that, darling, and I'll find a use to occupy it."

She smirks and turns back to her food, "Willow is coming here today," she tells me. "To get ready for the event."

I tilt my chin down in a nod, "Okay."

"You don't mind?"

"This is your house. Invite whoever you like." I take the plate Louis passes over, "Thank you, Louis."

"Well, okay," She says quietly, "I've got to pick up my dress too."

"I'll take you. I have to go into the city anyway."

"No!" She blurts.

My brows lower, "No?"

"I mean, Dennis can take me. It'll be really quick anyway," She rambles, "And I don't want to hang around."

"I'm only picking up legal papers," I wave my fork around, "I'll take you for coffee after."

"I'll just go with Dennis."

"Dennis is taking a personal day," I lie.

"Well, I'll just take one of the other cars."

"No can do," I shrug, "You'll come with me."

I swear I see her wince.

"Have something to hide, wife?"

"Nope!" She blinks rapidly, "Nothing. Not a thing."

My mouth quirks, so fucking adorable.

Ten minutes later she's fidgeting in the kitchen door, eyeing the front door as if she's contemplating fleeing out of it. I'm curious to know why she's this shifty and it only leads me to believe she's fucked with me again. It's highly probable after I left her wet and needy last night.

I almost look forward to whatever creative way she comes up with to fuck with me. She's inherently not violent so she finds other ways to get her revenge.

"Come on," I guide her with my hand, letting the warmth of her skin brand me through my palm. Her sneakers tap quietly, and her nerves keep her head down.

"What is it?" I ask.

She shakes her head but follows me into the garage, the car beeping as it unlocks, lights flashing.

Rolling her lips, she loosens her breath and slides into the passenger seat when I open the door for her. What the hell is wrong with her?

She has an hour trapped in a car with me, I'll get it out of her.

I hit the button to start the car before I then click for the garage doors to be opened. It's fucking cold today and when I look over to Olivia she is shivering in her seat, her body however is pressed right up to the door, as far from me as she can get.

My eyes narrow but I'll deal with that in a moment, I need to get her warm first.

"Wait, Malakai!" She suddenly blurts at the same time I hit the button for the heat.

And get blasted in the face by a shit ton of bright pink glitter.

It explodes through the car from all the vents, covering me, Olivia and the black suede seats. It's in my fucking mouth.

I suck my lip between my teeth, but fuck, I can't stifle it. Fury rolls through me.

Out of everything she could have fucked with, she fucked with my car.

I turn my eyes to her, seeing her in much the same state as me, covered in glitter. It sticks to her cheeks, and lips, covering her dark hair and clothes. It's all over the fucking windows. And she's barely containing her amusement. Her eyes crinkle at the edges and she rolls her lips together, but her dimples have already sunk into her cheeks and her eyes are watery with amusement.

I lick my teeth, nostrils flaring.

"Run." I growl out.

The humor fades, "What?"

"Run, Olivia." I switch the car off. "If I catch you, I'll tan your ass so red you won't be able to sit for a week."

"Malakai," she reaches for the handle but doesn't get out.

"Now, Olivia."

Something in my tone gets her moving, she throws the door open, straight into the car parked next to this one, scratching the paintwork.

"Fuck!" I growl.

"Shit!" She squeals and then slams the door, her feet squeaking on the floor as she bolts, throwing herself through the door back into the house, leaving a trail of glitter behind.

I'm covered in glitter, more falling off me as I exit the car, shoes a steady thump as I walk through the house. My palms itch to slap her ass like the little brat she is, my cock rock fucking hard ready to bend her over so I can rail that rebellious streak right out of her.

My fucking car.

I follow the trail of glitter, the specks getting fewer but out of all the things she could have done, she chose the one that leaves a trail. When the fuck did she even get into the garage? Probably sometime last night while I was fucking my fist because I refused to fuck her.

"God fucking damn, woman," I growl under my breath, noticing where the glitter trail stops.

There's pink glitter stuck to the handle of the door leading into the games room. Silly girl, she's smarter than that.

I push open the door hard enough it swings open and hits the back wall, rattling picture frames where they hang.

The room appears empty, quiet and cold and for a minute I stand, and I listen.

Her breathing is heavy, I hear it even from here coming

from somewhere by the bar.

I step quietly inside, grabbing the door as I push it softly closed. Without the light of the hall, it's dark in here. Reaching over blindly, I flick the switch which turns on the soft LED strip lighting that's installed into parts of the wall. It only illuminates the room a little, leaving pockets of darkness scattered throughout the space.

There's a shuffling noise, like shoes dragging across the floor and my mouth kicks up into a feral grin.

"No where to run in here, kitten," I say to the room, "Should have been smarter than that."

I start the slow walk through the room, just rounding the pool table when she jumps up from behind the bar, glitter sparkling on her cheeks, stuck to her bottom lip and hair. She's frozen, like a deer in headlights, wide eyes focused on me. I pause, waiting for her next move.

"You wanted to play games, Olivia," I tell her, "Let's play games."

38
Olivia

Oh shit.

Oh, shit, oh shit, oh shit.

My eyes flick to the closed door and he's currently on the opposite side of the pool table. There are two exits to this long bar, am I quick enough to get out of one and sprint for the exit?

With the way he's looking at me, tracking my every move like a predator with its prey, I doubt it. His eyes are dark, his body poised, and his mouth is notched up at the side, the smirk anything but kind. It's full of promise.

Even with the glitter on him, neon and pink and sparkling, he still looks lethal. Ready.

Maybe I pushed him too far?

In my defense, I wasn't actually supposed to be in the car with him. I figured he'd have enough time to calm down before I got back so *this* wouldn't have happened. I suppose I could have given him a heads up but that wouldn't have been nearly as funny as watching him get glitter bombed. It was worth getting glitter all over myself too.

But this reaction, this chase wasn't something I had expected.

But it's now or never. He's moving closer, toward the entrance to the bar on my left, leaving me no choice but to bolt out the right.

Like a goddamned frightened animal, I run, throwing myself around the corner and beelining for the door. I don't even make it halfway down the pool table.

An arm snags around my waist and the next thing I know, the felt of the pool table is being pressed to my cheek, my body hitting the table hard enough to move the balls out of the triangle formation.

Malakai's chest presses into my spine, his hand on my neck. It's a very similar position to last night but I don't think he'll be walking away from this one. Despite only having been on the green material for a few seconds, pink glitter already sparkles against it.

This shit really does get everywhere.

His breath is heavy, his fingers flexing on my neck.

"My wife," He rasps, the hand not currently pinning me to the pool table moving down my body, "My pretty little brat. Did you have fun?"

Say no, Olivia. Tell him you're sorry.

"I had a blast," My voice comes out strained. "Pink really is your color."

He chuckles and leans in, his nose burying into my hair as he inhales, "I hope it was worth it."

"I'd do it again," I admit. Let's be honest, I really

would.

"You fucked with my car," He growls.

"You noticed, huh?" I try to push up, but he allows no movement. His hand captures my waist, and he squeezes before he moves up beneath the cropped sweater I have on, fingers toying with the band of my bra.

"You have such a fucking smart mouth," He moves away from the bra and back down my body. I am hyperaware of every spot his fingers touch, very aware of how hard he is. He gets off on forcing my submission. He can make my body submit all he likes, with his force, his body, his will, but me? The very thing that makes me who I am, more than my body, is my soul and the fight it gives me. He'll never have that submission.

Ever.

"All the better to hurt you with," I growl, gathering all of my strength as I shove up from the pool table. He moves this time, seemingly caught off guard but it isn't enough to get away. He forces me back down with a grunt.

"Never, not once," He rasps, "In my life, have I been tested the way you test me, Olivia."

"Do you hate it yet, Malakai?"

His body shivers above mine and a breath leaves him as he groans.

"I find with you; I don't hate anything at all."

My breath leaves me in a whoosh as his weight is suddenly lifted from me, but he's pressed to my ass, cock slotted between my cheeks above my sweats.

"I've seen you in many outfits, kitten," A hand runs down the center of my spine, "But I think I like this one the most."

"What!?"

His fingers hook into the band of the sweats, "You're comfortable. At ease."

Well, he's not wrong.

"Unguarded."

My lashes flutter as he starts to drag my pants down. I should have probably worn underwear.

"You wear all your outfits like armor, but this one," He groans, a hand smoothing over my bare backside, "No panties?"

"I wore a bra," I point out.

He chuckles, the sound warm.

I am trying really hard not to be turned on but there's no denying the wetness between my legs. He yanks a bit harder until my sweats pool around my feet and then he leans down and taps my calf, asking without words for me to lift my foot.

I do and then do the same on the other side. I hear the swish of material as he grabs the sweats and tosses them to the side.

Bare for him and bent over the pool table, I'm at his mercy and it just makes me hotter, wetter, more aroused. My pussy clenches, that ache returning tenfold, like my body is punishing me for not letting it have him last night or any type of release for that matter.

"You're already soaked, kitten," His voice comes out strained, "Is it pissing me off that gets you going?"

I stay quiet. My willpower isn't as strong as it was before. Not when I'm already clenching and at the verge of begging for it.

"Did you fuck with my car because I didn't fill this greedy cunt last night?" He cups me, groaning as he smears my wetness over his hand, "Are you that needy, Olivia? Need my cock that badly?"

My teeth sink into my lower lip as I push back on his hand, earning that delicious chuckle from him again.

"My needy little wife," He praises before his hand pulls back and reconnects with my ass cheek.

I let out a loud moan, the spasm in my pussy almost enough to force an orgasm.

"You want it that bad, then fine. You can have my cock, Olivia. You want me to fuck you, fill up this needy cunt until I'm dripping down your thighs, I'll do it. I'll let you lie to yourself, tell yourself you don't want me as much as I want you, but you and I both know the truth of it." He yanks me up, spins me and his hands instantly go for the sweater, tugging it over my head before his fingers hook into the bridge of my bra between my breasts.

He's rough as he tugs, the bra biting into my skin.

"You'll snap it," I warn.

"That's the point." He growls before he yanks hard, the stitching and fabric popping and snapping and does it again, the material finally snapping in two.

With my arms down, the straps slide right off. He steps

back, eyes traveling down the length of me, his thumb swiping over his bottom lip before he reaches for my cheek.

I hold still as best as I can, but I can feel my body trembling, my knees shaking as the ache only blooms bigger, hotter.

His thumb moves over my cheek and comes away covered in pink glitter.

"Stunning," His voice scratches, the deep timbre rising goose bumps on my flesh, dropping the thumb to my nipple, smearing the glitter over the peaked bud.

"Malakai," I breathe his name, needing him.

His eyes bounce to mine, the sound of his name on my lips seeming to pull him apart at the seams.

He lunges for me, his mouth crashing against mine in the next breath. His fingers thread into my hair, holding me to him, the other going to the nape of my neck as he manipulates me into a position that allows his tongue to go deeper. He kisses me like he's starved, pouring his entire being into it. And all I can do is hold on, kissing him back just as hard and heavy.

He devours me entirely and doesn't break the kiss when his hands start to move down me. He grasps my waist, lifts and throws me down onto the pool table. Balls scatter as the whole table shifts with the momentum, his body slotting into the cradle of my thighs the moment my elbows catch myself on the top.

I gasp before my eyes roll back at the grind of his cock, even still covered, it feeds the fire inside of me, begging for more.

"Fuck me, Malakai," I demand, nails scraping across

Playing with Fire

the felt of the table.

His jaw pops as he grinds his teeth and then he begins to undress. His fingers move lazily over the buttons of his shirt before he tugs it off, along with the jacket and then he unbuttons his pants. I can see the outline of his cock, the length of him straining against his slacks.

"Such a greedy little brat," He muses as he shoves out of his pants, shoes and socks, leaving him as bare as me.

He really is a damn work of art. All muscles carved as if made from stone. I want to lick him.

He steps back between my legs, hand going to my breast as he palms them and flicks my nipple with his fingers.

The head of him nudges at my pussy, clenching already.

"Open up, baby," He growls, and when my thighs widen further, he thrusts forward, filling me completely.

I let out a groan, part pain, part pleasure, the sting of the stretch and the satisfaction making my spine arch and my eyes flutter closed.

His hand pins me down just above my hip, my arms keeping me steady as he thrusts forward with hard slams of his hips.

The balls bounce and move around the table, knocking into me as he fucks me hard and fast.

"That's fucking it, Olivia," He growls, "Look how fucking good you take me. Look at me when I fuck you, Olivia. Look at the man you belong to."

I hook my legs above his ass, keeping him in me as I open my eyes and meet his. Lips parted, I keep my eyes on him, watch as his brow lowers and his mouth parts, slackened by pleasure. He fucks me hard, rough and fast.

Our skin slaps together, the sound of my moan joining the obscenely loud noise in the otherwise quiet room.

Fingers bruise where they hold, to the point of pain but it keeps me here, I want the bruises his fingers leave, want the marks and the ache.

I'm getting tighter, I can feel my orgasm just at the surface, right fucking there.

I drop a hand between my legs, the tips of my fingers rolling over my clit.

Malakai groans, his thrusts turning slower but harder, he goes deeper when he hooks his arm beneath my knee and shifts my leg and it's enough.

My head throws back as I come, crying out as my pussy clenches around him, convulsing as I prolong my own orgasm with my fingers, convulsing around him as he continues to thrust.

But then he suddenly pulls out of me, and hot spurts of come land across my lower abdomen. Hooded eyes focus on his hand as he jerks himself, spilling himself onto my skin.

"You look so pretty with my come painting your skin," His fingers push through the come on me, smearing it in. His eyes bounce away from his claiming, to mine, the blue of his so dark and full of promise. I need more. I'm not done.

"I want to mark you, Olivia," He rasps, "Paint you

mine so the whole fucking world knows that I am *yours*."

39
Malakai

She sits on one of the stools at the bar, my shirt falling halfway down her thighs and glitter still shimmering on her skin. Raven black hair mused and disheveled, falls over her shoulders as she sips on the water I grabbed from the fridge behind the bar.

I'm back in my slacks, giving her a rest. I was far from being done with her, but I did need her to stay conscious, so here we are.

My hands easily organize the balls on the pool table, putting them back into formation before I grab the cue and chalk.

"Come here, kitten," I order gently.

Lazy eyes follow me before she caps her water bottle and slides off the stool. I watch her long, toned legs eat up the space between us, a sensual, flirty little smile playing on her lips.

I hold a cue out for her, "Winner gets a prize."

She quirks a brow, the smile on her mouth turning

smug, "You sure you wanna play this game, Kai?"

Time stops.

The world stops spinning.

Kai.

The only people to call me Kai are those closest to me. My grandfather. My friends.

She's only ever called me Malakai, if she uses my name at all, and hearing her call me something so intimate, like we were more than enemies, more than a man who forced a woman to marry him, feels like an ending to my universe and a beginning all the same.

"I want to play, kitten," I swallow, pretending it doesn't affect me the way it does. Like my cock isn't already getting hard, like my heart didn't skip a beat, like I'm not looking at her like she's the very thing that makes my world spin.

It's not been long enough. We don't like each other past fucking or getting on each other's nerves. But when she says my name, either version of it, I can't help but feel like the sun has just risen after several days of night, like the clouds haven't just parted after endless days of rain.

I feel like I've just been shot – it's happened – and this burning, all-consuming pain is flowing through me. It was a few years ago now, an ex-employee who had escaped my inner circle after he tried to betray me to my competition. I found out, ordered his demise and everyone involved, but he tried to take me out first.

The bullet sliced through me, at my hip, though he was aiming for my heart, and it was a through and through, it went in and came out, but it still felt as if I was about to die.

That's how it feels with her.

With Olivia.

Like the next moment with her might be my end.

And I anticipated it like a drug. If there were any way for me to go, at her hands, it would be with a smile.

"Fine," She grins, taking the cue and circling the table.

She eyes the formation, the white ball and the table itself like she hasn't played before. It's obvious she has, and I don't doubt her skill, I just know I am better.

"Who breaks?" She asks, fingering the collar of my shirt.

"Go ahead," I give her a grin.

"And what do I get if I win?"

"Anything you want." I tell her, "But if I win, I get you for one day. Twenty-four hours. With no rules."

She quirks a brow and gives me a lazy half smile, the confidence oozing from her pores. "Fine." She flicks her hand as if that isn't a big deal. She thinks she's going to win.

She lines up, bending across the table. My shirt slides up her thighs, teasing at the crease of her ass. I'm so focused on her, on where the material of my shirt whispers on her soft skin that I don't see her take the shot. The sound of the white slamming into the ball's jolts me from my trance on her body and I look to the table, seeing her pot two of the red balls.

"I played in college," She tells me, "Willow and I made it our goal to out play the frat guys since they believed women shouldn't be able to play. We always bet a lot of money and pretended we were awful to get them to play along. It brought me an immense amount of joy to crush them."

She flutters her lashes.

"That's called hustling," I point out, watching her take her second shot. She pockets another red easily, a cocky little smirk pulling on her mouth as she analyzes the remaining four reds on the table.

"Hustling," She shrugs, "I call it being fifty grand richer."

"That's how much you earned?"

"Throughout college, yes. Those guys didn't care about the money though, they were more pissed that they were beaten by a couple of girls. Eventually they stopped playing with us because out of all the games we played, we lost maybe two or three. We didn't need the money, but it was fun taking it from them."

I chuckle, "I can imagine."

She lines up and sinks a ball.

Three reds left and all my yellows are still on the table.

The white ball is positioned in such a way that she has to bend across the table directly in front of me. The shirt rises, leaving her bared to me. My cock strains behind my zipper. Fuck I need to be in her again.

I fist my hands to stop me from reaching for her. I want to finish the game even if fucking her right now is the only thing on my mind.

She strikes the ball but the red bounces off the corner of the pocket, rolling up the table.

Straightening, she throws a wink over her shoulder as if she knows exactly what she just did and did it, just to throw me off my game. I grab my cue, eyeing the yellows.

Time to bring this home. Having her for twenty-four hours, no rules, no restrictions is not something I'm going to lose the chance to have.

She leans on the bar, watching as I take my first shot, pocketing a yellow. Then I clean up. I pocket every ball without issue, leaving her three reds and the black on the table.

I look up, giving her a grin, "Not so cocky now, Olivia?"

Her eyes narrow, "You have to get the black," she shrugs, "And that shot isn't easy."

Not easy but doable.

She pushes off the bar and strolls casually to the head of the table. The black is sitting behind her three reds, the white almost on the cushion in front of me. She stands directly in front of me, the table between us.

The easiest pocket would be corner left, so that's how I line it up.

I pull the cue back at the same time Olivia decides to stretch. The shirt rises, lifting up and over her pussy and I fuck the shot up. The white strikes her red, a foul which gives her two shots.

Fuck.

She drops her arms and attempts to hide her smile but fails.

Playing with Fire

She pockets her last three balls and eyes the black currently sitting dead flush against the cushion and between two pockets.

I have no doubt she'll be able to get it in.

She lines up and strikes and I watch, focused on the ball as it bounces off the cushion and heads for the pocket only for it to bounce off the corner.

"Shit!" She hisses.

I walk around the table slowly, stalking her until I can brush my fingers up her thigh, reveling in the way her skin pebbles in reaction to my touch.

"Twenty-four hours," I muse, "And at least half of that will be spent with you naked with my cock buried inside of you."

Her breath stutters as I line up, strike the black and sink it, winning me the game.

"I'll be cashing in for those twenty-four hours soon, Olivia," I turn to her, pressing my chest to hers as my fingers go to the hem of my shirt.

Her lashes flutter as I let my fingers crawl up her thigh, over her hip until I can curl my hand around her waist.

"Malakai," Her voice is a whisper against my lips as I lean in, tasting her. I don't kiss her enough, I think, as I lay my mouth on hers a lot firmer, my tongue testing at the seam of her lips.

She opens for me, granting me access so my tongue plunges into her mouth, stealing her breath and her whimpers. I press her back against the bar before I lift. Her legs come around my waist as her fingers grip on my hair. For a few more blissful seconds she kisses me with as much demand as me but then her fingers curl and she tugs my head back, forcing me away from her mouth.

"Olivia," I growl.

Kiss swollen lips press to the corner of my mouth, "I have to get ready. And I still need to pick up my dress."

Lifting a little higher, I plant her ass on the bar and when she tries to unhook her legs, I tug them back. "You stay." I order before I pull out my cell. "Dennis." He answers immediately. "I need you to collect Olivia's dress."

"Where?" Is his response.

I look to Olivia for the details and when she gives them, I pass them over to Dennis.

"Now you don't need to pick up the dress," I tell her, triumphant that I get to keep her for a little longer.

"I thought you said Dennis was off today," She challenges, hands coming back to me.

"I lied," I whisper, "I just wanted to keep you close."

She searches my eyes, for what, I'm not sure but then her face softens, "Not sure you could be any closer."

A wicked grin pulls on my mouth, "Wanna bet?"

40
Olivia

I smooth my hands down my stomach, the silk of the dress sliding against my palms. My hair is dead straight, pulled back away from my face so it falls down my back. Diamond earrings dangle from my ears and a choker style necklace adorns my throat, complimenting the deep sweetheart neckline of the dress.

"Fuck me," Willow whistles, entering the room with two champagne glasses, "You look hot babe."

I eye her own dress, a full black number with a tulle skirt that has a subtle glitter to it and a corset style bodice which pushes her breasts up. Her long hair is up in curls, leaving just a few strands to fall around her face. A pair of black stilettos are on her feet which she walks in expertly as she passes me a glass.

I take a sip of the bubbles, turning back to the mirror, "Are you sure it looks okay?"

I'm not sure where the sudden insecurity has come from, especially since I love the dress and how it looks.

"Am I sure?" She scoffs, "You're gorgeous."

Perching on the edge of the bed, she watches me for a minute, "So you and Malakai?" She hedges.

I haven't told her about the mind-blowing, earth-shattering sex we've been having. I'm not keeping it a secret, I just… I don't know.

Something has shifted in me, granted, I still want to make his life hell but for an entirely different reason now. If I piss him off, maybe he'll chase me through the house again and fuck me ten ways to Sunday like he did this morning.

The last I heard his car was being taken off to be professionally cleaned though he'll be finding glitter in his car for ages, no amount of cleaning will get it all.

I hate him less than I did a few days ago.

Which is terrifying because if I don't hate him, then what is it? He's a dangerous, brutal man, a man who takes choices and lives, he isn't a man I should even consider, let alone catch feelings for.

And how far do I even let myself feel? How far does this go?

But he's a drug I can't get enough of, a presence I need. His hands on my body feel like they belong, his voice a soothing balm when it should be alarm bells.

He is the devil.

A monster.

So why do I want to call him mine as much as he calls me his?

I drain my glass of champagne and grab the purse I've chosen for the evening.

"What about us?" I play it down like my heart isn't skipping a beat.

"How are the both of you?" She asks.

I shrug, "Fine."

"Do you still hate him?"

"A little less than yesterday," I admit, "You ready?"

She purses her lips but ultimately drops the conversation as a smile comes over her face, "Absolutely. I can't wait to see the guys faces when they see us."

I shake my head, but I have to admit I'm looking forward to it too.

She links my arm as we walk toward the stairs, hearing the guys laughing from the kitchen. So normal and every day that I pause on the stairs, listening to the rich sound.

"You good?" Willow asks.

But of course, Willow doesn't understand. She doesn't know who these men actually are, doesn't realize we're about to join a room full of killers.

"I'm good," I give her a tight smile, "Let's go."

We make it to the bottom of the stairs, and it's as if the sound of our heels on the tile stops their merriment because their laughter ceases.

Willow enters the kitchen with confidence oozing from every pore. She knows she looks good and if the low whistle that comes out of Sebastian is anything to go by, he thinks so too. The damn man has hearts in his eyes. He eats her up, his thumb running along his bottom lip as he checks out every inch of her.

"Give me a spin, sweetheart," He purrs, "Lemme see all of you."

Willow throws him a wink and gives him the spin he requested before she refills her champagne glass and slots herself between Killian and Dean, who are checking her out appreciatively.

It's not until Willow says my name that I realize I've stopped just shy of the door, in a way that hides me from them but not them from me.

"Oh right," I half skip into the room, which almost makes me trip over the lengths of the dress and makes me wobble on the heels on my feet.

"Damn," It's Killian who speaks and I snap my eyes to him, feeling a blush creep up my cheeks when I see him obviously, and very appreciatively checking me out. I don't know why I'm blushing; I've been checked out plenty but in front of these guys – I don't know, feels different somehow.

"Olivia," Malakai's voice, a deep rumble that shoots awareness through me has my eyes flicking to him.

He's staring at me, eyes moving over all of me like he can't pick a spot to see first.

"You are devastating," He breathes, taking a step toward me.

He's handsome himself, in his all-black suit. His shirt is unbuttoned on the first few buttons at the top of his shirt, showing off tan skin. The suit fits his body like a glove, made for him to show off the lines of his body, strong arms, thick thighs and wide shoulders.

He's looked at me like this before, like he's in awe, wonderstruck but right now, it's more intimate, even with the four other people in the room with us. It's like they don't exist though.

Someone clears their throat and I snap out of whatever trance I was just in. I drop my eyes from his and cross to the champagne, giving myself a little more liquid courage before I check out the other guys too.

Sebastian is in a black and white suit, vest, and tie and all, Killian's is a deep navy, almost black but in this light the blue shines through and Dean is in white. I almost do a double take since I wasn't expecting that. His white suit has been paired with a blood red shirt, unbuttoned at the top like Malakai's.

All the guys are ridiculously attractive, unfairly so and all in different ways. Sebastian has his playboy charm, dimples and blond hair, where Killian and Dean, similar in looks with their darkness but where Killian is more open, Dean is reserved. The brothers both have a mysterious bad boy air about them which is an instant draw. Then there's Malakai, God like Malakai, with his own devastating looks.

I swallow down my champagne thickly, glancing at the clock.

"Our ride will be here soon," I say to the room. I'd booked a limo for us all, giving Dennis a night off and the opportunity for us all to travel to the event together.

I feel Malakai watching me still, feel every place his eyes touch but I don't look at him for fear of him being able to read every emotion on my face.

At six exactly my phone buzzes to let me know our driver is here.

Everyone goes ahead and I hang back, hoping to be the

last one out but Malakai is also waiting.

Before I can escape out the door, his hand slides across my back.

"This dress, Olivia," He purrs in my ear, "You really look beautiful tonight, kitten."

Swallowing, I will my cheeks not to bloom with color. His fingers play with the ends of my hair, "I like your hair like this." He tells me.

"Thank you," My voice shakes when I speak. What the hell is even wrong with me?

"Save me a dance tonight?" He asks, a flicker of vulnerability coming over him and this feeling inside of me only intensifies. I don't expect real with Malakai but it's the only thing he has ever given me. He doesn't hide.

I nod, "All of my dances are yours."

I almost bite my tongue when the words come out but then his face lights up, the smile stretching his sensual mouth boyish and playful. My heart stutters but then he's guiding me out the door and into the cold. I've forgone a coat since I'll be inside all evening but this quick stroll to the waiting limo has a chill biting in deep. Malakai ushers me into the limo and I take a seat at the end of the couches set up in the back. Sebastian is pouring champagne while Willow is squished between the two brothers, laughing at something Dean said to her.

Malakai climbs in behind me but instead of sitting in the vacant seat at my side, he takes my hand and pulls me up before he seats himself and tugs me onto his lap.

I'm so stunned by the move that for a moment, I freeze,

but then I realize everyone is watching us and I start to squirm.

Malakai holds me tighter, "You're where you belong." He whispers.

"They're all staring." I hiss back.

"I don't give a fuck."

"I can't sit on your lap, Kai." The shortened version slips out for the second time today and I clam my lips shut. I'd heard Sebastian call him it and I liked how it sounded though I never had any intention of using it. It's intimate. Much too intimate for us.

His eyes heat at the sound, dropping to my lips that I have painted red to pair with my dress.

"I like it," He tells me, "When you call me that."

"It was an accident."

"An accident is breaking a vase," He grins, "Calling me Kai is a natural progression between us."

I roll my eyes at how ridiculous that sounds.

"That's one red handprint on your ass."

"Sorry?"

"Roll your eyes at me again, you'll get two."

Warmth blooms in my core which makes me pulse, only reminding me how hard he took me only hours before. But with his threats I always feel defensive and rebellious, so I lean in, "Is that supposed to scare me, Malakai?" My lips are at his ear which I subtly take between my teeth, "You'll be disappointed to know, spanking me only gets me more excited."

He makes a low rumbling sound like a growl as his fingers squeeze my hips, "Everyone is watching, Olivia." He warns, "I have no problem showing them all that you're mine, but do you?"

I pull back and clear my throat, "Can I sit on my own chair?" I say it louder, making sure they all hear.

He smirks, "No."

"Fine."

I spin on his lap, facing the rest of the party, making sure my ass is right over his cock.

"He always this controlling?" I ask the guys.

I ignore the way they're all looking at us, pretending nothing has changed.

"Always," Dean is the one to answer, leaning back with a grin. He throws an arm around Willow which has Sebastian growling but ultimately, he does nothing.

The rest of the ride to the hotel is had in jokes and banter, mainly between the three guys and Willow while I wiggle and move every so often against Malakai. I feel his cock twitching under my ass and satisfaction comes over me.

We pull up to the hotel and the driver opens the door. Sebastian is out first, then Willow, followed by Killian and Dean but as I get up to move, Malakai pulls me back.

"Are you trying to kill me?" He rasps.

"Next time," I kiss the side of his mouth now we don't have an audience, "Don't tell me what to do."

He lets me go this time and I climb out but when he

doesn't follow, I pop my head back in, "Are you coming?"

His neon eyes meet mine and his hand adjusts his dick, still hard and tenting his pants, "I just need a minute."

A giggle escapes me, "I'll meet you inside?"

"No, you wait there. Just give me a second."

"Malakai, it's cold." I complain.

"We go in together, Olivia. You're my wife, you shouldn't be alone."

"Yes, well you seem to have an issue right now," I point out.

"An issue I should be getting you to fix," He growls.

"You started it, Malakai," I flick back my hair, "I just finished it."

"You forget," He lets out a breath, adjusting himself again, "I have a whole, unrestrained day with you to claim, and I don't forget things, Olivia."

"I'm terrified," I deadpan.

He glares at me and then mutters, more to himself than to me, "She's trying to fucking kill me."

41
Malakai

Olivia in that dress…

I can barely focus. Barely think.

This is a woman I'll go to war for.

I'd burn the whole world for her, die for her, *live* for her.

I'll give her everything she could ever want and more just for a moment with her.

Now my cock is down, thank fuck, I climb from the car, seeing her waiting for me. Seeing her, even after only a few minutes apart, hits me like a truck. Fuck me, she's so damn pretty.

The glow from the hotel windows lights up one side of her body, giving her a golden aura. My breath is stolen as I take her in, the dress, the hair, the makeup…

She's a queen.

A goddess.

And I'm ready to get on my knees to worship at her altar.

Playing with Fire

I pull her to me the moment I'm close enough, crowding her with my warmth to chase away the chill. My lips press to her head before I steer her toward the doors. Cameras start to flash, and while we were using this night as our first official public appearance as a married couple, I don't want her uncomfortable, so I protect her with my body. The articles weren't kind to her the first time, and I already have a list of names to visit.

She'll never be embarrassed again. Not with me.

I get her into the hotel, already packed with guests. The staff buzz through the crowds, serving drinks and food on silver platters. The city mayor is here, the chief of police, and every other important figure that has sway in this city. It's an event for the rich and powerful, a night to let loose a little without the need to donate or give, save for the thirty-minute auction taking place later this evening.

Nonetheless, it's still political.

A steppingstone, no matter how you look at it.

A red carpet is laid out leading into the ballroom where the event itself is taking place.

The Lauder hotel is stuffy, I've always thought it. It's classic wealth, with burgundy and gold, everything added to make it look like money was spent but it feels as if the walls are closing in. The building itself is beautiful but inside… gaudy.

But this room? The one Olivia took over and planned in a week?

Stunning.

Black silk, gothic touches, candlelight, and roses.

It's all tied together one way or another, from the people donned in designer clothing in red, black or white, to the slight glittery shimmer splashed through the black in the room.

"You did this?" I say close to Olivia's ear.

"I did. Do you like it?"

"You've outdone yourself," I smile down at her, "Well done."

"I'm proud of it," she says quietly, a soft smile on her lips.

We find the rest of our group a minute later, ordering drinks from the bar. I get myself a whiskey and Olivia a wine, letting her go so she can mingle with a few of the guests vying for her attention.

Willow stays with her, but Olivia seems at ease, her shoulders are relaxed and her smile light.

Sebastian drops onto the stool next to me. I glance at my best friend, noting the grin and choosing to ignore it.

But of course, it's Bast, and the fucker doesn't know when to keep his mouth shut.

"Damn, Kai," He muses, watching the girls, "Never seen you so…" He trails off his words, tilting his head as he watches Willow move, "Enraptured."

"Pick up a dictionary, did we?" I jab.

He cuts me a scathing look, "Bit close, isn't it?" He hits right back, "You gonna miss that hundred K?"

His words remind me of that stupid bet we made a couple weeks ago. I don't tell him I've already won. I didn't sleep with Olivia to win that bet. I forgot all about it until right fucking now and the reminder turns something sour in my stomach.

"I'm not in the bet," I tell him, "You can have the money."

His head snaps to me, "Shit."

"What?" I growl.

"You have feelings for her." He points out.

"Shut the fuck up, Sebastian."

"Holy shit," A laugh bursts from him, "You have actual, real to fucking god feelings for her."

"That's enough."

"Have you fucked her?" He asks.

So polite.

It's none of his damn business though, I won't tell him I have. I won't tell him that being *with* her is like taking a breath. It's more than sex. It's home. It's the feeling that all my puzzle pieces have finally found the matching set.

"No." I lie.

"Either way," He chuffs, "I'm gonna be hundred grand richer. Maybe I'll get a new car."

"Buy whatever the fuck you like with it," I grumble.

"You're giving up?"

I turn away from him, waving a hand to flag down the server to refill my glass.

"Olivia is more than a bet, Bast." I admit, giving him a raw version of myself. It doesn't happen often, and he knows it.

"Shit." He widens his eyes, "You're in love with her."

I shake my head, I didn't think I was quite there yet but close? I was damn sure close. And I don't even really know when it happened.

Was it the salt in the coffee? The neon socks?

Was it her fight and then submission?

Can you even fall in love that quick?

I throw back the whiskey and immediately order another one.

Either way, I know being in love is a problem, whether I am there, or not.

Olivia will forever be a target regardless, but if people know the depth of my feelings toward her, she will have a big fat bullseye on her forehead. She'll be used, exploited and then spat back out.

You don't get to where I am now without enemies, and I have a lot of them, both within my organization and outside of it.

She is not safe if I love her.

But I can't not be with her. I can't not touch and feel, can't not breathe her in and drown in her. There's something so damn special about the woman in the red dress that it has my attention and no matter the threat or the danger, I gravitate toward her.

She's an obsession...

"Don't be ridiculous," I snap at my friend.

He side eyes me, not believing a word I say.

I don't *love* Olivia... There's just so much about her that captures me. Her attitude drives me crazy, but her laughs send me wild, her body ends me, but her smile? Fuck me, her smile is the one thing that might just very well kill me. Everything about her captures my attention and she's quickly becoming the reason to breathe.

"Okay, man," He scoffs, "Whatever you say."

Granted I'm not being very convincing when I'm following her every move, cataloguing her every smile. I can tell when they're fake, when they're real, can sense when she's uncomfortable based on the way her shoulders lower, like in defeat and when she's excited by the creases that sink in around her eyes when she smiles.

There's so much depth to Olivia that drowning in her is merely an inevitability.

Dinner is called around thirty minutes later and when she makes her way back to me, her hand resting on my chest, a level of calm comes over me that I've never experienced before.

We are seated at one of the front tables, all six of us. Olivia made sure we were the only table to seat so little when every other one is packed.

"Why the event?" Willow asks me.

I shrug, "Why not?"

She tilts her head back and forth as if in contemplation, "Most throw a party for a reason, Farrow." She points out, "What's your reason? It isn't charity, that's for sure."

I lean across the table just as the appetizers are being served, "I wanted to show off my wife, Willow. Tell the world she is mine."

42
Olivia

"I'm so sorry I'm late!" A beautiful female rushes up to our table, her long flowing blonde hair falling over bare shoulders. She's stunning, with tan skin and a light dusting of freckles over the bridge of her nose and cheeks. Big, blue eyes, framed by lush black lashes, flick between the six of us sitting around the table, the first course already completed and cleared away.

"Savannah!" Sebastian shoves out his chair, enveloping the blonde in a tight hug. She's in a floor-length, off-white gown, simple in design but on her, she makes it look elegant and intricate.

I see my best friend wince and look away quickly from the two of them embracing, but then Malakai also stands and hugs her, followed by Dean and then Killian, who holds onto her far longer than the others did.

"You said you weren't coming," Sebastian says, glancing at me.

"I know!" She dances between her feet, "I wasn't sure I'd make it back!"

"Shit," Sebastian turns to me and Willow, "Olivia,

Wils, this is Savannah, my sister."

"Oh!" Willow stands quickly, offering her hand, "Hi!"

I shake her hand after and quickly find a member of staff to bring up another chair and place setting for her, putting her next to Sebastian and Dean.

Malakai leans back in his chair, throwing his arm over the back of mine. I almost jump when I feel the brush of his fingers down my spine.

"Did I tell you how beautiful you look?" He leans in and whispers.

I watch Sebastian and his sister catching up across from me, purposely keeping my face blank when the rest of me is in riot mode, "You did."

"This place looks amazing," He tells me, "You did all of this on your own?"

I glance at him, "Yes, the previous planners quit before it was done."

"Did you enjoy it?"

I nod slowly, "More than anything else I've done." I admit. "Not sure I'm cut out just to sit behind a big desk, all alone in a stuffy office."

"You're not," his fingers continue to move across my bare skin, ignoring the rest of the table in favor of providing me with his undivided attention. "You have far too much energy to sit behind a desk all day."

I nod in agreement, "I'm thinking of taking it over completely. My managers already run this place fine without me and all I need to do is paperwork every now and then. They don't need me to manage this place like my dad did."

He nods, completely invested in what I have to say, even with the riot of sound all around us.

"Olivia!" Savannah calls for my attention and breaking eye contact with Malakai, I turn to face her. She's young, maybe early twenties and now I know she's Sebastian's sister, I see the resemblance.

I fall into an easy conversation with her, trying to keep my attention on her words when Malakai's hand is still brushing across my spine.

"You're a dancer, wow!" I beam, "I always wanted to dance but two left feet stopped me."

She laughs, "It's a lot of discipline," she nods, "But I love it. It's why I was late; I was on tour and we weren't due back for another week but our last show was cancelled so it was chaos to try and get on a flight. I got back maybe two or three hours ago and then I had to find a dress!"

"Well, I'm glad you made it." I glance around the table but my attention snags on Killian. He watches Savannah the same way Malakai watches me. Like nothing and no one in the room matters more than she does.

Interesting.

No one else has seemed to notice but he follows her every move, listens to every word and I wonder what *that* story is.

The main course is served, stopping the conversation momentarily as wine is refilled and plates are placed in front of everyone. But while we eat, everyone still talks, laughs, except for Malakai who appears to be favoring watching and listening over joining the conversation.

It goes that way for much of the meal, even through

dessert, and when the tables are fully cleared and dinner complete, Willow and Savannah get up from the table to go to the bar.

"She's lovely," I say to Sebastian.

"She's young," He grumbles, "And doesn't understand how dangerous the world is."

I snap my head back, "I'm sorry?"

"He doesn't like her traveling so much," Dean explains.

"Oh."

Sebastian shrugs and then grimaces when he sees something over my shoulder.

I try to turn but Malakai wraps his arm around my shoulder, stopping me, but he's stiff, alert.

"Malakai," the overly sweet voice churns my stomach. I've only been in her presence a couple of times, but I know the voice. Know the sound. "You look handsome." Regina comments.

The cloying scent of her perfume stuffs itself up my nose but still, Malakai keeps a tight hold on me, stopping me from looking at her. I turn panicked eyes to Bast, but he shakes his head at me, curling his lip when his eyes snap to Regina. Glad to know I'm not the only one at the table who dislikes the woman.

"I didn't realize you were still coming," Malakai says flatly.

"I wouldn't miss this," She giggles, "It's your event after all. And the Lauder hotel is one of the nicest hotels in the city. I'll never pass up the opportunity to be here."

I make a note to ban her account. Petty? Absolutely. Do

I give a fuck? Nope.

But it also makes me wonder if she knows who I am. Surely if she knew this hotel belonged to me, she wouldn't be so willing to be here since her dislike for me is pretty clear. But I'm not important enough to her for her to do even a little bit of research. I'm just in her way and a problem to clear.

She wants Malakai.

Jealousy turns over in my stomach and it's a feeling I despise. He told me I had nothing to worry about with her, and maybe I don't, and maybe I shouldn't feel any kind of way toward her, but that little envy monster inside of me disagrees.

There's no way I can deny my feelings toward Malakai have shifted, not when the idea of her being so close to him makes me want to pull her hair out.

"Will you save me a dance?" She asks, and I can imagine her fluttering her lashes.

"No." Malakai answers in a tone filled with disdain. "Now please excuse me, my wife needs a drink."

He gets up, bringing me with him and still, I haven't laid eyes on her, nor does it appear I will as I'm steered away from the table and walked to the bar.

"She doesn't belong in the same space as you," Malakai whispers, "I apologize if you thought that was rude."

"I don't like her. Does she not realize this is my hotel?" I ask.

He chuckles, "Not many do. Unfortunately, I work closely with her father, but clearly, she hasn't put your surname and this hotel together."

"My sympathies." I grimace, joining the girls at the bar. "I actually need to go to the bathroom."

"Oh, I'll come!" Willow pipes up, "Sav?"

"Nah, I'm going to catch up with the guys," She smiles before she plucks up her drink and makes her way back to the table.

"She's nice," I say to Willow.

"Mm," Willow agrees, "Not going to lie, thought she was someone else when she came to the table."

"You thought she was *with* Bast?"

She nods, "I didn't like it which is weird because we're just friends."

I purse my lips and don't say a word. I push open the door to the bathroom, locking myself in a cubicle to do my business and Willow does the same. The door opens a few seconds after, and the woman's heels click on the marble tiles of the floor. There were only two stalls so she's waiting for one of us to finish.

I'm the first one done, so after I flush, I make sure my dress is all in place and hurry out of the stall only to stop abruptly when I see who is staring back at me from the mirror.

Regina looks gorgeous in a full black dress, the cut low and risqué but on her body, it looks incredible. Sheer panels work up the sides of her dress, revealing no panty line and her strawberry blonde hair tumbles in waves around her shoulders.

Her makeup is all glam, bright red lipstick and smoky eyes. She has this femme fatale vibe going on and it annoys me.

Cooling my expression, I choose to drop her glare and step up to the basin, turning on the water before I reach for the soap.

"He'll get bored." She says. I still feel her eyes on me but choose to keep mine down, watching the soap work into a lather between my palms.

"We all know it. I don't know why you keep trying."

I don't correct her that, I am, in fact, not trying anything. Malakai wanted this marriage, not me. Things may have changed a little since then, but we started because of him.

"Being the other woman is not a pretty look." She continues.

I can't help it, I laugh.

"Firstly," I meet her stare in the mirror, "To be the *other woman* would imply Malakai was with someone else." She curls her lip, "Secondly, I'm the one with his ring on my finger and his last name attached to mine, which would suggest any woman that isn't me, would be the *other woman*."

"You can put a collar on any stray," She spits, "but it doesn't make it a pedigree. We all recognize trash when we see it. You don't belong here." This bitch did not just refer to me like I am a dog.

I can hear Willow scrambling to get out the stall, but I don't need her to back me up on this.

"I don't belong here?" I laugh without humor, "Where do I belong, Regina?"

"Wherever it is you crawled out from."

"Do you know who I am, Regina?" I ask her seriously.

Playing with Fire

"You're not worth knowing."

"Look, I don't know what weird claim you think you have on my husband but fighting with me is not going to win you any battles. Desperation is not a good look."

"Malakai is mine. So how about you just disappear." She shrugs and gives me a fake as fuck smile.

"Malakai is not an item one can pick up and put in their pocket. That man can't be owned."

"And that right there is why you're not right for him."

She's so sure on her answer she drops my eyes and goes back to touching up her red lips.

"Why don't you go tell that to him?" I challenge, "I'm sure he'd love to know."

"We were good before you turned up." She meets my eyes again, venom and hate radiating from her. "He would be married to me right now. So, you need to leave so I can have what is rightfully mine. Know your place before you get hurt, honey."

"You like this hotel?" I lean on the counter just as Willow exits the stall, going straight for Regina. I grab her wrist and drag her back, shaking my head at her. She relents but not before her eyes cut through Regina as if she could end her with a look alone. For me, she would, which is why I stop her.

"It's going to be mine." She tells me, "I know Malakai is working on procuring it. Just for me."

Now *that* is funny.

"Is that right?" I glance at Willow whose eyebrows have shot up to her hairline.

"Yes."

"I wonder when that meeting is going to go ahead," I say as if thinking out loud, "Did you know the hotel was for sale?" I ask Willow.

"News to me."

"Why would you two know anything?"

This is juvenile. And boring.

"This hotel belongs to me, Regina. If you had bothered to look into me at all, you'd realize my last name isn't just Lauder, it's *the* Lauder. I am Olivia Lauder, the current and only owner of the Lauder Hotels and Resorts. This is mine, and I'm not really sure how you didn't make the connection."

Shock crosses her face before she masks it quickly and steps away from the basin. She closes the gap between us, looking down her nose at me.

"Leave him," she warns in a low voice, "Before you get hurt."

I shake my head and step back, putting the space back between us. "Your desperation is ugly, Regina." I turn my back on her, ready to end the conversation there but my hair is suddenly yanked, hard.

My scalp burns with how hard she's just pulled me back and I almost lose my footing, barely managing to catch myself before I fall on my ass. I swing around, startling her enough that she lets go of my hair.

I don't even realize I'm doing it when my hand swings back and I clock her straight on the mouth with my fist.

I was aiming for the nose.

Pain bursts in my knuckles and I'm pretty sure something just cracked, but Regina is on the floor, cupping her lip in shock.

"Oh shit." I whisper.

I've never hit anyone before.

"We gotta go," Willow grabs me, shock on her face, "Now."

I'm cradling my throbbing hand when Willow hustles me out the door, only to run right into Malakai and Sebastian.

43
Malakai

"I think it's broken!" Olivia cries.

"Shut up, Olivia!" Willow hisses, bundling her friend in her arms as she gives us a smile that I'm sure is supposed to be innocent.

Watery eyes meet mine, her hand clutched to her chest, "I don't want to go to jail."

"What the fuck is going on?" I demand, reaching for my wife who comes willingly. If that doesn't puff out my fucking chest then I don't know what will.

I take her hand in mine, gently removing her fingers to see bruising on her knuckles, the swelling making me pause. "What did you do?"

"We gotta go," Willow rushes, "Now."

"What. Happened?" Sebastian demands.

I keep Olivia close and when Willow opens her mouth to talk, the door to the women's bathroom opens and Regina storms out, looking a little less put together than when I last saw her. Makeup smudges beneath her eyes and that's blood trickling from a small cut on her bottom lip.

"She assaulted me!" Regina accuses loudly, drawing the attention of some lingering guests in the hall. "Call security! I want to file a report!"

"She tried to attack me," Olivia whispers to me, turning her back on Regina. "I didn't mean to."

I place a palm on her back, offering her some silent comfort.

"Did you see anything, Willow?" I ask.

Willow's wide eyes meet mine, "Um. No. I didn't see anything."

"What!?" Regina screams, "You saw it all."

"No," Willow shakes her head, "I didn't see anything. Olivia wasn't even in the bathroom."

"That's right," Sebastian agrees, "She was with me."

"What!?" Regina hisses, "No, she wasn't."

"Have you had a bit too much to drink, Regina?" I ask. "Should I call someone to collect you?"

"What?" She hisses and lunges forward as if to grab Olivia.

I move her back quickly, shoving her behind me.

"I don't give a fuck who the fuck you are," I warn, "Come near her and I will end you."

Regina stops dead and Sebastian takes her arm. "Time for you to leave."

"She attacked me!" She screams, "She assaulted *me*!"

"Everyone thinks you're lying, Regina." Sebastian tells

her lazily, starting to drag her out, "Time to leave."

She fights and struggles the whole time until the ruckus draws more attention, including that of some of the men here I know work with her father. She stops screaming when she sees them but doesn't cease her fight to get away from Sebastian. He'll have her gone so I turn back to Olivia, her eyes wide.

"I didn't mean to hit her." She tells me, "I'm sorry. I just... she..."

"Shh," I soothe, curling a finger under her chin, "Let me see your hand."

"Girl," Willow whistles, "While decking the bitch is what I was rooting for, you do not have a good swing."

"I've never hit anyone before!" Olivia defends. "I don't like confrontation."

Willow softens, "I know, babe."

"Go on," I tell her, "We will be through in a moment."

"You good?" She asks her friend and when Olivia nods, she rubs her arm and then turns, following the path Sebastian just took with Regina.

With no more eyes on us and only the dull hum of music filling the hall, I lift Olivia's hand, running my thumb over the swelling, the bruising darkening by the second.

"Is it broken?" She asks.

"I'm not sure," I tell her, "Perhaps we should go to the hospital. Get it checked."

"Absolutely not!" She pulls away from me, "I can't leave yet and how am I supposed to tell them what happened? I'll go to jail!"

"You're not going to jail, Olivia."

"No," She shakes her head vehemently, "No hospital."

My teeth grind, "Olivia you're hurt. In pain. If it's broken, we need to know."

"I can't believe I hit her." She shudders.

"You defended yourself," I smooth a hand down her hair, "I'm proud of you."

At my words she melts a little, her dark eyes turn soft and round, "You are?"

"I am, kitten," Cradling her injured hand, "But please, I don't want to fight on this, let's go to the hospital."

She shakes her head, "Malakai, I don't want to."

"And if it's broken?"

She looks down, not answering.

"How about this," I offer as much as it pains me. I want to throw her over my shoulder and take her out of here kicking and screaming, "We get some ice and I give someone a call who can come check out your hand?"

She looks up at me, "And?"

"If he says you have to go then we go."

"Fine." She relents.

I nod, "Good girl."

Another shiver.

I add praise to the list of things that make her weak for me.

Guiding her back toward the main room she hesitates at the doors, "Is she gone?"

I nod, "Sebastian would have forced her to leave."

"I'm banning her," Olivia pouts, resuming her walk back into the room.

"Banning her?" I guide her toward the bar, waving down one of the servers.

"From my hotel. She isn't welcome."

"Okay," I soothe. "Ice. In a towel. Now." I order the guy who comes over.

He immediately nods, rushing off to get me what I need.

I accept the ice from him and take Olivia's hand, gently laying it over her swollen knuckles. Holding it there, I meet her eyes, "Did she hurt you anywhere else?" I ask, pushing down my temper.

"No," She shakes her head, "I mean she pulled my hair, which is how the punch happened but no. She didn't do anything else."

"If I knew she was going to attack you, Olivia, I would have never allowed her near you."

"I know," She breathes. "But that woman has a weird obsession with you."

I nod, "I know."

"It's borderline stalking," She cringes.

"Don't worry about it," I say, "She won't come near you again."

I lay her hand down on the bar, keeping the ice on it, "Hold this." I tell her. When she takes it, I pull my cell from my pocket, "Don't move, I'll be back in a moment. I'm just going to give doc a call."

At her nod, I start for the exit, looking back to check on her once more before I get outside and dial doc's number.

44
Olivia

The ice isn't comfortable but to keep Malakai sane, I leave it on my knuckles, even though it burns.

I'm still waiting for him to come back when a man steps up next to me at the bar.

"Olivia," He says my name like he knows me but when I look at him, I don't recognize his face.

"Um, hello?"

"Accident?" He asks, referring to my hand.

I pale, "Yes. Nothing to worry about."

"I do hope it isn't too bad."

"I'm sorry," I turn to him fully, "Do I know you?"

"Oh, no," He shakes his head, "Apologies, I'm Stefan. Malakai's cousin."

"Oh, right, okay." I frown, "Hello."

I look past him, waiting for Malakai to return. There's something about this guy that I don't like, not sure what it is but I'm instantly on alert.

"Malakai hasn't told you about me?" He asks.

"Um," My teeth gnaw at my lip as my eyes keep flicking to the door, waiting for him to return. "Maybe? I can be forgetful." I lie.

Stefan smirks, "It's okay, Olivia. It would not surprise me if my cousin failed to mention me. Our relationship is a little strained."

"Why?" I blurt.

"It's a long story," He tells me, "Can I get you a drink?"

"No," I rush, "I mean, no, thank you. I've had enough."

Even though a drink right now would be delightful. Especially since it'll likely ease the pain in my hand.

He asks for a beer when he's served but doesn't leave after he's been given his drink.

"I have to say," He leans on the bar casually, like we're old friends. "You don't seem to be Malakai's type at all."

Hackles raised, "I don't think that's any of your business."

Brows shoot up at my tone and I resist the urge to shrink. I feel incredibly vulnerable right now, with an injured hand and already a little emotional over the fact I just hit someone. I could cry. I want Malakai.

It's that realization that has my spine straightening. I want him. Right now.

He's strength and safety in the most profound way considering he's the most dangerous man I know. But for me? He isn't a monster.

He isn't the devil.

For me he is a rock. He is a net to catch me, a crutch to hold me up.

He's never once made me feel weak.

Though he absolutely could if he wanted to.

I've been looking at him all wrong, like having him by my side is a bad thing. But in fact, him as my husband, no matter how it came about, is a strength I didn't know I was missing. My heart starts to pound inside my chest, and I glance at the door again.

"How interesting," Stefan comments, drawing my attention once more. "You're falling in love with him."

He says it in a way that makes it appear like a weakness, like it's a plight.

"I wish you well, Olivia."

His words hold no warmth. There's an undertone of violence, a bite of something that makes me incredibly wary.

Since Malakai isn't coming back and I can't see him, I search for anyone else, thankfully capturing the gaze of Killian who isn't looking at Savannah for the first time tonight.

I plead with as much as I can for him to come to me and it must be enough because his eyes move to Stefan who still hasn't left, even though his last statement was one said in farewell and then he's getting up, striding toward me, long legs eating up the space.

He is darkness and violent intent, "Olivia," He says, slotting himself in the space between Stefan and me, "You okay?"

I shake my head subtly, but lie and answer, "Good. How are you?"

"Parched," Killian answers, before he gives his attention to the other man, "Stefan."

Stefan doesn't answer but does push off the bar, glancing once more at me before he starts to head for the door.

"Stay away from him," Killian warns me.

I quirk a brow, "You think I wanted that conversation?"

"What did he say?"

"Nothing," I shift the ice on my hand, "I just get bad vibes from him."

"Good." Killian nods. "Heard you smacked Regina."

"Sebastian?"

Killian grins, "Gave her a nice bloody lip. But how the fucking hell did you damage your hand so bad?"

I roll my eyes at him, "I've never hit anybody! I don't know how to!"

Chuckling, "So defense lessons?"

"Apparently I need them."

Malakai rejoins us, sliding up to the bar, "He'll be here in five."

"Can you move your fingers for me, Olivia?" The doctor asks. He's an older gentleman, with silver hair and deep wrinkles. We've moved into one of the side rooms used for conferences for some privacy while he checks my hand.

I wiggle my fingers the best I can and while it hurts, I can move them just fine. Malakai watches with rapt focus, cataloguing every wince so I try to stifle them, so he doesn't flip out.

"Good," the doctor says, "Now squeeze." He slots his hand into mine.

I wrap my fingers around his palm, suck in a breath and grip, knowing my nails are digging into his skin.

"Good, very good," He comments, withdrawing his hand only to grab mine and begin to move around my fingers, pulling and stretching. I wince and gasp, but they move without issue and while it hurts, it's not unbearable which tells me already that nothing is broken.

"I don't think we have any breaks," The doctor confirms what I was just thinking, "Just some bad bruising."

"So, we don't need a hospital?" I ask.

He shakes his head, "Painkillers. Maybe some compression and ice. The swelling should go down in a few days, but this bruising will last a little longer."

"But I definitely do not need a hospital," I repeat.

"No," He smiles, and I flick my eyes to Malakai who is stiff and glaring at where the doctor holds my hand, "I can prescribe some medicine," He tells me, "Would you like me to?"

"Yes please," I bring my hand back to me, the throb a little uncomfortable but I'm relieved there are no breaks.

He writes out a prescription before he stands. "If that

will be all?" He asks Malakai.

"Are you sure?"

"I'm sure, Mr. Farrow," He assures him, "Your wife is just fine. A little pain meds and rest on her hand and she'll be as good as new."

"Very well," Malakai sighs, walking him to the door.

"I can see myself out. You have a good evening."

He leaves us, the door clicking closed behind him.

"See nothing to worry about," I tell Malakai.

"Let's go get you your meds."

I laugh, "No. We're going to enjoy the rest of the evening, Malakai. The meds can wait. I have some pain meds in my purse that'll work just fine for now."

"Why do you have meds!?" He demands.

"Fuck me," I sigh, getting up, "In case I get a headache. Or cramps. Stop worrying. You'll go grey." I pat his chest and open the door, breezing through it and hear him follow. I smile when his arm snakes around me.

He pulls us to an abrupt stop and then his mouth is on mine.

I'm breathless when he pulls away, heart pounding, "What was that for?" I breathe.

"Because I can, wife. Because you're mine."

45
Olivia

The lights have been darkened, the tables have moved a little further away from the dance floor and soft music now plays for the room.

There are crowds of people dotted throughout the space, some talking quietly, others laughing, all dressed in their finest as cameras flash and people dance.

I've taken meds which have taken the edge off the pain in my hand making me feel a little lighter. No one mentions what happened, they ask me if I'm okay but that's as far as it goes.

"Dance with me," Malakai leans in.

"Not many people are dancing right now," I point out.

"So?"

"Everyone will stare."

"Please give me another pointless reason," He deadpans.

I glance at the dance floor and try to tell myself why

this is a bad idea but I can't think of a single reason, so I slide my uninjured hand into his.

His eyes light up as he helps me to my feet and then he's guiding me to the dance floor.

Hozier, *Work song,* plays softly over the speakers as Malakai draws me in close. I place my injured hand on his shoulder while my other rests in his, and his hand spreads across my spine, keeping me flush against him. His eyes are on me as he begins to move us to the music, his every step in beat to the song. The lyrics flow through me, slamming into me more and more as his eyes hold mine, never wavering.

We don't speak as we dance, the attention is purely on the way we move, on the way our bodies talk and join, like they know, like it's built somewhere deep inside of us to read the other. Nothing else matters right now, I don't see the hundreds of other people surrounding us or the other bodies dancing. I only feel *us* as we dance, like the two of us are part of the same puzzle, pieces coming together to form an entire image.

A beautiful, messy painting built upon carnage, deception, and violence.

He holds me like I am precious, like I am the sun in his life and the way he looks at me completely devastates me.

"Olivia," He rasps my name, the sound almost lost to the music.

"Don't," I warn.

I see him swallow and a touch of his hardness shutters over his eyes, "Later, then."

"Later," I agree. Or never.

He finishes the song with me, his touch not changing despite the shift in our conversation and the hardness remaining in his eyes. I'm not ready to have such discussions with him. It's just sex. Just a mutual loathing that manifested in some great fucking, but too much reflection has now ruined that.

This between us, it's just a contract, that's all marriage is. I have to ignore what I feel.

But no matter how much I say it in my head, I can't get myself to agree to it.

Fuck, when did this get hard?

I pull out of his arms, "I need some air."

He moves to come with me, but I shake my head, "Give me five minutes. I just need five."

"Olivia," He whispers.

"Please," I breathe.

I can see he doesn't want to, can see he is warring with himself, it's all over his face but eventually, he dips his chin and lets me go. I flee, my heels eating up the space to the door. I feel him watching me the entire time, right until I slip out the door. There are a few guests mingling in the foyer and beyond the doors I see snow is falling. I don't have a coat, so I change direction and head for the staff entrance behind the desk, slipping into the empty hall.

I press my back against the wall, close my eyes and let out a breath.

It was all the little things. The crusts on my bread, the need to know I've had water, had food. It was the forehead kisses and light touches, the smiles he threw me when I tried to piss him off. It's the attention and care he provides, the softness I see in him when he's trying to hide it behind a wall of violence.

It's him in his entirety, the hard, brutal parts of him, the dominant possessive edges that have been softened by the way he cares for those close to him. It's his laughter with the boys and his mischievous, playful grins.

Fuck.

I'm falling in love with my husband.

Conflict works through me; how could I love him? He took my choices away, threatened my family. My sister is the only family I have left, and he would have taken her too if I didn't agree to marry him. It makes everything that happened to her seem small, not important but it almost destroyed her.

It feels disloyal.

I should call her. I pull my cell from my purse and bring up her contact information but before I can press the button, the staff door opens. I'm expecting one of my employees but it's two men who enter the hall.

"Sorry," I lock my phone again, "You can't be back here. This is a staff only area."

"Olivia Farrow?" The one on the right asks.

"That's right."

The two men exchange a look and then they're coming for me. I stumble back, dropping my purse, along with the phone which they step on, crushing it.

Shit.

I turn and I run, heading straight for the office. If I can get there first, I can lock myself inside.

I'm pulling on the handle when arms come around me, dragging me back from the door.

I let out a scream but a hand slams across my mouth hard enough, my teeth cut into my lip and I instantly taste blood on my tongue. He lifts me off the floor and begins to drag me toward the door that leads back to the offices. There's a fire exit that way and no one to see them.

I can't let them get me there. I fight in his arms, kicking out with my legs and landing a blow to his shin with my heel.

"Bitch!" He hollers, dropping me. I land hard on my knees but I'm up a moment later, and sprinting as best I can with the lengths of the dress and my heels. I need to get to where there are people, where someone can see me, but the door is so fucking far away. My mouth is still bleeding and my knees ache, my hand throbbing anew.

Shit. Shit. Shit.

A hand grips my arm tightly, stopping my forward motion. I'm yanked back once more.

"Knock the bitch out!" I hear the other one say.

"Help me!" I scream before he can quieten me. A hand strikes me across the face and bright light bursts behind my eyes, stunning me enough I feel my body go lax in the arms that hold me.

Fuck. *No.*

But I feel useless, like I can't fight even though my mind is telling me to. My body doesn't listen, it does nothing.

"She's still awake," I hear them say, the voice like an

echo inside my head.

He'll hit me again. Any second now.

I feel my spine hit the wall, hands holding me up but my head rolls to the side, eyes flicking to the door.

"Pretty little thing," he says, grabbing my cheeks in his fingers. My lips pucker as my teeth bite against the inside of my cheeks. "Be a good girl and go to sleep."

He jerks my head forward and then slams it back, knocking my head into the wall.

Fog drifts into my vision but still, I look to the door. To safety that's just too far out of reach.

But then it opens, and a body fills the frame.

My vision is too dark to make out who it is but there's something so recognizable in the way they stand and then they speak, in a voice filled with murderous intent, the roar filling the space all around me.

"Get your fucking hands off my wife!"

46
Malakai

My eyes haven't moved from the door since she left. I'm waiting for her to return.

I'll give her five minutes exactly, when that's up, I'm going for her.

She's scared.

I see it all over her, but I won't let anything hurt her, won't let anything come for her.

When the five minutes are up, my legs are eating up the distance between us. I ignore everyone as I stride through the hotel, heading for the doors in the foyer but it's snowing out and when I look, she's nowhere to be found on the sidewalk.

Heading back inside, I glance around the few faces lingering but they pay me no attention.

And then I hear it.

A scream, filled with so much terror it chills the blood in my veins. It's muffled and barely audible and it doesn't appear anyone else heard the sound, but I did. I know I did.

I'm moving before I even register it, shoving open the staff door.

And there she is.

But she isn't alone.

She's being pinned to the wall, an arm across her chest, a hand gripping her face. She's lax in his grip, there's blood on her lip, a smear of it on the wall.

Rage unlike I've ever felt before consumes me. It makes my blood boil, my heart pound as red overcomes my vision.

"Get your fucking hands off my wife!" I roar and begin to thunder toward them. One man runs in the opposite direction immediately, whereas the one holding my wife drops her and begins to move too.

But I'm already there, grabbing him by the neck to slam his head into the wall. He goes down, dazed as I reach into my suit pocket and grab the knuckle dusters I always carry. I could beat him with my fists, but these hurt worse, these guarantee agony. It's the only thought in my head, the only thing keeping me moving is ensuring he suffers for what he has just done.

They're on my hand in the next breath, and my fist is rearing back on the next, the cold black metal slamming into his face with a satisfying crack.

I hit him again, and again, blood coating the metal and my hand, splattering up and onto my face. It takes no time at all to leave him a fleshy, bloody mess, face split open as blood pools beneath him, a couple teeth scattered in front of his face. I can see bone and muscle, his skin torn and mangled.

"That's my wife!" I growl but the guy is dead.

Behind me I hear footsteps and I rear up, ready to take on the new threat but it's Sebastian, his eyes wide with shock as he moves them between me, the guy and Olivia who is laying on the ground, eyes closed.

Shit.

I drop the guy and move to her immediately, the rage pulsing like a living breathing thing inside of me. The dusters fall with a clang to the floor as I drop to my knees next to her.

"There's another one," I growl to Sebastian, pulling Olivia into my arms. She's limp, her arms falling heavily at her sides as a thin trickle of blood runs down her chin. "Escaped through the office." I tell him, eyes moving away from Olivia just for a second to make sure he understands this is not a request but an order, "Find him. I want him in the cells by the end of the night."

Sebastian jerks his head in a nod, and pulls out his phone as he moves past us, following my orders.

"Olivia, baby," I move her hair away from her face, my thumb swiping over the blood on her chin and then notice the blooming bruise on her cheek, darkening her pale skin. "Wake up, kitten."

I smooth a hand down the back of her head only to find it wet and warm. My palm comes away stained red.

"No," Panic consumes me, my heart slamming against my rib cage. She's breathing, her chest rises and falls steadily and it's the only thing that keeps me centered.

Sliding my arm beneath her knees, my other under her torso, I lift her carefully, making sure to cradle her head against my shoulder. There's enough blood leaking from her skull that I feel it soaking through my shirt.

Carrying her in my arms, I kick the door open at the end, leaving the body of her attacker behind. The guys will handle it.

I ignore the gasps of horror as I break out into a jog in the foyer, keeping it steady so I don't jolt her. I don't feel the cold as I make it outside. The hospital is a block from here, there are no cabs or cars around for me to use.

So, I run.

I hold her tight as I sprint down the sidewalk, the snow crunching under my feet. I ignore the burn in my lungs, the scream in my muscles as I push myself to go as fast as I can, curling myself around her to shield her the best I can from the elements.

It's when I can see the hospital ahead of me, the lights shining against the snow on the ground, when Olivia stirs in my arms.

"Almost there, kitten," I rasp to her.

I storm into the ER, drawing everyone's attention, "Help her!" I roar.

Nurses rush toward me, a bed is pushed in front of me, which I lay Olivia on. She's still dazed but she's groaning, almost fully awake, lashes fluttering against her pale cheeks.

"What's her name? What happened?" All the questions

blur into one, everyone's voices sounding the same.

"Olivia Farrow." I answer, "She was attacked."

"Who are you?"

"She's my wife."

They start to take her away from me, toward a set of blue double doors. "Sir you can't come." A nurse stops me from following but quickly removes herself from my path when I glare down at her.

"You will not keep me from her," I warn, slamming through the doors after Olivia.

"Sir, I will call security!" The nurse yells, "You can't go back there!"

"Fucking watch me!"

"Sir!"

Sudden arms are yanking me back, tackling me back toward the waiting area.

"Get your hands off me!" I growl.

"Sir! Mr. Farrow!"

There are three guys holding me back and I glare down at the nurse who ordered them to stop me. I memorize her face, the steel in her eyes.

"You cannot go back there. There is nothing you can do," She tells me sternly, "You will have to wait in here."

"That's my wife!" I growl, trying to get free. I'll fucking kill them all.

"I understand," She softens a little, "When there is news, we will come get you."

Playing with Fire

"No, she needs me!"

"Sir," She sighs, stepping back a little when I snatch away from one of the arms holding me. "You need to calm down. You have blood on you, are you also injured?"

"It's not mine," I growl.

A flicker of fear joins the steel in her eyes. *That's right, be fucking afraid of me.*

"Sit down, Mr. Farrow." She hides that fear quickly, "I will come get you when there is news. Is there any medical history we should know about? Allergies to any medicines?"

"Let me back there!"

"I will have you removed if you do not calm down."

Fuck.

I have no fucking control here.

I stop fighting the arms, "Please." I beg.

"She's in good hands," The nurse sighs, "Please just take a seat."

"You'll get me?"

"Immediately," She assures me.

"Fine." Forcing myself to relax, the arms hesitate for a few more seconds before they release me, and though I itch to find her, protect her, I resist. The whole waiting room is watching with wide eyes, but no one says shit as I take a seat closest to those doors Olivia just disappeared through.

Elbows on my knees, I lean forward and drop my head, staring at the blood on my hands. Hers. His.

I wanted to go find his fucking body and mangle it some more. They hurt her. *They hurt my wife.*

Someone is going to fucking pay for this. Painfully.

I reach into my pocket for my cell, dialing Sebastian.

"News." I demand when he answers.

"The event has been shut down. Everyone is leaving now. The body is being cleaned and Killian has the second guy and is taking him back to the cells. He's a little bloody."

"Keep him alive," I order quietly, "I have questions."

"Already told them," Bast assures, "What the fuck happened, Kai?

"I don't know." I admit, "She went out for air, didn't want me to come with her. I found them like that."

"Is she okay?"

"I don't know," I feel my voice shake, "She was bleeding."

"You at the hospital?"

"Yeah."

"See you in five." Bast hangs up so I drop the cell from my ear, gripping the device in my hand.

Sebastian shows up four minutes later, Willow, Dean and Savannah in tow.

"Killian will be here when he has–" Sebastian cuts himself off knowing he can't say shit with the girls there. Savannah knows some but not all, and as far as I am aware, Willow is oblivious to our business.

I nod, understanding.

"Where is she?" Willow demands, her voice shaking.

"They're working on her," I tell them.

"What's wrong with her?" She asks.

I shake my head because I don't know. I don't know the extent of her injuries or what they had managed to do before I got there.

A hand lands on my shoulder when the same nurse from before comes back through the doors, "Mr. Farrow. She's awake."

I shove away from the chair, "Can I see her?"

"Only one of you," she eyes the group, "This is an ER not a damn café."

"Where is she?" I demand.

"Follow me, please."

I say nothing to the rest of them as I follow the nurse down a long, sterile corridor. She stops at a door to a private room but doesn't let me inside.

"She's okay. A little bruised, she has a concussion and a small wound on the back of her head. It's been glued shut, no stitches. She'll be kept in until tomorrow because of the concussion."

"Let me inside," I demand, "Let me see my wife."

47

Olivia

Fuck me, I hurt.

Everywhere.

The door to the private room they're holding me in opens, and Malakai storms in. His neon blue eyes land on mine immediately before he crosses the space and cradles my face in his hands.

"Hi," I croak.

His eyes jump between mine, a war within them, a battle of rage and panic.

"I'm okay." I whisper.

"Shit, kitten," his mouth presses on mine softly, nothing like the all-consuming kisses we've shared before. This is tender, as much for me as it is for him. He tells me he's here while also reminding himself that I am okay.

My body is still shaking, fear making it impossible to fully relax. They attacked me, tried to abduct me from my own hotel. If Malakai hadn't found us, where would I be? What were they going to do?

"Shh," Malakai soothes, "You're safe."

His forehead rests on mine and the touch of him quietens everything else. I still hurt, my head aches and my body feels as if I've been hit by a damn truck, but the fear eases a little.

He's here. They didn't win.

He saved me.

"You came for me," I say, feeling the sting of tears.

"I will always come for you, Olivia. *Always*, you hear me?"

Swallowing, I gently pull back, letting out a breath as I lay back on the pillows to give my muscles a break. "Who were they?" I ask because I know he will have that information.

"I'm finding out," He growls, hardness entering his expression. "One of them is dead."

I widen my eyes, "What?"

"I killed him." He says it with no shame, regret, or guilt. He says it like he had no problem doing it and would do it again easily. I shouldn't be surprised by it, but I am.

"There were two," I stutter.

"Yes," He agrees, "They won't be a problem for you again, Olivia."

"Did you kill him too?"

"No. But I will."

Malakai takes a seat in the chair next to the bed, and I get a proper look at him now. I don't know how I missed the blood all over him, it's splattered over his face, his hands are stained with it. Swallowing, I avert my eyes to the window, seeing white flakes drifting down from a pitch black sky. It's much too peaceful when there's so much chaos inside me.

"You don't have to be afraid of me, Olivia," Malakai's words are spoken softly, a whisper, "I'd never hurt you."

I let my eyes fall closed against the sting, "I'm not afraid of you." I confess honestly, "I'm afraid of everything that surrounds you."

"You're safe," He repeats.

"Did they target me because of you?" I ask him bluntly. I have to know what I am facing, and then I have to decide if I want to continue allowing myself to fall deeper with him. How much risk is too much?

"I don't know, Olivia." He reaches for my hand, curling his strong fingers around my much smaller one. The blood is a malevolent reminder of the monster he is but when he touches me like this, so gently like I'm fragile and precious, I don't see the monster at all. "But I promise it'll never happen again."

"How can you make that promise, Kai?"

He shudders, it's gentle and subtle but I feel it where our hands are connected, "Because there is nothing I won't do to make sure you're protected. I will burn every city to the ground to eliminate any threat to you. I am your shield, Olivia. Your bullet. I am your husband."

My lashes flutter but words fail me.

"Rest, kitten," Malakai stands, leaning over the bed. His hand smooths back some hair from my forehead, the callouses on his fingers scraping on my skin.

"Are you leaving?" I panic.

"I'll be right back," He promises, "I need to change and wash off the blood. I'll send Willow and Sebastian in, okay?"

"The nurse won't let them both in," I remind him.

"Don't worry about that," he says, gently pressing his mouth to mine before he then kisses my forehead and strides from the room.

A few minutes later Sebastian enters the room, "Well damn," He whistles, "She's alive."

He clicks the door closed behind him and comes to the bed, staring down at my face in concern. "You good?"

"Yeah," I answer, "Sore."

I reach for the water on the bedside, but Sebastian is there first, grabbing the cup and guiding the straw to my mouth.

"I have a concussion and a few bruises," I deadpan, "I didn't lose the use of my limbs."

It doesn't stop him though and knowing I won't win, I take a few draws of water, wetting my lips and tongue.

When I'm finished, he puts it down and takes a seat just as Willow sneaks into the room, quickly shutting the door behind her.

"Shit Oli!" She gasps, rushing over. Both hands grab one of mine as watery eyes flick around my face, cataloguing my injuries. "Well tonight didn't exactly go to plan." She winces, her thumb brushing over my knuckles.

"No," I agree. "What a shit show."

Sebastian scoffs but says nothing as Willow climbs onto the bed to lay down next to me. She rests on my shoulder, and I lean my cheek down on top of her head. "I lost my phone."

"I'll get it sorted," Sebastian answers.

I was going to phone my sister, but now I think I'll wait. If she finds out about this, she'll be on the next ferry over, and I didn't want her or her new boyfriend near Malakai just yet because of how angry they both were that I was doing this.

Willow stays in the bed with me and ends up falling asleep there, but I stay awake, watching the snow while Sebastian sits quietly beside me. I know he's only here as a bodyguard, but it's nice to have his company. I like Sebastian. I like them all.

I blow out a breath, almost wanting to laugh since this is not how I expected any of this to go.

Malakai returns about two hours after he left, dressed now in a pair of dark denim jeans and a sweater, hair still a little damp from his shower but his skin is clean, hands too.

"Well then," Sebastian stands, shaking Willow gently, "I'll get this one home."

Willow groans and buries into my side further, refusing to wake.

"She'd sleep through an earthquake, I swear," I laugh.

Rolling his eyes, he gently lifts Willow from the bed, and she snuggles right into his chest. His arms happen to curl just a little tighter, not that I let on that I notice. Malakai opens the door for them before he takes the seat Sebastian just vacated.

"How are you feeling?"

"I'm okay," I tell him. I'm not in too much pain, though I am worried about looking in the mirror. I know my face is bruised but I don't know how bad it is.

"You understand you won't be able to go anywhere alone now?" He says softly.

I nod. Figured as much and I didn't much mind having company if it meant never experiencing what I did today again. I've never felt so helpless, not even when my ex blindsided me with that damn video.

"I'll assign a bodyguard once we get home," He tells me, "He will be with you whenever I am not. Even at work and with Willow. He'll be trained."

"Trained like you?" I hedge.

"Yes."

"Okay."

"When you're ready," He continues, "I will train you in self-defense and how to use various weapons. I won't have you at risk."

"I hope I never have to use it." I confess.

"If I have anything to do with it," He leans in, "You'll never have to."

48

Malakai

I take her home late the following day. Willow had come by earlier this morning and dropped off some clothes for her to change into, and now she's sitting in the now clean passenger seat of the Maserati, watching the city pass outside the window.

She's gone quiet on me, reflective but she accepts my hand when I reach across to take hers within mine, her thumb brushing up and down my finger.

"What's going on inside that pretty head of yours, kitten?" I ask when the landscape around us changes from grey buildings to lush greenery, the scenery like something from a painting, covered in white snow with only small peeks of green breaking it up.

"Do you think it could have been Regina?" She asks, turning to me.

"What about her?" My hand turns hard on the wheel.

Playing with Fire

"Well, we had that altercation," She watches me intently, "Do you think she could have hired someone?"

"Regina isn't brave enough," I answer honestly, "She's all bark."

I see her purse her lips out of the corner of my eye, "I'm not sure."

"I will find out," I assure her, "I'll find whoever was behind it. You have my word."

"I believe you," She answers, "I just never expected anything like this to happen to me."

My stomach twists. Of course, this never would have happened if it wasn't for me. If she didn't have my last name, wasn't tied to me with that wedding band on her dainty finger, this never would have happened.

But I never thought about this when I decided to take her as mine, it didn't cross my mind when I kissed her at the altar or forced her to share my bed. But back then, I didn't realize how quickly I'd become enamored by her, how much I would crave her.

I haven't had the chance yet to interrogate the second man since I've spent the last several hours at the hospital, but I plan on doing it the moment Olivia is settled in back at the estate.

The cells are in the basement of the house, deep beneath my home and are made up of several rooms. They've been used for various reasons over the years, but it's mostly been for traitors.

I have a feeling I'd be using them a lot over the coming weeks.

I am ready to tear my council apart, weed out the rats

and snakes with these changes coming. Olivia thinks
Regina had something to do with it, but I know different. I know one of the members of the council is involved in this. But who, I didn't know.

Iwan and Hank are prime suspects but without sure evidence, I could lose any remaining members on my side if I outright accuse them. I couldn't risk taking revenge on them without knowing exactly what it is they are doing.

The council needed me more than I needed them, *but* they are still required. I just needed to change how it runs and how decisions, votes and changes are made.

It's been run the same way for generations but time changes all and these outdated traditions and rules put in place by my predecessors must change.

Olivia goes to bed earlier than usual, but she looked exhausted. I sat with her until she fell asleep which hadn't taken long at all and then I'd switched out the light, closed the door and ordered one of my most trusted men to sit close by to keep watch.

I won't make the mistake of risking her life again.

Sebastian, Killian, and Dean are waiting in the drawing room for me when I come downstairs, their clothing dark and leather gloves already covering their hands.

"Ready?" I ask them, opening the top drawer for my own gloves.

"Let's go." Sebastian moves toward the hidden door inside the drawing room. It's the only way to access the cells beneath and unless you knew it was there, you'd never find it.

I press on the panel on the wall which clicks to show a metal door with a pin lock. Entering the code, the locking mechanism begins to click and whirl before the door releases straight onto a set of stairs leading down.

The walls are concrete, and the air cold, stale, the sound of our steps echoing as we make our way down the stairs and then the long dark hall which opens into a large room. The room is divided into several small rooms surrounding a much larger area that's stained red with aged blood. It doesn't matter how thoroughly it's cleaned; the blood never comes out.

All of these rooms are empty right now except the one holding my current *guest*.

I can hear him, voice raw from screaming, begging to be let out, but this room will be the last one he sees. It'll be my face that shows him to hell.

Sebastian heads straight for the room, unlocking it while I take a seat at the table in the middle of the space. The top of it is scratched and dented, stained like the floor is. There's a drawer with all my *toys* but I don't get them out yet. While torture is handy and useful in getting what I want, I do try to be civilized first.

The guy is dragged from his cell, his face a mash of broken skin, swelling and day old, crusted blood. His clothes are torn, and he has a limp, but he fights like he hasn't already taken a beating even when he knows there is no way he could win.

"Connor Lane." I say his name, "Let me introduce myself."

Sebastian forces him down in the chair opposite me,

grabbing his hands as he slams them onto the table, using the chains to keep them there. He does the same to his ankles, locking him to the chair.

"I know who you are," The guy spits, struggling past the swollen lips and missing teeth.

"Good." I lean back, throwing an arm around the back of my chair, "Makes my life a little easier."

"What do you want?" He snaps, keeping his fight.

"Isn't it obvious?"

"I don't rat."

I roll my eyes, everyone talks eventually. And men like him, hired for a purpose, talk far quicker than they like to believe. This one though isn't part of my organization. Of course, there are smaller businesses like mine, little fish that have no bearing on me whatsoever, but every now and then paths cross, lives become tangled, and I have to do a little clean up.

"Then I'm sure you know where this is going." I open the drawer, looking down into it as I contemplate my choices. Keeping it simple, I pull out the butcher's knife, the edge of it glinting in the white lighting above my head.

It's nothing fancy, I don't need anything like that for what I am about to do.

Connor's eyes drop to the knife I lay on the table, a flicker of fear there but it doesn't remain.

"Last chance, who hired you?"

"Go to hell, Farrow." He spits down onto the table.

"Fine." I get up, walk around and toward him, the knife dangling from my fingers. "You hurt my wife."

"I don't give a fuck."

"You laid your hands on her."

"Yeah?" He grins manically, "I was gonna do more than that."

"I'm sure," I don't show a reaction even if I burn within. I flick my eyes to Sebastian who steps up, grabs the guy's fingers and flattens them against the table. I don't hesitate to swing, the knife coming down across all four fingers, cutting them clean off his hand.

He screams, blood splattering onto the shiny surface.

"That's for touching her." I tell him, waiting for Sebastian to straighten out his other hand. He thrashes, trying to get free but the chains are flush to his wrists, allowing no movement. The metal rattles with his fight and spittle flies from his lips as he screams but it does nothing to me, it's like music.

I bring the knife down across his other fingers, cutting them off just like I did before.

"That's for hurting her."

Connor thrashes in pain, his fingers pouring blood onto the table, the severed digits scattered across the top. I pick one up, his middle I think and examine it.

"Open wide," I order, moving the finger toward his fucked-up mouth.

His eyes widen as he thrashes his head side to side, but Sebastian does what is needed, not even fazed by what I am about to do. He forces the guy's mouth open, and I shove the finger inside. Before he can spit it out, Bast is snapping his jaw closed.

He cries out but can't get the finger out, leaving him no

choice but to swallow it.

"How does it taste?" I ask when Sebastian releases him. "Do you understand now? Do you understand who you've fucked with?"

Finally, fear twists his expression and this time he can't hide it.

My hands land in the blood as I lean on it and get close, "That's what it tastes like when you come for a Farrow. This is what happens when you come for my wife."

"I-I'm sorry!" He stutters, blood leaking from his mouth, mixed with saliva that drips off his chin.

"It's a little late for apologies," I wave a hand, pushing up from the table as I start to pace, bored, "But I will give you one offer."

"Anything." He begs.

"The name."

"I don't know!" He cries, "I swear man, I wasn't given the details, I just tagged along for the job!"

"You didn't think to ask?"

"No!" The chains rattle some more, "It doesn't matter much. You know that! I just wanted the money!"

I nod, "Did you know she was my wife?"

"Not until we found her in the hall, and she confirmed her name."

"Yet you still went for her?"

"She was alone man," he admits honestly, "It was easy."

I flick my eyes to Sebastian who looks as angry as I

feel.

"Last chance, Connor. I want a name."

"I don't know, I swear! I don't have a name!"

I shake my head in disappointment, "Then my offer is off the table."

"What!? No!"

"No name, no freedom." I pull the gloves off my hands, throwing them onto the floor at his feet, "Gentlemen," I say to the guys, "Finish the job. Make sure he understands the severity of his mistake of crossing us before he dies, yeah?"

They nod and I start to walk away, the sound of my steps joined by his screams. They grow quieter the further I get from them until I'm walking out the door and shutting out the sound.

49
Malakai

I walk into the room with my running sneakers in my hand, "Olivia."

She's still in bed, sitting with her back resting on the headboard. She looks adorably disheveled, hair sleep mused while she cradles a cup of coffee in her hand. The bruises are darker today but they're not as bad as I originally thought they would be. It's mostly contained to her cheekbone and her lip is still a little swollen, the cut healing.

She was still soundly sleeping when I came to bed last night, so I have no idea when she found the time to do this.

"Mm?" She turns her attention to me.

"Where are the laces for my shoes?"

A smile stretches her mouth, but she shrugs innocently, "I have no idea."

I cock my head, "When did you do this?"

Playing with Fire

"I didn't do anything."

Chuckling, I drop the sneakers and cross the room, climbing onto the bed. I take her coffee from her, placing it on the bedside table as I grab her thighs and slowly begin to drag her down, careful not to be too rough as I'm sure she's sore.

Her dark eyes watch me the entire time, following me as I lay my body over hers, wedging my thigh between her legs. She gasps as I press it up against her.

"I have methods to get what I want, Olivia," I warn her, "Where are my laces?"

She giggles, "I have no idea."

I could have chosen a different pair, but she's taken *all* the laces for my sneakers.

"Are you going to be a little brat, kitten?" I kiss the uninjured side of her mouth as I move my thigh, rubbing it against her through the little sleep shorts she wore to bed.

She lets out the sweetest little moan and tilts her head, giving me access to her neck. My hand roams up her body, over the mound of her breast until I gently tease the peak of her nipple through her top.

So effortlessly sexy, nipples straining against the thin cotton, pussy warm and inviting against my leg. My cock jerks in the sweats I have on. I had been hoping to release some of this tension in the gym with some cardio but I'm finding myself relaxing right here.

She is the balm on my soul. She makes breathing so fucking easy.

"Malakai," She whimpers my name, eyes fluttering

closed as I continue to pepper kisses all over her, going light over the bruising before I move back to her mouth, my tongue licking across the seam of her lips. She opens for me, her tongue meeting mine and while I want to devour her, swallow her down I can't while she is still injured.

I kiss her languidly instead, a complete contrast to the need that burns within me and when she reaches between us, palming my cock through my sweats I almost snap.

"The laces, Olivia," I growl, as much to remind myself why I'm here. Like the fucking laces even matter.

"Bathroom counter." She gasps as I shift and move my body between her thighs, grinding my cock into her. "Under the basin."

Fingers claw at my back, trying to pull the t-shirt on my body. I let her take it off me, reveling in the feel of her fingers on my skin, touching, caressing, scratching. My mouth drops to her neck, and I suck her skin into my mouth, freshening up the fading bite I had left there previously.

"Please," She begs, hips rolling against me.

I can't fucking say no. I don't even shove the sweats all the way down when I grab the hem of her tiny shorts, forcing them to the side to show me the slick center of her. She moves her hand to mine, holding the shorts to the side so I can grip my cock, moving the head of my dick through her pussy, coating myself in her before I slip down to her entrance, slamming into her to the hilt in one, quick thrust.

She cries out, widening her thighs for me. She's so fucking perfect.

I drop my eyes, watching where I sink into her body, my shaft covered in her.

"You take me so well, baby," I rasp, "Look at us together."

"Please don't stop," she begs.

"So pretty when you beg for my cock, kitten. Your body is made for me, isn't it?"

"Yes," she gasps when I shift, allowing the head of me to brush up against that sensitive little sweet spot inside as I pull out almost all the way and thrust back in several times. She only gets wetter, the slide of our bodies sounding erotic and messy.

"Fuccckkkk," I groan, "Eyes on me, kitten."

Dark eyes latch onto mine as my hips continue to work. "Come for me," I demand, "Let me feel you."

Her brows lower as I thrust harder and drop my hand to her clit, giving her that stimulation I know she needs. She jerks under me, a gasp leaving her but like the good girl she is, she keeps her eyes open, and I get to watch as she shatters for me. Her pussy spasms around my cock, squeezing me so damn tight and I snap. My teeth grind as I come, head dropping to watch as I fill her up, pumping my hips to get every last drop of pleasure.

Gently, I pull out of her, pressing a kiss to her forehead before I roll off. She remains lax on the bed, watching me move with just flicks of her eyes. I head into the bathroom and quickly clean up, ready to get a warm washcloth to help her but she's followed me in and turns on the shower. She strips out of her clothes, the crotch of her shorts soaked with us, but my eyes are focused on the drip of come currently running down the inside of her thigh.

She doesn't appear to notice me looking, not when she spins, giving me a view of her perfect ass before she climbs into the shower.

Fuck me. She's going to kill me.

Shaking my head to try and clear it, I leave her to shower and crouch, opening the cupboard beneath the sink in search of the missing laces for my shoes.

It's while I am rummaging through the clutter that I spot the red bottle hidden at the back. Pulling it out I stare in confusion before I stand and turn to Olivia.

"Olivia," I call loud enough for her to hear me over the water. She pauses and pops her head out the door, water dripping down her face.

"Why the fuck is there ketchup in our bathroom?"

A beautiful burst of laughter erupts from her, and she continues to laugh and not answer me as she resumes her shower. Shaking my head, I put the ketchup down and locate my laces, leaving her in peace to lace up my sneakers.

"Olivia!" Louis greets her with a big grin, putting a huge plate of food in front of her. "You didn't eat last night!"

"Sorry, Louis," She smiles at him gratefully, taking her seat next to me. "This looks great!"

"How do you feel?" He asks her.

I leave them to their conversation as I read the paper

and drink my coffee. We got no information from Connor last night and my last hope was hanging on Dean hacking the guy's phone. We have two, from both the guys that attacked Olivia, but they're under lock with some incredibly tough tech to get through which tells me they might have the information I need to locate exactly who it was that targeted my wife.

I need that damn evidence.

Putting down the paper, I pull out my cell, leaving the room to dial Dean.

It's not even been twenty-four hours, so I doubted he'd have anything.

"Malakai," He answers on the third ring.

"Anything?"

He sighs, "The encryption is strong," He explains, "It has several layers that take time to get through."

"What do you need?"

"Honestly?"

"Yes, Dean," I grumble.

"I need a whole fucking team. Know anyone?"

"Not that I trust," I admit. With the council riddled with traitors, I don't know how far the betrayal goes. How many are corrupted?

"Exactly," Dean says, "It could take days, Malakai, if not weeks."

"We do not have weeks, Dean." I glance back to Olivia, her shoulders shaking with laughter at something Louis just said. "We barely have days."

"We will keep her safe, Kai," he says as if reading my

thoughts.

"I'll kill them all if I have to," I warn him, "But if I can avoid a mess, I will."

"Just leave it with me," He sighs, "I'll get in. We will get the information we need."

"We better. For everyone's sake."

50
Olivia

It's been a week since the attack.

My bruises and cuts are healing, the aches and pains almost non-existent now. The evidence of what happened is fading but my nightmares remain.

Arms band around me, my skin slick with sweat, hair stuck to my forehead and heart still pounding inside my chest, so hard I can feel it thumping.

Malakai's hand rests above it as he uses his other arm to bring me in closer. "Shh," He soothes, voice roughened with sleep, "I've got you."

I let my hand curl around his arm, letting the warmth of him seep into my skin and the feel of him bring me back to earth.

"You're safe, Olivia." He whispers, more alert now. I turn, knowing his face is right next to mine, making our noses brush.

"I'm sorry for waking you."

"Never apologize for needing me," he rasps.

I can't even correct him. I do need him.

"Does it go away?" I ask.

"I don't know," He admits, tightening his arms.

During the day it's easy. I'm so busy I don't have time to think about it. I've taken over the event planning at the hotel full time, and between that and the general running has kept me focused. In the evenings, I'm wrapped up in Malakai or spending time with Willow or the guys, but it's in my dreams, when I'm most vulnerable, I'm back in that hallway.

True to his word, Malakai assigned me a bodyguard who follows me *everywhere*. Including to the bathroom though he waits outside. It had shocked me when he first followed me there thinking he was actually going to come inside, but he'd laughed at my horror and stationed himself against the opposite wall.

The only time he isn't with me is when I am with Malakai. There's been a few days when Malakai hasn't been here and I'd thought I'd be alone, but my bodyguard turned up not five minutes after Malakai had left.

His name is Carl, an ex-veteran in his late forties who is, quite honestly, terrifying to look at. He's nice enough though, a little quiet but I hadn't expected much conversation from him.

It almost felt silly to have him, to have to explain to people who he was, especially since nothing at all has happened since that night at the event. There hasn't even been a sniff of danger.

I'd said all this to Malakai, but he'd refused to let him go. How long will I need a bodyguard?

What even is the threat?

Malakai has his secrets locked up tight, I know they have something to do with the long evenings he spends up in the meeting room. He tells me to stay away, and I do, but I see the men coming in, so many of them, all suited, most older with a few younger ones around Malakai's age dotted within.

Were they all part of the organization Malakai owns? The one where he controls hired killers and makes a profit from people dying? How deep do his crimes go? Just how *evil* is the man currently holding me to shelter me from my nightmares?

He killed two men for me.

Have there been more I don't know about? My thoughts wander to Bradley, my ex, and his sudden death after I told Malakai about him. Surely, it's coincidence, right? It was a tragic accident; he fell off a damn cliff for goodness sake. Malakai didn't have anything to do with it, right!?

Why isn't that terrifying me like my almost abduction is?

"I can hear you thinking, Olivia." He grumbles.

"Oh, stop it, no you can't."

"Wanna bet?" He shifts onto his back, pulling me with him so I'm now laying across his firm, warm chest. His heart beats steadily beneath my ear, his fingers running up and down my naked spine. It's something he does a lot, touches me this way with light moves, like a feather on my skin.

"Don't be ridiculous, Malakai," I chide softly.

He chuckles, the sound of it rumbling and vibrating beneath my ear, further chasing away the lingering fear left behind by the nightmare.

"You grind your teeth when you're thinking too hard," he says softly.

"Sorry, what?" I try to move off him so I can see his face, but he holds me down.

"I didn't think much of it at first," He says, "But whenever you're thinking really hard about anything, you grind your teeth."

"I do not."

"You do, kitten." His voice is light, full of amusement. "So, what are you thinking about?"

I swallow, "Did you kill Bradley?"

I feel his body stiffen beneath mine and my eyes go wide, all the confirmation I need. I start to wiggle and squirm to get off him, not in fear but so I can process the information.

He does not let me go. "Olivia."

"You killed him!?"

"Yes."

"Oh my god." I keep fighting but I know it's no use. Malakai isn't the type of man to let go. Ever. "They said he fell off a cliff!"

"Technically, he did," Malakai says, loosening his arms just a touch so I can push up and look down on him. There's a dim glow in the room, enough for me to make out some features but mostly, he's covered in shadow. "He just had a little help with the fall."

"You pushed him." I accuse.

"*I* didn't."

Playing with Fire

My eyes narrow even though he can't see it, "You hired someone to push him."

"Yes."

"Who?" I ask, needing to know everything but also wanting to know nothing at all. I shouldn't have asked. His death doesn't affect me in any way, I wasn't and am not sad about it, the guy was a prick but still... he died because of me.

"Is that important?" He counters.

"Yes," I breathe, "I need to know."

"Sebastian and Killian were hired to do the job, Dean helped." He sighs, "I requested it to look like an accident, so no one asked questions."

"Why would you do that?"

"Because he hurt you," He answers immediately, the promise and conviction in his tone stealing my breath.

"You can't kill everyone that hurts me in some way, Malakai!"

"I can and I will."

He suddenly flips us until his very naked body is pressing mine back into the mattress.

"You do not understand, Olivia. There are no lengths I will not go to."

"You're crazy," I breathe.

"No, you're just mine."

His mouth crashes against mine with fervor, it stuns me enough that I don't fight. And then I'm kissing him back with as much demand since he's been treating me like a fragile little doll all week.

But this? Now?

He's acting like a man who's been starved and I'm his first meal.

Hands grip and bruise where they hold, rough and possessive as he grinds his hard cock against my pussy, teasing me. It would be so easy for him to just sink inside, to take what he so clearly wants right now but he doesn't.

"My twenty-four hours is starting now." He growls into my mouth.

"What?" I push him away a little, trying to ignore the way his dick is pressing against my throbbing clit, "No, I have things to do!"

"Tough shit, kitten," he nips my lip, "The prize was a twenty-four-hour period of my choosing, to be taken when I want it. I want it now."

"Right now!?" I gasp.

"Right now. The next twenty-four hours belong to me, Olivia." He starts to move down my body, kissing and sucking my flesh, "And I intend on starting them by eating your cunt until you beg me to stop."

I cry out as his mouth latches onto my pussy, sucking and licking against my clit until I can feel myself dripping and my knees start to shake. His fingers join his torture, sinking into me as he flicks his tongue on that sensitive bud until my head throws back and I cry out, my orgasm shattering through me so unexpectedly, I can't help but scream.

The intensity continues, my muscles contract as he keeps going, keeps working until the pleasure almost becomes painful.

"Malakai!" I cry his name, fingers tugging on his hair.

He only intensifies his ministrations, fucking me harder and faster with his fingers, moving his mouth messily over me and that one orgasm rolls into two.

"Oh fuck!" I scream.

My legs tighten around his head but still, he does not stop.

And that promise of eating me until I beg him to stop becomes a little bit more real.

51

Malakai

My fingers brush over the several dresses lined up on Olivia's side of the closet. I pull out three summer dresses, a blue number with a deep plunge and pretty floral pattern, a yellow that I think will look incredible against her skin, and a more formal one for the evening. I add in a couple pairs of shorts and some tops too, just in case. She doesn't need this much but I don't know exactly what she'll want to wear.

She's still sleeping, leaving me to do this in secret. I fold it all and place them into the case I have open on the bench inside the closet. Next, I pick her some shoes and underwear, finding a few lacy lingerie pieces inside, near her bikinis, which I also pack.

I'm quietly thankful she has all her makeup in a bag because fuck if I know what I'd need to pack and shove that inside, forgoing toiletries since I've already taken a picture of every bottle, lotion, spray and cream she owns and sent it to the staff at the house to procure.

I pack a couple sweaters before I pack my own belongings, zipping up the bag to place by the door. Then I grab a shower, leaving her to sleep for a little longer.

My twenty-four hours started two hours ago, and she's only been asleep thirty minutes. She can sleep a little bit on the plane, but I plan on using every minute, down to the last second of this time with her.

Perhaps I shouldn't have been so impulsive since I'm going to lose time on the flight but it's a private plane. I can do just as much to her up in the air as I can down on the ground.

Showered and dressed, I cross the room to where she still sleeps and gently shake her awake.

She grunts and rolls away, "For every minute I wait for you, I'm adding it to the twenty-four hours." I tell her.

She grumbles something that sounds an awful lot like *fuck you* and snuggles deeper.

"Wake up, kitten or I'll fuck you awake."

Now that I've said it, the idea is appealing.

But she flops onto her back and scowls at me, "I only just went back to sleep!"

I check my watch, "It's seven a.m."

"Exactly!"

"Shower, get dressed and meet me downstairs in thirty minutes." I start to walk away, bending to pluck up the case from the floor, "I'm serious about the time, I will be adding thirty minutes onto my time."

I look back to find her sitting on the edge of the bed, naked back to me, "Control freak." She grumbles.

"Thirty minutes, Olivia." I remind.

She flips me the middle finger and I leave the room,

chuckling.

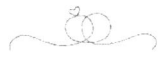

I flip my wrist and check the time on my watch. Seven Forty-Two.

"That's an additional hour for me." I grin.

Twenty-two hours left.

"Forty-two minutes." She snaps back. Twenty-one hours and forty-two minutes then, if she wants to be pedantic.

My eyes lick down her. She's in a pair of blue jeans and a sweater with knee-high boots. She'll be too warm in that when we get there but for now it's fine, she can change on the plane.

"Dennis is waiting," I get up from the chair I was waiting in and start walking to the door.

"I haven't even had coffee!"

"We'll get coffee on the way."

She jogs after me, her shoes squeaking on the floor, "Where are we going!?" She demands, "Why do you have a suitcase!?"

"No questions, Olivia." I guide her out the door and into the cold with a palm against her back. Dennis opens the back door for her, and she slides in, me following behind after he takes the case to place in the trunk.

"Where are we going?" she asks again, chewing her lip nervously.

"Just trust me, kitten," I bring my thumb to her lip, popping it out from her teeth.

Her wide eyes search mine before her shoulders lighten and she nods softly. My chest swells that she gives me it, my heart doing this weird little gallop in my chest that has my free hand moving to rub against my sternum like something is wrong.

She tracks the movement, frowning before she averts her eyes and watches out the window.

"Why are we getting on a plane!?" Olivia half gasps, half screeches.

"Because we're going on a trip."

"What!? I can't just leave."

I stare at her. She opens and closes her mouth a few times but gives up the fight, stomping away across the tarmac to where the private plane waits.

One of the flight staff welcomes her on board and she gives a half-hearted response, her nerves getting the better of her.

I place our bag in the storage and take a seat next to her on one of the plush couches.

"You're mine right now, Olivia." I remind her, "To do whatever I want with."

"I didn't know that included getting on a plane!"

"We have six hours to kill," I lean back, "I'll allow you some rest for a couple of them."

"Ass," she snaps, and I grin, knowing that would get at

her. "You're not going to tell me where we are going?"

"Not yet." I say, "Just trust me." I say for the second time in the past hour.

And whether she wants to or not, she does.

52

Olivia

"Barbados!?" I gasp.

"Yes," Malakai grins at me, "Now get changed."

I stare down at all the clothes he packed for me, "How warm is it?"

He pulls out his phone and checks before he answers, "Eighty-two."

A bubble of excitement works through me. Heat. Sun. Time away with him.

Granted, a trip away was the last thing on my mind but now we're an hour out, I'm starting to realize I might just need it.

Despite his little taunt of only allowing me a couple of hours sleep, I fell asleep an hour in and slept for four hours. There's now only an hour before we land.

Grabbing my Levi shorts and a tank, I skip toward the oversized bathroom. This plane is all luxury. There's a shower in the bathroom, a bed at the back and a fully stocked bar and fridge.

The chairs are made of the softest material, which had made it so easy to drift off even though I had no intention of sleeping.

"Not in there," Malakai startles me when he pushes the bathroom door closed and guides me further back, toward the bedroom with the full-sized bed inside.

He clicks the door closed and sits on the bed, leaning back against the headboard.

"Strip, Olivia." He purrs.

I'm starting to regret not giving him any rules for this twenty-four-hour claiming of his.

Hooking my fingers beneath the hem of my sweater, I pull it off and then drop my hands to the button on my jeans. I kick off the boots before I slide them down my legs, leaving me in my bra and panties.

His eyes devour me like it's the first time he's getting to look.

But that's how he always looks, with unabashed desire and appreciation.

"Such a good girl when you're not being a little brat," He praises, "Come here."

Swallowing, I round the bed and place my knee to the soft mattress, climbing on but he grabs me quickly, pulling me onto his lap so I'm straddling him.

His hands go to the cups of the bra, tugging until they're away from my breasts, sitting beneath them so they're pushed up. His fingers tease over my nipples, eyes on where he touches me.

"I fear I'll never get enough," He whispers, as if speaking more to himself than he is to me. My heart thumps wildly, warmth blooming that I could disguise as desire, but I'd be lying.

I was no longer just falling in love with Malakai.

I *am* in love with him.

Every jagged, sharp edge of him.

"Kai," The shortened version of his name, the version I know he loves to hear, stutters from my lips. A rumble that can only be described as a growl of approval sounds from his throat as he squeezes more forcefully on my breasts, not painfully but it's enough to feel, to know what I do to him. How much control he lets go of when he is with me.

His cock, hard beneath me, twitches behind the constraints of his pants, my center pressed against it, my legs spread as wide as they'll go over his hips. I rock gently over it, applying just a little bit of friction. It won't take much, I'm wound so tight already, a wet, needy mess for him. I should be unnerved by the control he has on my body, how I yield to him without much fight but I'm not.

It's like my very soul feels safe with him. Like it inherently knows this man, touching and caressing and feeling me, would never do a single thing to bring me harm. I want walls to protect myself, but he brought them down, crumbling them with his dominance with half a thought.

Malakai just *is*.

He's a king among men, an apex predator – *the* predator – and despite the morally grey lines he dances upon and the evil he controls, he's someone I am willing to worship. For a taste.

"You don't come unless I tell you to," He groans out, hands now at my hips, aiding the grind of them over the solid length of him. Fuck, I want it inside of me. I want the deep, powerful thrusts, the glide as he pulls almost all the way out only to slam right back in, burying so deep I feel him everywhere and still yearn for more.

I nod mutely but I know I won't obey. He makes me so hot, so highly strung I wouldn't be able to deny myself even if I tried.

"I mean it, Olivia," There's a hint of steel to his tone, a commanding bite that I have no doubt he uses in every aspect of his life to get what he wants. He has his schemes and his manipulations, the hidden forces that back him, but it's the control bred into him, the leadership, the threat, that makes people listen.

And as much as I could worship him, get on my knees for him, I won't allow him to control me. And I think he likes that. I think he likes the defiance, the rebellious streak, and tests I throw at his patience.

"Mm," I moan, as he lifts his hips a little from the bed, adding just a touch of pressure. If I move just right, slip a little further down…

I'm suddenly flipped, landing with a slight bounce atop the mattress before his whole body is pressing over mine.

"You were close," He breathes, dropping his face to my neck where his tongue then takes a long, slow lick over the fluttering pulse point.

I nod, unable to deny it.

"I told you no," He rasps as he moves down my body, teeth grazing over my collar bone that sends a delicious zap through me.

"I don't take kindly to the word no," my words end on a moan as his lips latch around a sensitive nipple, drawing it into his mouth, his tongue flicking against the very tip of it.

I feel his chuckle against me, the warmth of his breath as it pushes out of him with the sound. "I know you don't," He presses a tender kiss to the mound of my breast, "So I'm going to teach you it."

Alarm races through me but the warning is squashed as he moves down my body, kissing and nipping all the way down to the band of my panties. He presses his forehead to the soft swell of my lower abdomen, his breath just a whisper against that intimate part of me. Hands glide up the insides of my thighs, parting them further and then his breath his blowing against the wetness beneath my panties, his nose running up the seam of me. The material grates but it also feels insanely good.

"You're so wet, Olivia," He praises, looking up at me from between my legs, the wicked, erotic dance in his eyes coiling something hot and tight in my stomach. "All for me." The tip of his finger slips in at the edge, a whisper against me but enough to have my hips bucking.

God if I don't come in the next two fucking minutes…

He pulls away from me, standing as his hands go to the button on his pants. He strips out of his shirt, letting it drop to the floor before he kicks off the trousers and boxers. I watch with a lust filled fog filling my vision.

The impressive sight of him makes my pussy clench with need.

He pumps his shaft as he surveys me, and a wicked smile curves his mouth. "Turn on the bed, Olivia, dangle your head off the edge."

Confused with the order but willing to do just about anything to sate this need, I obey, shifting until I'm laying sideways across the bed, head leaning against the edge. He steps behind my head, hand going to my mouth. He pushes his thumb inside, eyes heating as he watches me draw it into my mouth, sucking on it.

"What a good girl you are, Olivia." His thumb pops from my lips but as he pulls away, he draws down my bottom lip, opening my mouth, "Come a little closer," He commands, "Dangle your head off fully."

I shift using my feet until I'm upside down, moving my eyes so I can still see him.

"Very good," He commends as he drops my lip and moves his hand to his cock, taking it into his fist before he guides the head of it to my lips.

I open without him asking, my tongue licking up the bead of salty precum from the very tip of him. His eyes turn hooded as he presses forward, my lips parting wider to fit.

"I'm going to fuck your throat," He tells me, gliding his cock in a little before pulling out, "You're going to take it, Olivia. All of it."

I nod.

"Don't touch yourself."

I feel my eyes widen a little at his command. I am so fucking desperate.

But I don't have time to contemplate or argue, he shoves his cock into my mouth, all the way until I feel the head of him at the back of my throat. And then he's fucking my mouth, thrusting in deep. I can barely breathe, water wells in my eyes, dripping from the corners and down my temples but fuck, more wetness heats me from between my legs, I feel it, my pussy throbbing. I ache.

He groans, his own hand wrapping around his throat as he tilts his face to the ceiling, the sound and the sight only adding to the burning desire within me. My toes curl against the urge to sate this need, to end this pain but when one of my hands slides down my stomach, it's suddenly captured. His hips don't stop, not even when he grabs my other hand, bringing up my arms to stop me from touching.

"Swallow," He grinds out before his thrusts turn jerky and he spills himself into my mouth, his dick so far in, it hits my throat. I swallow awkwardly, considering the angle and he stills, cock remaining there as he breathes.

Slowly he slides out and then he crouches, taking the back of my head into his palms as he gently lifts it from the position. He holds the weight as he stares into my face, satisfied as his eyes flick to my mouth, at the pearl of come I hadn't managed to get down my throat seeping from the corner of my mouth.

"Dirty girl couldn't listen to one command," Shifting the weight to one hand, he slides his thumb up, capturing that bead. He brings it to my mouth and my lips wrap around it. "For that, pretty girl, you're going to have to earn your next orgasm."

53

Olivia

He cleans up my face, wiping away the tears and the saliva before he helps me to stand. I'm still throbbing, still wet, the ache so potent between my legs I could cry. He helps me into the shorts, pushes my bra back into place and pulls my tee over my head, dressing me.

I'm in some dazed, confused state, unsure I heard him correct or catching up to the fact that he is, in fact, denying me an orgasm when he knows how tightly strung I am.

My body physically reacts to every touch, every brush of his fingers, but even when he smooths hands down my hair, tucking an errant strand behind my ear and then strolls out of the bedroom with the swagger of a man who had just been fully satisfied, I still stand there, *confused.*

It's only when the captain's voice comes over the speakers, announcing our imminent descent that I snap out of the stupor. My knees feel like damn jelly as I

Playing with Fire

walk out of the cabin, straight to where Malakai rests in a chair, a fresh glass of whiskey in his hand. His eyes flick to me and his brow quirks in challenge.

"Are you serious right now?" I feel the rasp in my voice as it scratches against my throat.

"Deadly. Sit down."

I glower at him and choose to sit in the seat over from him, crossing my arms.

"Here." He commands.

"I am not a dog." I snap at him.

"I still have," he checks his watch, "Fifteen hours left."

"You're taking this time watching very seriously," I note.

"I get you, without restraint, I'm using every second of it."

I roll my eyes. I never should have made that fucking bet, but my damn pride won't let me call this quits. Not even sure he'd allow a bow out anyway.

Grumbling and pissed at my denied pleasure, I get up, purposely knocking into him so whiskey splashes over the rim of his glass, getting little amber droplets onto his white shirt and throw myself into the seat next to him. But he just chuckles, placing his whiskey down as he leans over me.

He straps me in with the belt, tightening it before his lips whisper over my jaw, to my ear, "There's my little brat."

"Fuck you," I breathe.

"Soon, baby," He vows. "Soon."

How soon is *soon*?

Now? I wonder as we sit in this expensive black Mercedes cruising through a palm lined street, huge villas on one side, the ocean, a glimmering beautiful sight on the other.

I would give up the view, the awe in which I'd gasped at it when I first saw it if I could climb into his lap right now to end this throb between my legs.

"We're here," Malakai's voice is a deep timbre, a purr calling to some deep primal part of me he had stirred to life back on that damn plane. I can only think about sex.

Prick.

I turn my attention to the front, watching as we pull through a set of open gates and onto a small round courtyard, big enough to fit two cars at a push, that sits in front of a modern, white villa with a black tiled roof and large, floor to ceiling windows to let in as much natural light as possible. Palms sway in a gentle breeze that flows in from the ocean across the way, white sand beckoning, the surf gently lapping on the shore barely a hundred feet from where the car stops.

Forgetting the ache, I move my hand to the handle but find it locked. I roll my eyes, waiting for the driver to get out to come and open it for me.

"Such impatience," Malakai tuts but there's a lilt of amusement.

I slide my eyes to him, noting how his shoulders aren't as tense, how the lines in his face, deepened because of the constant scowl are smoothed out. He appears younger.

He didn't change on the plane and still wears the same suit he traveled in, but if the heat bothers him, he doesn't show it. I felt it the moment we got off the plane, it hit me right in the face and after the last several months of icy cold, it was a shock to the system, and I've been sweating ever since.

The door opens and, despite the heat, I eagerly get out, feet on instinct heading to the gate we just pulled through.

A hand gently circles my wrist, "Later," Malakai softens, "I'll take you down to the beach later. I'd like to show you the house."

I nod, turning with him as I take in the building before me. Well looked after with manicured lawns and pruned hedges and trees. It's much smaller than the estate back home, much more modern too. He opens the front door, gesturing for me to enter before him and I'm struck stupid by how different it is to Silver Lake Estate.

"Is this place yours?"

"Yes." The door clicks closed behind him.

The entire downstairs is open space, to the left is a den, a huge sectional sofa sits facing windows that look out onto the ocean, a large TV on the wall with abstract art in blues and greys and soft yellows framing it. Greenery has been scattered throughout, giving color to the otherwise white décor. But while everything is light and white, it's not sterile. Little blooms of color break it all up, like the plants and the art, bright orange cushions set up like a little reading nook in front of some shelves in the corner. A large kitchen is directly opposite the living room, white cabinets and grey countertops, the appliances matching with an oak dining table set up in front of the windows. Beyond that, there's another smaller couch and coffee table, a bar stocked completely and a set of double doors that lead out onto a terrace. An infinity pool glimmers as the sunlight bounces off the top of the water and the garden beyond is set in tiers. I can't see it all from here, but I can see a sun deck, a jacuzzi and a hammock that swings between two palms.

"This way," Malakai guides me toward those doors, keeping quiet since it's fairly obvious what is what without pointing it out. We stop at a door I hadn't noticed, and he opens it to reveal a large bathroom, including a walk-in shower and clawfoot tub but we don't linger, and we don't go outside. He guides me to the wide staircase, the railings made of glass and silently we walk up.

There are two bedrooms, the master suite that looks out onto the sea with an ensuite and a smaller one across the way which only has a bed and desk in it, the space clearly used the least.

"This is modest for you," I point out, unable to stop comparing it to the estate.

He quirks his mouth into a smile as he hauls our case onto the bed, unzipping it.

"If I had a choice," He starts to unpack everything inside, folding it neatly into piles onto the sheets. I don't comment on the amount of clothes he's packed for me even though he's brought enough for a week. "I would not have chosen Silver Lake as a home base. But it has been in my family for generations, and I have a strange fondness for the place."

"It's your family home," I cross to him to help with unpacking, "It's not strange to be fond of it. It's like the hotel, I used to hate going as a child. All the gold and red, I just didn't like it but now as an adult, I walk through the doors, and it feels a little bit like home there. Even if I loathe the color scheme."

"Why not change it?" He asks. "It is your hotel now."

"I've thought about it," I admit, "But it feels like erasing parts of my history. My family's history."

Something uneasy stirs in my gut as I remember the man before me had a part in erasing some of that history. My father died because of his actions.

I roll my shoulders, trying to shift the tension that's suddenly formed.

And as if he can sense where my thoughts have gone, he steps closer, "I had a hand in your fathers' death."

My nostrils flare as tears sting my eyes.

"Apologies don't change what's happened." I say, "my father died because of whatever game you were playing at the time, I know you didn't pull the trigger but every event after that was orchestrated by you."

Sorrow twists his face, there one minute, gone the next, "I don't make decisions lightly." His voice holds no emotion, it's flat and steady, "The choices I make are to protect my organization and everyone within it. It is to ensure my legacy."

I scoff, "The choices you make kill people."

"Let's not pretend your father was innocent here," Malakai glares at me, "He hired one of my best killers to take me out."

My sister's new boyfriend he means.

"So, you got there first."

"His life or mine, I chose mine." He says it so simply, so easily.

"Have you never thought about anyone but yourself?" I snap, "About the lives your choices effect?"

"No."

I shouldn't have been surprised by the answer, I really shouldn't have, but that's sadness weighing down my chest. I am in love with a monster. Could he ever love me back?

His selfish thinking suggests not, but what about the man I've seen beneath this cold exterior I'm seeing right now. That man isn't selfish.

That man saved me when I was attacked. Supported me when I chose to defend myself. Sat with me in a hospital and never left.

"I think that's a lie." I pick up my pile of clothes and head to the drawers, "I think you pretend not to care but you do. I just don't understand why you hide it."

"I don't hide from you." I hear his whisper though I'm not sure he intended for me to.

I don't answer him and despite all the evil things he has done, a little bit of light chases away that heavy sorrow in my chest. If I can love a man who did all those atrocious things, see past it, then I know there's more to him than he leads people to believe.

"I want to swim," I declare loudly, changing the subject completely.

Playing with Fire

I turn to find him already dangling my bright yellow bikini from his fingers. There's tension back in his shoulders, a small frown creasing his brow. I walk toward him, swallow my apprehension, trusting my instinct as I reach up and smooth out that little line between his brows. He relaxes at my touch, eyes closing for a moment before his blue eyes open and pulse when he looks at me.

"Are you going to ask my permission, kitten?" he purrs, holding the control.

Fuel, meet fire.

"May I go swimming?" I flutter my lashes, looking up at him as I widen my eyes innocently.

"Fuck me," He groans, dropping the bikini into my waiting hands.

I don't bother going for privacy to change, choosing to strip right there and then. I'm naked in a matter of seconds, reaching for the bikini.

"*Fuck me.*" He groans for a second time and storms from the room.

54
Malakai

Olivia swims elegantly toward the edge of the pool where I wait with a cocktail, the bright pink concoction gently fizzing in my hand.

"Is that for me?" She asks.

That bright yellow bikini is doing things to my brain, I swear.

"Yes." I answer. I'm still tense from that earlier conversation in the bedroom. Quite frankly, I'm not sure how she can bear to touch me after everything I did to her family. When I manipulated her into this marriage, I didn't worry about such things but now…

Will it cost me in the end?

Or will it be one of the many other evils I've committed?

Water sluices down her delicate frame as she uses the edge of the pool to pull herself from the water, sitting herself so her feet are still submerged. She reaches for the cocktail as I hand it down to her.

I changed myself into a pair of navy swim trunks but hadn't gotten in, too content in watching her glide through the water like some tempting little siren.

I don't tell her I scoured the cocktail recipe books stashed at the bar, that's never been touched before now, to make her this drink, flipped through the pages until I found one I thought she might like, but then realized there isn't enough I know about her.

I want to know it all.

So, I picked the one I thought she'd like the most, and hoped I was right.

She takes a sip from the straw and makes a sound that shoots straight to my cock.

"This is delicious!" She takes another hearty sip, "Did you make this?"

"Easy," I warn her, "That has a lot of alcohol in it."

Her eyes light up, the sorrow and guilt that was written on her face barely an hour ago completely gone, or hidden, I didn't know which.

"Where's yours?" she asks, placing the drink down onto the tile next to the pool and leans back onto her palms, tipping her head back to look at me.

I flick my eyes down her body, the water clings to her skin, the wet material of her swimsuit molding to her shape. My damn mouth waters. She has a hold on me, a hold so tight I'd crawl across burning coal for her.

"I'll have one later." I tamp down the urge to spread her out on the deck by stepping to the side and diving into the water.

I take a few seconds to come back up, opening my eyes beneath the water to see her still sitting on the edge, staring down at me. I swim toward her, pushing up off the bottom to come up right between her legs. My hands curl around her ankles as I bring my head above water, flicking hair out my face. Water droplets stick to my lashes, running down over my face and lips. I grin at her as one of her brows jumps up, a smile pulling on her lips.

"What's that smile for?"

She cocks her head, "Not sure I've ever seen you..." twisting her lips side to side as she thinks of her answer before she continues, "Have fun, or even relax."

"I have fun."

"Do you?"

"I play poker."

"Oh," she rolls her eyes, "So much fun."

"Did you just roll your eyes at me?"

"Malakai!" She screams before I haul her into the water. She goes under and comes up spluttering, her glare one for the history books. If looks could kill, she would have killed me time and again.

I chuckle when she splashes me but quickly grip her wrists before she can swim away. I can touch the bottom here, but she can't, so I bring her close, gripping her beneath her ass to wrap her legs around my hips. I wade further into the deep, deep enough the water now comes to my shoulders, but it would completely cover her if she were to stand.

The sun warms her face, showcasing the lighter flecks of gold hidden in the depths of the brown of her eyes. I run the tip of my nose down the bridge of hers before I capture her lips with my own.

I only have twelve hours left where she is completely mine, it's about time I start using them wisely. We are here, we are alone, and she is all mine to do with whatever I like. The possibilities are endless but right here is a good start.

She opens for me, sweeping her tongue into my mouth, the taste of that fruity cocktail on her tongue, so sweet and mixed with the taste of her, could be a dangerous drug. I rumble into her mouth, my cock hardening at the feel of her pussy pressed to my lower abdomen, grinding softly.

But again, she won't be coming for me just yet. I have a few more hours I want to wind her up for.

She trembles in my arms, I can feel the speed of her heart thumping against my chest, her breathy little moans landing on my tongue.

I can only imagine how pent up she is already after the plane, a little caressing, a slide of my fingers where she's desperate for me most, will likely detonate her. It just makes me harder, my cock aching like I didn't come down her throat only a few hours ago.

But I am punishing her with this denial as much as I am punishing myself. I won't bury my cock in her until I am ready for her to come, and I doubt she'll be willing to get me there if I don't get her there first, she made that mistake once, Olivia isn't the type of woman to make it twice.

So even though the tip of my cock leaks, my balls pulsing, I will deny us both because when it happens in just a few hours' time, when I strip her down and lick every inch of her, she'll shatter into thousands of pieces for me, over and over again.

But for now, I let her work herself up because the reward will be that much sweeter. I revel in the way she uses my body to find pleasure for herself, how her moans taste in my mouth, how the water feels as it ripples around us both. But when she is right there, right where I want her to be, I still her against me, clamping my arms tight so she's stuck and can't move.

"Ah, ah, kitten," I purr, licking across that kiss swollen bottom lip, "Not yet."

"Malakai," She cries softly.

"Not yet," I whisper, "Wait, baby. A little patience."

I gently unwrap her legs from my waist, holding her so she doesn't dip beneath the water, "We're going to take a walk."

"Now?"

"Yes, now," I start to swim for the edge of the pool, feeling and hearing her follow, far rougher than she was swimming earlier, like a little tantrum. I'd expect nothing less from her. I hoist myself from the water, turning so I'm sat at the edge and wait for her to come to me. She does which pulls up my mouth in a satisfied smile, then I grab her, hauling her out with me. I pull her over me, so her breasts are squashed against my chest, the length of her covering me and I capture her mouth one last time before I send her off with a quick slap against her ass.

To save temptation, I grab a shower in the downstairs bathroom while she uses the one in the ensuite and get changed, waiting downstairs for her to arrive.

I almost choke on my own tongue when she does.

I don't know what it is about us being here, but something feels different. Like there is no static or interference.

She beams at me when she hits the bottom step, dressed in the cobalt blue dress I had packed, the one with the deep plunge neckline and delicate floral pattern. It swishes around her knees, loose from the hips down but tight everywhere else, it sticks to her curves like a second skin, leaving nothing for my imagination. Her breasts have been pushed together, giving them a tempting swell that makes my fingers and mouth itch for a feel, for a taste.

Her hair, left down and flowing, is nothing like it is back home. There are glorious waves to it, volume and shine and her face is clear of makeup, not that that mattered. Either way, she is gorgeous, whether her dark eyes are framed by smokey shadow or left clear and bright. There are freckles that dot her nose from an afternoon in the sun, a slight burn that reddens her cheeks.

"Hi," she chirps cheerily.

"Hi," it comes out as a rasp.

I need to touch her so the moment she is in reach, I grasp her hand. Shock passes her expression when my fingers wrap around her delicate ones, my hand enveloping hers. Such an intimate move but not one I haven't done before. Perhaps it feels to her like it does for me.

So, I hold her hand as if I can tether her to me, like I can hold her permanently to me in fear that one day she may leave. And despite being the selfish asshole that I am, I know I'd let her go. But with this link, with everything I am, I hold her, I show her without words that I need her like a rope to the earth, grounding me.

It'll only take one sharp knife to cut it. I know that. But I cling because inside, I am terrified.

Olivia demanded I take off my shoes the moment we hit the sand.

She pretended like I hadn't been here before, hadn't felt the sand between my toes or experienced the waves against my skin as I walked where the sea met the earth.

I didn't have the heart to tell her no.

I thought myself heartless. Without a soul.

Until her.

She's unearthed a precious rare gem within me, something I long thought dead. And I want to treasure it, keep it safe.

Olivia walks by my side, her own sandals, hooked by the straps, dangling from her fingers as she takes easy slow steps through the white sand beneath her feet. Her chin is angled toward the sea, where the sun is setting, casting a brilliant pink and orange glow atop the surf that rolls toward the land.

The setting sun kisses her skin, so lovingly lighting her up as if it has waited eons to do so, touching every line of her body with a stroke of pure light that makes me ache from within. I still have her hand in mine, her dainty fingers curled tight like she believes I'd ever let her go.

The sand filters between my toes, grainy and rough and yet soft, a cushion as we walk. The ocean sings the song of its tides, the foamy white edge drawing close but never touching where we walk.

"This is beautiful," Olivia whispers above the roar of the sea.

"It is one of the only places I feel myself," I admit.

"No weight," she comments, "Nothing to drag you down."

I nod though she isn't looking, still staring out at the wonder of the sea. "I've only been to the beach a few times. It wasn't a vacation our family took often but whenever I did, I always found myself near the water. It's like music."

"Music?" I question.

"Yes," She answers, "Can't you hear it?" Her deep brown eyes turn to me expectedly.

I shake my head, hating the disappointment that contorts her face. "Listen." She says.

My breath stalls, shallowing as I obey her command.

I hear the grain of the sand shifting beneath our feet, like sugar emptying into a pot, but more than that, I hear the roar of the ocean, starting out low, an echo that draws closer before it crashes against something solid. It howls as it slams against the shore, hissing as it withdraws to try again, as if in a bloody, endless battle. The sea against the land.

"Music," Olivia repeats, sighing, "It feels endless. Like no matter where we are, the past, the present or the future, that sound will never age."

The ocean. The sea.

She likes the sea.

I tuck away that kernel of information, changing our direction. It isn't dark yet, the sun is still making her descent which has set the waves ablaze, dipping beyond the horizon ready for night to reign, but she still clings on. Giving a lasting impression, a last war cry before she submits to the power of the night.

I can't help but compare the two, the sun and moon, to me and Olivia.

"What is this?" She breathes.

I look toward the intimate table, set for two, placed beneath the clear skies and separate from the packed restaurant further up from the beach.

"This is our first date," I say, full of confidence yet underneath, I don't feel that way at all.

"You did this?" she asks with a breathy laugh.

"Yes, Olivia, for you."

55
Olivia

The waves crash against the sand as the sun sets, dipping beneath the horizon, casting a longing golden glow across the surface of the sea as if saying goodnight.

It takes some time before the night truly reigns, a kernel of daylight clinging to the clouds before wielding to the power of the moon.

A small table has been set up at the edge where the sand meets soil, stone paving cutting it off, a thick line that travels miles both left and right, a clear divide.

A candle flickers within a tall glass vase, a polite server showing us to that very table. A chair is pulled out for me, and I delicately start to lower myself into the chair until…

"Absolutely not." Malakai snaps. "Get your hands away from my wife."

The server jumps back, hands going up as shock crosses his face.

"Malakai!" I scold.

But Malakai doesn't listen, he steps up to me, his hand going to my back, "No one touches you."

"He wasn't touching me." I glare at him.

His eyes plead with me, and I soften a little, "Go on then."

His face breaks out into a smile, beaming and then he grabs the back of my chair, waiting for me to resume lowering into the seat. I'm shaking my head at how ridiculous it is, but I can't help but smile too. When I'm sitting, Malakai takes the chair opposite me.

"Now apologize," I say.

With a frown, Malakai opens his mouth, likely to ask why but I cut him off.

"You snapped for no reason," I explain, "He did nothing wrong. Apologize."

"Olivia." He warns, the rumble of his voice sending goosebumps over my skin.

"The way you treat wait staff says a whole lot about you. They're human too."

"It isn't because he's our server, it's because it's *you*."

"I'm so serious, Malakai."

He huffs out an apology and turns his eyes to the waiter still awkwardly standing to the side. "My apologies for snapping." He says, "But keep your hands away from my wife and we won't have a problem."

My mouth pops open but he just grins smugly at me.

Prick.

"Can I get you started with some drinks?" The server asks nervously, and I note how far away from the table he is and shake my head. This is ridiculous.

We order our drinks, and he hurries off, heading toward the restaurant a few hundred yards away.

"Did you pay them to set this up out here?"

"Yes." Malakai answers, turning his face toward the sea.

"Thank you," I tell him, "This is thoughtful, Malakai."

"I wanted to take you on a date." He repeats.

"A date could have been inside," I laugh.

"But there's people in there. I wanted you alone."

We order our food when the drinks arrive and are quickly left alone again. A string of fairy lights is hanging close to our table, and the candle in the center flickers in the slight ocean breeze. The air is still warm despite the lack of sun, and the dark skies above us turns the water inky.

"How much time is left?" I ask.

He checks his watch, "Seven hours."

The date, as far as dates go, was the best I had ever had. It was normal, we talked and laughed and ate, and now I have his jacket on my shoulders and my shoes dangling from my fingers as we walk down the beach, listening to the sound of the waves lazily lapping against the shore. His hand is strong and firm in mine, his thumb idly stroking over my skin. Goosebumps pimple across my body, the slight wind rolling off the ocean teasing a few strands of my hair.

The villa is up ahead, I can see the golden light spilling out of the many windows, and anticipation rolls through me.

I've been on edge all day, waiting for his electric touch. During our date I was distracted, but now we're alone I know where this night is going to lead. I'm not sure I can handle being denied again.

He opens the doors and steps aside, letting me enter first. I drop my shoes just inside and head straight for the fully stocked bar. Malakai follows casually behind me, and while I fix a couple of drinks, he steps up close to my back, pressing his chest almost against me.

"Thank you," He rasps as he bends and kisses me, sweetly, softly, on my cheek.

My hands shake when I pass him his two fingers of whiskey, having picked up on it being his go to drink.

"I had fun on our date," I tell him honestly, "I've had fun all day actually." Minus the no orgasm shit. It's been wonderful, the heat, the pool, the house and time away. I needed it.

"Yeah?" He grins when I turn to face him, cradling the bowl of my wine glass.

I nod and place my wine down, a plan forming in my mind.

Just because he controls my time right now doesn't mean I can't play with fire a little. "I'm just going to get changed." I tell him. "Be right back."

I spotted the white lingerie he had packed for me earlier while we unpacked, the full set, and even though I didn't plan on putting it on, that's now changed.

Playing with Fire

Malakai is a relatively simple man when it comes to me. I can play him at his own game.

I grab everything I need and dart into the bathroom, stripping out of my dress and underwear before I place the lingerie on my body.

It's from my sister's boutique, a small business she put together some time ago now where she designs and manufactures lingerie. It's stunning, a bright white lace number that leaves nothing to the imagination. It covers everything but with it so sheer, the pink hue of my nipples shows through on the bra, and you can clearly see the small triangle of hair at the apex of my thighs.

But I feel sexy in it. I leave my hair as it is, tumbling like glossy black waves over my shoulders and run my finger beneath my bottom lip, cleaning up the smear of gloss there. Then I grab the robe from the back of the bathroom door and head back down to find Malakai.

He's out on the sun deck, his whiskey in one hand, the other buried in the pocket of his slacks as he looks down onto the lit yard. The ocean roars around us and the lingering warmth presses against my skin.

I pause a moment, running my eyes over him, appreciating the pure masculine form in front of me. He's so effortlessly attractive, with his sharp jaw, dusting of facial hair, and his mop of dark brown hair that almost boyishly falls over his forehead like he's just mused it with his hands.

"Hi," I whisper, stepping out onto the deck.

He turns to me, eyes softening as he takes his hand out of his pocket and opens his arm to me. I go, tucking in tight as it comes around to hold me to him as he continues to look out across the yard.

"What are you looking at?" I ask.

"Nothing," He answers immediately, "Just thinking."

His hands steer me toward the set of patio seating near the house and he pulls me onto the wicker couch. I sink into the cushions, tucking in tight while my heart goes a million miles an hour inside my chest.

I don't know why I'm so nervous. Sex with Malakai is easy. Explosive but easy.

Perhaps I'm just scared of being denied.

He tries to grab me when I move to stand up, not a minute later. Now or never.

"Come here," He frowns, wondering why I've gotten up so soon.

I keep my eyes on his, my brown to his blue as my fingers go to the tie holding the robe closed. I tug the lose knot open, the slightly colder air hitting my naked skin, my nipples reacting to it and peaking beneath the lace.

Malakai lets out a hard breath, his jaw popping as he lets his eyes glide down my body. I shrug the robe off my shoulders, letting it drop to the floor at my feet.

His eyes burn as they look at every inch of me, my chest moving rapidly as I breathe heavily.

"Olivia," His voice is all growl.

My pussy clenches at the sound, my stomach knotting. So damn easy for him, my body is not my own when it comes to Malakai Farrow, it belongs to him.

My husband.

"I ache," I whisper, swallowing.

His eyes bounce to mine and a slow, seductive grin

pulls up his mouth, "Then let me fix that for you, kitten."

56
Malakai

She is the most stunning woman I have ever seen.

But I knew that before I saw her standing before me in white lingerie.

The low lighting out on the deck kisses her skin, highlighting every curve and dip of her and that little lacy number does nothing to hide what is underneath.

Color blooms on her cheeks as I look at every inch of her. There is not enough time to explore it all, not enough minutes for me to get on my knees and worship her.

My cock is hard, my blood humming through me.

She aches. She told me so herself and I'm ready to relieve her of her pain, to make her come for me repeatedly. I want her pussy on my fingers, in my mouth, on my cock. I want to stretch that tight little cunt until she can't fucking walk, until all she can think and breathe is me.

Her eyes drop to the obvious hard on I have, the bulge

at the front of my pants stretching the material around the outline of my cock.

"Spin for me, kitten," I order on a rasp, "Let me see it all."

There isn't a second of hesitancy as she slowly spins, showing me every angle, the curve of her spine and the firm globes of her ass cheeks.

"So pretty, Olivia." I praise, "And you're wearing this just for me."

She gives a small nod, capturing her lip between her teeth while her eyes drop to the glass on the table, still full of the whiskey she poured me.

"Can I have a drink?" She asks.

"Go ahead," I lean back on the couch, watching her hips sway as she closes the short gap between her and the glass. Her long, delicate fingers pluck the glass from the table and then she swirls the whiskey.

"Is this your favorite way to drink your whiskey, Kai?"

My cock jerks.

"Yes."

She nods and then takes a swig, taking at least half of it into her mouth before she drops the whiskey to the table and strides toward me confidently.

I adjust my position as she climbs onto my lap, stretching her legs over my thighs to straddle me and then her fingers are on my jaw, nails biting in just a little. I tip my head back, lids hooded with lust but then she shocks the shit out of me.

She brings her mouth close to mine before her thumb pushes on my bottom lip and forces my mouth to open.

And before I can question it, can take control, she's lining up her mouth to mine and emptying the whiskey onto my tongue.

I swallow every drop down.

"How about now?" She breathes, her tongue darting out to capture a drop caught at the corner of my lips.

My fingers flex on the flesh of her thighs, her body yielding to my grip as a new wave of desire floods my system, making me impossibly harder for her.

"You're like a drug, Olivia," I confess, "I cannot get enough."

"Kiss me, Malakai."

And I oblige, crashing my mouth against hers as I lift a hand to cradle the back of her skull, holding her to me while my tongue plunges between her lips. Nails bite at my scalp as she too holds me to her, her pussy grinding over the length of me.

"Are you wet, kitten?" I pull away from her mouth, letting my teeth nip at her bottom lip.

"Yes," she hisses on a breath, "Please don't make me wait."

"Don't worry, my pretty little wife," I slide my hand from her head over her neck, wrapping it around the delicate column before I give it a gentle squeeze, "I'll take care of you."

My hand trails from her throat over her collar bones, down to her breasts where I take one peaked nipple between my thumb and finger. She gasps when I squeeze, rolling the bud before teasing the pad of my thumb over the very tip.

"So pretty in all this white lace," I praise, "And all fucking mine."

"Malakai, please," she begs again.

"Stand up." I order.

Slowly and with a shake, she stands from my lap, and I lean forward, grasping her behind her knee as I bring one leg up to rest her foot against the pillow of the couch.

I glide a finger down the seam of her above the lace and she lets out a harsh breath, but when I hook a finger at the edge of the panties, pulling it to the side to expose every dripping inch of her, she moans.

"You're so ready for me to fill you up," I rasp, scissoring my fingers through the heat of her, "To stretch you open and fuck you raw."

"P-please."

"Such beautiful manners," I commend before I lean in and run the flat of my tongue over her, tasting that slick arousal.

I hold her against me, my fingers digging into the plump skin on her ass, likely leaving marks but fuck if I don't want to see my brandings on her.

Her fingers claw at my hair, tugging while I continue to lick and suck at her, covering my chin and lips with her come. It's so easy to bring her to the peak, she's wound so tightly already that it only takes me a minute to apply the right attention to the right place before her cunt is pulsing against my face, her moans filling the night around us.

I can't fucking wait to be inside of her.

But my girl is aching. She needs more.

So even when she stops contracting, when her whimpers quieten, I continue, this time inserting two fingers into her pussy, listening to the sweet sound of her moans mixed with the sound of her arousal as I fuck her with my hand.

I've never tasted anything better than Olivia. I eat her cunt like a man starved, worshipping the center of her like I may die if I don't. Messy and raw and primal, I coat my face in her.

"Malakai!" She screams as I bring her once more to the edge, grinning when she comes again, softer this time, quieter.

I give a quick kiss to the sensitive bud when the last of her orgasm shakes her body and look up at her, "Bedroom, Olivia. Now."

"I don't know if I can walk," Her voice shakes, lids hooded with satisfaction.

Not waiting a minute, I stand, hauling her up with me. Her legs wrap around my waist, arms looping around my neck. There's a lot to unpack in the way she is looking down at me, in the way her eyes are soft and relaxed, open to show me every raw and gritty feeling.

I know mine are a mirror.

I carry her through the house, her body locked to mine, taking the stairs slowly until I reach our bedroom. I lower us both to the bed, lining up my body with hers just so I can kiss her. I cradle her face in my hands as I do, melting against her and the feel of her on my body.

"Kai," She breathes my name, her emotion so open, so clear…

Playing with Fire

I feel it too. Feel the intensity of our connection, know the words in my bones before she ever has a chance to say them.

"I know," I whisper, kissing her softly, "I know, Olivia."

Her eyes bounce between mine before I lift off her and begin to strip her down for me, removing the barriers between our bodies and when she is finally bare for me, I strip off myself, leaving us both in just skin. Hands touch and lips taste, a frenzy of the two of us needing it, needing each other until the head of my cock punches at the entrance of her.

I capture the gasp she breathes, sucking it in like it's the oxygen that fills my lungs.

"I –" she breathes into my mouth.

But as much as I crave to hear it from her lips, want to hear the words from someone when no one has ever said it to me, I can't hear it yet. It'll end me. Weaken me.

So instead of letting her finish the three words, I crash my mouth to hers, stealing it. I suck it in, consume it instead, pour my own confession back.

I am in love with my wife.

And it might just be the very thing that kills me.

I glide my cock into her, the thrust smooth and slow, feeling every inch as I fill her up, her body stretching to accommodate mine. Her nails score my back, her head tipping as if what I am doing to her is pure ecstasy. I pull almost all the way out before I thrust back in, quickening the pace a little more with each pump of my hips.

She makes me want to lose control, like with her, there are no strings to hold me back.

"Olivia," I growl her name, "Eyes on me, kitten. Watch me while I fuck you."

Dark lashes flutter open and I adjust, pushing up a little so I can see between our bodies. A fine sheen of sweat lines her skin.

"Arms up," I order. Her limbs shake as she obeys, placing both hands above her head where I can grab them with one of mine. I let my other fall to the dip of her waist, painting the image inside my brain so I can always remember how she looks when she is in my hands. This perfect woman. My perfect wife.

Her thighs widen a little as I thrust harder, my teeth grinding as pleasure shoots throughout my entire body. My cock is soaked with her, her arousal coating her inner thighs, a small little wet patch marking the sheets.

"Kai," She breathes, "I'm going to come."

"Then come, kitten," I grind out, "Come all over my fucking cock, Olivia."

Her brows twitch down, eyes rolling back as her body shivers beneath me, so I move faster, harder, fucking her so damn thoroughly, her body shifts up the mattress.

"Yes!" She hisses. "Like that!"

I chuckle, keeping that rough, brutal pace, our bodies slapping together, her pussy fucking weeping for me.

"Come for me," I order when I feel her start to pulse around my shaft but it's my words that fully tilt her off the edge. She cries out when her orgasm grips her fully, the walls of her cunt fluttering chaotically around me.

"Fuuckkkk," I groan, "You feel so damn good, Olivia, you know that?" My words are strangled, rough, "You're made for me. You drive me fucking *wild*."

Her body relaxes as the last of her orgasm leaves her but fuck if I'm done. Letting go of her hands, I pull out of her abruptly, and then my hand is right there, fingers thrusting back inside. She cries, body bowing up from the mattress as my fingers thrust and my thumb circles her clit.

"Stop, stop," She writhes on a moan, "Too much."

"Not enough," I groan, reveling in how wet she is for me. Drenched and dripping, soaking the bed sheets, coating my hand.

She lets out a deep moan as I continue, paying more attention to that bundle of nerves at the apex of her slit.

"Look how pretty you are, Olivia. I need more from you."

"I don't think I can," she breathes, her eyes opening and finding mine. They're glassy, like she's on the verge of tears.

"You can and you will." I demand. "Give me more, Olivia."

She whimpers as I keep with the stimulation, thrusting into her with my fingers at the same time, forcing what I want from her.

"Malakai," she cries before she detonates again for me, the scream ripping from her throat.

"Good fucking girl," I praise and while she's still pulsing, her cunt dripping for me, I grab her hips, spin her on the bed and lay myself over the length of her, straddling the backs of her thighs as I guide the head of my cock back inside of her.

Her moans are like music to my ears. I hold her down, hands against her back as I thrust into her. Hard, brutal fucking, my fingers leaving marks, her pussy still pulsing from her orgasm.

Her nails claw at the sheets as I fuck her into the mattress, seeking my own pleasure. I watch myself as I disappear into her body, loving the way I fit against her and a zap of pleasure shoots down my spine.

"Fuck," I groan, keeping the pace until my balls draw up tight, my cock jerking inside of her. My chin dips, my body trembling as my climax barrels through me and I empty myself into her, fucking her through it, wanting to feel every second of this.

Spent and dripping sweat, I pull from her body, letting my hands glide down, following the curve of her ass until her cheeks are in my palms. I spread her, my thumb swiping through the wetness between her legs as I watch my come leak from her body.

"I need more, Olivia." I warn. "Always more."

57
Olivia

Pleasure stirs me from my sleep. Whole body pleasure, the type that sets every nerve on fire in the best possible way.

Sleep still clings to me, even when I hear myself moan, even when I can feel him pumping in and out of me, his thick cock stretching me open for him.

I force my eyes open, but I'm met with darkness. I only feel him, behind me, one leg thrown between mine as he holds mine up, parting my thighs so he can easily thrust between my legs.

"Malakai," I moan, voice edged with raspy sleep.

"I'm sorry, kitten," he growls, "I couldn't wait."

"Don't stop."

I don't know how I can possibly go again, not when he squeezed every drop from me only hours before. He forced my body to do things I didn't think possible.

And then when we were done, spent and sleepy, he picked me up and we showered, the water falling onto us as his hands gently cleaned me up, worshipped me and loved me.

My heart had swelled. And then we got into bed, and he cuddled me, holding me close where sleep claimed me quickly. I didn't expect to be woken in the middle of the night to him fucking me. Not that I minded.

His fingers flex where he holds my thighs apart, cock gliding in and out of me at a sleepy but deep pace.

"Touch yourself," He demands, "*Please*. I need to feel you."

My hand falls between my legs, instantly finding my sensitive clit and I begin to circle it, my breath stuttering from me as a new wave of pleasure has my pussy fluttering.

"Yes," Malakai hisses, "Fuck, you feel so damn good."

"I'm close," I whisper.

"Give it to me, baby," He begs and it's enough, to hear him like that, the plea in his tone, the desperation. My orgasm barrels through me, bursting stars behind my eyes. He groans into my neck, thrusts turning jerky as he finishes himself, coming hard and fast into me.

For a few long seconds we lay there in the dark, sweat on our skin, our breaths hard and rough but then he starts to chuckle.

"What's so funny?" I breathe.

He presses a tender kiss to my neck, "My twenty-four hours are up and if there was any way it should have ended," Another gentle kiss, "Like this is the only way I'd want it to."

"You can have my hours, Malakai. All of them." I smile, which then promptly falls off my face when I realize what I just said.

"Olivia," He rasps, arms coming around me, "You have all of mine, too."

Tears sting my eyes. Those words may be the closest thing I'll get from him that expresses his feelings. He knew what I wanted to tell him earlier, knew them, I saw it when he realized, but he didn't let me say them.

We lay in the dark, our breathing now steady, hands still touching and caressing but softer, explorative. I needed to go clean up, I can feel the stickiness between my legs, but I don't dare move just yet, too content to be here.

It's a bubble. Nothing can touch us here, nothing from the past or the fucked-up things that landed us here, no dark secrets and death, just us, in a cocoon.

"I can't believe you flew us out here," I laugh. "Just for twenty-four hours."

"Worth it." I feel his smile.

"Can we come back?" I ask.

"Any time you like, Olivia."

Despite it only being twenty-four hours, it feels like everything has changed. *Monumentally*. Malakai holds my hand against his thigh in the back of the car as we travel to the airport, absentmindedly stroking his thumb against it while he checks his phone with the other.

I'm too busy watching the scenery out the window to

mind.

But his cell rings, drawing my attention.

"Dean." He answers.

I hear the tinny sound of Dean's voice but it's too low to make out the words but whatever it is, has Malakai's hand tightening on mine.

"We will be home in about eight hours." Malakai says.

"No. Wait till I am there. I can't do shit here, Dean, and knowing right now will fuck me up. I'll meet you at the house."

I'm watching him now, seeing the stress on his face, the anger now lining his body.

"I'll call when we land."

He hangs up the phone, curling his fingers around it as he turns to face me.

"Everything okay?" I broach.

"Fine," He answers but I immediately know it's a lie.

"Is it about…" I pause, swallowing, "your business?"

"It's about you."

My lashes flicker, "What about me?"

"The men who attacked you," He turns away from me, but his hand still holds mine tightly, not letting go, "They were hired. Dean has just found out who hired them."

Fear pumps through me, spiking my heartrate, "Who?"

"He'll be letting me know when we get home."

I let out a stuttering breath, swallowing.

Playing with Fire

Malakai turns to me again, "Whoever it was, they won't get another chance. No one will be able to hurt you again, Olivia."

"I believe you." But it didn't stop the very real, very potent terror in my blood.

"Would you like to be with me when he meets us?"

I think about it, trying to squash the fear in me. What would knowing do? I already know this isn't inherently about me, but him…

"No. I don't want to know."

"Okay, kitten." His hand loosens and he strokes my skin again, "Okay."

The flight home goes without incident. Malakai is in his head, quiet and brooding so I've tried to distract myself. I scrolled endlessly on social media for the first two hours of the flight, but that started to get on my nerves so I opened my kindle app and tried to read, but my mind cannot focus. So now I'm looking out the window, sipping on a wine and watching the fluffy clouds beneath the plane. We'll be home soon, and Malakai will know who targeted me.

I still stand by not knowing.

What good will it do me? Why would I need to know? It'll be a name I don't recognize anyway, and if it's something Malakai thinks I need to know, he'll tell me.

"I'm sorry," Malakai's voice startles me. He's been quiet this whole time so hearing his voice is a surprise.

I turn to him, "Why?"

"This isn't how I wanted this trip to end."

"It's okay," I shrug, "You need this more than I do."

"Why?"

"Because knowing doesn't change anything." I say, sipping my wine, "Knowing won't take it back. And this is your domain, not mine. Knowing will make me spiral when I know none of it was my fault."

"It wasn't your fault," He confirms. "It's mine."

"It won't happen again," I say confidently.

"Never." He assures, placing his phone down on the table in front of us, "And I will handle it."

"I know you will," I swallow, "Just don't tell me, okay?"

He softens and reaches for me. I put the wine down and let him drag me closer, tucking me into the side of him as he presses a kiss to my forehead. "You're much too good for me, Olivia."

I laugh softly, "We both know that already."

His chuckle vibrates through my body, "Good thing I'm much too selfish to let you go."

I turn my head up, letting him see my expression, my emotion, "Good job I don't care if you think you're not good enough or if I'm *too* good. I want you regardless."

Against my better judgement. Against everything I know of good and evil.

I can't help it.

My heart sings for him. All of him.

His eyes bounce between mine before he lifts a hand

and traces my bottom lip with his thumb, eyes dropping to watch it.

"I'll give you the world, Olivia, you just need to ask."

But I don't want the world.

Just this with him.

58
Malakai

The steady thump of my shoes is the only thing that keeps me sane. It's the rhythmic tap of them against the hard wood flooring that keeps my pace the way it is.

I'll know who tried to hurt my wife in less than five minutes, I'll have the name and the details, and I'll be plotting my revenge.

I didn't come straight here when we got home, instead I spent the time with Olivia, touching her, holding her, just to make sure she is still with me even though we are home.

She is, her kisses are just as passionate, her touch just as soft. She is now mine completely.

I push open the door to the drawing room, finding the guys waiting for me immediately. Dean sits with a laptop open and resting on his knees, while Bast nurses a whiskey – from my fucking stash – and Killian scrolls on his cell.

"Name." I demand the moment I close the door.

"Hank."

I nod, having known it all along.

"Give me the details," I take a seat behind my desk, opening the laptop.

"I've sent all files to you," Dean advises, "Voicemails, texts, it's all on there."

I look up to see Dean looking a little nervous.

"What else."

"There are more people involved but we don't have their names. I can't find their details anywhere. Hank is the one who hired the hitmen to attack Olivia but it's obvious in the message it was more than just him."

My nostrils flare, "It's okay."

"How is this okay?" Bast bursts, suddenly standing, feeling just as slighted as I am. "These fucking members answer to *you*. You lead this whole fucking thing, and they think they can do this?"

"It's okay," I answer, opening the text log Dean managed to get hold of. "Because the things I am going to do to Hank will have him singing like a canary. We will know who is involved and when we do, the purge can begin."

"It's about time the council changes," Killian says, "We adapt, or we'll be dead."

I nod in agreement, eyes scanning over every text that was sent and received.

They had been trying to get Olivia for weeks, never

finding the right moment until Hank spotted her wandering off alone at the event at the hotel. The hitmen were on standby, close always, in case an opportunity presented itself. And it did when she decided to take a minute for herself.

I click out of the message and open the voicemails.

"What the fuck am I paying you for!?" Hank's distinctive voice sounds through the speakers. "Why hasn't the girl been acquired yet!?"

Acquired. Like she's some object to be used as a pawn.

Hank sighs, "Be on standby. An opportunity will arise where she is alone. We need her alive."

He hangs up and I flick to the next message.

"Olivia has just walked from the event hall. Follow her, you know what you need to do. I don't care what you do to her, just keep her alive."

That's the only two messages available so I go back to the texts, trying to dig through them to see if there is anything Dean may have missed, a hint at another name or names that may have been involved.

It's just a lot of *us* and *we* but no names. That's enough to tell me there are others but not enough to say who.

I'll get him to confirm them all.

I can guess at least two, but it could be more. The council is riddled with snakes and thieves which have been allowed to continue for too long. The leader before me turned a blind eye to all the traitorous ways the council has been allowed to work but with me, I will not let it stand. I've needed a reason to purge, and this is it.

I just fucking hate that it's my wife they're targeting.

Why?

Why Olivia?

What are they hoping to gain by going after her?

I close down the messages and shut the laptop, steepling my fingers beneath my chin.

"Call a council meeting," I order, "I'm not sitting on this."

"When?"

"For right now." I get up, turning toward the window. Olivia is upstairs right now and the threat against her is present, it's right fucking there. I want it done. Over with. "I want them in the council room within the hour."

"What's the plan Malakai?" Sebastian asks.

So, I tell them, knowing they won't question me. It won't be easy, getting Hank to talk but *talk* he will.

While they call in for the meeting, I leave them, heading through the house to satisfy the craving deep within me.

I find Olivia soaking in the tub in the room across from ours, music on so loud she doesn't hear me enter. She sings along while bubbles come up to her chin, eyes closed and head bobbing to the music. The girl cannot sing but I'd listen to that voice every minute of the day.

I creep into the bathroom, leaning on the wall across from her, waiting until she notices me.

The song changes to a new one, and she sits up, the water sluicing down her body. The fine hair at the nape of her neck sticks to her skin and sweat rolls down her brow, her mess of dark hair pulled into a bun that wobbles on top of her head.

"Olivia," I growl out her name.

She lets out a scream, water splashing over the rim of the tub to soak the floor. Her wide eyes find mine immediately, the fear washing away to show her agitation.

"You could have knocked!" She snaps.

"Why would I knock?" I stroll toward the tub, "You belong to me, wherever and whenever."

With a roll of her eyes, she leans back into the water, watching me approach.

"Have we not learned what rolling our eyes will get us?" I crouch at the edge, dipping my hand into the scalding water. How she can sit in a tub with water hotter than the depths of hell is beyond me, no wonder she is sweating.

"Will you spank me?" She flutters her lashes, innocence, and filth colliding.

"So fucking hard, you won't be able to sit."

"Don't tempt me with a good time," She grins, lowering herself until her mouth is submerged in the water.

My own smile pulls at my mouth, despite what is about to go down.

"You tease me, wife," I dip my hand further into the water, finding her body.

Her eyes heat but she grins mischievously, "You're so easy, Kai."

I stop moving, "What?"

"I have you wrapped round my little finger." To show

Playing with Fire

her point, she wiggles her pinky, "Who knew the big bad man could be so easily tamed?"

She's so fucking right.

Grinning like a damn maniac, I grip the edges of the tub and then I hop inside, splashing scalding water over the edges as the added body pushes the water level up. I'm dressed, shoes and all but that doesn't stop me. She squeals, moving to let me in.

I cradle the back of her head as I drop myself closer to her, nose brushing hers, "Let's get a few things clear."

"You're dressed!" She tries pushing at me, but I don't budge.

"There's only one person who owns me," I capture her bottom lip between my teeth before I let it go, "And she's currently naked and wet beneath me. You want to tame me, Olivia, consider me tamed. I'm yours."

"No one can tame you," She breathes.

"You can." I admit.

"I don't want to," she shakes her head, running her hands over me, the sopping clothes clinging to my skin, "I want you how you are."

There's water in my shoes, so hot it's almost unbearable, "How can you sit in this?" I shove out, pushing the water from my face as I sit on the edge of the tub and then climb back out. "It's fucking hotter than hell in there."

I begin to strip out of the wet clothes, watching her settle back in the tub.

"It's not hot enough," She sighs, "But this is the hottest I could get it."

"She devil," I mutter as I strip completely down to my boxers, them soaked through too and clinging to me. Her eyes drop to the outline of my cock, clearly defined by the wet material. I shake my head with a grin.

But she just beams at me, and I leave her to soak in the tub while I go dry off and get ready for the meeting with the council.

59
Malakai

The table is full when I enter the meeting room, every seat filled and brimming with conversation which silences the moment the door closes behind me.

Bast sits where he always has, opposite to the head and Hank, Iwan and Stefan are in their same chairs, their scowls at me heated and filled to the brim with disdain.

This will be fun.

"Gentlemen." I address them all.

There's a grumble of responses as I take my seat at the head. My grandfather watches me curiously, I should have filled him in but there wasn't time.

"You're probably wondering why I've called you all in so abruptly." I continue.

"Well, yes," an older man says from further down the table, his name alludes me, "This is the second time in only a matter of weeks."

"I understand but please know these would not be called if not for a matter of urgency."

"You just got back from Barbados," Hank scoffs, "What possibly could have happened in a matter of hours that required this level of response."

"Well, it's good to know you're keeping tabs, Hank." I address him personally, "And since this is about you, it's fitting for you to comment."

His eyes turn wide, but the fear isn't there yet.

Bast turns to the monitor attached to the wall behind him and flicks it on, all the messages from Hank and the hitmen on display.

"Where did you get this?" Hank snaps, standing.

"My warning clearly wasn't taken seriously," I address the room, "I have no tolerance when it comes to my wife."

"This is fake!" Hank bellows, shoving out his chair as if to leave.

But Killian and Dean fill the door, blocking his only exit. He knows better than to test the two brothers.

I nod to Sebastian who rolls the two short voicemail messages I have recorded, watching Hank's face go from bright, infuriated red, to a terrified shade of white.

"Is that not your voice, Hank?" I ask.

He sputters, turning back to that red shade. "This is a set up!"

But the whole room is looking at him, my guys are ready to take him. It isn't this easy, but this part right here is a piece of cake. Segregating him, turning the very people he has worked with for the majority of his life against him, is easy.

"Killian, Dean," I address the two hanging back in the doorway, "Take Hank for questioning."

"You can't do this!" Hank fights, "There must be a trial!"

There are some grumbles of agreement which I squash immediately.

"I warned you all." I tell the room and I don't bother to disguise the pure rage and murderous intent from my voice. It consumes me and they all hear it.

"I gave notice of changes to come. This is one of them. I am now judge, jury and executioner. I will not tolerate treason to our organization, regardless of where it comes from. Hank will be questioned based on the clear evidence provided. For those who oppose, please stand."

No one stands.

I'm not blind to the fact there are more traitors in this room, I'm certain of at least one other, if not two, I just needed to get the names from Hank. This must be handled fragilely from here on. While no one stood to defend Hank, I see them eyeing me skeptically, and now we're all balancing on a scale.

I have to ensure it tips in my favor or it won't matter what I do or how I handle these threats, because one wrong move and everything I have done up until this point will have been for nothing. Do I think they have the power to get rid of me? No. But it'll make things very difficult in moving this organization in the right direction if the men who hold all my secrets are not on my side of the line.

"As no one will defend you, Hank," I nod to Killian who closes the final step and grasps Hank, followed by Dean and they drag him away from the table. The chair is knocked over in the process and while Hank has always been a fighter, he doesn't compare to two of the most lethal men this business has ever seen. "Take him to the cells."

His bellows echo through the room long after my guys have removed him.

When silence finally falls, I look to each face around the table, "He will not be executed until I have provided further proof of his treason."

"Hank has been with this organization for nearly thirty years," One of the men says, "What of those years of loyalty?"

"I don't give a shit about the years before this," I tell them, "I will not tolerate betrayal of this organization. And I'll make it clear now, there are more of you involved in this, I will find out who. This is your one and only chance to step forward and I will make it swift."

No one moves an inch.

"Death is the only outcome to betraying this organization. Consider yourselves warned."

My phone buzzes in my pocket and I pull it out, reading the message from Killian advising Hank is ready for me.

"Be on standby," I step away from the table, "I expect everyone here within an hour if I call until further notice."

As I leave, I hear them all start to shuffle around, preparing to leave while Sebastian follows me down to the cells. Somewhere in the house, Olivia is relaxing, having no idea what I'm about to do beneath her feet.

Killian and Dean are standing when we finally enter the cells, seeing Hank already attached to the table and chair. He scowls at me when he sees me arrive, not nearly as bloody as I'd hoped.

"Hello, Hank." I greet him with a smile.

"They'll all turn on you for this!" He seethes.

"Will they?" I reply, a little smug, "Because there wasn't a single person ready to defend you back there."

"They're not blind to your uselessness, Malakai. I only did what they were all too fucking scared to do."

"And what is it you did, Hank?"

He closes his mouth, glowering at me from across the table.

"Tell me, was it you who also dug into Olivia's past?"

He scoffs, "You won't get anything from me, boy."

I glance at Sebastian who heads to one of the locked rooms, pulling out his keys. He inserts it into the lock and opens the door, instant wailing filling the room.

Regina is currently tied to the wall, completely unharmed if not a little put out.

"Regina!" Hank gasps.

"So, here's how it's going to go, you're going to tell me what I need to know, and she'll remain unharmed for the duration."

"You'll torture a woman!?" Hank seethes.

"Please," I scoff, "As if you have any respect for the fairer sex."

"That's my daughter!"

"Why did you dig into Olivia's past?" I ask.

"He didn't!" Regina interrupts with a hiccup, tears on her face, "I did!"

"Shut up, Regina!" Hank bellows.

I laugh, "What else do you know, Regina?" I turn to the woman, contempt rolling off me as she pleads with her eyes, trying to convey innocence which falls flat. This woman is not innocent in anyway and now I'm wondering if I've just caught two prey in one trap. I didn't think Regina had it in her but maybe I was wrong, I can admit as much when I am.

"Regina," Hank warns.

"I – I don't know anything," she stutters, "But I had a PI look into Olivia. It was me who left the files. I just wanted you to see what you were getting yourself into, Malakai. She isn't right for you."

Even Hank cringes at the whine, at the desperation.

"It was always supposed to be me, Malakai. We were made for each other."

"Close the door, Bast." I order.

"What!?" Regina screams, "No! Please!"

"What will you do with her?" Hank asks.

"She'll be buried next to you."

"Let her live," Hank pleads, "Banish her. Send her away but let her live."

"You're in no position to request anything of me, Hank."

"Twenty-seven years," His fingers curl in anger atop the table, eyes burning with rage, "I have been loyal to this service for twenty-seven years and this is how I am repaid!?"

"No one is questioning your length of service, Hank." I stand from the table, opening my drawer of toys, "but let's not pretend it's the organization that you serve, it's yourself. Tell me why you had Olivia attacked."

"Fuck you, Malakai." His chains rattle, "You may as well kill me now, you won't get anything from me."

I pull the hammer from the drawer, "You ever broken a bone, Hank?" I judge the weight of the tool in my hand, watching as his eyes follow my every move, throat working on a swallow.

He doesn't answer, not that I expect him to, but he follows me with his eyes as I walk around to his side of the table.

"Last chance."

"Fuck you." He spits.

I bring the hammer down, fast and hard, straight across his knuckles, shattering them on impact.

His scream of pain fills the space around us.

I bring the hammer down once more, straight across his knuckles again, further crushing his bones. His skin splits beneath the impact, covering the hammer and the table in blood when I bring it down a third time.

"Please!" Hank screams.

"You ready to talk?"

"You made it easy!" He cries, face wet with his tears, "Olivia was your weakness. You showed it to the whole fucking council!"

"What did you hope to achieve by taking her?" I ask.

He whimpers, staring down at his mangled and bloody hand, his fingers now pointing in every direction, the hand so beaten, bone and muscle stick out from between the brutalized skin.

I don't hit him again, instead I take the head of the hammer and I start to move it through all that mangled tissue, the sound of the bone crunching and muscle squelching loudly in the quiet room. Hank cries, the pain unbearable. I can only imagine how it feels.

"Talk Hank, what was taking Olivia going to achieve?"

"Blackmail," He cries. "We knew – we knew," He cries as I keep moving the tool, keeping him motivated, "We couldn't kill you. The council wouldn't respect us if we did. We had to get you to stand down."

I bring the hammer away, dropping it onto the table. Droplets of blood lay against the shiny surface as I turn to the guys, cocking a brow.

"So, you were going to use Olivia as blackmail." I nod in understanding, "You were going to dangle her in front of me and do what? Kill her?"

"Yes."

"Who else was involved?"

"It's too late," Hank sucks in a breath, "It's too late now."

"What do you mean it's too late?" I growl.

"Any means necessary." He rambles. "By any means

necessary."

"What are you talking about!?" I snap.

"To get Olivia alone." His eyes are clearer than a few seconds ago, as if he was putting on a show. Not with the pain, that can't be faked, "I'm an old man, Malakai. This organization has been my life and to see it in your hands." He shakes his head in disgust, his face still wet with his tears of pain "You're soft. You won't do what is necessary to keep us thriving. I never wanted the seat, but you'll be damn well sure I'll put my life down to make sure it continues for another century. You're too late."

Panic works through me. Olivia.

I'm moving before I can even register what is happening. My legs carry me quickly back through the halls beneath the house before they take the stairs two at a time and I'm shoving through the doors.

"Olivia!" I roar her name but only silence greets me.

60
Olivia

I don't like how silent the house is.

After the bath, Malakai disappeared, and I took a nap, but I woke up with this feeling of dread sinking into my stomach. Now I'm wandering the house, finding no staff in any of the rooms, or any noise at all.

It's like the place is empty but I know that isn't true. If Malakai wasn't here, my bodyguard would be…

Where is everyone?

Shaking off the unease, I continue down the hall to the kitchen, finding only the spotlights on beneath the counters. No Louis or Miranda, no Malakai drinking coffee at the kitchen island.

Coldness sweeps through me as I walk barefoot through the kitchen, toward the coffee machine.

"Olivia," a voice says from behind me.

Playing with Fire

I startle, spinning around to find Stefan standing in the threshold. "You scared me!" I clutch my chest, my heart pounding something fierce beneath my rib cage.

"My apologies," He smiles though it's unkind, a little menacing.

"Where's Malakai?" I ask, looking beyond him as if my husband will magically appear.

"Dealing with some internal issues," He waves a hand like it's no big deal.

"Oh, I'll go find him," I tell him, wanting to get as far away from this man as possible. He gives me the creeps, especially with the way he is watching me right now.

"I find it very surprising," He continues like I didn't say anything, blocking the way out of the kitchen. "I figured a woman like you would have more respect for herself."

Hackles raised, I position myself behind the kitchen island so it's between us, something he notices too.

"What are you talking about?"

"Fucking a man who is only doing it to win a bet."

I look beyond him again, his words settling in, but I refuse to show him what they do. I don't believe him. Malakai and I may be like oil and water but everything we have shared has been raw and real. There's no faking what we have, all the cracks and splinters and all.

"You don't believe me," Stefan cocks his head.

"Why would Malakai make a bet like that?" I cross my arms, "It's not like he needs the money."

"It's a pride thing, I don't expect you to understand."

I narrow my eyes at him, yeah, I really don't like this guy.

"Here," he says, "Let me prove it to you."

"And how do you expect to do that? Ask Malakai himself?"

He slowly reaches into his pocket, "Just let me show you. I think it's only fair you know the kind of man you're dealing with."

Rage like I've never known before boils up in my blood. This man doesn't like Malakai, his own cousin and he'll use me to get at him. No, I don't believe this.

"Save it."

"Just listen Olivia."

"*Give it some time,*" Malakai's voice sounds through the speaker on Stefan's phone, "*It won't be long before I have her on her back.*"

"*Now this is a bet I'd like to put money on.*" Sebastian's unmistakable voice answers.

"*Yeah, how much?*" The smugness in Malakai's tone makes me feel sick, my stomach churning as the conversation plays out in front of me.

No, he didn't. He wouldn't.

"*Five thousand.*" Sebastian suggests.

Oh god. This is real.

"*Is that it?*" Malakai scoffs, "*Come on, make it worth my while.*"

My head empties out, tears burning behind my eyes.

"*As if bedding that woman would be such a hardship.*"

Playing with Fire

Bast laughs… "*Fine, a hundred.*"

I am going to be sick. He put money on sleeping with me. He played me the entire time and for what? To win money he won't even notice or was it to prove just how stupid I could be? That he could fuck the woman he ruined for fun?

"*A hundred grand?*" Malakai continues but his voice from the speaker sounds like fog in my mind. How have I been this stupid?

Malakai is a monster. Everything he's done this past month has been a lie. He doesn't love me, he never did and never will. It's a fucking game.

And I walked right into it. I played with fire and now I'm being burned.

My hand clutches my stomach as nausea rolls through me. I gave everything to him. My body. My time. My heart.

And now that's shattering, the pain in my chest blooming until it feels like it may actually crush me.

"*Sure, why the fuck not,*" Sebastian laughs.

"Turn it off," I beg, "Please."

"*Time frame?*" Malakai asks as the recording continues.

"Please. Turn it off."

I am going to be sick. Oh god.

"*A month.*" I hear right before Stefan switches off the phone and puts it back in his pocket.

"I need to leave," I say, more to myself than anything else. The gestures. The kisses and caresses. The trip. All a lie.

But that's our marriage, isn't it? Why am I surprised this happened?

I just... *fuck*, this hurts.

"Would you like me to drive you somewhere?"

My eyes bounce to Stefan, seeing he's edged closer. The island is still between us and despite the whirring emotion within me, the rage and the despair, I'm not completely gone to it. And I have enough common sense in me that has me shaking my head.

"I can go myself."

"Perhaps you shouldn't drive while you're upset," He suggests.

I know there are tears on my face, that my emotions are written all over it. "I'll be fine."

Within the grief turning over inside of me, there's anger, enough of it that makes me want to lash out. Making sure to keep the distance between Stefan and I, I turn to the cupboard where Malakai keeps the keys to all his cars.

The Maserati key is the first one on the hooks and my fingers close around it, pulling it down.

I know Stefan is watching me, waiting to see what happens next and I also know he only told me about the bet to get to Malakai. I should be mad at being used like a pawn, but that recording was real. I know Malakai's voice, I dream it, hear it when he isn't around. He haunts me.

My spine stiffens when I have to pass Stefan, unsure what he's going to do but he lets me go and then I'm running.

I have no shoes on and only the clothes on my back, but I can get to Willow's. She'll let me stay there, let me use her things and I've driven in worse conditions than this.

I throw the door open to the garage, hitting the button on the key to unlock the Maserati. The grit on the garage floor bites at the soles of my feet and the fresh clean smell of the car hits me when I open the door. Of course, he just had it cleaned because of the glitter…

"This may hurt a little," Stefan's voice sounds from right behind me. I spin around, wondering how I didn't hear him following me but then I see the needle, the syringe.

He plunges it into the side of my neck and then his palm slaps over my mouth, stifling my scream.

"Shh," He hushes, arms wrapping around me as my heart pumps hard and fast, only working against me to push whatever drug around my body quicker.

And quickly it does, I can already feel it taking hold, feel my limbs go numb, my heart start to slow as dark shadows creep in at the edges of my mind.

"Go to sleep, Olivia," Stefan coos, his face twisted and cruel as he watches the effects of the drug take hold. I can't fight it even though I claw at him, each swipe of my nails turning heavier, softer.

I shake my head, tears stinging my eyes before everything goes black.

61
Malakai

"Where is she!?" I demand, "*Where is my wife!?*"

"Malakai," Sebastian urges from behind, "Calm down. We'll find her."

I've searched the entire house. She isn't here, not in any of the rooms or outside, I've roared her name until my throat is sore, but she is gone.

"Malakai," It's Dean who speaks, his face twisted in grief.

"What is it?"

"Stefan."

"What?"

My legs eat up the space between where I was pacing and where he sits at the kitchen counter. He was looking at the cameras while we searched so he must have found something. Relief softens the tension in my shoulders. He's found her, she's safe.

He turns his laptop around, hitting play on the recording.

There she is, my beautiful wife, in the garage, getting into my car. I'll punish her later for taking the Maserati, but then I pause. There are tears on her face but before she can get into the car, something startles her.

She spins as Stefan plunges something into her neck.

Ice works through me, my heart stopping inside my chest. He holds her, hand across her mouth as the drugs start to take hold. I see it happening, as her body starts to go lax, in the way her eyes turn hooded. She fights to the very end, clawing at him but whatever he gave her is stronger.

And then she collapses, unconscious. My nails bite into the palms of my hands as I watch him manhandle her sleeping body into the car before he climbs into the driver's side, hits the button for the garage and drives away with my wife.

"Where?" I don't bellow. I don't shout.

The type of fury working through me turns everything else quiet. I feel myself shaking with it, the promise of violence warming my blood.

He has my wife.

He *drugged* my wife.

I am going to kill him. Rip him to fucking shreds until nothing is left.

"I'm tracking the vehicle now," Dean says, turning the laptop back around, "The location will update soon."

"How soon?" I demand.

"Right now." Dean grins triumphantly, his eyes promising the same kind of violence I feel. "He's taken her to the warehouses by the docks."

"Let's go."

"What about Hank and Regina?" Killian asks, following me as I make my way to the garage.

"I'll deal with them when I get back."

"Do you think there's anyone else involved?"

"Yes. One other."

"Who?"

"Iwan," I confirm, "He didn't speak up, but I guarantee we'll find him at the warehouse."

"Fucking kill them all," Sebastian growls.

"Plan to."

I take the corners at speed, pushing the car to its limits. It's not the Maserati and doesn't match it in speed but it's fine, I make it work. Dean keeps an eye on the location to make sure they don't move or change locations which they haven't in the past twenty minutes.

"They haven't given demands," Sebastian notes.

"Because they've had to change tactics now that we have Hank. They were always planning to do this." I say, my head working a million miles a minute, "Finding out about Hank and taking him just moved up their schedule. *Any means necessary*. They knew Hank would talk so used the opportunity of our distraction to get to Olivia."

"Where was she going?" Killian asks, "Why was she in the garage in the first place?"

That, I didn't know. She knows better than to leave alone, especially since the attack on her back at the hotel, so what prompted her to try and leave?

"Stefan was speaking with her in the kitchen," Dean tells us, "The cameras in the house don't have audio for obvious reasons."

Too much is discussed within the walls of that house for audio to be recorded. If it were to fall into the wrongs hands a lot of things could fuck up.

"So, I don't know what they were talking about," Dean continues, "I didn't show you because I found the garage footage after and that was more important but whatever he said prompted her to run for the garage. He followed and used that to his advantage."

The tears. The grief. What could he have said to her for her to react that way?

"Call Willow," I order Sebastian, "Make sure she's safe."

Bast nods, pulling out his cell to dial. He speaks a minute later, confirming Willow is fine. He then calls Savannah who is also okay.

I finally pass the city limits, not slowing despite the heavy traffic. The car weaves chaotically between lanes, a chorus of honking horns and angry shouts following as we force our way through traffic until I take a side road, the roar of the engine echoing down the street.

I can see the sea up ahead, rough and turbulent. The skies are an ominous grey and snow still lines the earth, leaving the roads icy and treacherous. I slam the brakes on just outside of the lot for the docks. The warehouses are further up but I don't want to make them aware we are here yet.

"The only plan," I tell them, "Get her out alive. Kill them both."

"And if there are others?"

"Then take them out," I demand, muscles stiffening as I force my heart to slow. I could rush in. I could shoot first but there's a risk to my wife and I am not willing to make a mistake.

"And if Olivia..." Sebastian trails off.

If Olivia is dead...

A moment of grief stabs me right in the chest. There is no world to live in if Olivia is not in it. I don't answer him because I don't have one. All I know is that if Olivia is not here, not with me, then I won't be in control of my actions.

I push the door open, refusing to believe that is a possible outcome. She's their bargaining chip but they've rushed, they're sloppy now they've been forced to do this too soon and that is their second mistake. Their first was going for Olivia in the first place.

We walk toward the warehouses, ignoring the curious looks the few dock workers give us until we get to the rows and rows of warehouses. The alleys between each building give us the shelter we need until we get to one of the smaller warehouses closer to the water. None of the buildings have windows, making it impossible to see where exactly they are holding her but right there is my Maserati, parked directly in front of the shutters, the water beyond smashing against the concrete wall that keeps the sea from flooding the city.

"Move in as one," I order, withdrawing my weapon and preparing, "Do not take the shot if you risk Olivia."

"Understood," One of them replies but the only thing in my head is getting to my wife, it's all I hear and see so I don't know which one of them it was.

Silently, as a unit like we've worked a thousand times before, we move toward the entrance to the warehouse. I pause, noticing the shutters are open and from within I hear voices, two males arguing softly. With no one around to hear, their guards are down.

I pause before the main entrance, at a door to my left used for when the shutters are down.

I try the handle, finding it unlocked and gently push it open, stepping inside. The stench of rotting fish stuffs itself up my nose and fishing gear is piled high across the entire space, old nets and rods, crab cages and rusty knives laying across the gritty warehouse floor.

I keep my steps light, careful not to disturb the loose dirt on the ground and the guys behind me do the same until I use some old crates for coverage and peer over the top, seeing both Stefan and, as I guessed correctly, Iwan. They argue quietly, the older man's face twisted in a mix of worry and anger while Stefan looks bored.

"Send the demands!" Stefan growls, "The sooner we do this, the better. Malakai is smart Iwan, if we don't do it now, he'll only find us first and then what!?"

"It wasn't supposed to happen yet!" Iwan snaps back.

"We do not have the backing of the council. It is just us!"

"They'll back us," Stefan says nonchalantly, before he disappears from view by crouching, "Because this little beauty is going to help us, aren't you sweet Olivia?"

My spine straightens at the sound of her muffled cry. "We don't need the backing when Malakai will step down and when he does, we will end him. We will not have the respect of the council if we kill him first."

I needed eyes on Olivia so I knew how to take the shot.

Olivia cries again and I hear shuffling, like she's struggling on the ground. I dampen down the rage pushing me to thunder for her, to save her and shelter her.

"I'm not so sure the organization will be better off in your hands," Iwan grumbles, typing on his phone, "We should have waited."

"And let Malakai sniff us out?" Stefan snaps, "It is now or never."

I couldn't agree more. I signal for the guys to get ready to aim and follow, keeping my eyes on the two of them as I prepare to show myself.

"I have to agree with Iwan here," I walk out from between the crates, gun drawn and aimed at Stefan. The guys follow quickly behind, Sebastian aiming at Iwan and then I finally see my wife.

She's tied at the wrists and ankles, laying on her side in the dirt with tape covering her mouth. And a gun is pointed at her head. Stefan was quick to draw, something I hadn't counted on which tells me he already had his weapon out.

I ignore it though, he won't shoot her. Not yet.

And even though everything in me tells me to go to my wife, to cover her from the threat, I don't.

I don't even look at her bar that first glance when I stepped out from the crates.

She whimpers and my teeth snap together, grinding painfully, "Get your gun away from my wife," I warn Stefan, my aim true.

"Do you think you can shoot me before I shoot her?" He asks with a menacing grin.

"Should we find out?" I ask. Fuck. Fuck. Fuck.

Sebastian edges toward Iwan who has his hands up, his gun still holstered but I don't hear Killian or Dean behind me. Where the fuck did they go!?

Olivia shuffles on the floor, trying to get away but the ropes restrict her. I keep my eyes on Stefan though, but I can see her out of the corner of my eye.

"Let her go."

"Step down," Stefan counters.

"There is no road here where you win, Stefan." I warn him.

"Do you not love your wife, Malakai?" He taunts, "Is the organization more important to you than her life?"

"Get the fuck away from her."

"Choose, Malakai," Stefan clips, "Her or the throne. You can't have both."

"I will kill you, Stefan," I vow.

"And I'll kill her," he shrugs indifferently, "You don't get both, Malakai. Isn't that right, Olivia?" He asks her directly. Whatever answer she gives is stifled beneath that tape.

"I'll count to three," Stefan continues, "By three, I expect your choice."

Movement beyond Stefan captures my attention and I just about see the shadow of one of the guys moving between the crates behind Stefan.

"One." He starts.

It's Killian, he has his eyes on Stefan. He won't shoot in case he misses and Stefan fires on Olivia. He's planning on disarming him.

My heart thumps wildly inside my chest.

"Two."

Olivia screams beneath the tape, the sound of it, no matter how stifled it is, twists inside my gut.

"Th–" Stefan is cut off before he can finish the number, his breath rushing from him with an oof.

A gun goes off.

And it wasn't one of ours.

62
Malakai

Blood.

There's blood. So much blood

Olivia is screaming, the sound muffled behind the tape but it's a sound I'll never forget, edged and soaked in agony. There are tears on her face, streaking through the grime and dirt clinging to her skin.

She's been shot.

Panic consumes me as I drop to my knees, finding where the bullet entered her and press my palms to it to stem the bleeding. It's in her thigh, there's a hole where it has sliced through her, the blood bubbling and streaming out of her, seeping through the fingers I hold to her wound.

"Dean!" I yell frantically, the shake in my voice clear, "Get the ropes off!"

She thrashes under my hands, trying to move, to cry out but she can't.

Dean hurries over, cutting through the rope before he gently takes the tape from her mouth and then her scream rips clearly through the warehouse.

"Stay still, baby," I whisper, "Shh, I've got you."

"You didn't choose me," She screams, trying to move away from my hands despite the amount of blood pumping through my fingers.

"I did. I'll always choose you, Olivia." I tell her. It wasn't a case of not choosing her, I would choose her over and over but if I gave him what he wanted, he would have shot her anyway.

Tears stream from her eyes, her skin reddened from the tape, wrists, and ankles raw from the chafing of the rope.

"Stay awake," I tell her when I see her lids starting to droop. "Call an ambulance!" I demand.

"The police," Killian hesitates, looking to where Iwan and Stefan are restrained.

"Then get them the fuck out of here," I growl, "But call a fucking ambulance."

I don't pay attention to what they do or who fucking does what, I keep pressure on the bullet wound and lift her leg above her body, trying to stem the blood flow.

"Stay with me, kitten," I tell her, "Olivia!"

She mumbles something, her head lolling to the side. The shock, the blood loss and the trauma all wreaking havoc on her body. Sirens wail in the distance.

I'm covered in her blood and when I lean forward, gripping her face to try keep her awake, the red smears across her pale skin.

"Fuck," I hiss, hearing my voice crack. "Wake up, baby."

"It's two minutes out," Sebastian advises.

I flick my eyes to him, pleading.

The brothers are nowhere to be seen and neither are Iwan or Stefan. It's just us in this rotting warehouse, the stench of fish now threaded with the smell of her blood, metallic and hot.

Sebastian adds pressure with me, looking desperately toward the door waiting for the paramedics.

"Olivia," I croak, "Olivia, wake up, kitten."

But she doesn't. She looks too pale; her chest moves too slowly.

"She's losing too much blood," Sebastian says.

"I choose you, Olivia," I beg, "I will always choose you."

"Kai," Sebastian whispers.

"She's my wife," My voice cracks, "I need her."

"Hello!?" Someone yells.

"In here!" Sebastian bellows. "Hurry!"

I hear them rushing, I hear them asking questions, but I just kneel here, silently begging for her to wake up but she never does. There's so much blood.

"Sir we need you to move."

I can't get my body to work.

"Sir!" The paramedic yells.

Someone grabs me – Sebastian – and drags me out of the way while two paramedics drop to Olivia. They work quickly, efficiently, speaking in terms I don't understand.

And then Olivia is hauled onto a gurney and rushed from the warehouse, but she still isn't awake.

I've seen people bleed out before; I've watched the life drain away quickly because of it but I don't remember there ever being that much blood.

I try to follow into the ambulance, but the paramedic closes the doors before I can get inside, the lights flashing as the sirens echo through the industrial estate, but I don't have a chance to demand to be let inside. Sebastian controls the situation, hauling me to the Maserati as he shoves me into the passenger seat.

"Get fucking with it, Malakai," he snaps, gunning behind the ambulance to follow it to the hospital.

"That's my wife," I croak.

"Yeah, and she needs you right now." He snaps, pissed at me, "Not this useless version of yourself. She needs *you*."

I turn my eyes to him.

"So, either snap the fuck out of it or I'll drop you on the side of the road and go to the hospital myself."

"Like fuck you will!" I growl.

"Get your head out of your ass!" Sebastian hisses back. "Your wife needs you."

He's right. I look down at the blood on my hands, the stained cuffs of my shirt. Her blood. My wife.

Playing with Fire

The drive behind the ambulance clears my head. She doesn't get to leave me. Not like this. The moment we stop, I'm out of the car, running toward the ER doors.

"Where is she!?" I demand.

"Sir!?"

"Where is Olivia Farrow?" I growl, "She was just brought in. Gunshot wound."

"Who are you?"

"I'm her husband, where is she?"

They show me through to a quiet family room with Sebastian following, but then they close the door and provide no answers. I throw it back open, but Sebastian stops me.

"Malakai!" He growls. "Fucking stop. They will come to you when they have answers."

"She needs me."

"She needs the fucking doctors right now. She will need you when she wakes up so pull it together, wash off the blood and wait for her."

I nod mutely. Wasn't he the one who told me she needs me right now? Or was that just to get me to stop panicking? I have no fucking idea what is going on right now. It's like the years of training, of preparing for a life like this have all gone out the window. I don't know what to do, how to act.

But I start by washing my hands in the small bathroom attached to the room, watching the stained red water swirl down the drain. It takes five minutes to get it all off but the sleeves of my shirt are soaked with it so I can't completely get clean. Sebastian goes in after me, washing off the blood on his hands and then he sits in one of the chairs while I pace the room.

It's several hours later when a doctor comes into the room.

"She's stable. We stopped the bleeding and repaired her leg. She lost a lot of blood though, we had to give her a transfusion. She's awake."

"Where is she?"

"This way." We both move to follow. "Only one of you." The doctor says.

Sebastian stops, "I'll handle the mess at the house." He tells me before he turns on his heel and jogs out of the hospital.

I'm let into a small private room like the one she was in before and find her lying in the bed, her face turned toward the window.

"Olivia," I croak.

Blood shot eyes turn to me, but she doesn't smile, her expression doesn't change. If anything, she looks at me with contempt.

"Olivia?"

"I don't want to see you." She turns back to the window.

I step up to the bed, "What is it?"

My hand reaches for hers, but she flinches away, pain crossing her features.

"What's wrong, kitten?"

She brings her eyes back to me, glazed but she doesn't cry even though the tears sit on her water line. They never fall.

"I don't want to see you." She repeats, firmer.

"I chose you, Olivia," I panic, "It didn't matter what I said, they would have shot you anyway. I was trying to keep you alive."

She shakes her head and withdraws her eyes from me again, "Everything is a game. A scheme."

"What are you talking about?"

"I know about the bet, Malakai."

"The bet? What fucking bet?" I demand.

She laughs without humor and then flinches. I move for her again, trying to provide her with some comfort.

"Don't fucking touch me, Malakai." She snaps, "You'll never touch me again."

"What is happening right now!?"

"You made a bet, Malakai and don't try to deny it. You made a bet with Sebastian, to sleep with me."

The blood drains from my face.

"It was all a game to you," Her voice cracks, "You used me. And now this?" She gestures to her leg. "You can pretend you were going to choose me, but we both know you wouldn't. You only ever choose yourself."

"Olivia, let me explain," I don't move to touch her again though I am desperate to, "Please."

"I don't want to hear it, Malakai. I don't want to be near you right now."

"Olivia, you're hurt. You need me."

She scoffs, the laugh filled with disdain, "I don't fucking need you, Malakai. I never did." Bored eyes travel the length of me, "But I will admit I wanted you. That I fell for you. So, congratulations, maybe you can get an extra hundred grand since you managed to fuck me *and* make me fall in love with you, hope it was worth it."

"Olivia, please," I beg, "That isn't how–"

"Leave."

"Olivia…"

"Leave!" She screams, loud enough it'll draw the attention of the staff outside. "Leave!"

Tears fall freely from her eyes now, grief twisting her features, paling her skin.

"Leave!" She cries again, and fuck…

"Okay." I hold my hands up, "Okay, baby. I'll leave."

"Don't come back."

"We're married, Olivia."

"And I'll hate it for the rest of my life." She jabs, sniffling as those fat tears roll down her cheeks. I want to kiss away her pain, hold her until she no longer feels like she is falling apart, but I can't. She won't let me.

"This isn't over."

She swats at her tears, "We never even begun, Malakai. There is nothing to be over. We are *nothing*."

63
Olivia

I'm not sure what hurts the most. My leg or my heart.

It's been a week since I was shot and a day since I was let out of the hospital. I didn't go home, even though he tried to demand I did. Willow collected me from the hospital, apparently Sebastian filled her in on *everything,* and now she's walking on eggshells around me.

Malakai came to see me every day at the hospital, begged me to talk, pleaded with me but I refused.

He didn't choose me.

He can pretend he did all he likes but he didn't. Not from the very beginning. I just hadn't realized it when I was wrapped up in him. Us, we were always contractual, fake from the very start.

And laying on the warehouse floor, listening to them

while Stefan gave him the ultimatum, I saw the hesitation. It was there, just a flash. Me or his so-called throne.

For a second, he *hesitated*.

Fresh tears heat my eyes, but I quickly clear my throat and shake my head.

It didn't matter that no matter what he decided, it would have ended with me dying anyway, and he got us out, or rather Killian and Dean fixed it to be that way.

And then the bet with Sebastian, the ego and cockiness that he was so sure he'd be able to get me into bed. Well, I guess it wasn't misplaced. He did get me.

All of me.

I use my crutches as I move through Willow's penthouse, heading for the fridge to grab some water. I have a shit ton of pills to take and I'm not even mad about it. The painkillers are strong enough they knock me the fuck out, and for the few hours of dead sleep I don't think of him. I don't dream of him.

It's only when I'm awake that he haunts me.

I take the water awkwardly back to the couch where my pills are, abandoning the crutches as I carefully lower onto the plush cushions, reaching for the pills.

I pop the antibiotics first and then grab the pain meds, shaking two of the pills into my hand. I'm swallowing them down when Willow gets back home, a bag of groceries hanging from her hand.

"Hey," she says, placing it on the side.

"Hi," I croak, voice raw. I've barely spoken, and I've cried a lot so now my throat is sore, to add it to the long list of shit that hurts right now.

"I got us ice cream," She pulls two pots from the bag, "I was gonna get wine but figured with all those meds…"

I nod, "Can't drink right now."

"How are you doing?" She continues, placing the ice cream in the freezer before she unpacks the rest of the groceries and puts them away.

"Fine." I answer, turning around to stare at the wall of windows, waiting for those meds to kick in if only to drag me into oblivion for a few hours. I'll take anything if only to avoid this conversation. I love Willow. I appreciate her and need her, but I can't talk about this. Especially when she is still seeing Sebastian and she's on the fence between me and Malakai. She says she's on my side but the '*just give him another chance to explain*' tells me she's more on his side than mine.

That man doesn't deserve another chance.

And I know I'm stuck in this marriage now. He won't allow a divorce and has enough power to stop me from getting one in any form. He controls all.

Prick.

"Have you taken your meds already?" She asks and I nod, laying down on the couch, ready for it to hit.

"You're about to pass out on me, aren't you?" She huffs, stepping in front of me with her hands on her hips. She looks pretty today, in her tight leather pants and red knitted rollneck sweater, her red hair bundled on top of her head.

"I am," I agree. And I can't fucking wait.

I miss him despite my better judgement. Miss his

chuckles and his kisses, miss the way he holds me at night and cares for me. I just miss him. And it hurts so fucking bad, like I left my heart with him.

But he crushed it.

A single tear slips from the corner of my eyes as the pills finally take hold, dragging me swiftly into sleep.

When I finally wake it's dark beyond the window, the city around me alive with lights. It's nothing like the estate, with its fathomless dark and endless starry skies. You can't see the stars here or hear the wind in the trees or smell the earth. It's just smog and city traffic.

I can hear Willow somewhere in the house, speaking softly and figure she's just on the phone until I hear a very male voice reply.

"He's going fucking mad, Wils." Sebastian says, "He needs to see her, just so he knows she's okay."

Slowly, I sit up on the couch. I can feel my hair standing up, stuck in the same position I fell asleep in. Those pills really do make me dead to the world, I don't even move when I sleep.

"She's not ready." Willow replies.

"Have you tried talking to her?" He asks.

I rub my hands over my face, running my fingers over my eyes to remove the sleep, "I'm awake." I grumble loud enough for them to hear.

"Olivia!" Sebastian comes barreling over, full of restless energy.

"Hello, Bast," I give him a small smile, as much as I

can muster.

"It's good to see you," He sits on the coffee table, his face full of compassion and I know he isn't just saying it to be kind. "You're looking better. How do you feel?"

"I'm not seeing him," I get right to the point. "I can't."

"That bet…" He winces.

"Don't Sebastian," I warn, "I don't want to hear it."

"Olivia," his shoulders sag, "He needs you."

"Yeah, well," I snap, grabbing my crutches, "He should have thought about that before he tossed it all on the ground and set fire to it."

"He didn't," Sebastian argues, "He never meant for any of it to happen."

"But it did happen, Sebastian." I hobble to the kitchen though I've no idea why. I guess just to escape the conversation. "He didn't choose me, Sebastian. We all know this was never going to work anyway, so why don't we all move on from it."

"He won't move on, Olivia. Ever."

"Then it'll be a lonely life for him."

"He killed them all." Sebastian lowers his voice, but I know Willow is listening. She knows anyway but I haven't had the confidence to ask her how she feels about it. She hasn't brought it up so neither have I.

"He killed them because they were a threat to his organization and a threat to his leadership."

"You know that isn't true."

"All I know, Sebastian," I level him with a glare, "Is that Malakai only cares about his needs. It's how I ended up here in the first place."

"You're as stubborn as he is," He grumbles.

"Him and I are nothing alike." I snap.

"You're right," he huffs impatiently, "You're not alike in anything but that damn stubbornness. No wonder you fought all the time in the beginning."

I roll my eyes, "Is that all?"

"Just think about it," He pleads, "Just think about seeing him."

"No," I answer immediately, "Tell him it's over and if he has any respect for me, he'll send me divorce papers, so we never have to see each other again."

"I'm not telling him that."

"Coward."

"Olivia," Sebastian warns.

"It's over, Sebastian. Over."

64
Malakai

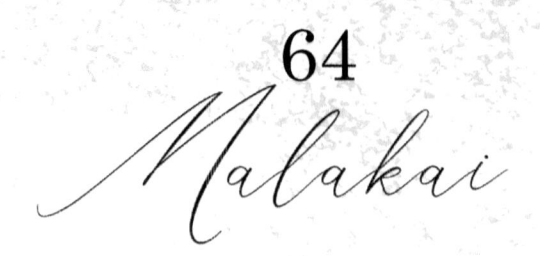

"Divorce papers!?" I roar, the glass in my hand shattering against the wall, "She wants a divorce!?"

Fuck, it feels like I'm having a damn heart attack. I rub at my sternum as if it can help with the pain there, but nothing helps. No amount of alcohol numbs it, the gym doesn't help, sparring with the guys just angers me more.

The only time it dulled to a bearable pain was when I ripped them all apart. I was frenzied when I killed Stefan, remembering the way her blood looked on my hands because of him. It wasn't quick. I literally took him apart, piece by piece to the chorus of his screams. I made the other two watch.

But then it was over, and the pain began anew. I haven't slept. I've barely eaten a thing.

She doesn't want to see me and while she was in the hospital, I didn't respect those wishes. I went every day to beg her to listen, but she never did. I tried to get her to come home with me and she refused. I would have dragged her regardless of her wishes if she wasn't still recovering.

She doesn't answer my calls. My texts.

She doesn't talk to me at all.

And now she wants a divorce.

No. Absolutely fucking not.

It would have been impossible for me to give her one before but now I've changed all the rules for the organization, signed them off with the approval of the council that divorce is a possibility now. But still, she isn't getting one from me and I'll block every opportunity for her to get one.

We are not over.

She is mine.

My kitten. My little brat. My fucking wife.

"She's hurting, Kai," Sebastian says softly, Killian and Dean watching, "She doesn't mean it."

I scoff. She does. It's Olivia, and if anything, that woman is honest to a fault. She thinks I wouldn't choose her, but I would. I'd give it all up if that's what she wanted.

That fucking stupid bet didn't mean anything, I never would have taken the money and Sebastian knows that too. He never even brought it up again after the event because he knew then too. He knew Olivia was more to me.

That she was it.

But why can't she see that?

Why won't she let me take care of her? She's hurting and I am not there.

"I'm going over there."

"Malakai, that's probably not the best idea." Killian winces.

"Do I look like I give a fuck, Kill?" I bark at him, "I need to see her."

"It's late." He tries. He's right on that, it's almost two in the morning but it doesn't stop me.

I grab the keys to the Maserati and storm to the garage, getting in the driver's seat. They don't join me, and they don't try to stop me as I peel out of the garage and speed down the drive, the gates barely open by the time I'm barreling through them.

My head is only filled with images of her, her smile and her laugh, her body and the way she sounds when she falls apart. I see her sleeping and dreaming, can picture vividly how she looks when she's playing with me. I see her in that red dress and her wedding dress, how she looks when she watches the stars.

Her name is a prayer I repeat inside my head.

The drive passes in a blur and then I'm pulling into the garage beneath Willow's apartment building, parking up and crossing the lot to the elevators to take me up to the penthouse. I know the code thanks to Willow, but she only gave it to me for emergencies and made me promise I wouldn't just show up like I'm doing right now.

It feels like ages pass by the time I reach the very top floor, the doors opening to the foyer of the penthouse. Brightly colored art hangs on the wall and beyond this hall, the lights are off. The sound of my shoe's echoes on the tile beneath my feet and the hall then opens into a large open plan living room and kitchen space, windows on either side looking out onto the sleeping city below. There's a lamp on in the living room and from this angle, I can only just see the dark head of hair resting on the couch pillows.

I move toward it, toward that sleeping body, inherently knowing it's her.

She sleeps soundly, her lashes fluttering against the apples of her cheeks and seeing her soothes something deep within me. It makes the pain in my chest just a little bit more bearable.

She looks a hundred times better than when I last saw her, her skin now brighter, her hair washed and shiny.

A sigh leaves my lips as I slowly and carefully take a seat on the coffee table ahead of her, letting my eyes scan her completely. She's in a pair of sleep shorts, the blanket she had been using now half on the floor, showing the gauze wrapped around her thigh. The markings on her ankles and wrists have almost faded but I can still see the extensive bruising at the very top and bottom edges of the bandage.

I'd lost my shit when I'd first seen it back in the hospital what feels like weeks ago now when in fact, it's only been a few days. And logically I knew the bruising was normal considering the trauma but seeing it on her, seeing her beautiful skin marked like that – I wanted to kill Stefan all over again.

Playing with Fire

Unable to stop the craving, the temptation to touch her, I reach forward, letting my fingers trail over her warm cheek, the whisper of her skin against mine like a song for my soul.

She stirs beneath my touch, moving toward it when I start to bring my hand away. Even in sleep she knows my touch, even in sleep she needs me like I need her. I can't breathe without her.

My hand remains still, not quite touching as her lashes begin to flutter.

"Olivia," I rasp her name. There hasn't been much time since I last saw her, a couple of days at most but fuck it feels longer. I fucking miss her.

She blinks a few times, sleep still clinging to her before those stunning dark eyes land on me.

And then she bolts up and cries out at the same time, her hand going to her leg as pain contorts her face.

"Fuck!" I jump, lunging for her. "What can I do?"

"What are you doing here!?" She screams, one hand cradling her injured thigh, the other trying to push up from the couch to get away.

"I needed to see you," I follow her, ready to aid her in anyway as she hobbles away, physically trying to put space between us, "I miss you, kitten."

"Get out!" Tears fall from her eyes, but I don't know if it's the pain or if it's me but seeing her cry rips me apart inside.

"Olivia, please," I speak through the burn in my throat. "What can I do?"

She shakes her head rapidly, breaths coming in hard,

rough pants.

"You want me on my knees, kitten?" My voice shakes, "You want me to beg? I will for you. You want the world? Let me give it to you, but please, I need you. I need you to come home."

She clutches the side as she continues to cry, stifling her sobs even when those tears continue to fall.

"I know you feel it too," I tell her, "I know you need me just as much. It's us, Olivia. You're my wife."

"I – I can't d – do this." She stutters.

"There is no end for us, Olivia. I won't allow it."

Anger twists her face, "Get out!" She bellows, her rage, something I've never witnessed before. Not like this. Not this raw, sharp fury that even whips warnings through me.

"I'll prove it to you," I say calmly, even as I step away, giving her the space she needs in this minute, "I'll prove to you that it's only you, Olivia. That bet? It was a fucking stupid game that started before we were even married. It meant nothing."

Her anger simmers in her eyes, the heat of it heightened by the sudden quiet tears that now fall. There's no more sobbing, no heaving breaths, just this quiet simmering rage.

At me.

"I will always choose you, Olivia." I vow. "You might not see it right now, but I will always choose you."

65
Olivia

It's been two weeks since Malakai showed up at Willow's house in the middle of the night, and the pain in my chest has not eased in the slightest.

It feels like a physical, living thing, so much so I had to ask the doctor to check me over on my last checkup. He told me I was fine, healthy but it didn't feel like it. It feels like my heart is dying.

My leg is healing well, I don't have to use the crutches anymore, but I still have a slight limp and the bruising is still there but healing slowly too. Physically, I am on the mend, apart from the nasty scar I'll now have and the trauma that haunts me every time I sleep now, it'll be like it never happened.

I don't have the pills anymore to keep my mind clear of nightmares or dreams.

I've woken every night reaching for Malakai even though I know he isn't there. He hasn't tried to contact me, hasn't showed up, not even the guys try to convince me to see him anymore.

It hurts even though I asked him for it.

Now I have it, I'm not sure I want it.

I wander down the hall toward the offices in the hotel, smiling at everyone who says hello, and then I close the door to the office and take a seat behind the desk. My new office. The old office is being renovated into a new staff area, it's plenty big enough and since I'll never use it, it seemed like a waste to leave it gathering dust. I thought it would have been hard to say goodbye to that piece of my father, but it didn't. It's now stripped to the bone, not a single speck remains to say it used to be my father's.

Shaking my head to clear my thoughts, I load up my laptop and open my emails.

Since I've taken over the event coordination for the hotel, we've been inundated with requests to book but I've taken it slow, accepting only the events I know I'll be able to manage so there are only a few in the books for now. As I grow my team, I'm sure it'll grow with it, but while it's only me, this is how it'll be.

There's a new email in my inbox when it finally loads.

Dear Mrs. Farrow,

I wince at the name.

Firstly, I would like to commend you on the winter event that was held a few weeks ago. My wife and I thoroughly enjoyed our evening – though it ended far too quickly for my liking, and now a few weeks have passed, I'd like to take this opportunity to request your services.

I will be frank here, Mrs. Farrow, my wedding to my wife was not what it should have been, and she deserves more, which is why I would like you to organize a vow renewal ceremony, including an after party to be held at the hotel.

Please understand I will simply not take no for an answer. My wife deserves the world and I plan to give it to her. There is no amount of money I will not pay to persuade you to help me with this.

I fully trust your judgement to make the day in the same way you made the event.

She does not know about this yet, it is a surprise for her.

So, can I expect your help with this, Mrs. Farrow?

With hope,

Mr. M. Levine.

I read the email again before I hit reply.

Dear, Mr. Levine.

Thank you for your high praise, however I am currently not scheduling new events for the coming months.

I wish you and your wife a very happy marriage.

Best,

Olivia Lauder

Sickness works through me. I could totally schedule a small vow renewal, but do I want to?

My computer dings loudly in the quiet office, a new email popping up. That was quick.

Mrs. Farrow,

I do not think you understand, I will not accept no as an answer. Money is not an issue; I will pay whatever is needed to make this happen and to make my wife happy.

Please understand there is nothing in this world I will not give her.

I request you to please, reconsider.

I blink at the screen.

I will draw up an invoice once I have received quotes.

Please provide the date of the ceremony.

Olivia

The reply is almost instant.

Seven days from now.

I will make a deposit of fifty thousand to the hotel now, please charge the remaining to the card.

Thank you, Mrs. Farrow. I look forward to it.

Seven days!?

Okay, maybe I spoke too soon. Who the fuck organizes a vow renewal in seven days!?

I'm still staring at the screen five minutes later when Helen, one of the ladies from finance knocks on my door, "Um Mrs. Farrow?"

That fucking name. It's both a curse and a treasure.

"Yes, Helen?" I paste a smile on my face, hoping like fuck it looks somewhat genuine.

"We have just received a rather large sum of money however it does not tie to anything."

"Shit," I hiss. He works fast.

"Mrs. Farrow?"

"Fifty thousand?" I ask. It's a big deposit considering the guy has no idea what I will plan.

"Yes, that's right."

"Open a new account for a M. Levine. We will be hosting his vow renewal ceremony in seven days. Now please, excuse me, I apparently have a lot of work to do."

66
Olivia

Seven days later…

"Wow, Oli," Willow breathes, "You really fucking pulled it off."

I stand in the entrance to the grand hall that very rarely gets used here and smile. I really fucking did pull it off. It kept me so busy I almost didn't have time to think about Malakai.

I say almost because that man is in my soul, and I can't figure a way to get him out. I'm not even sure I want to anymore. I miss him.

So much it *hurts*.

I didn't expect love to feel like this.

It's all consuming, a physical thing inside of me. I feel

it in my bones, in the very threads of me. How did it become so strong in such a short amount of time?

I stare at the room I've managed to transform. It's a rare sunny day which I'm thankful for since all the curtains are open to let in as much natural light as possible. I decided on a rustic, natural theme with fresh blooms spread out across the room, wooden accents threaded throughout. Rows of white chairs have been set up ahead of a stage that's been decorated in moss and white Gypsophila. It's simple but elegant, a long white carpet spread down the center to create an aisle.

The after party will be held in one of the restaurants. While Mr. Levine wasn't too forthcoming, he had given me a head count which had allowed me to organize the meal and set up the room to allow dining and dancing. I followed the same theme, but I added fairy lights and a lot of candles.

"So, what happens now?" Willow asks, hands on hips as she watches my staff buzz through the space excitedly.

"Nothing," I shrug, "Now we wait for the happy couple to arrive."

"Great!" She claps her hands, "I booked us to get our makeup done."

"What?" I gasp, "I can't leave and why an earth would you do that!?"

"Because it's Sophia Carlton!" She widens her eyes, "She's only in town for like a couple of days!"

"What?"

"You know that huge makeup artist who does all those celebrities for the red carpet."

"How do you know she is in town?"

"Stalked her IG," She rolls her eyes, "Anyway, I begged an awful lot to get this so you're coming."

"Willow, really, I can't leave. Everything is set up, but I need to be here when guests arrive and stuff. It won't just run itself."

"I can help," Nora strolls over, a smile on her face, "I helped, remember, I know what to do."

I narrow my eyes, detecting something else is happening here. "What's going on?"

"Nothing!" Willow answers too quickly, "Come on, let's go."

"Willow!" I pull back but she continues to drag me toward the foyer.

"Our appointment starts in like five minutes, she's right upstairs so it's not even like you're leaving."

"Willow, this doesn't make sense."

"I know it doesn't," she stops suddenly, and my nose bounces off her back.

"Ow," I rub at it.

"But I need you to trust me right now."

"What are you up to?"

"Can't I do a little something to make my bestie feel better?" She pouts.

"Well, yes," I start.

"Exactly," She cuts me off, "Let's go."

I grumble the entire way up to the twelfth floor where several of our luxury suites are. Willow knocks a few doors down and then opens without waiting for an answer. My scolding is on the tip of my tongue but then I see a whole team inside with Sophia.

My mouth clamps shut.

"There you are!" Sophia smiles sweetly, "Come, sit, sit! There isn't a lot of time."

Willow shoves me toward her and then she bolts, the door slamming closed behind her.

"What the fuck is going on!?"

"Come," Sophia ushers me, not answering me. I doubt she even knows but still.

"Such a pretty face," She compliments as she holds my chin, tilting my face side to side as if wanting to get all my angles. "I know exactly what to do."

And then she does it, and I sit silently, accepting it in utter confusion. And when she's done, my hair is tugged and brushed and pinned.

"Stunning," She breathes, "Absolutely stunning."

"I'm sorry," I blink rapidly, "What the hell is going on?"

She checks her watch, "Oop, would you look at the time! I've gotta run, you look beautiful though. Have a great day!"

What the hell!?

Before I even realize what's happening, I'm standing in the hall outside the bedroom, the door firmly closed behind me.

This is starting to freak me the fuck out, so I do a Willow and I bolt, heading back down and rushing toward the offices. Sweet isolation beckons a few feet away and I lunge, closing the gap as my hand tugs on the office door frantically, and then I slam it behind me.

I don't like this.

I don't like this at all.

I rest my head on the door, careful because you know, make up, and take a breath.

But then it gets lodged in my throat when I hear the voice from behind me.

"Hello, kitten."

I spin around, eyes wide, hands shaking to find Malakai sitting behind my desk.

And he looks utterly devastating.

In a three-piece light grey suit, he relaxes in my chair, hands resting behind his head which stretches the material of that suit over every expanse of him.

"Malakai," I breathe.

"Did you miss me?" His mouth cocks up into a half smile but behind it and swimming in his eyes is hesitation, fear… longing.

"What are you doing here?" I ask.

"Choosing you," He's suddenly standing, closing the space between us. My spine hits the door and then his arms are caging me in. "Choosing you, kitten. Right now."

"What do you mean?" I breathe.

"This is our wedding, Olivia."

"It's not a wedding," I point out, unsure what I am actually saying. "It's a vow renewal."

He cocks his head, eyes flicking around my face as if waiting…

"Oh!" I finally catch up.

He chuckles, "For us, Olivia. It's for us."

"But you're not Mr. Levine." I point out again uselessly. My brain is not working.

"Levine is Sebastian's last name. I just borrowed it. If you knew it was me, you wouldn't have arranged for this."

"Wait," I gasp, "You had me plan my own vow renewal!?"

"Yes."

"Why?"

"Because I wanted to give you the day you wanted. We can't have the wedding again, but this, I can give you this. I can give you the day you would have wanted."

"Malakai, I–"

"There's more, sweetheart," He says quietly, sorrow lining his face, "I am choosing you now," He steps away, and I swear that's tears in his eyes, "I am choosing you even if you are not choosing me."

He walks back to the desk, "I've signed them already."

I stare at the brown envelope in his hand.

"I am choosing you to be happy, Olivia." He swallows and I wasn't mistaken, those *are* tears. That's a tear rolling down his cheek.

If I thought I was heartbroken before then I was wrong because this – this is excruciating. I can't fucking breathe past it.

"And if being happy means being without me, for now, then sign the divorce papers and don't meet me at the end of the aisle."

"Malakai…"

"But I need you to know, even if you sign these papers, I won't stop. I will earn your love again, Olivia, whether we are married or not. You are my wife. You will always be *my wife*."

He places the thick envelope on the desk, turning to me once again, letting me see every raw and gritty emotion on his face, letting me see those tears on his cheeks.

"I never told you." He whispers. "I never told you that I love you."

My lip's part on a breath as my heart hammers in my chest.

"But I do," He promises, "With every fiber of my being. I love you, Olivia. I think I loved you from the moment you stood in my office that first day you moved in."

He's back in front of me, finger curled under my chin, "And I *knew* I loved you," He breathes, "the moment you fucked up my closet and put ketchup in my shoes."

A watery laugh bursts from me but hesitation works in too.

"I want it all, Olivia." He tells me, "But now, it's up to you."

Icy cold sweeps through me when he takes a step away,

"Your dress is behind you and my pen is on the desk."

I turn and almost choke when I see my wedding dress, the very same one from our wedding day minus the big red wine stain.

"I bought a new one," He explains, "After the wedding."

I step away from the door as he reaches for the handle.

"Whatever you choose," He pauses, his back to me, spine straight and shoulders stiff, like walking away right now is physically paining him. "I will understand, but please… choose me back."

And then the door closes, and he leaves.

67
Malakai

"She'll be here," Sebastian says but even he's nervous. Willow fidgets at the other end of the aisle, waiting for her friend, and I can sense her anxiety too.

I left Olivia in her office to decide twenty minutes ago. Willow had gone in after her and came back out within ten minutes, she didn't say anything to me, and her face gave nothing away.

I don't know if Olivia is coming.

When another ten minutes pass and there's still no show of her, despair starts to weigh me down. She hasn't chosen me back.

My throat feels raw and my stomach rolls. I've never felt this way before, never felt this crushing weight of sorrow, the loss a physical weight I feel pinning me down.

But then Willow whips her head around to me, eyes

wide, and even from here, I can see they're glazed.

And then the music starts, a soft melodic sound and my breath catches in my throat when Olivia steps through the doors.

She was stunning the first time she wore that dress but now, she's devastating.

Willow links her arm as she escorts her down the aisle and all eyes are on her, but her eyes are only on me.

But I simply cannot wait.

My legs are already moving, closing the space between us, closing that distance until she's in my arms, her face cradled in my hands and my mouth on hers.

"You came," I whisper against her lips.

She nods slowly, "I choose you too, Kai."

"I have vows," I tell her urgently.

Her lips pull up into a breathtaking smile but before she can speak, someone clears their throat.

I snap my head around, glaring at where Sebastian tries to hurry us along. "Fuck you!" I snap at him, "My wife was talking."

He just grins.

"Come on," Olivia whispers, "Everyone is staring."

I walk her the rest of the way, her hand in mine and while the ceremony begins, I don't hear a word of it, not until it comes to the vows.

I have a piece of paper in my pocket but they're not the words I want to use anymore.

So, I step up to her, lean in until my mouth is at her ear

and she's the only one who can hear me.

"For the rest of my life, Olivia, I will love you. Every bratty, rebellious side of you. I will laugh with you, and hold you when you cry, will worship you, and look after you. I will continue to choose you, no matter the outcome because you are it. It's not the sun I seek after the storm, it's you. Always you."

Her breath rushes from her as I gently kiss her cheek.

"And when my time comes, there will be no place that will be able to hold me from you. I will find you in every existence. I love you, Olivia Farrow. Always."

68
Olivia

"Olivia," The feminine voice sounding from behind me has my spine stiffening.

It's been a few hours since the ceremony and I haven't yet had a chance to see everyone, but I don't know how I missed *her*.

I spin to find my sister standing with a soft smile on her face, Everett, her partner, at her side. He looks uncomfortable as shit, but my sister looks happy.

"Arryn," I gasp, voice breaking on a sob.

"Hi," She opens her arms and I immediately step into them, folding myself around her as she holds me just as tight.

"You're here."

"Well, when Malakai Farrow calls and begs for us to attend, we can't really say no."

"He called you?" I wince. After everything that happened, I can't imagine that went down well. We only got married because he threatened her.

"He did." She cocks a brow, "You've got some explaining to do."

"I–" I snap my teeth together, cringing, "Are you mad?"

"Mad?" She scoffs, "I'm hardly mad, just confused. You said you were going to make his life hell."

"I did," I laugh, "I still do."

Everett remains a quiet stoic presence, a complete contrast to the playful charm I was used to from him from my time spent with them.

"But you love him," She points out.

"Yes," I look away, the guilt for doing so trying to eat me alive. I shouldn't. But I do and I can't deny it or stop it.

"It's okay, Olivia," Arryn soothes, "If anyone should know about falling in love with the one person you least expect, it's me."

Everett scoffs, "Please, you loved me the moment I bent you –"

"Everett," Arryn snaps.

I clamp my mouth closed, "I'm surprised you're here."

"You deserve to be happy, Olivia," She shrugs, "No matter where it comes from, and I don't care how it happens as long as *you are* happy."

I wasn't for a while but now… "I am, Arryn."

"Good." She smiles, "Now, wine. You need to tell me

everything."

So, I do, leaving out certain parts, telling her it all.

"You got shot!?" She yells, eyes wide.

"Just in the leg." I try to calm her, but she swings her gaze around as if looking for the person to blame.

"Malakai killed him." I tell her quietly, "Stop."

"Why didn't you call me!?"

"I had some things to deal with," I pull her back to me, trying to stop her from causing a scene, "And I didn't want to worry you. With everything anyway, it didn't seem right."

She softens, "No more." Arryn declares, "You don't keep things from me, Oli."

"I know, I'm sorry."

"I'm sorry too," She sighs, "I haven't called either."

I shrug, "Life happens. People get busy."

"Or shot," She grumbles.

"Or shot," I agree. "How are you and Everett? All okay?"

She sighs dreamily and I grin, "Perfect."

"Can I steal my wife?" Malakai's voice sends warmth down my spine and then his hand presses against me and his scent invades my senses.

"Be my guest," Arryn grins, "I'll catch up with you tomorrow," she says to me.

"You're staying?"

"For a few days," She nods and climbs off her stool,

turning ready to go search out Everett but before she leaves, she turns back to us, "I'm glad you're happy Olivia, but Malakai, if you ever hurt her again, I don't give a fuck who you are, I *will* kill you."

She ends the sentence with a smile and trots off before either of us can reply.

"I think she just might," Malakai agrees, sliding his arm around my waist. "I missed you."

"I've been gone an hour."

"You were gone for three weeks, one day and seven hours before today."

"What?"

"That's how long it has been since I last saw you, until today."

"You kept count?" I blink up at him.

"It's all I could do," he kisses me gently, "Let me take you home."

I nod mutely, my heart speeding up inside my chest. He doesn't wait a single second before we're moving toward the door, ignoring everyone who tries to speak with us. Outside, the chill bites at my skin but the car is right in front of the hotel, the engine already warm and purring.

"You knew I would say yes?" I laugh, pausing.

"I hoped," He shrugs, "And I didn't want you to be cold."

I move to the passenger door, ready to sink into the warmth but he stops me, "Olivia?"

I turn back to where he is still waiting on the sidewalk.

Playing with Fire

He tosses something at me, and I fumble to catch it, only just managing to and look down into my palm.

He grins at me, walking around to the driver's door to hold it open but he doesn't get in. With a wink, he says, "You can drive."

69

Malakai

The moment she is in the house, the door closed behind us and silence fills the space, I'm on her.

Like an addict needing a fix, I soak her up, my mouth crashing against hers with a need so hot it consumes me. And she kisses me back just as desperately, tongues and teeth clash, hands grabbing and pulling.

She moans into my mouth, fingers threading into my hair as my tongue sweeps in.

"I love you," I drag myself away from her lips only to attach myself to her neck, sucking her flesh into my mouth to leave her little bites and marks. Her fingernails scrape against my scalp as she holds me to her, her legs working to keep her upright as I move us through the house blindly.

"I need you," My mouth moves to the open cleavage of her dress, teeth grazing over the soft mound of one and then the other.

"You own me, Olivia."

"Malakai!" She gasps, "Please."

"Get upstairs," I order, following close behind as she hurries as fast as her dress will allow. I'd rip it clean off if it didn't hold sentimental value, but I'd like to see the dress survive. Whatever is underneath, however, will not.

The door to our bedroom opens abruptly, slamming against the back wall and then I'm on her again, fingers working at the buttons on the back of the dress.

"Hurry," She urges on a whimper. When the last button is popped, her hands fly to the straps of the dress, tugging them down and I help her step out of it.

She stands before me in just a pair of lace panties, nipples peaked, makeup smeared from my mouth.

"Fucking stunning," I growl, hands cupping her waist to lift her. She slots against my body like a puzzle fitting in, breasts squashed to my chest as I suck on her throat. Her body bounces when I drop her on the mattress and fall between her legs, covering her entirely. It's been too long without her, without her touch and her kisses.

She tugs at my jacket and shirt, and I shrug out of it the moment I can, my breath shuddering from my lungs at the feel of her hands against my burning skin. My cock is hard and aching behind my pants, throbbing.

I grind it against her, shooting pleasure through both of us but then I peel myself away, looking down on her as she watches me.

Red marks dot her skin from my fingers and teeth, and I

get my fill of her, tracing over every inch as if it's been years and not weeks since I last saw her. I'm gentle as I peel away the lace and pull it over her thighs, careful not to hurt her still healing thigh that looks better, but I know it is still sore.

And then she is completely bare for me, pussy weeping, breath heaving while her eyes follow my hands as I unbutton my pants and shove out of them, grasping my hard cock with my fist.

"I fucking missed you, kitten," I rasp, letting my dick go to bring my hands to her thighs, carefully pushing her open for me before I let a single finger run through her wet folds. She bows off the mattress, my sensitive little kitten desperate for me.

I get to my knees at the edge of the bed, ready to worship her just like I vowed. I press a tender kiss to her clit before the flat edge of my tongue licks up her entirely.

"Yes," She hisses, hands flying into my hair to hold me in place as if I'd want to be anywhere else. I lick and I suck, and I bite, working her into a frenzy with my tongue and when I push two fingers inside of her, thrusting them in deep and hard, she shatters for me. Her cunt pulses against my mouth, her cries echoing through the room.

I don't allow the orgasm to recede when I grasp my leaking cock and thrust into her, stretching her open wide to fit me. She screams again, her pussy fluttering around me as I fuck her into the mattress, needing to be in her skin, in her fucking soul.

"Kai," She cries, her nails leaving welts on my arms as she claws at me.

Playing with Fire

"Eyes on me, kitten," I growl, "Watch me as I fuck my wife."

Her eyes jump to me, heavy with pleasure.

"Who do you belong to, Olivia?"

"You."

"Who do I belong to?" I ask, balls slapping against her body as I continue to thrust hard and fast, muscles tightening with my impending orgasm.

"Me." She gasps, "More. Please."

I grasp her beneath her knee, pushing her leg up higher as I adjust to go deeper, as deep as I can get.

"Fuck!" She cries.

"Touch yourself," I demand, "Come for me again, Olivia."

Her delicate fingers land between her legs, gently circling that little swollen bud as her lips remain open on her moans.

"Yes, yes," She chants.

Her cunt pulses, her arousal coating my cock and then her second orgasm explodes through her, forcing mine from me. She clamps around me tightly, her head thrown back on a cry as my thrusts turn jerky and my climax barrels through me. I empty into her with a long groan and when my arms are no longer able to hold me and my heart feels about ready to burst, I collapse down onto her, holding my weight with the strength I have left.

Her fingers gently stroke through the short hair at the nape of my neck, her breaths whispering against my ear.

We shower together before she climbs into her side of the bed and I pull her close, her back to my chest, my hand resting atop that steadily beating heart.

I came into this expecting nothing and yet here I am, with the whole damn world in my arms.

Nothing else matters but her. I don't care for the organization, for the men and women in my employ or the city down the road. It's just her.

There are no choices to be had, nothing I wouldn't give up to make her happy though I know she'd never ask such a thing.

This woman here in my arms, the one gently caressing my skin as I hold her close, is the only thing I need.

She is the air in my lungs, the very thing that keeps my heart beating.

"Thank you," I whisper, running my nose down the shell of her ear before I press a soft kiss behind it.

"What for?" She murmurs sleepily.

"For letting me love you, Olivia. For giving me the chance."

A content little sigh works out of her before she turns in my arms and is facing me directly.

Her eyes bounce between mine, so full of honest love and just as much need as me.

"I choose you Malakai," She whispers, kissing the corner of my mouth, "I love you."

I bring her closer, holding her tight.

"Always."

EPILOGUE

Olivia

One year later...

Shit. Shit. Shit.

I sprint from the room, shoving the tools into one of the closets in the hall outside the drawing room.

I can hear him calling my name.

He's back early.

"There you are," He smiles at me, that dazzling kind of smile that makes me lose my breath a little.

"You're home early," I struggle to catch my breath, trying to hide what I've just been doing.

The smile drops and his brows lower, "What's wrong?"

"Nothing," I huff, "Nothing. I'm fine."

"What were you just doing?" His eyes flick to where

the door to the drawing room – his office, has been left ajar, suspicion working its way in.

"Oh, I was just looking for something." I lie.

"You're a bad liar, kitten," He curls his finger beneath my chin, bringing his lips close to mine. I inhale the scent of him, melting at his touch and despite the hold he has on me, I won't be telling him anything.

He should know this by now, the last year has been full of moments just like this.

"What did you do to my office, Olivia?" He asks.

I flutter my lashes, "Nothing."

"Come with me." He doesn't give me an option as he leans down and hauls me over his shoulder like a damn sack of potatoes. I guess he has learned something because this way I can't bolt and hide. His hand squeezes my ass while he walks the short distance to the office, opening and closing the door with a kick.

Before he puts me down, he surveys the room, "Show me what you did."

I giggle, "I didn't do anything."

A quick, sharp slap lands on my ass cheek, forcing a short scream as my ass tingles with the sting.

"Ow!" I complain.

He massages it better, "Tell the truth, kitten."

"I didn't do anything!" I plead my case and for a moment, I almost believe myself.

"Pretty little liar," He slowly lowers me, making sure I keep in contact with him the entire way down, "Are you being a brat today, Olivia?"

I flutter my lashes, "Never."

"I said I was sorry," He grumbles, not believing a word I'm saying. "I was stuck in traffic!"

I narrow my eyes at him, "It was our anniversary."

"So now I'm being punished?" His eyes flick back and forth between my eyes and lips. He apologized extensively last night, first with his anniversary gift, and part of the reason he was late was because he was picking it up. I'm now the owner of my own Maserati, a match to his but mine is blue, where his is black and then he worshipped me all damn night. My knees were still weak this morning. So, no I am not punishing him for being late, I wasn't even annoyed about it last night but it wouldn't be me, it wouldn't be *us*, if I didn't do *something* because of it.

"You're not being punished," I tell him gently, cupping his face, the coarse hair of his beard scratching at my palm. He leans into the touch before he kisses me gently and steps away.

"Sebastian and Willow will be here soon," He advises, walking toward the desk and my heart notches up in speed, a little panic setting in. What if this goes wrong and he gets hurt like the water bucket incident!?

That went bad and we ended up in the hospital because of it, and this has just as much risk.

Shit. But before I can say anything and back track, he's already sitting down.

The chair collapses out from beneath him with a huge crash and he disappears with it.

"Olivia!" He roars.

"Shit." I look between the desk and the door wondering if I should make a run for it now. But I don't know if he's hurt.

Maybe I went too far. It is the water bucket incident all over again!

In my defense, I didn't realize it would hit him in the head when it fell off the door, so along with drenching him in ice cold water the moment he walked through the door, the bucket whacked him, splitting his brow. So, he was wet and bleeding.

I hop from foot to foot, waiting with bated breath to see if he's hurt as he grips the side of the desk and hauls himself up, the chair a pile behind him.

Not hurt. But mad. Like furious mad. Like I'm about to have my ass slapped until I can't sit down *mad*.

Shit.

"Love you, bye!" I yell out, bolting for the door. I throw it open but he's already behind me.

Nope. I sprint away, skidding on our floors as I use the wall to propel my body around the corner and toward the stairs, a laugh bubbling out of me as I hear him gaining pace.

I'm almost at our bedroom where I plan to lock myself in, but before I can make it there his arms circle around me and he hauls me back, the breath rushing from my lungs.

"You little brat," He growls in my ear.

"I'm sorry!" I yell struggling in his grip but he just chuckles. It isn't filled with humor but the promise of revenge.

It's what we do. I fuck with him, and he gets his pay back in some sick way.

He walks us toward the bedroom, locking us inside.

"Don't forget our friends will be here soon!" I say breathlessly, hoping to worm my way out of this.

"I don't give a shit," He continues walking us toward the bed until the backs of my legs hit the edge of the mattress. He turns me swiftly, forcing me to the mattress with a hand at the back of my neck.

"What should I do with you, wife?" He contemplates. "Spank this pretty ass until my handprint is tattooed on your skin?"

A shiver works through me, the rough desire in his tone waking up every nerve ending in my body. His hand strokes down my spine before he cups my ass and then keeps going until his fingers are at the hem of my skirt and he's tugging it up.

"Did you wear these panties for me, Olivia?" he asks, toying with the strap of the lacy thong I have on.

"Yes," My voice shakes as his hand works between my legs, cupping me. As far as punishments go, this isn't too bad.

"Dirty, dirty girl," He rasps, moving his hand to apply friction to me above the lace of my underwear, "You're wet for me."

"Always." I admit.

He chuckles, "Good girl."

His hand comes away from my center to go to the straps, tugging my thong off, leaving my skirt flipped up my back and my ass in the air.

With anyone else I might feel vulnerable, but with Malakai, it's only empowerment that consumes me.

"Please," I beg, pushing back on the hand he places back between my thighs.

"Needy little thing," He whispers, voice roughened with his own desire.

"Yes," I agree, "More."

He slowly thrusts a finger inside of me and I moan into the sheets, my breath whooshing from me as he moves his hand faster and harder.

"Just like that."

He doesn't remove his finger or stop fucking me with it as I feel him shift behind me. I'm so ready to be full of him, to feel his cock stretching me open and that's what I'm expecting.

What I am not expecting, however, is the sound of a vibrator and then said vibrator being pressed to my clit.

I cry out at the sudden sensation, my pussy throbbing, preparing for the orgasm I can feel tightening every muscle in my body.

"Fuck," I hiss, "Yes."

"You're dripping, Olivia." He praises, "All over my fucking hand."

"Fuck me, Kai," I beg shamelessly.

He lets out a rumbling sound but doesn't oblige but that's okay, because I'm right there.

"Yes, just like tha–"

He pulls out and away, leaving my pussy clenching around nothing, the orgasm ebbing away.

"What are you doing!?" I screech.

But the bastard chuckles, "You really think I'm going to reward your little stunt, kitten?"

I flip around, glaring at him, not bothering to fix myself as I let my hand fall between my legs, fully prepared to finish myself.

He suddenly yanks my hands above my head, laying his body over mine, the weight of him against me soothing something inside of me. I'm irritated but I need him like the air in my lungs.

His tongue traces the seam of my lips and I open to let him in, hoping to seduce him into fucking me and dulling this ache.

But I should know better, "You're going to have to work for it, Olivia," He rasps.

"Malakai," I plead.

"No chance, baby," he kisses me, his smile playing against my own mouth. He holds both my hands in his one while the other moves back between my legs. I gasp, so tight and ready, the mere touch is almost enough. Almost. I could fucking weep with desperation. But then he is pushing something inside of me and drawing away his hand the moment it is completely inside.

"You're going to keep that in for me," He tells me sternly, "Take it out and I won't let you finish for a fucking week."

And then his body is gone, and I'm left squirming on the bed, the foreign weight between my legs both pain and pleasure.

He casually straightens his shirt and looks back to me on the bed, "Straighten up, kitten, our friends are here."

"Malakai!" I scream but he just leaves me on the bed, his chuckle spiking goose bumps over my skin. He'll know – I don't know how – but he'll know if I finish the job.

So, I get up and I fix myself like nothing happened. Like I don't have an object inside me right now, an object that suddenly vibrates and makes my knees weak but immediately ceases again like it didn't even happen.

He wants to play?

Fine.

We can play.

We never did learn our lesson after all, or perhaps we did, and we both enjoy playing with fire too much, if only to revel in the burn.

MORE FROM RIA WILDE

TWISTED CITY DUET

LITTLE BIRD – BOOK 1
TWISTED KING – BOOK 2
TWISTED CITY – THE COMPLETE SET

WRECK & RUIN

WICKED HEART
SAVAGE HEART

NO SAINT UNIVERSE
(INTERCONNECTED STANDALONES)

NO SAINT
ALL THE BROKEN PIECES
PRETTY RECKLESS

RAVENPEAK BAY

THESE ROUGH WATERS
LIKE A HURRICANE
BENEATH THESE DARK SKIES

MORE

PLAYING WITH FIRE

ABOUT THE AUTHOR!

Ria Wilde is an author of dirty, dark and dangerous romance. A lover of filthy talking anti-heroes and sassy AF queens! She's always had a love of reading and decided to pursue her passion of words in late 2021 and hasn't looked back since! Little Bird and Twisted King, Ria's debut dark romance was the start of something amazing and she now has plans for several new series and spin-offs with some of your favorite characters as the main stars!

She currently resides in the UK with her husband, daughter and 2 dogs. You can often find her daydreaming or procrastinating with her head buried in a book!

www.riawilde.com

Printed in Great Britain
by Amazon